Reality Kicked

R. D. Chapman

Copyright © 2023 by Reneé D. Chapman
ISBN: 979-8-9906998-5-4

Editor: Ray Rhamey
Cover Design: SelfPubBookCovers.com/thrillerauthor
www.ShadesOfFall.com

A warm thank you to my family for their support. A very grateful thank you to my editor, Ray Rhamey.

Chapter 1

A dark, damp, foggy night: the perfect setting to wage a small war. Thick fog had turned early evening into midnight. At least the downpour common to Midgard's winter had let up about an hour or so ago. Jem Wilmont spared a glance at the light on the top floor from the shadowed doorway she huddled in.

Thom Danford, the head bastard of Azusa's planned bloodbath, should be getting escorted into Brower's office about now. He and his security guard had entered the building across from her a few minutes ago. They were to keep Kenneth Brower and his security chief engaged while his men quietly eliminated everyone in the building.

Everyone. Even a visitor.

Ah! It's started.

Jem shifted into ghost-mode, invisible and untouchable, as a form approached the building's corner and paused. Her lip curled. The traitor on duty in the Security office would have shut down the building's security feeds as soon as Danford entered. His coworker would have been powerless to stop him because his family was being held hostage. Or had been. Boyd's text thirty minutes ago had verified he'd taken down their two captors.

Having all the cameras shut down happened to make things easier for her, too.

Walking over, she watched the man perform a thermal sweep of the area, checking for any guards Brower may have deployed outside. He wouldn't find them; they were hidden several streets over. Neither would his radar detect her, as she no longer existed in his "reality" but on a different plane of existence.

Or non-existence, since she wasn't breathing or pumping blood. She'd long ago quit trying to understand it.

Sweep completed, he made a hand motion and more forms slipped from the shadows. A number of them skulked around to the back while the rest filed through the front door. She flashed a humorless grin they couldn't see. They were in for a surprise.

She rematerialized behind the man as he started another sweep and fired a drugged dart into his neck. He crumpled. Jem texted *go* to Brower's men. The ones outside would move in and take care of the enemy coming in through the rear. Those inside would move into position, since emptying the building completely would have alerted the invaders, who would have alerted Danford.

No sense in postponing the inevitable.

Moving stealthily through the door, she spotted one man sneaking into a room. She left him collapsed on the floor, then shifted back into ghost-mode to continue her hunt. She found three more hunched outside the guard's lounge, laz-guns held ready. The voices heard inside were decoys, with two hidden on either side of the entrance with stunners.

One of the creeps held up a hand. *Great signal.* She materialized, firing as she called out *"Now!"* Her first dart hit, but the second one missed as the thugs dropped to the floor.

A laser bolt sizzled past as she dived into a side hallway.

Z-ping, sizzle, z-ping-ping.

"They're down," one of Brower's guards called out softly.

She scanned the three bodies, then the guards. Two moved past her to stare down the hallways, ready in case the sounds had alerted the others. The other two quickly shoved the laz-guns away and searched the bodies. She caught the eye of the one with a laser burn across his arm.

"I'm okay, for now," he told her.

True. The wound was cauterized.

"There's another one down on this floor and at the front door," Jem told them as she broke open her weapon and tilted out the remaining dart. She reloaded with what the old-fashioned tech manual had called a 'quick reloader.' It shoved five more darts into their slots in a single motion. The empty reloader and the extra dart went back into a small pouch hanging from her belt. Her modified dart gun was as quick as a stunner but quieter, and the drug contents could be varied as needed. For these assholes, she'd chosen a powerful, painful cocktail.

Leaving the men to take care of the downed thugs, she headed for the nearest stairwell. Once out of their sight, she shifted. Running up the stairs, she phased through the door and one of the two guys standing in front of it. *Oh, yuck.* She hated when that happened.

"I don't like it," the tall one said, sotto voce. "We should've found more people by now."

The other guy shrugged, his attention locked on the hallway. "They wouldn't need many at night, counting on security to alert them. Luckily the other guy only had a stunner. Our guy will wake up soon."

Dammit. They'd lost one.

"Let's check these rooms."

Jem dropped the shift as soon as they were in the first room. She reached the doorway at the same time one was coming out. His yell was cut off as her dart slammed into him. She lunged sideways as a laser bolt blackened the doorframe and the wall opposite it.

Shit, damn, crap. She couldn't give the guy time to warn Danford. She *poofed* to ghost-mode, phased through the wall, and jogged quickly to a position behind the man. Intent on the doorway, he never realized she'd rematerialized until her dart pierced his neck.

Jem hurried out the door and down the hallway. Ten had entered the building; three more to go. At least one would be headed for—she dropped into a squat as a laser bolt passed over her head. She dropped the guy firing at her before he could redirect his aim.

Dammit, dummy—shift.

She did, while running for the Security Office two hallways away. The SOB she found there had burned a hole through the traitor's head and was about to do the same to David Ashbridge. No time to worry about exposure, she fired as soon as she materialized in the doorway. A laser bolt blackened an equipment rack as the thug collapsed.

Ashbridge blinked. "Where—never mind. Thanks. My family?" he asked, anxiously.

"Safe. Where's the last guy?"

"Headed for Mr. Brower's office. They were to be the last ones."

Jem flashed her teeth. "Then Mr. Danford is in for a surprise. Bring security back online." Wheeling around, she raced for the stairwell and the third floor.

* * * * *

"You have one more day to make a prudent decision," Thom Danford said, sneering at the man behind the desk.

Did Kenneth Brower really think he could stand against him? With the Dragonfly's organization backing him, he was unstoppable. All of Midgard's major cities would be under his control within a year. The rest he'd take at his leisure.

The man is a fool. Soon to be a dead one.

Danford glanced at the security guard standing behind and to the left of Brower's desk. His own guard stood on his left, too, leaving Browser's guard exposed to the door. His people would take him out as soon as they came in. They should be close to clearing the building by now. He detested dragging out this useless conversation.

"You're wasting your time, Danford," Brower said, glowering. "I am not handing my organization and people over to you. That's final."

There came a double rap on the office door.

Perfect timing. "Well, then," Danford said, rising casually. "I guess we can dispense with any further talk. To tell the truth, I didn't expect anything different from you," he said, hearing the door opening behind him. "Your cooperation is no longer required. Only your death."

Several things happened simultaneously.

Both guards went for their weapons, his guard collapsed, and a female voice said, "That's a bit dramatic."

Danford whipped around. A pair of cold bi-colored eyes stared into his. *Jem Wilmont?*

"Joe, would you mind getting his weapon?" Jem said.

Brower surged to his feet. "How did it go?"

Danford swallowed. Brower worked with the Ghost?

"Last one," Jem said, nodding backward at a body splayed in full view through the door.

"I'll see to things," Brower's guard said. He scooped up the other guard's laz-gun and handed it to Brower. He grabbed the first man by an arm, then the other unconscious one in passing and dragged them unceremoniously away.

Jem made a mental note to never arm-wrestle the guy.

"My team's dead?" Danford said, stunned by the unexpected turn of events.

"No," Wilmont replied. "They're experiencing the pleasures of Fire and Ice. You seem to like drugs. Why don't you join them?"

* * * * *

Kenneth Brower looked down at Danford's unconscious form. "Fire and Ice?"

"A drug created primarily for Law Enforcement to control rioters and misbehaving prisoners. Instant takedown followed by short-term paralysis. Lasts about one, two hours normally." She grinned. "I regret to say that the pain is extreme. Think molten fire."

Brower grunted and toed Danford. "What do we do with them?"

"Your office building was invaded by a team wielding illegal laz-guns. You have casualties among your employees and were personally threatened with death. You call Law Enforcement, like any other law-abiding citizen."

"And when LE asks *why* they invaded?"

"Simple. Tell them you were contacted two weeks ago by Danford. He requested you and your resources facilitate moving their products into Azusa. You refused. He said you'd regret it and this, evidently, is their retaliation."

Brower's grin stretched face-wide by the time she finished.

"All true. You had that in mind all along," he said. "That's why you insisted my men wear only licensed stunners and you used darts."

"Yes, and it cost one of your people his life." Jem shook her head. "I'm sorry. I had hoped there would be no fatalities."

"You saved a lot of lives tonight. If the man has a family, they'll be taken care of."

"Oh. The two guys in Security? The dead one sold you out but David Ashbridge was coerced—his family held hostage. My associate freed them a short while ago."

They both turned as the guard she'd called Joe came in.

"We've dumped all of them in the lounge on the first floor. Nineteen all together, unconscious but alive. The way our guys are grumbling that might change soon. I believe these are yours, Miss Wilmont." He held out a handful of darts. "And the name is John."

"Thanks." She accepted them, along with the two Brower plucked and handed over.

"And the explanation for how they were taken down?" Brower asked, his tone curious.

"Again, simple," Jem said, sliding the darts in with the two empty reloaders. Her level gaze met his. "An ally learned about the attack and came to your aid." She ignored their shocked expressions and walked out. Behind her, she heard John's voice through the open door.

"*Allies?* Should we be happy or worried, Boss?"

Chapter 2

Thane Baron sipped a wimpy whisky in an upscale bar—*lounge*, his snickering brain corrected—and pondered his next move while keeping an unobtrusive eye on his client's daughter. Marissa Rawleigh was laughing and drinking in a circular booth filled with the young and affluent and…he'd be polite and call them immature. Babysitting spoiled children wasn't something he normally did. Yet, here he was.

Joseph Rawleigh had approached him at Coleman Two's spaceport as he prepared to head home. The maniac's trial that had brought him back to the planet had ended as expected: confinement in a psychological ward. The one the knife-welding idiot shouldn't have been let out of in the first place. Thane had initially declined Rawleigh's request. But the man's obvious worry and his claim that she'd been lured away by a group of trouble-hunting Earthers—especially one Timothy Altman—had swayed him. He'd mailed off a quick message home to explain his delay and headed for Sol Three: Earth.

Thane had found Altman already acting like a significant partner. He'd generously paid for their shuttle trip here to Portland from the Mobile Spaceport and for their hotel suite using his bank card. *Thank you, Universe!* If the guy had been using a cash card like Marissa was, well, Earth was a big planet and covered with people.

His Tracker license had an auxiliary law enforcement clause. While it'd only been activated once in his fifteen years of tracking, it did provide a number of civilian benefits. It authorized requests for financial and Port Authority information, which was the most effective way of tracking a person between star systems—cities, in this case. It also authorized his stunner and laz-gun, both secured in his ship back in Mobile. He'd rarely used the latter, but the former had been quite handy on a number of jobs.

Cash cards were the simplest—and anonymous—way to carry funds, especially between systems. They were slightly oversized T-drives that fit comfortably in pockets or bras. Squeezing the sides could light up a miniature screen on the bottom to display its current balance. Most types were refillable; some were single use.

Marissa Perkins Rawleigh was of a legal age, barely, and therefore entitled to flit through the Republic's systems and party if she wanted to. However, after watching and listening to their inane prattle for the past two hours, Thane had to agree with her very wealthy father. Marissa was inexperienced and naïve enough to end up in a questionable relationship with the calculating blond snuggling against her. Timothy Jones Altman had plenty of experience. According to Thane's comp brain's search of Earth records, he had swaggered through three short, progressively profitable-for-him marriages in the past seven years.

Guess that's why he had to go off planet to find his next victim.

Thane ignored the woman getting up from a group on his left until he realized she was heading in his direction. He groaned inwardly as she slid onto the stool next to him.

"Thane Stohlass Baron," she said in a low-voiced drawl.

He glanced over. Hawk-black hair, brown eyes, soft brown completion that showcased the diamonds and rubies dangling from ears and layered around her neck. Ugh. Could she be even more ostentatious? That was answered by the numerous matching bracelets hugging the arm she laid on the counter top. Disinterest probably wouldn't work, but it was worth a shot.

"Yes," he acknowledged and stared down the bar's length with what he hoped was a boring-enough attitude. He caught her quick frown in his peripheral vision. She leaned forward, her shoulders slightly twisted. The better to see her well-exposed cleavage or her jewels, he assumed. He wasn't interested in either.

"I'm surprised to see you here."

Is that husky-purr supposed to be sexy?

"I would have expected it to take longer to get Baron Financials settled on Midgard."

This time he gave her a disdainful look. "Got managers for that."

Thanks to the new consolidated news outlet on Polaris One, word of BF's move from Milania, Romanique Three—and his inheritance of it—had spread to news media in almost all the Republic Systems in very short order. His name and image had probably been plastered across more vid-screens than Jem's had been when the Enforcers were hunting her.

"I'm Tia Rockefeller Lexington," she said, arrogance replacing the purr.

Was that supposed to mean something to me? He ignored her, realizing his target's group was breaking up. The blond leech had a possessive grip around Marissa's shoulders. Instinct told Thane the guy had to make his move quickly. He needed to coax Marissa from sig-ner into another beneficial-for-him prenup and marriage before someone local informed her of his hobby.

Thane slid off the stool. "Miss Lexington," he said, keeping his eyes on the exiting couples. "I am not interested. Why don't you go back to the guy at your table giving me a death-glare who obviously is."

He walked out, needing to catch them before they disappeared. Marissa had undoubtedly had the birds-and-bees speech. She was about to get the leech-and-vulture one.

***

"Come on, Marissa, finish packing."

Thane couldn't keep the exasperation out of his voice. Standing in the bedroom doorway, he bounced his attention from the suite door to the wailing and crying woman he'd been trying to get out of Altman's suite for over thirty minutes. He'd pried Marissa away from him about forty-five minutes ago. Thane expected him to come stomping through the door when he couldn't find her anywhere else.

"I c-c-can't believe Tim would do this. How could he? He said I was the only one for him. *He said he loved me.*"

Thane winced at the high-pitched whine. How many times did that make? She plopped down on the bed, blabbering something about her father being right. *No frigging time for this.* Yanking two blouses out of the closet, he threw them in an open suitcase.

"Those are Ramona Silks," Marissa squealed, jumping up. "You don't *wad* them up!"

"Then *pack them* or we're *leaving them*," he yelled into her astonished face. Well, fancy that. Threaten her clothes and she starts moving. He'd have to remember that for the next spoiled brat. Assuming he was idiot enough to take the job.

"*Why* are you in such a hurry?" she said pouting, folding a pair of striped pants.

The suite's door opened, then slammed shut. Thane sighed. "That's why."

Altman stared daggers at him from the doorway. "You again? What are you doing here?"

"Helping Marissa pack." He went into the bathroom, grabbed a bunch of bottles and hair things off the counter. He threw them on the bed, keeping a wary eye on Altman.

"You're not taking my fiancée anywhere."

Fiancée? Thane watched Marissa's eyes widen. Yep. The asshole was stepping up his plans.

"Marissa, honey, there's been a misunderstanding," the asshole continued, giving Thane a hard look. "Why don't we go somewhere quiet, have a drink, and talk about this?"

Thane couldn't believe it when he saw her hesitating. "You mean have a quiet drink or three—maybe spiked with something that'll make her amenable to signing prenup papers you just happen to have ready? Followed by a quick trip to a judge to finish out your marriage plans?"

Altman's jaw tightened. *Nailed it.* Marissa's expression told him she realized it, too. Finally.

"If you really care about me," she said in a trembling voice, "then come home with me. Meet my family."

"We'll go. Right after the ceremony. I promise," he said with a sly smile.

Marissa surprised Thane by shaking her head and taking a step back. The girl was learning. Thane took a step forward. "We'll be out shortly ass—

Altman. In the meantime, leave."

Furious, Altman marched out of the bedroom. Thane watched him leave the suite, not trusting him. The man gave up too easily on what would be his most profitable bride to-date.

It took another twenty-plus minutes to pack Marissa's bags. Fortunately, she'd never unpacked the other three. Thane set the last one down in the suite's main room and reached for the phone to call for a hotel steward. The door was thrown open. Altman wasn't alone this time. He'd evidently recruited a couple of street thugs and one of them had a baseball bat.

Note to self: Never go anywhere without a stunner while on any *job.*

Thane yelled at Marissa to call security as Altman dodged around him, his focus on the two thugs and the bat. He dodged their first blows, his greater Midgard-gravity speed an advantage. A scream from the bedroom distracted him and the bat connected, a last second twist changing a home-run to a second-base blow against his ribs. He staggered. A quick glimpse showed Marissa fighting off Altman with a sequined purse.

The second thug took advantage and closed in. This one had martial arts training and Thane's head snapped backward from the blow, the taste of blood in his mouth. *Shit!* Teeth gritted, he blocked and countered their blows. Mostly.

Marissa was screaming. Altman was yelling.

Where the hell is Security?

The suite door slammed open again as he kicked the bat-guy into a side table. It wasn't Security. Two women in loose shirts and drawstring pants came charging in. After one quick assessing look, Thane's opponents were bounced off the wall, ping-pong style. Altman ran for the door and straight into someone who did appear to be hotel Security.

Chapter 3

"Dawson is escorting a couple of Law Enforcers in from the gate," Stuart said. Nicholas O'Daniel's Security Second took up his boss's favorite position of standing at the window.

Jem figured his and Gordon Stohlass's dour expressions were more from not being informed ahead of time about their night's activities than being awakened to it afterwards. Both men's features were suitably neutral by the time the two LE officers were shown into Gordon's library—aka the War Room, as Jem called it.

Gwendolyn Williams, Gordon's wife, stood. "Captain Kelding, I realize it's late—or early—but would either of you like something to drink? Coffee, perhaps?"

"Thank you, no," Captain Kelding replied. "This is Detective Janice Bristol, Crime Unit. We're partnering at the moment as tonight's events cross both our doorsteps."

Jem sighed internally as Bristol's unfriendly brown eyes met hers. Another day, another I-know-you're-a-criminal enforcer.

They settled into chairs, Gwen in her usual to the left of Gordon's desk, and the enforcers in front of it. Jem and Boyd were seated facing the right side. Catching Boyd's eye, Jem rolled hers in a 'here we go' sentiment. That got her a stern look from Gordon.

Definitely not happy with me.

Gordon cleared his throat. "Captain, Detective, my clients have informed me of tonight's events that have undoubtedly brought you here. And, I'd like to ask, why the head of Homicide Division is here instead of another detective?"

"If Jem Wilmont is involved, I'm involved," she replied tartly, earning a sideways glance from Bristol.

Limiting information about me as much as possible. Kelding was aware of her ability. Well, part of it.

"The family appreciates, and will note, your professional attention," Gwen said smoothly.

Jem pressed her lips together. No one did polite threats better than Thane's grandmother.

Kelding ignored Gwen and turned to her. "I'm surprised you didn't give your lawyer more time to prep for your defense."

"Defense for what, Captain?" Jem asked politely. The Enforcer had come a long way since their initial meeting. Kelding's original hostility toward her had mellowed into a wait-and-see attitude, especially after the chaotic events of seven months ago. Tonight, that may have slipped to dubious trust. "We've done nothing wrong. In fact, I believe we stopped a major wrong."

"You left the scene," Detective Bristol said sharply. "We need answers about what went on at Mr. Brower's office building."

"I'm sure Mr. Brower and his people have told you *exactly* what happened." Jem hoped Gordon appreciated her cool, professional tone. "I also knew you'd be interviewing me at the first opportunity."

Kelding gave her a sharp look then turned to Boyd. "According to statements, Mr. Ashbridge's wife and son had been held to force his cooperation. From Charlene Anson's description, you were their rescuer. You also left before Enforcers arrived."

Boyd shrugged.

"If you wish to be petty, both of my clients will pay whatever fine a judge sets. If one so chooses," Gordon said briskly. "As I understand it, their actions tonight prevented a mass killing. Wouldn't you consider that more important?"

Captain Kelding's grunt could've been interrupted several ways. "Miss Wilmont, when you became aware of the moves against Mr. Brower, why didn't you come to Law Enforcement for us to handle it?"

Finding Brower on her doorstep six days ago had been a surprise. It would have taken something important to risk the hour-long boat trip in heavy fog to her fjord home. It had been. A request for help.

"Because you wouldn't move against unsubstantiated rumors. Because LE doesn't consider Mr. Brower an upstanding citizen," Jem said bluntly, "and probably would think 'good riddance.' Mostly because it could have resulted in Charlene Anson and her son's deaths and Danford slinking away to strike another time."

Silence. Gordon had acquired his lawyer-neutral face.

"While Mr. Brower's business and ethical codes may be abhorrent to many," Jem continued, keeping her tone civil for Gordon's sake, "he adheres to what is, mostly, a low-violence standard. His men could have been more heavily armed and my darts could have contained a more potent drug. We left them for you to deal with, *legally*. I left to take care of a few additional details that were related to tonight's main event that couldn't wait," Jem added with acerbity.

The two enforcers shared a look.

"Would that involve the disturbances we heard about in the Port Circle?" Kelding asked dryly, referring to spaceport's support area.

Azusa's spaceport was a private extension of the main airport and primarily for the benefit of its local citizens. Though small in comparison and crescent-shaped, the traditionally-named Circle provided the same amenities as its big brothers.

"I needed to retrieve a few things I'd left hidden in several places. Being in a hurry, we couldn't wait for the areas to be empty." Which is why she'd taken Boyd. She'd been surprised at how he'd perked up at the thought of trashing those two would-be drug dens. And maybe a few of their inhabitants. She pulled three items from the bag at her feet.

"Captain Kelding, Detective Bristol, I think you both will be interested in these."

"Crystal recorders?" Kelding said, as Jem passed them to her.

The expensive crystal recorders were a one-time use, their contents permanently embedded into them. No deleting, tweaking or overwriting. With no transmission capability, they were invisible to electronic sweeps. Perfect for clandestine monitoring.

"You may want to add someone from Narcotics Division to your team. Two of them have Danford's employees discussing preparations for their drug and other illegal operations. From the sound of it, they may have some product already on hand. The third crystal has Thom Danford himself on it, planning tonight's expected takeover of Azusa. That one is a couple of days old and how we learned of and prepared for tonight."

"I'm assuming these were gained using those well-touted traits of yours to infiltrate their rooms?" Bristol said, just short of sneering.

"Yes, Detective Bristol," Kelding said, "Miss Wilmont has stealthy feet. That and her relationship with the Stohlass family are two things the rumors do have correct. You'll do well to remember that going forward." She handed the recorders to the startled detective. "I'll take care of the interviews. Contact Narcotics, get warrants, teams. Take everyone down that you can."

Kelding waited until Stuart escorted the detective out. "So, you approve of Kenneth Brower?"

Jem shrugged off her suspicious tone. "Of the man, yes. Of his business, I'm nonjudgmental. Tell me, Captain, would you prefer to dance with the devil that's light on his feet or stomps all over your toes?"

"I'd rather not dance with either," she replied, voice heavy with disapproval.

Jem wasn't surprised. "There will always be those who will gamble, or seek out black market or other questionable deals. Mr. Brower does not deal in murder, mayhem, or drugs. He does not actively seek to ruin people—not counting business rivals. And he keeps his word once given. Remove him, Captain, and someone probably a lot worse—like Danford—will slither into his society niche."

After giving her an enigmatic look, the captain apparently decided to ignore the whole issue.

"Ms. Williams, if it's not too much trouble, I could use a cup of coffee. This long night isn't over yet." Kelding pulled out her hand computer and set it to record. "Interview with Jem Seaborne Wilmont and Boyd Perez Papagiannopoulos," she began, stumbling over Boyd's full name. Then she added date, time, and place.

"Miss Wilmont, could you provide a summary of the events, from your perspective, occurring earlier tonight at Mr. Kenneth Brower's office at 37902 Stanton Street?"

Chapter 4

Reginald Kurzvall closed the files he'd been reviewing and stretched. He had enough information about three of the board members he was meeting with tomorrow to ensure their cooperation with his proposal. While merging the Stanfordson Mining Company with one of his subsidiaries would benefit them both, it was another step in his and his partners' long-term plans.

Granted, the Consortium could buy most of its ore needs from the Euphrates System. Its Independent status had eliminated any hindrance from Republic meddlers. But once he gained control of the Argus System's mines, he'd have a controlling interest in the metal ore trade for the entirety of Sector Three. A stab in the Republic's side.

The humiliations he endured at the Republic's hands, past and current, were not going to go unpunished. Since the Consortium's succession, their offenses had escalated. The port delays. The idiotic *interviews* by enforcers. The watchers. Pure harassment, all of it. Nor had he forgotten about Midgard. *Midgard.* His lip curled at the mere thought of the planet and its people. They were another source of humiliation he'd not soon forget. They'd all regret it.

Unfortunately, he needed Jem Wilmont to do that. At least she would be easier to find now. The woman had settled down there, unlike her previous habit of unpredictable drifting from one system to another.

Too bad his Midgard informant had been arrested for murder several months ago. His last messages had provided some very interesting news. From the rift he'd reported between the Feds and the military, it looked like they'd learned Wilmont's invisibility secret and were fighting over who got control of her. Fools. Like that team he'd hired two months ago. He'd been assured they could infiltrate and seize Wilmont from her fjord home. Good thing he'd kept the arrangements anonymous as they were currently sitting in an Azusa prison cell on a number of charges. The three incompetents never made it past her dock.

Jem Seaborne Wilmont. His lip curled. The woman was infuriating, her and her asinine morals. With her skill, she could be the wealthiest, most influential thief-spy-assassin in the Galaxy. Not some…some introvert going around doing good deeds, he fumed. Setting up a foundation to waste more money on more good deeds. Except where *he* was involved, seeing as how she'd sabotaged several of his companies. And refused to work for him. Willingly, at least. A smug smile crossed his face, remembering her fury the one time he'd managed to trick her into a contract.

The smile faded. He'd have his people arrange for new informants. There were always plenty of people looking for additional income. He needed to know what was happening in Azusa. What *she* was doing. Only then could he make plans. With professionals this time. His finger tapped the tabletop. There had to be some way to force her hand. To gain control of that unique ability. And that data she undoubtedly had hidden somewhere. He couldn't see her destroying it.

But how?

Kidnapping someone in the Stohlass family wouldn't work for long. Wilmont would use her freaky way to learn where they were and free them. Then he'd have to put up with ridiculous attempts of retribution from a family of morally inflexible fools. Foolish fools. As a Consortium citizen with diplomatic standing, any legal charges brought against him by their insufferable lawyers wouldn't be enforceable.

There had to be a way to keep…*what if there was no way for her to find them?*

Chapter 5

"*Lone Tracker*, you are cleared for Azusa Spaceport, landing pad 2-A. Airways are clear. Of aircraft," the port traffic controller added with a chuckle.

Thane grinned, appreciating the woman's humor. "Thanks. Beginning descent for 2-A," he confirmed. He closed the comm link. "Thor, assume auto-nav control and begin landing procedures on beacon 2-A." It felt good to be back on Midgard. Even better, having a comp brain he could turn the ship's operations over to.

He'd never figured out how his father had managed to get one tucked into a small ship like the *Lone Tracker*. More than a computer but not quite an AI, it was akin to using a fusion plant to power one city block. It also lacked the digital undertones one usually heard in most computer-generated voices.

Thor acknowledged the command and, several seconds later, Thane felt the first atmospheric vibrations. He leaned back in his seat and let out a deep sigh. He was so looking forward to being home. To give Jem a big hug. Maybe not too big. His ribs were still sore. He checked the chronometers above the viewscreen. The center one was always set to Earth time, the left one to Midgard time. The one on the right displayed local time for whatever planet he was at.

Not quite noon, according to both the Midgard and local clocks.

Excellent. He should be able to snag lunch from his grandparents' cook. Merle might even have some fresh shard chowder on hand. He licked his lips in hopeful anticipation. They needed to figure out a way to tastefully freeze the meaty fish so he could stock it on his trips.

The rumble of the ion engines grew deeper, indicating the ship had breached the denser stratospheric layer. Soon now. He'd call the house after landing and ask for a car to pick him up. Have lunch and a quick visit with the relatives. He wondered if Andi had popped yet. His genius cousin's first baby should be due any day. Once the familial obligations were observed, he'd head for home in the fjord and his beautiful sig-ner.

***

There she is.

Thane's grin spread wide on seeing Jem. Standing in the well-lit entrance, the fog-diffused light created an aura-like glow around her. Emily Barker, the family security guard that had picked him up, had told him she was currently staying at his grandparents. Good news, as it would have taken hours to reach the fjord in this. And his old bedroom was now their second home whenever they needed it.

Climbing out of the car, he hurried to the open doorway. Dropping his travel bag, he enveloped Jem in his arms. Then flinched when her arms tightened around him.

Jem drew back and in a resigned voice said, "Okay, what kind of injuries do you have this time?"

"Sore ribs, mostly," he replied, as she drew him into the house. He fidgeted as her scrutiny swept over him.

"Is that black eye the rest of it?"

"Mostly," he repeated. Good thing he'd lost the puffy lip, though the hip bruise would linger a bit longer. "I promise to tell all. Preferably at one time. Is GG home? Andi? Has she had the baby?"

GG was the family shorthand when referring to both his grandparents. Non-blood related members occasionally used it also, as it matched their first names.

"Yes, GG and a few others are here." She held up a hand. "Due warning. Miss Andrea Sullivan is in a prickly mood. Nicholas is in danger of being castrated if she doesn't give birth *real* soon."

Thane was still laughing when they got to the family room. Both grandparents rose and came toward him, but stopped short of their usual hugs.

20

"We can see the eye, Jem. Anything else we should know about?" Gordon asked.

"Sore ribs, and since he didn't stop at a MedCenter, they weren't broken or badly fractured," she replied matter-of-factly.

Pretending to be offended, he said, "What does it say when my injuries are taken so…"

"Lightly?"

"Unsurprisingly?"

"Routinely?"

"Par for the course?" Seth Sullivan said, laughing.

Thane glanced at Andi, whose contribution was a glower. Oh, boy. Nicholas must be hiding out in Security.

Jem poked him in the stomach, gently. "Come home with another laser burn, it'd be a different story and you know it."

He did. A Tracking job could be anything from dull to extremely dangerous.

"Well, sit down and rest," his grandmother said. "Plenty of time to hear your story. You aren't going anywhere in this fog and Merle says she'll have shard chowder in half an hour."

Thane lowered carefully onto the short couch, Jem curling next to him. They clasped hands and exchanged a private smile. "Believe it or not, this came from a simple babysitting job."

He grinned at the multiple raised eyebrows before launching into his tale.

"…and we ended up staying in the suite as Altman and friends were spending the night at Law Enforcement. The hotel medic verified my ribs were only bruised and the hotel manager wanted to avoid any, uh, publicity issues."

"Surely the guy didn't think he could sweet-talk her back," Gordon said in disbelief. "Especially with the two others whaling on you."

"Who were the two women who helped out?" Jem asked.

"Altman evidently thought he could manage Marissa. As for the women?" Thane grinned. "Daphne Davis and Hatsu Bevington had the room next door. They'd just returned from the day's competition and heard Marissa screaming."

"Competition?" several listeners chorused.

That's what he'd said, too. "Portland was hosting Earth's Female Body-building and Weight-Lifting Contest. They both had qualified for the finals."

His listeners burst out laughing. Thane sneaked a quick glance at Andi. She wasn't laughing with the others, but the glower was gone. A prickle of worry tugged at him. A quiet Andi was not normal.

"They were better than Security," Gwen finally said.

"The rest is boring," Thane said. "I got Marissa back to Mobile and on the first liner that stopped at Coleman Two. She wasn't happy at having to share a room with someone and could only take *three* of her bags—who needs six suitcases?" Thane shook his head at the pouting he'd had to put up with. "We shipped the others by UPMS. To say I'm glad to be home is a gross understatement."

The Otanak Drive had opened the galaxy for humans, but it had a time-vs-size quirk: the larger the vessel, the longer it took to get anywhere. Universal Postal and Messaging Service's mail and courier pods were the glue that kept the Republic together, utilizing that baffling TVS feature. Their small, autonomous Class One drones transported their cargos to even the farthest systems in hours. Everything from electronic data files to specialized cargos to people in a hurry. In recognition of their importance, the systems that had separated from the Republic over the last two years had negotiated contracts to continue their service.

"What, no touring?" Jem teased. "No visiting the old-home region?"

Thane gave her a you're-kidding-me look. "No, I didn't feel like being a tourist, especially to a place that's too many generations distant for nostalgia."

A large number of Midgard's colonists had come from Earth's Scandinavian region. Many of their towns, businesses, and physical features reflected that heritage. Some, like General Kowalski, even spoke one of the old languages.

"Well, it certainly sounds like you had an interesting trip," Seth said.

"Enough to last me for a while. How's things been here?"

"Well," Jem said, drawing it out. "Margo and Saul were here last month—they still haven't decided where to settle. They had planned to look around Azusa but with the fog… I'll paraphrase Margo to 'can't see a damn thing.'"

Thane's cheek twitched. Jem's friend from Pappia had no filter on her mouth.

"So, they visited a couple of cities on Stockholm before going on," Jem continued. Their largest continent was basking in the Southern Hemisphere's summer. "Margo did tell me that Midgard is in the top three before they left."

Midgard, Wotan Two, was a beautiful green-blue world slightly larger than Earth that, astrophysically speaking, could be its twin, not counting its extra moon. The days were a bit longer, the years a bit shorter, the gravity a bit higher, and a constant wind that was a main source of power.

Jem cleared her throat. "Then things got, uh, a bit hectic a couple of days ago."

"Which is what I'm here to discuss," Seth said, raising a finger.

Thane looked over sharply. While anyone from the family law firm could represent her, Andi's oldest brother was Jem's primary lawyer. "What's happened?" Had someone made another attempt against her?

Jem grimaced. "We need to bring you up-to-date."

Van, the head steward, materialized in the doorway. "Lunch is ready," he announced.

"Which we can do while we eat," Jem added, popping off the couch.

Uh-huh. This was going to be interesting.

Van turned to Andi. "Miss Sullivan, Mr. O'Daniel is picking up a vegetable and sandwich tray Merle has fixed for you to take home. He'll meet you at the front door."

Thane bit his lip as Seth and Gordon jumped up to help Andi out of her chair. Evidently her pregnant susceptibility to fish odors hadn't decreased. Thane watched worriedly as Van assisted her out of the room. His cousin was huge.

"She's really having just one?" Thane asked Jem in a low voice, getting a nod in return. Multiples did run in the family. He even had triplet cousins.

* * * * *

Jem lay contented in Thane's arms, her back to his chest. They were both naked, sweaty, and satiated.

"So," Thane drawled lazily, "is everything settled like Seth said?"

"More or less. Law Enforcement isn't happy that we handled it, but they're ecstatic at stopping Danford. Everything they collected here also gave Odinheim Enforcers what they needed to go after his organization there."

Thane nuzzled her ear. "You know helping Kenneth Brower has solidified your standing with certain groups."

Jem winced. "It certainly didn't help Captain Kelding's opinion of me. At least she hasn't reverted back to full-on hostile. Suspicion about what I've done or may do is rampant, especially among law enforcement. 'Where there's smoke there's fire and it's pretty thick around her,'" Jem quoted.

Thane's arms tightened. "Who the hell said that?"

"A detective on Stromli Four. He also said people around me were going to get burned, one way or another. That's proved—" She let out a small *yelp* as Thane's powerful arms whipped her around.

"The problems we've experienced have nothing to do with you or me," he said, "but with others who are *reacting* to us in their own twisted way to suit whatever purpose *they* want. You didn't set the Branson Hotel Fire, or ask to be kidnapped and forced to steal. My cousin and her lover attacked the family so she could inherit Baron Financials, which I never wanted in the first place."

The miserable undertone in his voice tore at her. Jem shoved her arms around Thane and held him close. The Stohlass family would always grieve the senseless loss of several members that Katherine Baron and Ahrymani Carpenter's greed had caused. No, they weren't responsible for the deaths and other problems that swirled around them. Not directly, yet the deaths would always weigh on them.

"We've done what we can to protect ourselves and those we care about." Thane rested his chin on her head. "We'll deal with whatever comes our way."

Together. But would their precautions be enough?

***

A loud pounding on the door brought Jem awake. Thane had already pulled on pants and hurried toward it as she sat up. It was Stuart.

"Nicholas called. He and Andi are on their way to the hospital. I've already woke GG. Better hurry if you want to ride with them. Head for the security entrance," he said, slapping Thane on the arm before disappearing down the hallway.

They threw on whatever they could grab and ran for the side entrance, boots in hand. They almost collided with Gordon and Gwen at the door. Everyone climbed into a double-seated sedan, the driver barely waiting until they'd settled before taking off.

"Woo-hoo!" Gordon crowed, his grin stretching from one ear to the other. "Another grandbaby."

"That's *great*-grandbaby," Thane said, chuckling.

"Irrelevant," Gwen said, wearing a wide smile of her own. "They're all great."

Chapter 6

Jem and Thane gave another round of congratulations to the new parents and their goodbyes to everyone crowded around Andi's hospital bed. On the way out, they made a detour to see Dante Sullivan O'Daniel. Thane's sister and cousin were there, staring through the nursery's observation window. Picking out the two-day old infant was easy. At twenty-four and three-quarters inches in length, he was the biggest one. Not unexpected, considering his parents. Andi was a six-foot-plus Valkyrie and Nicholas was even taller, over seven-feet of muscle.

He's beautiful. Jem stared at him wistfully. Would she and Thane ever have a child? With her messed up DNA, could she even get pregnant? And if she could, should she?

After a few more window taps, they all headed down the hallway.

"Can Katrina and I catch a ride home with you?" Shiloh Stohlass asked. "We rode in with Mom, but she wants to stay longer."

"Sure," Thane replied.

"Have you heard who won the weight pot?" Katrina Baron asked.

"Dante," Jem said, grinning at their '*huh?*' expressions. "None of us guessed it, so the unanimous decision was that, technically, the baby had won. Nicholas said it'd come in handy buying extra-large diapers," she added.

They piled into an elevator, laughing.

"Got settled into the apartment, yet?" Jem asked. The two girls had recently signed a lease together. She tossed her hair back over her shoulder, having left it hanging loose in a long ponytail tonight instead of its usual braid.

"Mostly." Katrina's nose scrunched. "We're still shifting things around, figuring out the best place for them. Shiloh and her mom where right about getting a place with a third bedroom."

"It's our everything-else room right now," Shiloh added as they stepped off the elevator and into the main lobby.

Outside the hospital entrance, they stared at the thick wall of fog.

"I hope you can find the car, Thane, because I can barely see the parking lot," Jem said, squinting.

"Fog is projected to be exceptionally bad for the next week," Katrina said. "That's why we rode in with Shiloh's mom and her driver."

"Of course I can find it," Thane scoffed. "I'm a highly trained Tracker," lights suddenly blazed off to their left, "with a remote button."

Katrina punched him in the arm.

Laughing, they made their way through the swirling fog. They were sliding into the car when Shiloh suddenly said, "Do you hear something? Like a hissing?"

"I don't feel so good," Katrina said, leaning sideways on the seat.

Jem's head began to spin, and she saw Thane stagger. She tried to stand, but her legs gave out. *Oh, shit,* was her last thought.

***

Jem fought bile down, trying to think through the dizziness and nausea. The car. A hissing? *Gas.* They'd been gassed with something odorless and quick-acting. She was slumped in a sitting position, her knees drawn up in what felt to be a confined space. Cracking her eyelids open cautiously didn't help. It was totally dark. She confirmed the cramped space by trying to move her head and elbows. Neither got very far. She appeared to be in a Jem-sized shipping container.

Who was kidnapping her this time?

Muffled voices. Vibrations.

Shuttle? Taking her who-knew-where. What had they done with the others? She didn't dare shift, not with her brain mimicking a kid's whirligig. She squirmed; that was a mistake. The movement aggravated both her symptoms. She won the battle to keep her stomach contents but lost the one with the whirlpool dragging her into its depths.

Chapter 7

Thane paced from one side of his grandfather's library to the other. Two hours had passed since he'd awakened in the front seat of the car, nauseous and dizzy, as Stuart banged on the window. Once people had realized they were missing, Stuart called LE who had in turn contacted Dykstra Communications. Dykstra had triangulated their phones to within a few blocks and two cars, one filled with Stohlass guards and the other with Law Enforcers, had crawled through zero visibility streets to find them.

His unconscious sister had been taken to the hospital. His mother had called an hour ago to let them know she was awake, doing okay and would be going home with her. Katrina's system, still recovering from the ordeal she'd gone through this past year, had been more sensitive to the drug they'd been sedated with *after* they'd been gassed. Utica gas was odorless and quick-acting, but the effects were short term, usually no more than an hour.

The drugs had given the kidnappers time to get where they were going before the alarm was sounded. They'd had over six hours now to get wherever that was. Thane stopped in front of a window, still fuming. General Kowalski had declined to shut down port facilities, saying it was undoubtedly too late and they had no way to know if the kidnappers were using air, ground, or water craft. Or what direction they were going if they'd left Azusa, despite the heavy fog.

He had, however, put Major Markowitz and his commando teams on alert.

Azusa Law Enforcement was quietly checking all airport departures, along with hotels and transit dorms in case the kidnappers were lying low locally.

Several worried family members and Boyd, Jem's stand-in father, had gathered at the house.

The sound of wheels had Thane turning. His grandmother pushed in a cart laden with plates and cups. She parked it beside the large desk.

"Coffee, breakfast rolls, and danishes," Gwen said. "We can all use something to keep us going. Gordon and Seth are in the conference room. They'll be here as soon as their call with General Kowalski and Director Raine is finished."

Thane poured a large cup of coffee, his stomach too snarled to eat. He sat down tiredly in a chair. Conferring in the secure conference room, with its classified comm line, meant they were discussing Jem and the possible targets she might be aimed at. Something extremely valuable with normally impenetrable security, undoubtedly. If it had been a ransom-kidnapping, all four of them would have been taken. Thane's hand tightened around his cup. No, it was another frigging opportunist. One who planned to exploit Jem and had undoubtedly taken Shiloh to force her cooperation.

Then his grandmother's words fully penetrated. "Director Raine? She knows about Jem now?" he asked.

Ankara Raine was Azusa's FBI Director, which also made her the Director of Oslo's Western Federal Law Enforcement Agency district.

"Only about her stealthiness. I do believe General Kowalski is thinking about giving her office a few additional details. Situations such as this could benefit from the FLEA's full resources."

Few knew about Jem's mutation, when a lab experiment on Earth went wildly out of control. The resulting DNA-slash-cellular changes had given her the ability to become invisible. More recently, she'd discovered that it linked to a teleportation capability, although that had serious side effects. Even fewer, including most of Thane's family, knew the full scope of those abilities. The truth was deemed too dangerous, too volatile. It had driven Director Raine's predecessor into attempting to kill Jem under the banner of Republic security.

Time passed slowly. LE called. Nothing found locally. No spaceport departures. Three cargo carriers and two shuttles had left the airport, all on routine routes and more or less on time despite the fog. Nothing new or last minute scheduled. Gordon and Seth joined their vigil.

"Thane, try to get some rest." Gwen laid a hand on his arm. "We'll wake you at the first news. Promise."

"You've been up for over twenty-six hours, son," Gordon said from his place behind his desk. "Not counting that four-hour nap."

"Yeah, well, I'm not the only baggy-eyed one here," Thane retorted.

"True," Gordon acknowledged. "But we're not the ones waiting to take off like a hawk dive bombing for dinner. Kevin, you might want to take that into consideration, too."

Grumbling, Thane conceded, as far as resting. But he did it on the couch there in the library. Didn't matter if his legs hung over the end. Shiloh's brother, he noted, kicked back in his chair. Neither of them were going anywhere.

Thane didn't think he'd be able to actually sleep, but there was nothing between wondering *"Where the hell are they?"* and his grandmother shaking him awake.

"Thane. Kenneth Brower is on the house comm. Says he needs to talk with you."

Thane rolled off the couch, almost knocking her down. "Sorry," he apologized hurriedly as he raced to his granddad's desk. There was only one reason the man would be calling him. His grandfather rolled his chair to the slide, exposing Brower's face on his monitor.

"I'm here. What do you have?"

"I heard about Miss Wilmont and her friend. My people pegged a hard-looking group of five men that came in about ten days ago and stayed to themselves in a transit dorm. I had them under surveillance in case they were Danford's backup. They've disappeared. I've got people scouring the Circle and other areas. If there's—hold on a minute." A blank screen replaced his image.

Thane leaned forward. *Come on, come on.*

Bower reappeared. "A night worker on Vanguard Avenue saw what she described as several tough-looking types loading something aboard a dark-colored cargo van. She couldn't see much in the fog and prudently didn't stop to stare. That's all I've got," Brower said.

"That's two streets over from where they found us," Thane said grimly. "Thanks. I owe you."

"No. We owe her. I'll be in contact if I hear anything else. Good luck." The screen blanked.

Thane straightened and found the desk surrounded. *Oh, hell. When did Shiloh's mom arrive?*

Susi Taft gave him a small smile, Kevin's arm wrapped supportively around her.

"That van could be anywhere," Boyd said grimly.

Yeah, it could. Worry tightened Thane's jaw as he contacted Law Enforcement to update them. Hopefully, they knew how to find a needle in a foggy haystack.

Chapter 8

Jem blinked as consciousness returned. Halleluiah. *Rats!*

She was back in the crate. The top was open, not that it would do her any good at the moment. According to the throb at the base of her skull, they were aboard a spaceship and the O-engine was running. Feeling an O's active field was an annoying facet of her mutation.

Crappy rats. How long had it been this time?

She remembered a bed and being so woozy she'd needed help to the bathroom. At least she'd been able to handle the rest herself. Then another prick in the arm after getting flat again.

"You were paid to get Wilmont and Baron. That is *not* Thane Baron," Jem heard an angry male voice say.

"The woman will be easier to control," a condescending male voice replied. "And force compliance by both Wilmont and Baron."

Dammit, they'd taken Katrina, too.

"It was not your decision to make, Myers. My employer—"

"Wilmont is awake," interjected a deep voice above her.

Jem looked up and into a face as expressionless as the voice had been. So much for eavesdropping. She pulled herself upright, using the crate rim to steady herself as she glanced around. A ship's plazo, the open space that was the ship's main access point. From its size, the ship was probably a Class Three or Four. She noted several men standing off to the side as the guard stepped back, then turned her attention to the two quarreling in front of another crate. She didn't recognize either, though one did seem kind of familiar.

She propped back against the crate to hide her slightly wobbly legs and crossed her arms. Drawing on lessons learned in numerous Port Circles—*show no fear, show no weakness*—she said, "What moron had the dumb idea to kidnap us?"

The vaguely familiar man wore an insolent smirk. That, and the way he ran his gaze over her, told her which voice he belonged to. Myers, huh? Ignoring him, she focused on the one wearing a scowl and the standard jumpsuit a lot of ship crews preferred. The conversation she'd interrupted said he was the one in charge of this fiasco.

"Well?" she drawled.

"Does it matter?" the man snapped. "The continuing health and well-being of you and your companion depends on your cooperation."

"I have been threatened by worse monsters than you," Jem said in her most bored tone. "Where are they now?" Richardson was dead and Beckett was in a federal penitentiary cell. Jem looked over at the other crate. Katrina must still be—no, wait, that's *black* hair. *Shiloh.*

"You got a name?" she said, turning back to the scowler.

"Farouk Henning."

"Well, Mr. Henning, you can save all of yourselves a lot of trouble and turn this ship around as soon as we drop out of O-drive and take us back to Midgard." She caught the guard's head tilt in her peripheral vision. Wondering how she knew they were in O-space? "I'll even let you, your crew, and Mr. Smirky there take off before reporting to LE," she finished.

"You don't seem to have grasped your current situation," Myers said, annoyance replacing smirk.

Why did this guy look familiar? She didn't know any Myers. "No, that would be you two. Thane—the Republic's best Tracker—will be looking for us. And so will others, some of whom won't be too particular about the condition they leave you in." Boyd would pound them into pulp.

Grasping the crate's edge, Jem swung over and out. The guard backed up several feet, his hand dropping to his weapon. She walked over to the other crate and laid a finger on Shiloh's neck. A pulse beat, slow and steady. "How long does the drug last?"

"Normally about four, five hours," Henning said, eyeing her. "You came out of it pretty fast."

Jem ignored that. "I'm assuming you have quarters for us. Since Shiloh is still out," she turned to the deep-voiced guard, "would you mind carrying her there?" Her nonchalant attitude had Henning off-balance. Good.

Myers stepped forward. "I'll take her."

Something in his voice chilled her. Instinctively, Jem stepped in front of the crate. "No."

"Get out of my way."

Jem spread her feet slightly and rebalanced her weight. She was about to put Thane and Stuart's lessons to the test.

Suddenly the guard bent over the crate. With very little effort, he swung Shiloh's limp body over his shoulder. "Where to?" he said.

Henning, nonplussed for a moment, motioned for them to follow.

The lift ride to the upper deck was a bit crowded with the four of them. After a short trip through the communal areas and down a hallway, they entered a suite. Several chairs, a couch, and two smallish side tables took up most of the room. A bathroom was visible through an open door to the left. The door on the right was most likely a bedroom. A large viewscreen hung on the wall beside it.

The guard carefully laid Shiloh down on the couch. Then he went to lean against the wall next to the entrance.

Jem faced Henning. "Do you serve meals here or do we get to use the kitchen?" Richardson had allowed her the use of his ship's public areas: there was nowhere to go while traveling through O-space.

Henning turned to the guard, said "Wait here," and stalked out.

Jem noted the guard's brief flash of irritation. "Thank you…"

"Rolfe."

"Thank you, Mr. Rolfe. How long have you worked for Henning?"

"Just Rolfe, and I don't."

"You're Myer's man?"

"Temporarily."

A hired mercenary, and a very good one instinct warned her. It'd taken experience and finesse to pull off their kidnapping as they had. From his tone, he didn't like his boss very much. *Hmmm.* That presented future possibilities.

Henning returned and demanded, "Put this on." He tossed what he held to Jem.

A tracker bracelet. Jem's heart sank. She couldn't shift wearing this. Henning and his guards would come running when its signal dropped off sensors. It also told her who was behind this operation, as his thugs had previously used the inch-wide band with a small transmitter case. At least it wasn't a zap band. That one included imbedded needles that would administer a potent drug at a remote signal.

She tossed it back to Henning. "No. And you can tell Reginald Kurzvall, Asshole Extraordinaire, hello for me in your next message."

Henning beckoned to Rolfe. "Put it on her."

The merc didn't move. "I'm not crew."

"You've got a contract."

"With Myers. We're still owed passage back to Toulouse and final payment."

"So? I'll pay you to keep an eye on Myers. I don't trust..."

Jem's breath caught as Rolfe's hard gaze locked on Henning. The idiot had insulted a professional mercenary who could probably kill him in less than five seconds and in twenty different ways.

Toulouse, Palmyra Two, had been the Republic's unofficial mercenary capital. That title had become official after the Palmyra System seceded and went Independent about four months ago. They had turned it into a business, their contracts considered sacrosanct with stiff penalties for failure to meet its terms. An ex-mercenary they knew had told them about the newly formed Mercenary Guild. Its code of ethics disapproved of taking multiple contracts at the same time, as that could create a conflict of interest between employers.

Which Henning should know, ignored at his own peril, and just realized his mistake.

His deep voice so low it was almost a growl, Rolfe coldly stated, "Under. Contract."

After a tension-filled pause that saw Henning still breathing, he turned back to her. Jem happily noted he was a bit paler than before.

"You will put it on," he told her, "or your friend will suffer the consequences."

Show no weakness.

"No, and the instant you, or anyone else, harms Shiloh, my cooperation ends." Jem used her most icy tone, the one she'd picked up from the Kid. She angled forward slightly. "I will also cut off your balls the first chance I get. Can you lock your door against a ghost?" she taunted.

Impasse. Anger and frustration warred across Henning's face.

Henning and Kurzvall had expected her to be compliant. To be fully cowed, obeying their smallest, dirtiest commands. To do that, to not draw any lines, would eventually condemn Shiloh. They'd claim her death was an accident or suicide. Then they'd go grab someone else she cared about.

Jem's teeth ground. This had to stop. She was frigging tired of it, especially when others were endangered because of her.

"Then neither of you leave this room," Henning spat. Throwing the tracker onto a chair he stomped out.

Rolfe gave her a brief nod. Jem was pretty sure that was a flicker of respect in his eyes. The door slid closed behind him, undoubtedly locked in its track.

Henning would post a guard outside. Kurzvall obviously hadn't told him about the invisibility. But her reputation for bypassing locked rooms and security systems—assumed by some secret physical means—had become well-known in various circles. She was constantly declining job offers from criminal organizations. Something else she was tired of.

"Well, that didn't go so good," said an unexpected voice.

Jem spun around. How long had Shiloh been awake? "How do you feel?"

"A bit woozy, but otherwise okay." She sat up. "Anything to drink? My throat's pretty dry."

Jem hurried over to a small refreshment bar in a corner and located several cups in the upper cabinet. Filling two of them with water from the small spigot, she gave one to Shiloh and drank the other down. She hadn't noticed how dry her throat was until Shiloh's comment.

"I am so sorry. You're here because of me," Jem said, sinking guiltily on the couch.

"To intimidate and force you to steal for them. Or worse," Shiloh said calmly.

"Yes," Jem said, miserable. "Sounds like they were supposed to grab Thane, but one of them—a smirky kidnapper named Myers—decided you'd make a better hostage. I'm so sorry," she repeated. "I'll…I'll get you away safe. Somehow. I'll think of something," she said, gesturing toward her ear.

Shiloh nodded, getting the message of possible listeners. "We'll both get away," she said firmly. "What happened and where are we?"

Jem provided a summary and that she had no idea where they were headed. "At least this is a nice suite. Looks like they combined three rooms. We even have our own bathroom. On the *Hidden Trove*, I had to use the communal bathroom and my room was the standard eight-by-fifteen crew quarters." She had been prisoner on the Class Five ship until she convinced the crew to mutiny.

"I appreciate you taking this so calmly," Jem said, rubbing her neck.

"I'm a Stohlass," she said quietly, "and the last couple of years have been…eventful."

Jem's gaze dropped. Eventful wasn't the right word. More like chaotic. Deadly. Soul numbing. Her own problems during that time were insignificant compared to their family's losses. She'd only had to deal with a couple of paranoid fanatics and the exposure of her abilities.

Crap. Jem dropped her chin on her chest and sighed. "I've broken contract." The five-year contract she'd taken with Midgard's Planetary Defense office in order to stay out of Earth's Military Command's clutches.

"What?"

"General Kowalski specified I had to stay on Midgard for a year. I've still five months left."

"Was there an extenuating circumstance clause?"

Jem blinked. Right. Lawyer family. "Kind of, yes."

Shiloh patted her leg. "If the general doesn't think getting abducted and hauled off planet while unconscious fits that definition, then he can take a dip in barnacle waste."

Jem couldn't stop the wide smile stretching her face. "Don't take this the wrong way, Shiloh, but I'm glad you're here."

"So am I," said a voice behind them.

Both women surged to their feet and whipped around.

Jem scowled at Myers, standing in the open doorway. *Stupid, stupid.* Not only had they failed to hear it open, she'd been sitting with her back to an enemy's door. He also didn't appear surprised Shiloh was awake. Yep, there were cameras.

"I'd appreciate you knocking before entering our room, Myers," Jem said boldly.

He ignored her. "Did you miss me, Shiloh?"

"*Myers?*" Shiloh said in a strangled voice.

Jem looked over. Shiloh's expression was a cross between horrified and furious. After a moment, it was simply furious.

"Allow me to introduce you, Jem. Meet Martin *Myers* Stohlass." Her voice was acidic enough to etch his name in steel. "The family disgrace."

"Really?" Jem drawled, now seeing the family resemblance. "I was trying to figure out why he looked familiar. Thane hasn't told me much about him, just that he was sentenced to six years on Fed-Pen planet Skewed for assault and stupidity."

His face flushed.

"By the way, I appreciate you using your maternal name," Jem quipped. "I'd hate to have to address you the same as Shiloh and others that I respect."

"You think you're so smart. Special," Martin bit out. "You think you can dictate terms? Let *me* tell you the way it's going to be." He took a step forward and jabbed a finger at Jem. "This is your prison. You'll be taken out when they need you to do something. Which you will do exactly as you're told to or she," he redirected his finger toward Shiloh, "will pay the consequence."

"You missed the part about me cutting off balls," Jem said coldly.

"You'll have to find them first," he retorted. "Shiloh and me. Nobody will know where we are, not even Kurzvall. Contact with him will be through one of Palmyra's anonymous mailboxes." His lip curled arrogantly. "I'll receive regular updates on your cooperation. You'll get the occasional timestamped video as evidence she's still alive. If you fail to perform or double-cross us, you—and her family—will get that video, too."

Myers gave Shiloh a smug once-over and said, "Later."

Jem waited until the door closed behind him before turning to study Shiloh. Her friend stared off unseeing, pale, her hands fisted at her side. "Well, that didn't go so good," she said, echoing Shiloh's earlier comment.

Shiloh gave a choked laugh. "No." She sank down on the couch, her hands covering her face.

Jem sat in the chair opposite her, which also let her keep an eye on that door. After a long pause of silent assessment, she said, "He's the reason you're here instead of Thane." She didn't need to make it a question.

Shiloh dropped her hands. "Most likely."

The resigned voice and shoulder slump were so unlike Shiloh. *This is not going to be good.* "Want to tell me about it?" she asked quietly.

It took a couple of seconds before she began. "Martin Stohlass showed up at my fifteenth birthday party. Normal family get-together, you know? After that, he kept showing up at family events he'd normally skipped. It was a couple of months before I realized he was *always* showing up wherever I happened to be. Sometimes with gifts."

"He was stalking you."

"Yes, but nothing overt or pushy. Just always *there*. Went on for almost a year, then he got arrested. I was so relieved, I spilled everything to Mom."

"You hadn't told them earlier?"

Shiloh shook her head. "I probably should have. But, you know, he was family and I didn't want to get him into trouble. He never pushed *too* hard, so I figured he'd eventually quit and go away. You'd think, after six years, he would have."

Jem's chest constricted. He'd keep her alive, all right. Myers—*never Stohlass*—would rape her every chance he got. Tall, willowy Shiloh was strikingly beautiful. Her father's black hair and deep blue eyes paired with her mother's soft golden skin had made a stunning combination. The asshole had fixated on Shiloh at that party, not caring she was a cousin.

"You were lucky, Shiloh. If he hadn't been arrested and sent to prison, he'd have soon become more than pushy. A year is a long time to be turned down…especially for someone with his ego. So, if you weren't the assault charge, who was?"

"Don't remember his name," Shiloh said, shaking her head. "Originally it stemmed from a bar brawl, then a second one was added when he punched the female enforcer sent to arrest him for skipping his trial."

"He didn't show up for court?" Shiloh's sudden giggle surprised her.

"When his lawyer contacted him by phone to remind him, the idiot told the lawyer to pay off the judge, the jury, and whoever else. Unbeknownst to him," she said, eyes dancing, "the judge had insisted the lawyer make his call in the courtroom with his phone on speaker so they could all hear his excuse."

"*Oooooo*. I'm guessing that's the stupidity part," Jem said, laughing.

"No, that was arrogance. Stupidity was him trying to intimidate the prosecutor's main witness after his parents bailed him out. Again. Needless to say, the judge refused a third bail and threw the book at him."

Jem shook her head. "No wonder Gordon refused to represent him."

"What do I do, Jem?" she said, a hitch in her voice. "I *can't* go with him."

"First, think positive. Since they were stupid enough to leave Thane behind, he'll be leading the hunt for us." Jem flashed a wicked grin then added sotto voce. "Not that we're going to sit around and wait." Shiloh knew about Jem's teleport ability.

Shiloh's eyes sparkled and her shoulders squared. "Second?"

Jem looked around. "We get rid of the cameras."

They found two in the sitting area and one each in the bathroom and bedroom. The perverts. Especially since they'd expected her to be *interacting* with Thane. The wrist tracker's hard case made a very satisfying mess of them.

Chapter 9

Gordon Stohlass sat at his library desk, trying to pretend interest in the document displayed in front of him. Finally, he gave up. He'd have to pass the case to…who? It was a *family* law firm. Everyone there was just as distracted, worried about Jem and Shiloh. This was the third day now and LE still had no clues.

Nor did Kenneth Brower, who had talked briefly again with his grandson last night.

The comm light on his computer lit as a chime sounded, announcing an incoming call. Gordon didn't recognize the number, but shock arrowed through him at the ID listed. He quickly switched it to comm mode.

"Beverly. Is everyone all right?" he asked as soon as a woman's image materialized.

The woman framed on the screen appeared startled for a moment, then flashed a wry smile. "Yes, everyone is alive and well," she said.

Gordon sighed in relief. He'd been afraid his niece was going to give him bad news about his brother or sister-in-law. His brother's family had ceased any communication with them years ago. He had kept track of them through financial and social news, silently cheering when his brother, Corwin, had finally released the day-to-day operational reins of their company to Beverly a year ago.

"I should have anticipated your reaction," Beverly continued, "and I appreciate your concern. I do have news. Martin was released from Skewed," she said, her tone neutral.

Gordon did a quick calculation. Yes, his six-year sentence on the Federal Penal planet would be up by now. His refusal to represent his nephew in court is what had caused the family rift.

"Thank you for the warning." He forehead wrinkled. "Does he appear to have moderated his behavior?" Or was Martin still the menace he'd called him?

"I don't know," she said. "He's only been home a couple of brief times since he was released six weeks ago."

Gordon stiffened. *Six weeks?*

"The company received an unexpected bill this morning from the Starfall Cargo Line for cargo and fuel expenses. I contacted the manager who put me in touch with the pilot. Captain Tara McKean says Martin reserved space on her cargo carrier in Azusa three days ago. It was last minute but she had the room. Three tough-looking guys with him stayed in the cargo section guarding three medium-sized crates they brought onboard. An hour out from Piscah, Martin insisted Captain McKean divert to Eastport. He claimed his cargo was time-critical for a company deal and we'd cover the cost of additional fuel. Since he was a *Stohlass*," Beverly said irritably, "and our company does use Starfall regularly, she complied."

Located on Oslo's east coast, Eastport was the second busiest port on Midgard. It primarily handled cargo shipments and UPMS pods.

Stone-faced, Gordon said, "Wouldn't want to alienate a well-paying customer."

"Precisely. They refueled in Swantown. Martin, his friends, and their crates got off in Eastport. McKean then continued on to Piscah."

The knot in Gordon's chest got bigger. Beverly gave him a few seconds to digest her news before continuing.

"I checked with Dad and Mom. I had to practically browbeat them to admit that Martin was gone again, probably for an extended period this time. He left about a week ago and took all his things with him. And, no, they have no idea where he's gone or that he had *friends*."

They stared silently at each other for several seconds.

"Have you heard anything more about Shiloh or Miss Wilmont?" she asked, an undertone of worry creeping in.

"No." She didn't want to say it. Beverly didn't want to admit she was afraid her brother was responsible for their disappearance. "Thank you, Beverly. Would you please send me the pilot's contact information?"

She nodded. "Please keep me updated. And for the record, Uncle Gordon, I never approved of Dad and Mom cutting off relations. You were right. My brother was a menace. Still is, I'm guessing," she said softly, right before the screen blanked.

Gordon spit out a couple of his grandson's more colorful cuss words. Martin's fixation with Shiloh was even stronger now than it was six years ago if he'd go to this extreme. Shiloh shouldn't have remained silent for so long. She hadn't told the family about him until after he'd been arrested on those other charges. They should have found some way to add a stalking charge too. Shiloh and her family would have automatically received an alert on his release.

Ping. A new email. He checked it, then pushed away from his desk. He hurried out of the library in search of Thane and Stuart.

***

A grim collection of faces gathered around Gordon in the family room later that evening. The day had been a whirlwind of activity since Beverly Stohlass's call. When Thane started to say something, he held up his hand. "Wait. One more is coming. I want to go through this just once."

They waited. The silence saying more about the room's mood than any conversation could.

Van materialized in the doorway. "Assistant Director Rafael Reis," he announced. He stepped aside to let the man enter then vanished as quietly as he came.

"AD Reis. Good to see you," Gordon said, "although I wish the circumstances were better."

Reis bobbed his head. "Director Raines is watching this closely and will assist in any way necessary."

Gordon looked around, took a deep breath. "We'll start at the top to ensure everyone has the same information. Beverly Stohlass called me earlier today." Gordon listed precisely all that his niece had told him. "I contacted Captain McKean, verified Beverly's information and asked a few more questions.

Timewise, Martin was contacting her for a ride at the same time as the kidnapping. Damn suspicious, that."

"Director Raines and I concur," Reis said.

Gordon continued. "Martin's three crates were approximately one meter square by one meter tall. Captain McKean didn't get a close look at them."

"That's big enough to pretzel a person into it," Boyd said grimly. "Want to bet the third one held all their specialized equipment? Port Security would have noticed even one well-armed individual."

"Thane?" His grandson had used his Tracker license to get port information.

"Cargo plane TY32087, operated by Starfall Cargo filed a routine flight plan—six hours earlier and straight to Piscah. It was thirty-five minutes late taking off. Reason given to Azusa Airport Control was that their last load was running late. With the fog, who'd question it?" Thane said, his face set in hard lines. "Piscah Airport Control verified McKean's plane filed an inflight deviation, landing there almost five hours past their initial flight plan."

"By waiting until almost to Piscah—a four-hour flight—Azusa Control was unaware of the deviation," Nicholas said. "We'd most likely have never known about it without Beverly's info."

"Thank Thor," Gwen muttered. "It's about time someone in the family showed some sense. *That* family," Gwen clarified when Gordon gave her a skeptical look. "Our side of your tree is quite sensible."

"Quite true. Did you get to talk with Eastport Control, Thane?" Gordon asked.

"Plane arrived. It taxied to a communal cargo hanger, idled for about twenty minutes, and then joined the out-bound queue. Plane took off," Thane said sourly. Atmospheric aircraft weren't bound to static in and out windows like spacecraft were.

"Twenty minutes. That's more than enough time for four men to unload three crates, even without a hover-cart." Boyd rubbed his chin thoughtfully. "Communal hanger…that time of night…it'd be hectic and workers would be focusing on their own loads. No telling where they zipped off to—a local vehicle or over to the spaceport side."

"Are we assuming they were taken off planet?" Stuart asked.

"Why not?" Gordon said, frustrated. "We're already assuming a lot. Martin's behavior is definitely suspect. We don't have proof the girls were in two of those crates. We don't have proof Martin is behind their abduction. We don't know if the five men Bower mentioned are our kidnappers. If they are, where did two go since only three accompanied Martin to Eastport? It's all circumstantial. Dammit!" He slammed his fist on his leg. "We don't *know* anything! We're guessing."

"Azusa Law Enforcement's investigation is continuing along their normal avenues," Reis said tersely. "We will conduct ours at the Federal level. I checked with the FLEA office in Odinheim. Martin Myers Stohlass did arrive there six weeks ago and reported to them as per protocol. That officially released him from Federal custody. Ninety minutes later, he was on a shuttle to his home of record, Piscah on Helsinki.

"Director Raines has sent an express messenger pod to Skewed— borrowed from General Kowalski—for Martin's personnel file from there. By the way, the general is a bit annoyed at being left out of the loop. Contract, remember?"

No, he hadn't forgotten. Defensively, Gordon said, "I planned to call him as soon as we had something definite."

"I'd suggest sooner than later," Reis said dryly. "Anyway, we should receive the file from Skewed soon."

"Why? I mean, what are you looking for?" Thane said.

"Anything that stands out," Reis said. "This wasn't planned overnight. Too organized, too well funded, too precise in execution. If your nephew is involved, as it certainly appears, things were already in motion before he was released. I'm willing to bet those three men with Stohlass, plus the missing two, were a very expensive mercenary team. Where and when did he hire them? Or were they provided by an interested third party?"

Like Reginald Kurzvall, Gordon thought grimly.

"Is Beckett still on Skewed?" Thane asked Reis.

"Yes."

"Why?" Thane demanded. "Why isn't he on Hellspawn with the rest of the lifers?"

"Perhaps your grandfather should ask General Kowalski that question when he speaks with him. Beckett is being kept there by military decree," Reis said tonelessly.

The room went quiet. Joseph Beckett, the psychopathic pirate-rogue responsible for countless deaths, including the hundreds who'd perished here in the Branson Hotel Fire. The military had finally defeated his fleet, but not before Jem had been kidnapped and forced to steal Jaguide crystals.

Cold snaked its way down Gordon's spine. It was conceivable that Martin had crossed paths with Beckett on Skewed. Surely, he wouldn't…the Universe help them if the monster was rearing his head again by proxy.

Chapter 10

Thane fidgeted in his chair, wanting to be out searching. Hunting. They were meeting tonight in the high-level security conference room down the hall from his grandfather's library. His granddad believed it provided a more 'dignified and professional' air and underscored the seriousness of their meeting. His eyes narrowed. Or else the wily lawyer knew more than he was letting on.

His granddad was conferring quietly with Stuart and Nicholas at the head of the table. Nicholas was supposed to be on leave for the next several weeks to help Andi with Dante. He'd strode in five minutes ago, his hard expression daring anyone to try and hustle him out. Thane sure wasn't about to try. Boyd, sitting on his left, might have a chance. The 3-Eg heavy-worlder was the only one he knew who could probably out-muscle their tall security chief.

AD Reis entered, accompanied by Federal Agents Jennifer Gaines and Leroy Twobears and, surprising him, Major Elijah Markowitz. Stuart closed the door before taking his seat.

Leroy Twobears had accepted a FBI job in Azusa after resigning a similar one on Earth and moving to Midgard. He'd ended up partnered with Agent Gaines, AD Reis's old partner. He was also Thane's stepfather. Markowitz was the ranking leader of the two commando teams that Admiral Gleason had attached to Midgard's Planetary Defense office. Publicly, their island base southeast of Azusa was for training. A number of units had cycled in and out over the past few months. In reality, Thane knew they were here to keep a helpful eye on Jem.

"As of two hours ago," Reis said, immediately taking command of the meeting, "the abduction of Jem Wilmont and Shiloh Stohlass has become a federal case. Due to Jem's status as a Midgard planetary asset, Major Markowitz has been attached to this investigation as representative of General Kowalski's office. Also, at that time, General Kowalski gave Director Raines a full in-briefing on Jem Wilmont."

Thane drew in a sharp breath. *Doubt that went over well.*

"You've learned something new and credible since yesterday to warrant this change?" Gordon said.

"Yes. Azusa enforcers found a dark van tucked in airport parking that had been reported as stolen. The thieves had been very careful. However," he said with a humorless smile, "they found a very long brown hair under the front seat and a single fingerprint on the driver's inside doorframe that matched to Martin Myers Stohlass."

Reis gave them a moment to vent. "We received Mr. Stohlass's file from Skewed earlier today. While he wasn't a model prisoner, he didn't cause any real problems either. What we found interesting was the visit by a lawyer five days before his release."

"Who?" Gordon snapped, leaning his weight on his forearms. "Who would want to visit that bastard?"

"According to the report, Naviere VanDyke Taylor. A senior partner in Abrahams, Hier, Taylor," the cussing resumed, "Bair and Gaspers, of Tricast Three, of the Consortium," he finished on a louder note.

"Son of a bitch. Son of a freaking bitch. Kurzvall!" Thane exploded.

The law firm was a founding member of the Consortium. Reginald Kurzvall was another and, in fact, the main force behind their secession. The sociopath knew of Jem's invisibility and had relentlessly hunted her after she fled Earth.

"Hold it right there, son," Gordon said. "We can postulate Consortium's involvement in general. Since I highly doubt Reginald Kurzvall is the law firm's only client, we cannot say who specifically is involved. And I can honestly say I prefer Martin's involvement with them over Beckett."

"Given Kurzvall's animosity toward our family, he'd love an excuse to sue us into bankruptcy for 'unfounded smears' to his reputation," Gwen added.

His grandmother's eyebrow arched. "Which means, young man, you need to watch your tongue."

Yeah, yeah, Thane thought sourly.

"With the additional information provided by Miss Beverly Stohlass and Captain Tara McKean, we're now certain that the two women have been taken off planet by agents of a criminally-minded individual, at minimum, or of a hostile foreign power at the worst. Given Miss Wilmont's abilities, General Kowalski isn't the only one that's highly concerned."

"Do you think Kurzvall has shared his *full* knowledge of Jem with these others?" Nicholas asked.

"Unknown," Reis said brusquely, "but it's highly unlikely. Right now, we're going on the presumption, and hope, that this act is primarily for Kurzvall's personal benefit. Which means that if Kurzvall has shared anything, it's probably limited to what will help capture and keep her. Her stealthy reputation is pretty much well-known.

"Director Raines is currently in contact with Eastport Control, requesting a list of all spacecraft that left there in the twelve hours after their arrival. We don't believe they would have risked hanging around much longer."

"Eastport's In- and Out-bound windows are two hours each," Stuart said. "Three exit windows will make for a lot of ships. How do you expect to find which one?"

"Not like they'd file a flight plan straight to a Consortium system," Boyd said darkly.

"Or even be registered to a Consortium planet or company," Thane added.

"Which we're well aware of," Reis said, shooting them both a dark look. "It'll be a process of elimination. Some will be easy, like the UPMS pods—they wouldn't be using them. Others can be deleted for other obvious reasons. The remainder will be scrutinized closely. Their information will be checked and verified, and we'll follow-up to ensure they arrived at their stated destinations, plus-or-minus standard transit times."

"That's going to take days…weeks," he said in a hard voice.

"That can't be helped, Thane," Reis said. "The galaxy is a big place and there's no guarantee they're being taken straight to a Consortium system. This act has been well thought out, even to using enviro-suits to hide their heat signatures from the hospital's security cameras' thermal imaging. Normal viewing was already blinded by heavy fog. You can bet they are using every means available to hide their trail.

"We have to have at least some idea of what we're looking for. Agents Gaines and Twobears will be task leads on this. In the meantime, an alert is being sent to all Federal and Port offices to be on the watch for them. We will follow all steps, document everything so we have solid proof of where they are, how they got there, and if they're no longer in the Republic, demand their return."

"You think the Consortium is going to comply?" Thane said bluntly. "They've protected Kurzvall from the beginning. We can't extradite him. Hell, we can't even touch him when he's here due to *diplomatic immunity*," he spit out. "They'll shrug and turn a blind eye to the whole mess."

Reis slowly turned his head and gave Markowitz an enigmatic look.

Markowitz favored the table with a very shark-like smile.

After a moment's speculation, Thane returned his smile. So did Boyd.

"Do you *want* to start an intersystem war?" his grandfather snapped from the end of the table. The intensity of his glare at the federal officers startled Thane.

"You want us to sit on our asses and do nothing?" Twobears retorted. "If we can prove a Consortium agent abducted two Republic citizens from their home and is forcing one of them into illegal acts against her will, and they turn that blind eye, what should our response be? Should Republic citizens be fair game to any individual or group that wants to extort them?"

Silence, as Twobears raked the table with a smoldering look.

"If we—and I include all levels of Law Enforcement and military," he continued in a cold tone, "do *nothing*, then we betray the oaths we took to protect and defend those citizens. We will undermine the Republic's entire foundation. Two years ago, we took a stand. We mobilized against a marauding pirate fleet. This threat is no different. We either face the reality of what this *is*, or stick our heads in a wormhole and leave our asses to be kicked."

Wow! Thane's respect for his stepfather went up several notches.

"I second that," Reis said bluntly. "With the formation of political entities outside of Republic jurisdiction, many aspects of our legal system must be re-evaluated. From Federal laws down to individual planetary regulations. One thing is clear: we cannot and will not allow agents of foreign entities/powers to operate within our borders with impunity. Due to circumstances, we have landed on the precedent-setting wave. Both Earth's Military Command and the appropriate Federal Senators are being informed of the situation. We can expect both oversight and assistance as needed."

"Assistance?" Nicholas scoffed. "More like swoop in and take over."

"Only if we do end up having to enact extreme measures." Major Markowitz shook his head. "Believe me, we do not want to start a war. Until such time, this will remain under the purview of Midgard's Federal Law Enforcement Agency, supported by its Planetary Defense Office." He flashed a grin. "And let's not overlook the very formidable Jem Wilmont. The Consortium may end up screaming for us to take her back."

Chapter 11

Transom Ode was a basic Class IV Drone, its Cargo sub-designation and basic shape inherited from the workhorse of its ancestors. Lounge and kitchen sections behind the flight deck were the communal living areas. The mercenary team was camped out in the plazo, the open space directly beneath those areas. A hallway ran from the kitchen to a supply/storage room at its end. Four pocket-style doors opened on both sides for crew quarters and the communal bathroom, located next to the kitchen. The area beneath the crew quarters held the ship's life blood, such as oxygen recycling and water and waste storage. The large, double-deck cargo hold filled the remaining space between those areas and the engines.

Jem and Shiloh had the bathroom side of the hallway to themselves, as the two doors on either side of theirs were false. Those areas had been used to build their 'suite.' She'd learned from her ghost-forays that the five crew members and Myers were double bunking in three rooms as Henning wasn't about to share his quarters. Myers, surprisingly, wasn't grumbling along with the crew. After six years in a cell, it was probably an improvement.

She'd been exploring the ship over the past week while her friend slept. After destroying the cameras and microphones, they'd formulated a plan. One that couldn't be executed until they landed on Argainn Two, the overheard ship's destination. Jem would sabotage the recycler after they landed if it was safe to do so. Neither of them knew anything about the planet. It'd be their luck it had a toxic atmosphere or was a barely established colony with little to no Law Enforcement presence.

Checking to make sure Shiloh was still sleeping, Jem *poofed* back into the normal universe and flopped down in a chair with a slightly guilty feeling. *I need to tell her about phasing.* That way, Shiloh would have more warning than Thane got with his first experience. But there was really no gentle way to ease her into it.

The throbbing at the base of her neck disappeared.

Jem straightened. *Yes.* They'd dropped back into normal space. After more than an hour passed with no indication they were landing, she shifted and went snooping. She'd held off, as she could only hold a shift for so long and hadn't wanted to waste it.

Argainn Two was a gas giant. *Shit, damn, double-crap.*

The pilot had matched the ship with the orbiting science station. The space-suited loadmaster was towing several large crates out the upper-level's cargo door and toward an opening in the nearest station arm where another suited figure waited. They manipulated the crates inside. Did she dare shift her and Shiloh over to it? No, she decided. It would cause too many problems, both for the scientists on board and for Admiral Gleason. Best wait until they landed, where she had a better chance of getting them away and without exposing her ability.

Disgruntled, Jem watched the loadmaster reappear and jet back to the *Ode* and into the hold. She phased through the decking in search of Henning. He was in the lounge outside the flight deck's door, arguing with Myers.

"—to Volpe Four," Myers said haughtily.

"I've already said no," was Henning's irritated response. "Our next stop is the Euphrates System."

"That can wait," Myers replied disdainfully. "Drop me and Shiloh off first—a quick in and out—and then you can go to Euphrates."

"Unlike your arrogant ass, I follow orders," Henning sneered. "Which means rendezvousing on Tigres with Wilmont and your Baron-substitute. And when were you planning to pay off the mercs?"

Ooooo. Sly jab. Rolfe and a couple of his men were observing the exchange from a corner seating. Jem grinned at the suspicious looks they aimed at Myers. Nothing like sowing discord between non-friends.

Myers made a dismissive gesture. "I'll pay them. No one will know you deviated."

"Like hell they won't," Henning snorted sarcastically. "Once they realize Wilmont is off-planet, they'll be looking hard at every transport that left within a close timeframe. That's why we waited then and are sticking to our schedule now. The *Ode's* normal transit time from Argainn to Euphrates is six days. You think they won't notice it took us thirteen? You're an idiot."

Myers's hands clenched.

"Wilmont was right about Baron and his reputation. He's smart, persistent, as fucking dangerous as they come, and you," Henning took a step forward and jabbed a finger almost up Myers's nose, "left him behind. Mr. Kurzvall will not be pleased."

"We'll see about that," Myers snapped.

"Yes, you will," Henning smirked. He walked onto the flight deck and shut the door in Myers's face.

Fuming, Myers whipped around to Rolfe.

Guessing what he was about to demand, Rolfe said, "Not in our contract." Standing, his men mirroring the fluid movement, Rolfe added in a hard voice, "Two of us will accompany you on Tigres to ensure your final terms of the contract are complied with. Properly and immediately."

Prison must have been hard for Myers and his ego, Jem mused, watching the man stomp off to his room. She'd seen that shade of facial purple once before…on another who also didn't think the word 'no' applied to him. Henning was right. After the way Joseph Beckett turned on him, Reginald Kurzvall had little tolerance for deviations from his royal commands. It would almost be worth staying to see the two mega-egos clash.

Jem returned to her would-be prison. Sprawled in a chair, she stared into the past.

Tigres, Euphrates Three. That's where they'd turned Beckett over to Law Enforcement. Where she'd fled the media circus that followed. Where her life had once again changed. Now, it's where she would be handed off to Kurzvall and Shiloh to Myers.

No way in hell was either happening.

***

She'd been gassed, drugged, and repackaged again.

Jem hung on to her nauseated consciousness. She'd been talking with Shiloh, anticipating their upcoming landing on Tigres and debating how to time a discreet escape. She had been about to launch into a phasing explanation when a sudden dizziness struck. No sound warned them this time.

The crate top hadn't been closed yet. Had they landed? Could she—no. Jem dropped her head back down on her knees, blackness threatening to swamp her. She'd been outmaneuvered.

"We have a problem."

Henning. Pissed-off, too.

"We can't land on Tigres."

"Why not?"

That was Myers. Naturally, he'd be overseeing the packing.

"Because they're watching for us," Henning all but snarled.

Oh? Concentrating on the voices pushed the blackness down.

"Impossible," Myers declared, sounding like the pompous ass he was.

"I got a comm from my contact there. A Republic-wide alert for a three-to-five-man mercenary team, two abducted women, and *Martin Myers Stohlass* has been shared with the Euphrates authorities. You arrogant, imbecilic piece of *spash*. They know everything."

Space trash, huh? Jem grinned into her kneecaps. Thane's impressive collection of swear words had probably called him a lot worse than that.

"An alert means they don't know it's us, then," Myers blustered.

"They will if I and my men disembark," came Rolfe's contemptuous voice.

"So, what? We're not in Republic territory. Slip the port guards a few thousand credits and—"

"Can I shoot him, boss?" said an annoyed voice she recognized as one of the mercs.

"We might not get paid."

Oh, boy. Jem wished she could have seen the various expressions in the pause that followed.

In a hard, icy voice, Rolfe said, "You want to bribe a Euphrates Port guard?

Go ahead, try it. They're notoriously unbribable and severely affronted when one tries. The Euphrates government maintains good relations with everyone—especially the Republic. As suspected kidnappers, we would be held for Republic Enforcers to arrive. If they have proof of said charges, we'll then be turned over to them."

"And since I and my crew are obviously complicit, we'll be sitting in the cell next to them and my ship impounded," Henning said in matching tones. "Looks like you get your wish, Myers. We'll have to divert."

"To Volpe Four," Myers said in a satisfied tone.

"Hell, no." Henning sounded disgusted. "Same alerts and it's a Republic system. Enforcers will swarm us at the first sign."

"Shift all the arrangements to Toulouse," Rolfe said. "Which will also serve to complete our contract."

There was a short pause before Henning agreed. "I'll get in touch with my contact, have him pass it on. Get the women back to their room. As for you, Myers—or should I say, *Stohlass*? You might want to ponder your future. Mr. Kurzvall does not like snafus and you've created two big ones."

Fifteen minutes later, Jem was staring furiously at Henning. She hadn't felt the bracelet until helped out of the crate. It'd been snapped around her left wrist while unconscious.

"Signal is now linked to the ship's internal sensors," Henning said, watching his hand comp. "Hall, lounge, kitchen. Anywhere else and I'll get a warning." He studied her for a moment. "You recovered fast again."

"High metabolism," Jem said, knees locked tight to keep from wobbling. Shiloh was sitting on the couch with her head in her hands.

"You can stretch your legs and get your own meals now. I'm in no mood to put up with shit so I suggest you don't give me any." With that grumpy warning, Henning turned and left.

Jem flung herself into a chair and stared at the offending item on her arm. Used a few of Thane's curses instead of her usual. Then she asked Shiloh how she felt.

"Okay. A bit woozy. You?"

Scowling, Jem held up her left arm.

"Oh. *Soooo*…we're screwed?"

"No. Not yet." She'd figure something out.

Chapter 12

Thane strode into his granddad's library and dropped into a chair facing the desk. "Our best bet struck out," he grumbled.

Gordon looked up from some notes he was making. *"Catford Two?"*

Thane nodded. "Reis got word about an hour ago. The ship's captain allowed Federal Enforcers onboard to search as soon as they landed. Nothing but a hold full of Midgard's finest lumber."

The *Catford II,* an independent Class III Cargo, was registered out of Riviera, Euphrates One. It had left Eastport three hours after Captain McKean's drop-off with a destination straight back to Riviera. That had earned it the top spot on their most-possible list.

The Euphrates System was a major hub, with a hundred ports scattered throughout the overpopulated system. That, and the independent status it acquired last year, made it an ideal place to interface with non-Republic Systems or slide nefarious dealings under their Enforcers' noses. AD Reis had sent a politely-worded alert to their FLEA offices about Jem and Shiloh.

Thane stared glumly at the floor. They'd waited over a week for the ship to arrive and the reply was disappointing. Looking up, he saw the same disappointment in his grandfather's face. "That leaves three ships on our list: *Star Trail, Bag of Stardust,* and *Rose Gold. Star Trail* should reach the Tardon System in the next day or so. The other two?" His granddad's grimace matched his own.

Bag of Stardust and *Rose Gold* were Class Fours headed out to Rim colonies. It'd be another week or two before they got word back about them.

Or not, if one of them deviated. Then it'd be a galactic-wide search. The *Lone Tracker* was fueled and stocked, ready to start that hunt. Once he got a starting point.

His ship was a Class II Globe, named for the old-fashioned snow globes they resembled. The main ship was over eleven meters in diameter, with the base housing its engines boosting its height past twelve meters. It was large enough to be comfortable, yet small enough to take advantage of the O-drive's TVS quirk. When tracking, it wasn't unusual for him to beat a quarry on a larger ship to their destination, waiting for them as they disembarked.

"Just heard the latest reports," Nicholas said, walking into the room. "Bummer."

Turning, Thane's response changed to a barked laugh. Nicholas's brows drew down.

"Sorry, sorry," Thane said, holding up a hand. "It's just that…" He waved it in front of himself.

"Most Security Chiefs don't walk around with a baby sling on their chest," Gordon said, chuckling. "It is a bit incongruent."

"A bit?" Thane said, another chuckle escaping. Dante was a big baby, but he looked like a miniature doll pressed up against his father's enormous chest.

"Do you know how little I've gotten to hold my son," Nicholas growled. He settled carefully into the chair next to Thane. "I'm taking advantage of it while I can. My folks left yesterday and Andi's will be here next week. For a whole two months."

Nicholas's family were foresters from the Achilles Archipelago, a cluster of islands northwest of Azusa. They'd spent over a week here, enjoying the sensation of first-time grandparents. Andi's parents owned, managed and often performed in the Valhallass Dance Troupe. Their performances were usually sold out wherever they played. The entire cast was taking a two-month break. Resting, developing new routines, and Dante-cuddling.

A touch of envy washed through Thane. "Andi sleeping?" he asked, watching Nicholas gently stroke his son's back. Someday. Maybe.

Nicholas shook his head. "Gwen took her to her postpartum checkup. Then they plan to do some shopping on Trade Street. No telling what she'll come home with."

That was true. The variety of merchandise offered there ran the gamut of Republic-wide imports to native products and crafts. Jem loved it and could spend a whole day wandering through it.

"I've been thinking," Nicholas said, catching Gordon's eye. "You've concentrated on Class Three and Four ships since they could easily absorb a group of that size *if*," he emphasized, "they remained together."

"We thought of that," Gordon acknowledged, "but decided that splitting into two or more groups would be unwieldy. Especially in providing multiple ships to get them and their equipment off-world covertly."

"Well, someone threw a lot of money on this operation. How did the mercenaries get here undetected?" Nicholas challenged. "According to Kenneth Brower, they were here for several days prior to the snatch."

Gordon's mouth opened. Closed. "Reis is looking into that," he finally managed.

"Uh-huh. They had to have arrived in ones and twos," Nicholas said. "I monitor the FLEA's Port Security reports. The last *known* armed group arriving on Midgard was Major Markowitz and the Commando Unit last spring."

"Agreed," Thane said with a touch of frustration, "but we had to start with the most likely, which is them staying together. Martin can't maintain control of Jem and Shiloh by himself. If none of these pan out, then we'll move down. Class Ones are too small. Twos would be doable if a bit squished on space." And that, Thane thought worriedly, still hinged on them staying as a single, noticeable group.

***

"I don't see why I need to be here," Thane groused to his mom several days later.

They stood in the Scarpello Banquet Hall, where the Hands of Hope Foundation was throwing a huge party to celebrate, belatedly, its move to Midgard. At least, Thane fumed silently and taking another sip of champagne, the wine and hors d'oeuvres were top quality.

Reyna patted the lapel of the formal suit he wore as little as possible.

"You needed to get out of the house and do something other than sulk."

"I did," he replied sullenly.

He'd made a trip to his and Jem's home in Spine Ridge Fjord. He'd even managed to spend a night there. But it was too empty. Too far away if news about Jem or Shiloh came in. He'd instructed Freya, the home's computer brain, to activate its Long-Gone program. The comp brain would keep the house functions at minimum and security levels at maximum. An alarm would be sent to Stohlass Security for any detected intrusions or other problems.

"Oh?" Reyna said, "I could have sworn that was you stomping and scowling all through the house this past week. Mom and Dad are talking about bonuses to the help for putting up with you."

Thane chose to ignore that as he nonchalantly maneuvered him and his mother next to one of the terrace doors. He intended to make a break for it at the first opportunity. Unfortunately, his mother knew him too well and, just as nonchalantly, maneuvered herself between him and it. His irritated glare got a twinkle of amusement back.

"Hello, Thane. It's good to see you again."

His mom's gaze slid away to his right. Both her eyebrows were an arched question when it returned. He rolled his eyes in answer and turned, having recognized the voice.

Her dress was a form-fitting green, matching the emeralds hanging from her ears. Several intertwining silver chains made up her necklace, with a single, large emerald dangling in the middle of cleavage that was, in his opinion, once again over-exposed. Her bracelet matched her necklace. Half her black hair was piled on top of her head, the rest cascading down her back.

"Mother," he said formally, "allow me to introduce Tia Rockefeller Lexington, of Earth. Miss Lexington, my mother, Reyna Williams Stohlass. We crossed paths on my last job."

"Ah, yes. The *Blue Strobe Lounge*," Tia said giving Thane a sultry smile.

His brow furrowed. Was she trying to imply something?

His mom had assumed her socially-polite-but-screw-you face, meaning she'd taken an instant dislike to the ostentatious woman. He was also aware of veiled glances and cocked ears in several of the nearby groupings.

He gave the woman a polite smile of his own. "Yes, that's right. I'd tracked my client's daughter there." Indifference hadn't worked on Earth, so he went with rude and turned his back to her.

"How are things going on Magnus, Mom?" he asked.

Reyna's face broke into a wide smile. "Excellently. The spaceport is fully functional and Port Royal is growing. A large number of the relief workers have stayed on as colonists."

The original colonists on Magnus, Cameroon Two, had nearly been wiped out by Joseph Beckett when he dropped three Delgados on its oil-based flora ecosystem. They'd generated firestorms that had merged to burn everything from the east coast to the Mangel Divide, a wide slash that nearly ripped the single continent apart. Port Royal was the new capital on the Divide's west bank.

"I've heard the Hands of Hope Foundation is assisting in several planetary issues. You are its current manager, I believe, Miss Stohlass?" Tia said. She took a sip from her glass.

Well, hell, rude didn't seem to be working, either.

"Yes, I am," Reyna said. "Are you looking to make a donation? I'd be happy to discuss it with you in my office tomorrow. Are you on Midgard for business?"

"Yes." Tia took another sip, her eyes locked on Thane. "With a side of pleasure."

She didn't just—yes, she did. His suitably rude response was forestalled by his cousin appearing beside him.

"Excuse us ladies," Seth said with a bright smile. "I need to speak with Mr. Baron."

"Let's step outside then." Thane handed his glass to his mother. Yeah, she knew he wouldn't be back. Shooting a veiled glare at Miss Lexington, he stepped out the terrace doors with Seth.

"Thanks for getting me out of there. You won't believe—Seth?" His cousin had grabbed his arm and was hauling him around the manicured shrubbery.

"I got a call from Stuart who got a call from Reis who got an alert from Euphrates. Two days ago, a ship called *Transom Ode* was on approach to

Euphrates Three when it suddenly veered off, nearly colliding with a passenger shuttle from their inner moon. It transitioned out of the system to who knows where."

Thane batted away a tree branch and lengthened his stride. "Dammit, it wasn't on our list." They emerged into the parking lot. "I rode in with Mom. You have a car?"

"Yes. Gina will fill your mother in and catch a ride home with—" Seth gave a short laugh as he slid under the steering wheel. "Scratch that. Knowing my wife, she'll be joining us with your mother."

Thane jerked his door shut as the engine revved. "Well, you did marry your equal. Isn't she the one that proposed?"

Seth looked over and grinned as the car shot out of its parking spot. "Yep."

"Eyes on the road!"

* * * * *

Reyna Stohlass pasted on an apologetic smile. "That was Seth Sullivan, a family lawyer. He must have information about an ongoing issue Thane has at the moment." Which she wanted to hear. Unfortunately, she couldn't leave for at least another hour. But that wasn't as annoying as the entitled brat in front of her.

"How long do you think they will be?"

"Hours, most likely," Reyna said blandly, setting Thane's glass on a passing server's tray.

"He left?" the brat's voice conveying disbelief.

Oh, my. Someone abandoned your jewelry and cleavage?

"I'm not sure what my schedule is," Reyna said, not deigning to answer the obvious, "but be sure to call the Foundation tomorrow. I'll let my assistant know to find a slot for you."

Seth's wife stepped up beside her. "Have you forgotten, Reyna?" Gina Geis said. "Tomorrow is pretty full. You have meetings planned with representatives for three Foundation candidates as well as that charity luncheon we plan to attend."

No, she hadn't. Forced to wait for an appointment like a common person would take Miss Arrogant down a peg. "Maybe the day after, then?" she said instead. "I'm so sorry."

Gina's cheek twitched.

Tia's eyes narrowed.

Huh. Not fooling either. "I'm sure you and my assistant can work out an agreeable time, Miss Lexington. In the meantime, please mingle and enjoy the evening's festivities."

Without a word, Tia turned and walked away.

"That is one irritated woman," Gina observed. She turned to Reyna. "Who is she?"

"A fortune hunter," Reyna snorted, "what else."

"You sure? She appears to have plenty of assets."

Reyna's finger tapped her glass. *Trouble is blowing in on the wind,* intuition told her. "The girl is more ballsy than most. She practically propositioned Thane right in front of me."

"Oh? Think she's going to cause trouble?"

"Count on in it."

Both of them studied the woman now surrounded by a group of admirers.

"Think she knows about Jem?" Gina asked.

"I don't think she cares. What Miss Lexington wants, she's used to getting. For whatever reason, she has set her sights on Thane. I don't like it," Reyna said, a worried timbre in her voice, "and I don't like her."

Chapter 13

Thane paced around the table, too wired to sit. They were back in the Stohlass conference room awaiting Reis's update. His granddad and Seth were talking quietly at one end while Stuart sat sphinxlike with crossed arms in front of the table comp. His grandmother had stepped out a couple of minutes ago, calling someone about something. He hadn't really been paying attention.

Thane whirled around when the computer signaled an incoming call.

Stuart answered it then said, "Wait a sec. I'm putting you on the main screen."

The large viewscreen behind the table's head lit up with Reis's grim image. The man scanned the room, checking who was on this side of the conference.

Thane slid into a seat. "What do you know?"

"We've been digging since the *Transom Ode* alert came in and—"

"Why wasn't it on our suspect list?" Thane interrupted sharply.

Reis flashed him an annoyed look. "Because it wasn't *here* until approximately twenty hours *after* Captain McKean's drop off, which put it well outside our *assumed* window."

His grandfather's glower at him said 'behave.' Mollified, Thane remained silent as his grandfather pressed Reis to continue.

"*Transom Ode* is a Class Four Drone Cargo approximately forty-five meters long. It's registered on Delmark Three as an independent carrier with a crew ranging from five to seven. Owner-Operator is listed as Farouk Cassell Henning. According to Eastport records, *Transom Ode* landed there twice in the last several weeks, always leaving in the next outbound window. The first one was nine days before Jem and Shiloh were abducted, dropping off several cargo pallets. The second one I've already mentioned. No record of anything offloaded, so they did a pickup."

All off-world cargo had to be logged in at its port of arrival, in case it needed to be backtracked later. Smuggling and sneaky varmints were the usual reasons.

"It's small for its class, but less cargo space is compensated by shorter transit times," Thane said, calculating. Still not as fast as the *Lone Tracker*, though.

"Its status is another plus. Independents can generate their own routes, showing up here and there without raising questions," Gordon said as Gwen retook her seat beside him.

"We're making a lot of assumptions—again. Hopefully, we won't get bit—again," Reis said grimly. "Our first two assumptions are that the *Ode* also unloaded passengers that nobody noticed on the first visit and that they and several crates left on the second one."

Thane could almost feel the intense focus boiling off of Reis. A hunter who's sensed his target. "That would match when the mercs show up," he said, rubbing his chin. "They must have split up, come to Azusa separately to avoid arousing any Enforcer interest." Which answered Nicholas's question.

"That's the way we figure it, too," Reis said. "Also, coincidently, that's the same time that Martin Stohlass suddenly shows back up at home according to his sister." He made a sour face. "His parents refuse to speak with any Enforcer."

"That sounds like the stubborn cuss," Gordon muttered.

"We tracked him through port records based on the dates she gave us, as much as possible. He left for Argus One by UPMS pod a week after arriving home from Skewed. Two days later, their records show Martin Stohlass leaving on a business class shuttle to Euphrates Three."

BC shuttles utilized the smaller class ships and provided transport options between the ultra-fast but cramped UPMS courier pods, and the slower, comfortable cruise liners. They were expensive, the cost depending on the ship size and the number of staterooms available. Also, their routes focused on major ports.

"We lose him there," Reis said, his exasperation loud and clear. "The Euphrates authorities' cooperation with the Republic only goes so far. It does not include sharing their port records. Assumptions three and four are that he hired the mercs during that gap and that he was onboard the *Ode* and dropped off with them. In regards to that…"

The screen blanked for a second, then displayed an image that wasn't Reis. The unsmiling man appeared to be mid-thirties, with cropped brown hair and dark eyes that stared out of the screen with a level-eyed confidence. He wore a Marine combat uniform.

"Meet Gunnery Sergeant Trystan Whitmore Rolfe," said Reis's disembodied voice.

The man was relaxed, poised, *and lethal as hell* Thane's hindbrain warned.

"Their Azusa rental had been cleaned by the time we were able to get a team in, thanks to Kenneth Brower's info, but they managed to get a few good fingerprints. On a hunch, I passed them to Major Markowitz who has now confirmed his identity through military channels. Sergeant Rolfe served twelve years, the last four in a Commando Unit. He was honorably discharged and returned home to Palmyra Two where, obviously, he went freelance."

Definitely lethal. "Explains their expertise. The merc leader?" Thane said.

"Undoubtedly. This is his last official photo, twenty-six years ago. He's fifty-eight now, but I do not recommend underestimating him." Reis reappeared. "Or getting in a fight with him, Thane. He was rated as expert-to-master in over two dozen different forms of martial arts."

Stuart let out a low whistle. "Which a mercenary would keep tuned."

"AD Reis, you said Martin was on Argus One four, five weeks ago?" Gwen asked. "Well, isn't that a coincidence. So was Reginald Kurzvall."

"How do you know that?" Reis demanded.

"I knew that asshole had to be involved," Thane said angrily.

"The *Republican Financial News*. They had an article last week about it. Kurzvall personally finalized the merger of Stanfordson Mining Company with KurzIndust Mining Corporation, one of his subsidiaries. The fourth such merger, actually, since the Consortium came to be."

Seth frowned. "Four? I don't like the sound of that."

"Neither did the article's author. It consolidates most of Sector Three's mining resources."

"We'll get a copy," Reis said, "and add Kurzvall's involvement to our assumption list."

It's more than a damn assumption, Thane fumed.

"We've put out an alert for the *Transom Ode*," Reis continued. "They had a scheduled stop at Argainn Two before Euphrates. We'll verify that and its transit time from Eastport. They can't go back into the Euphrates System without facing a stiff fine. We'll find them."

"Unless they ran straight into Consortium space after being warned about the alert," Thane said, pulling out his phone. Boyd answered on the second ring. "Get whatever gear you think you'll need and meet me at the *Lone Tracker*." He stood. "No, but I have a starting point now," he said before disconnecting.

"Wait. Wait." Reis waved his hands. "You can't go barging into the Consortium."

"I'm a Tracker tracking."

"Not in the Consortium," his grandfather warned.

"Gordon is correct. Your license is not recognized in any of the new, uh, republics. Which is something we need to look into," Reis added in a mutter.

Thane blinked. Damn. He hadn't even considered that. "Nothing says I can't be a very nosy private citizen," he said, jutting his chin out stubbornly.

"Well, if you insist." Reis's smile was suddenly all teeth. "I'll send what we have to your mailbox and any updates as we get them. Please keep us appraised of *any*thing of interest you learn."

Thane stalked out. Great. He'd gone from Tracker to Spy. According to old videos, they got shot.

***

Midgard was an hour and who knew how many kilometers behind them, as the ship was currently hurtling through O-space. They sat around the *Lone Tracker's* kitchen table, reading their hand comps. Well, Boyd and Markowitz were. Thane was reading Reis's information on the table comp. He'd provided

69

their hand computers access to the ship's computer for general information. Thor would keep them out of the other areas.

"Have you got to the last update?" Markowitz asked, breaking the silence.

"You must read faster than me," Thane replied surly, still annoyed at having to take the major with him. General Kowalski had overridden his argument about it and had cost him a two-hour delay in leaving for Hebros, Hermes Four. Kurzvall's home world.

"Eastport LE has confirmed a small motel outside the city rented two rooms for one day to a group matching our descriptions and the time gap. Six men and several crates that were taken into the rooms with them." Markowitz looked up. "The women must have been kept sedated or else Miss Wilmont would have teleported them away."

"Sounds like we found the two missing men," Thane said.

Boyd held up his comp. "He adds that they've added the Chadron System to their to-do list—the *Transom Ode* was there. They're guessing Martin Stohlass sent a 'come and get us' message either before they left Azusa or as soon as they hit Eastport. Since it's practically next door transit-wise, they played it smart and deliberately delayed their departure, knowing the outbound ships would be checked. And quit sulking," he added in an aside to Thane.

Thane scowled and crossed his arms.

"Gunnery Sergeant Rolfe's presence changed things," Markowitz said. "The general believed having someone who'd had the same training and skillset would be beneficial."

Beneficial, huh? "You think I can't handle him?" Him and a stunner.

Markowitz flashed an all-tooth smile. "We could find out right quick down in your plazo."

"Thane?" Boyd's cheek twitched. "You are good, but not commando good. Especially at Rolfe's level."

Markowitz shook his head. "I read Rolfe's jacket. *I'm* not at his level, but, if the situation arises, I'd stand a better chance than you."

Not yet ready to give up his irritation, Thane said, "I'm surprised you didn't bring your whole team."

"A team could be construed as an incursion. Cause political repercussions.

I'm a concerned friend helping out, same as him." He aimed a thumb at Boyd.

Thane ground his teeth. They were right and he was acting like a just-grounded teenager. Fine. He huffed out a breath and forced a smile. "A trained commando, a heavy-world brawler, and a badass Tracker. We'll be unbeatable."

"Excuse, me?" Markowitz's chin came up. "I believe I'm the badass in this group."

"Nope," Boyd rebutted. "No one out-badasses a heavy-worlder."

Thane's grin wasn't forced this time. "My ship, my title."

Chapter 14

"Your glare isn't working," Shiloh said, half amused. "It's still there."

Unfortunately. Jem had been glaring at it for two days and still hadn't come up with an idea of how to get around it. She couldn't sneak around the ship. She couldn't spy on Henning or Myers. She couldn't—*well, crap. When did I become so dependent on my ghosting ability?*

She could still remember the time when she was afraid of it. When she refused to shift unless absolutely, save-somebody necessary.

"Yeah," Jem finally said. "Guess my double-eye power isn't working." Her bi-colored eyes, one a soft amber and the other a deep emerald green, were her most notable characteristic.

Shiloh chuckled, then followed it with an annoyed grunt. "We should have tried smashing the case after using it to smash the cameras. He probably doesn't have another one."

"Probably not. If we could crack the case…" Jem's voice trailed off as an idea started taking shape.

"Well, I'm not about to try with it on you," Shiloh said firmly. "I could crack your arm instead."

"What if we made them think we had damaged it? They had to have seen us using it before the cameras failed."

Shiloh angled forward and asked in a conspiratorial voice, "What do you have in mind?"

In a low voice, Jem outlined her plan and her invisibility. Shiloh's eyes widened on that last part.

Twelve minutes and eighteen seconds later, a fuming Henning shoved their door open. "What did you do?" he demanded.

Jem gave him a grumpy look. "We got lunch, then came back. Shiloh is trying to talk me into a card game. Why?"

He looked down at his hand comp, up at Jem, then turned and walked out. As soon as the door slid closed, the two women exchanged grins.

"It worked," Jem said, doing an Andi-style bounce in her chair.

She had shifted in and out of ghost-mode twice, counting on the ship's computer to register the two brief sensor gaps and send a signal to Henning. The plan, now, was to stage more and longer 'gaps' in the hope he would remove it for a maintenance check.

"Jem, that was..."

"Weird? Spooky? Freaky?" And she hadn't told Shiloh the phasing part yet.

"A-*maaa*-zing."

"Let's hope it works."

Chapter 15

"How are things going at the Foundation?" Gwen asked, bouncing her grandson carefully on her knee. She'd stopped at Reyna's home on her way to her CEO office at Baron Financials. His boisterous laughter was the soothing balm she needed for the ache that she had woke up with.

"Great," Reyna replied, sipping on her hot tea. "We accepted Zorluma Two's petition yesterday. They've got a nasty fungus that's starting to coat everything, and I do mean everything. They'll wake up with it on their bed covers. I've started contacting agencies and coordinating support."

"Ugh. Another case of hidden or mutated?" Gwen said.

"Uh-huh. I've also decided to bring Susi on board as co-manager."

"Problems?" Gwen asked, frowning.

"Hmmm?" Reyna said, watching her mom cuddle her son. "No, no problem. I want to spend more time with Sam. Splitting days will give us both time with our families and Susi could use something else to focus on." She gave a heavy sigh. "We both could."

They all could, and it was a marvelous idea. Suzi Taft had weathered the loss of Cliff—*killed by those murderous bitches*—with grace, but, like the rest of them, she still mourned him. Gwen's heart panged again. Tomorrow would have been her son's birthday. And now Shiloh, their daughter, had been abducted along with Jem. Where were they? What had happened to them? What was happening to those that'd gone in search of them?

Just another worrisome day for the Stohlass family.

What? Gwen mentally slapped herself. Yes, the family had had a rough year or two, but wallowing in maudlin thoughts? Uh-uh. Tomorrow, she resolved, she and Gordon would cast a 'Happy Birthday' to Cliff on the winds he now rode. Maybe recite *The Liturgy of Passing*, too.

"I'm rather glad Thane isn't here at the moment," Reyna said, gathering in her son.

Gwen's gaze sharpened. "Oh?"

"There's a…I'm not sure what to call her." Reyna deposited Sam in his playpen. "She was dripping in gems and hubris, so not the usual fortune hunter or social climber."

"I take it she was hovering over Thane." His inheritance of Baron Financials had catapulted him up to Midgard's number one catch.

"She basically propositioned him right in front of me at the Foundation's party last week."

That was surprising. "Most moon over him from a distance while keeping a wary eye out for Jem."

"Those are intelligent Midgarders. Miss Tia Rockefeller Lexington is a spoiled Earther—you know her?" Reyna broke off when Gwen stiffened.

"Her specifically, no. The Rockefeller and Lexington families have been prominent in the financial news for over a year. Really, Reyna, you used to pay more attention."

"I don't deal with that end of the money spectrum anymore, Mom. They donate, I spend. So, what are they doing? Merging?"

"They did that about a century ago. Both families had extensive financial holdings and they took the core of them to create Lex-Rock Asset Management."

Reyna snorted. "Really? As in *let's rock* your assets?"

"They certainly did. They dominate the financial markets in the Sol System by a very wide margin. Meridan Securities and Investments was considered the Republic's oldest and largest financial body. After it became part of the Consortium, L-RAM and the Eisenberg Financial Group in the Coleman System started jockeying for the top Republic slot. For the past year, they've been establishing branches in other systems and inhaling smaller companies. Or putting them out of business.

"If you had been paying attention," Gwen admonished, "you'd know that Baron Financials is considered to be another of MSI's successors. In truth, it would have *competed* with MSI if Helga Baron hadn't been too narrow-minded to expand it externally to the Romanique System. With the change in management and outlook, Baron Financials is now poised for growth. And the experts have noticed." Her eyes held an anticipatory gleam. "They aren't debating if it will grow, but how far we'll take it." Into that top slot if she had her way.

Reyna's voice went flat. "And if a certain someone can get her hooks into Baron Financials through Thane…"

"Uh-huh. They'd absorb one major competitor and pole-vault past the other. Is the shark still here?"

"No clue. She didn't take up my offer to stop by the Foundation. And she was extremely annoyed when Thane deserted her and her boobs—assets."

Gwen stood. "I'll see what I can find out. I'm going to tap a couple of off-world contacts, too." Giving both daughter and grandson a hug, she hurried out to her car. This was just what she needed to take her mind off other things.

* * * * *

"Miss Lexington, I'm surprised to see you," Reyna lied as she stopped by the table. Her mother had learned some interesting tidbits about the family this past week and she intended to use them.

The *Jade Heights* restaurant was a swanky, snooty place she rarely visited. Its food and service were excellent and its prices ensured their customers didn't walk casually in from the street. Miss Lexington fit right it, with her expensive clothes, fancy updo, and enough jewelry to tempt even the most cautious thief. At least the blouse was buttoned.

"Mind if I join you?" Without waiting for a reply, Reyna pulled out a chair and sat. She spied the couple at the next table eyeballing her. Ah! There were the bodyguards. Not good enough to sit at the same table with their employer?

A server bustled up and Reyna declined to order.

"Why were you surprised?" Tia asked.

"You never came by the Hands of Hope Foundation to visit me. I assumed you must have run back home to daddy after you failed to wrap my son around

76

your bejeweled…finger."

"Daddy?"

"Franklin Jarvis Lexington, CEO of L-RAM. He sent you here to worm your way into Baron Financials since his usual tactics won't work."

"And what would that be?" Tia asked, one manicured eyebrow rising.

"The usual shark tactics, of course. Buy the company. Buy the board members. Buy enough shares to take over the company. Whatever will work," she said with a scornful expression. Except here. Not only was BF a privately held company, her mother had devised a unique corporate structure that severely limited compromises.

Tia met and matched Reyna's expression.

"Regardless of what you or my father thinks, Thane Baron is quite attractive and I find myself drawn to him. Why shouldn't I be? For that matter, why shouldn't your family welcome an alliance with mine?"

"We have no interest in your family and we quite like the woman Thane is with."

"A woman of no background and dubious reputation," Tia said, disdain dripping from each word. "The reputation of the Rockefeller and Lexington families goes back centuries."

"Uh-huh. A once-honorable reputation sullied by the self-serving, predatory, win-by-any-means it's now known for. Unacceptable. *You* are unacceptable." Ah, hah! There's the viper's true face. "You don't give a damn about Thane. You are *drawn* to what you will gain socially, financially, and politically through him. Your presence pollutes our city," Reyna said with disgust. "Go home. Baron Financials in not for sale and neither is my son."

One of the most thoroughly malicious smiles she'd ever seen had the hair on the back of Reyna's neck standing tall.

"That's not up to you, is it," Tia sneered. "Thane Baron is a man who makes up his own mind, as demonstrated by his choice of career and *current* partner. Perhaps he hasn't been made aware of other opportunities and their benefits."

"Oh, he's aware, especially since he inherited Baron Financials. Opportunists, like you, have been crawling out of the woodwork."

Tia placed her napkin on the table and retrieved her purse. Turning sideways as if to get up, she leaned close to Reyna. Sotto voce she said, "Family reputation aside, *bitch*, I always get what I want."

"Not this time. *Bitch*," Reyna fired back, not bothering to lower her voice.

Tia's mouth set in a hard line as she straightened. "We shall see."

Reyna watched Tia and her two guards walk out. Her mother had warned her direct confrontation wouldn't work. Foolishly, she'd insisted on it. The bitch was targeting her son, and she had hoped Tia would leave once she knew they were aware of her game. Resisting the urge to curse, she rose to leave. Not only had her mother been right, she'd inadvertently turned the conquest of her son into a challenge.

***

Reyna trudged through the front door, tired and wondering if she'd forgotten anything. Oh well, if she had, Suzi would take care of it. She had the chair for the next three days. The sight of her son cuddled in her husband's arms brought an instant lift to both spirits and lips. She kissed Lee's forehead and stroked Sam's head.

"I didn't think you'd be home until later," she said.

"We wrapped up our case and skipped out before they handed us another one. Is that all I get?" "Lee asked in a mock-hurt tone. He leaned his head back and pursed his lips up at her.

Reyna rolled her eyes, then gave him a soft smooch. "I'll make it up to you later. Is Lizzie already gone?" she asked, settling next to him.

"Uh-huh. I told her that if I get to go home early, so did she. Asked me to remind you she'd only be available for tomorrow if you need her."

Lizzie was a dear. A widowed and still spry eighty-plus, she adored taking care of Sam.

"That's right. She plans on visiting her daughter's family up in Granite Falls. Don't know what we'll do when Sammy here gets mobile," she said, getting the expected indignant frown. For some reason he disliked 'Sammy' and insisted on 'Sam' or 'Samuel.' But it was fun to tease him. "Fortunately, I don't have anything planned I can't take *Sam* with me."

"How did your day go?" Lee asked as the drowsy infant changed parents.

"More or less as usual," she said, looking downward at her son.

"Your voice says otherwise." His arm dropped around her shoulders.

She sighed. "I got a call from Jaes Oberlander about an hour ago." Lee's expression went neutral. "According to Jaes, Miss Lexington has boarded a BC shuttle bound for, among others, Earth."

Lee perked up. "You'll be releasing Jaes now?"

"Yes." He hadn't been happy with her hiring someone to watch Miss Lexington, which is how she knew to find the viper in *Jade Heights*.

"Your discussion yesterday must have worked." He took in her expression. "You don't appear happy about the news."

"I'm not. She's gone home to make plans and marshal her resources." Reyna chewed her lip. "Miss Lexington will be back and she'll be bringing as much trouble as she can pack in her fancy bags."

"Nothing this family can't handle," Lee said confidently, pulling Reyna against him.

"True," she murmured, snuggling into his warmth. It wouldn't be pleasant, though.

Chapter 16

"There is an incoming video call from Tylander Port Security," Thor announced.

Thane's fingers drummed on his forearm. Not unexpected. They'd gone through several polite *"Please state your business"* interrogations in the Hermes System. And that was *after* the frigging jerks had disabled his laser cannon. It was the only way they'd permit him to remain in the system, much less land on Hebros.

After confirming the *Transom Ode* hadn't made port on either Hermes Four or Three, they'd come to Tylander, Intervalic Three. After perusing the publicly available lists of arrivals and departures, he'd verified the *Ode* hadn't landed here in months. He'd started browsing the local news links, looking for anything of interest about Kurzvall specifically, or Consortium activities in general. So far, nothing. He hoped Boyd and the major were having better luck doing the same browsing in the Port Circle.

"Put it through, lower left quadrant," he ordered.

The face popping onto his viewscreen could be used for a recruitment poster. Pale blue eyes looked out of a dark-toned, narrow face whose features reminded him of Lee Twobears. His expression was a cross between curious and watchful.

"Captain Adam Igel Atkins, Tylander Spaceport Security," he identified himself.

"Thane Stohlass Baron, of Wotan Two," Thane replied in kind. No need to add anything else. The man would have already checked his ship's registration.

"We have an associate of yours in custody."

Okay, *that* was unexpected. "The charge?"

"Mr. Boyd Papagiannopoulos is not currently charged with anything."

Thane was impressed; he hadn't mangled Boyd's last name. "Then why is he in custody?"

"We're still gathering information from witnesses to the altercation."

"Altercation? Is Boyd injured?"

"No. But the three Borland gang members taken to Forest Hill MedCenter were," he said dryly.

Thane grunted. Tylander had Earth Standard gravity. Three locals wouldn't have been much of a challenge to a heavy-worlder. "I don't know why Boyd would be involved in a fight. He's not the aggressive type and we don't look for trouble."

Atkins's head tilted slightly. "What are you looking for? Your Tracker license isn't valid here."

Which rankled. "I'm not using it. This is a personal search for me and my friends."

Crap. He'd slipped up and the captain's expression said he'd caught the plural.

"Who are you searching for?"

It took a second's decision to go with the truth. He was frigging tired of dancing around it.

"My sig-ner and cousin were abducted from Midgard. We're pretty sure they were taken on the *Transom Ode*, a Class Four Cargo. It's disappeared from Republic space so, naturally, I'm searching the Consortium."

"Naturally?" he asked in a neutral voice.

Thane threw caution to the wind. "Because my sig-ner is Jem Seaborne Wilmont. Because the man who orchestrated their kidnapping was visited by a lawyer from an expensive Tricast legal firm shortly before he was released from Skewed." He couldn't keep his expression and voice from hardening. "Because Reginald Kurzvall is a bastard who has tried, repeatedly and using various methods, to obtain Jem's *cooperation*."

The captain's eyes had widened at Jem's name, then his whole expression went stiff at the rest of his litany. "You need to be careful about slinging out accusations."

"I speak from personal experience, Captain," Thane said coldly. "I first met Jem Wilmont when I was hired by Reginald Kurzvall, himself, to find and help capture her. When I succeeded, his head enforcer tried to kill me. Boyd can verify that. That same enforcer later attacked my grandfather and me on Midgard—threats of torture to be the incentive for her to 'join' his employment team. I don't care what Kurzvall's public image is, the man is a sociopath," he snapped, "with an ego and sense of entitlement that knows no bounds."

Thane gave Atkins a moment to process all that before continuing.

"You're aware of Jem Wilmont's reputation. *No one*," he stressed brusquely, "trying to force her cooperation is doing it for altruistic motives. Considering his past goals—such as ensuring secession—one has to wonder what he wants now."

Captain Atkins's expression was unreadable. "I'll keep you briefed on any changes in Mr. Papagiannopoulos's status." The screen blanked.

Thane ran a hand through his hair and his brain through several of his favorite curses. He had no way to contact Markowitz and could only hope he'd be back soon…without any altercations of his own. Next stop, he promised himself, they were getting kiosk phone numbers.

Each planet established their own communication network and, naturally, used the same phone numbers. Off-world visitors leased temporary numbers from spaceport kiosks so as not to interfere with the matching local one. Locals wishing to hide their true number, usually for nefarious reasons, utilized them, too.

Markowitz made it back two hours later, sans altercation. Thane was filling him in on Boyd's situation when Thor announced two individuals starting up the outside staircase. Given all the activity around the busy port, he'd limited Thor's monitoring to the *Lone Tracker's* immediate vicinity.

"Is one them Boyd?" Thane asked.

"Affirmative. Other is an unknown male. Single weapon detected, standard stunner."

Ah. An Enforcer was escorting Boyd back. They descended to the plazo as a banging sounded on the *Tracker's* outer hatch. The inner one was currently latched open. Thane ordered the outer locks released and both men entered.

"Captain Atkins, welcome aboard the *Lone Tracker*," Thane said, surprised to find it was the Port Security Chief following Boyd. He noted the man's quick assessment of the plazo, his attention lingering for a second on Markowitz. "Thank you for the escort. Are you releasing Boyd?"

"Yes. Witnesses have testified that Mr. Papagiannopoulos stepped in to assist another person that the three in custody were assaulting. I wanted to ensure he made it here without any other issues. And," the captain added smoothly, "I wished to speak with you."

Thane cocked his head, signaling for him to continue.

"Mr. Papagiannopoulos and I had a private conversation. I am aware of your current problem and he verified the previous ones you mentioned," he said curtly. "You're sure about the *Transom Ode*?"

"No," Thane said honestly. "But its behavior and timing are highly suspect."

"Agreed. Mr. Papagiannopoulos said you've investigated the Hermes System?"

"Call me Boyd," Boyd said in an annoyed tone, leaning against the stair rungs.

"Hermes was our first guess. The *Ode* is a small Class Four. It had two days head start from Euphrates. With the six days it took us to arrive, plus the three days we hung around the system, it should have arrived. It didn't. We came here next."

"Ten, eleven days should have been sufficient," Atkins said. "And since it's not here, you'll go on to the next Consortium system?"

"Yes, as a worried citizen," Thane said, missing the use of his Tracker license.

"Of a foreign Republic."

Foreign. That was really going to take getting used to.

"Who is, basically, popping in and out of our spaceports and mingling with our citizens. Your search would make the perfect cover to gather information about our ports and other infrastructure changes since the Consortium's separation." He pinned Markowitz with a sharp look. "And you are?"

"Elijah Drummond Markowitz, Tardis System," he said politely. Propped against an environmental locker, he returned the captain's look calmly.

"And what rank sits in front of that?" Atkins said.

The captain is no fool. Thane waited for a moment, but Markowitz continued to return Atkins's stare without replying. Okay. "Elijah, like Boyd, is here as my and Jem's friend." That might be stretching it a bit. "The Consortium may have separated itself politically, but, as far as I know, we're not enemies."

"Unless it chooses to make itself one," Markowitz added coolly.

Thane shot him a frown. He was trying to put the captain at ease and that comment didn't help. Especially since, even in civilian clothes, Markowitz's entire persona practically screamed *military*.

After a short, tense silence, Captain Atkins said, "I would hope not. I have sent a priority request for any information relating to the *Transom Ode* to all Consortium ports, both planet and space based."

All three men straightened. That would get them even more information than a Tracker's license.

"It will take at least two days to get a reply from all of them. In the meantime, please enjoy your stay." A small smile curved his lips. "If you do roam about, I ask that you don't *start* anything, and that any altercations that do ensue remain non-fatal."

Thane gave the captain's bland expression a calculating look. "Boyd, you planning on any aggressions?" he asked.

"No," he replied in a clipped tone. "But there's a bunch of those gang hooligans posted around the ship."

Huh. Markowitz had commented on seeing several suspicious lingerers on his way in. "That Borland gang giving you problems, Captain?"

"To be frank, yes," Atkins said. "Things were chaotic for a while during the transition. It gave certain elements time to get entrenched. The Port Circles have always had a reputation, but the Borlands have become more organized over the past six months. Not to mention vicious and vindictive. They've taken the Circle's underbelly over completely, either absorbing or eliminating the other groups. Informants tell us they're working with some off-world organization called Dragonfly."

"They've infiltrated critical areas," Markowitz said shrewdly. "How did they know, and so quickly, which ship he came off of?"

"Yes." Atkins's voice was grim. "They've started moving outward, into the city proper. They've also started pushing a new, nasty drug called *champ*, believe it or not. Any of you heard of it? No? Be glad. It's odorless, tasteless, highly addictive, and has a mortality rate of ninety-five percent for those trying to break free." He nodded at their shocked expressions. "I suggest caution in any of your movements. I'll inform you of any news as I get it."

Giving them a curt nod, he turned and left through the still-open hatch.

"Thor, engage outer locks." Thane ordered after Boyd swung it closed. There were several loud *thunks*.

"What do you think?" Boyd asked.

"I think Captain Atkins is hoping we'll put a dent in his gang problem."

"I got no problem with that," Boyd said angrily. "They were beating up an eighty-two-year-old man. If I had known they were drug dealers, I'd have pounded harder."

"Ditto," the major said. "I'm marked now, since they saw me enter the ship."

Thane gave them both a sharp look. "Garbage reduction is not why we're here."

"No, but we need something to keep us entertained for the next two days," Boyd replied, his voice holding an undercurrent of menace Thane hadn't heard before.

"And I could use a good workout. Call it a training refresher," Markowitz said.

Thane threw his hands up in surrender. "Fine. We do owe the man. Just remember the non-fatal part."

* * * * *

Boyd was lying on his bunk, eyes closed and hands tucked under his head, when he heard Markowitz enter. The major had sweated through one of his exercise routines, then gone topside for a shower. He listened absently as the man moved around in their limited space, preparing for bed.

"You okay?"

Markowitz's question caught him off-guard. Despite being on the top bunk, he still had to look upward to meet the tall man's scrutiny.

"Yeah." The major remained silent, unmoving. "Let's get some sleep." Boyd let his eyelids slide back down.

"Your whole mood has been off ever since Atkins brought you back. Not to mention, your reaction when he spoke about that drug."

"My reaction?" Boyd echoed. The man's training had picked up on it, no doubt.

"Like someone shoved an electric charger up your ass. Want to talk about it?"

Did he? Maybe he should. Maybe it'd stop the memories from repeating over and over. He'd figured out some time ago that the commando hid a soft heart under those hard muscles. Perhaps they were more alike than either of them cared to admit.

Without opening his eyes, Boyd said, "I lost a daughter to drugs. She was twenty-two. Shelly had come to live with me a couple of months earlier. She'd lived with her mother since she was twelve, after we'd gone our separate ways. Our visits had been sporadic, as her mother had taken a job in Winterset—a large city on the west side of Audabon. I worked in North Bay on its east coast. Her birthday was a week away and I was planning a big dinner."

His eyelids flew up, revealing the anger that'd simmered in him all evening.

"Her boyfriend of five weeks was the one who got her hooked. That nice, polite, well-mannered young man was a fucking drug dealer."

"Is he the one you did three years on-planet for?"

Should have known it would come out sooner or later, not that he'd tried to hide it. "Yeah. Defense pled it down to manslaughter. Said that I couldn't have known my punch would kill him." You don't contradict your lawyer, especially when he keeps you out of a Fed-Pen cell. "Thane tell you?"

Markowitz's expression had remained steady, neither softening with his story nor going hard at his admission. Very little probably surprised this man.

"No. After Ahrymani Carpenter's slip-through last year, Nicholas O'Daniel wasn't the only one running background checks. Don't know if he ran one on you since you were already part of Jem's inner circle. General Kowalski verified everyone around her."

"Everyone?"

Markowitz's face lit with laughter and he leaned a forearm on the bunk's edge. "Would you believe Gwendolyn Williams was once sued—unsuccessfully—for defamation? Judge told the plaintiff afterwards that, quote, 'if you don't like hearing the truth, then maybe you should consider some life changes.' It's part of the court records."

Boyd couldn't stop the laugh that burst out of him. He'd witnessed a few applications of Thane's grandmother's polite-but-deadly-accurate verbiage. He found the knot in his chest had indeed loosened so, yeah, talking had helped that. As for his worry?

"That drug Captain Atkins told us about? It bothers me," he admitted. "How widespread is the poison?"

"Don't care as long as it stays a Consortium problem. We have enough of our own," Markowitz added, unapologetic when Boyd gave him a withering look.

"Yeah? Well consider this," Boyd snapped. "If Dragonfly is what's empowering the Borlands, then it's the most likely source of their new drug. It's also the same off-world organization that Thom Danford had aligned his group with on Midgard."

"Danford." The major's voice turned thoughtful. "That's the would-be kingpin you and Jem took down in Azusa? And you're sure it's the same one?"

"Danford mentioned Dragonfly several times on that recording we got, and he was already setting up a couple of drug dens in Azusa. If he had that new drug, odds are he'd been pushing it in Odinheim."

After a couple of seconds, Markowitz did a chin-dip of acknowledgement before dropping onto the lower bunk. Thor blinked the lights out on his command.

Boyd stared up into the darkness.

Chapter 17

"Come on, Jem. I want something to drink."

Shiloh stood outside their door, ostensibly coaxing her to go with her. She was actually scouting the hallway, making sure no one else was in view. When her small hand signal said *safe*, Jem shifted and walked out. Shiloh hesitated before sliding the door halfway closed.

Jem would have sighed if she had the breath. Shiloh was still unaware about the out-of-phase-with-the-universe part and hadn't wanted to 'catch' her in the door. Jem was going to have to tell her soon. Should have already. Why was she putting it off?

Because she still looks at you as a person, not a freak, a small corner of her mind whispered.

Four steps down the hallway, Jem *poofed* back before someone popped out of a doorway. That should get Henning's blood pressure up. Shiloh gave a short start as Jem reappeared beside her but didn't break stride. The hallway opened into the kitchen area with the amenities on their right. A couple of crewmembers and mercenaries were on their left, some eating while others sat watchful with empty food trays in front of them.

Shiloh pulled a drink out of the cooler.

"Might as well eat while we're here," Jem said. Switching the food carousel on, she watched as the racks rotated, many of them empty. The unexpected diversion had made a serious dent in their supplies. She stopped on one, scrunched her nose at the description, and restarted it. Several more empty racks passed. *Finally!* Jem pulled out a tray labeled 'Vegetable pasta with

Tarlonia sauce.'

Shiloh looked over her shoulder. "Is there another one?"

"Uh-huh, but I have to warn you. Tarlonia sauce is pretty spicy."

She held up her drink. "I'll wash it down."

They pulled off the outer wrappings and set the frozen meals to heating in two of the four micros. Jem pulled out a drink for herself and they took a small table in a corner, which put the mercenary table between them and the *Ode's* crew. Jem cast a sideways look at them. What did it say when she trusted the mercenaries more than the regular crew members?

Henning came in from the lounge and stalked to their table. "Hold out your arm."

Jem gave him a scowl, hiding the leap of hope. "Why?"

"Arm."

Jem held it up. "Why thank you," she said, giving him a snarky grin as he unlocked it.

"Return to your quarters," he said sharply.

"After we eat," Jem replied, rubbing her wrist. The micros' double ding couldn't have been timed better. "How much longer? Food's almost gone."

Henning wheeled around without answering. Stopped at the two crewmembers' table. "Escort them back as soon as they're finished," he ordered before stalking out.

Jem and Shiloh ate their meals silently, both aware of the speculative looks they were getting from the crewmen. Dumping their trays in the recycle chute, they proceeded on to their room. The crewmen behind them crowded close as they approached the door. Tense, expecting it, Jem was ready when one of them grabbed her arm.

Instead of trying to pull away, she turned into him. Saw his flash of surprise, right before the heel of her free hand slammed upward into his chin. She followed it with a knuckle-punch to his throat. Grabbing his throat, he left himself wide-open to Jem's knee. She whirled around, looking for Shiloh while he was still collapsing into a ball.

The second thug had both of Shiloh's arms pinned to her side. Her head slammed backward and blood spurted from his nose. "You fucking bitch!" he swore.

Jem yelled *let her go* and jumped on his back, locking an arm around his throat. He shoved Shiloh face-first into a wall and she dropped to the deck. Failing to pry her arm loose, the bastard swung around and rammed her into the wall. She gritted her teeth and hung on. He whipped around and slammed her powerfully into the opposite wall. Jem struggled to breathe as he repeated the move. And again, her head snapping backward against the wall this time.

She fell to the deck, sucking in air, dark spots blocking half her vision. Dimly Jem heard a hard voice say, "You kick her and I'll finish it." Then it was Shiloh saying "Jem? Jem?" Jem got enough breath back to weakly say, "Here." The black dots were mushrooming.

"You disgusting offspring of an infected bitch!"

Shiloh? Definitely a Stohlass, was her last thought as yelling followed her down into blackness.

***

Jem woke to a semi-darkened room and pain radiating from head to hips. It took a moment to remember why. Carefully, painfully, she slid her legs sideways and pushed herself to a sitting position.

"Shiloh! *Shiloh!*" If those bastards had hurt her…

Her friend came hurrying into the room. "Jem! Thank Thor you're awake."

"Are you okay—did they hurt you?" Jem asked, holding her head in one hand.

Shiloh gave a short laugh. "All I have is a measly facial bruise. You've got one from neck to tailbone and a concussion."

That measly bruise ran down the whole frigging right side of her face. "How long have I been out?"

"About fourteen hours. We're currently sitting on the long-term ramp at Keosauqua Spaceport on Toulouse."

Belatedly, Jem realized the ache at the base of her skull was missing. Oh good, that was one less.

"Don't try to get up. Are you hungry?"

Jem started to nod, then wisely changed to "yes." Shiloh piled several pillows against the headboard and help her scooch—slowly—back against them. The jabbing pain at the smallest twitch of muscles was far worse than her pounding head.

"I'll be right back with something easily digestible. That's what the doctor recommended."

Jem leaned her head back. Letting the pain roll through her lessened the overall discomfort. Kinda, sorta. Something her teleporting experience had taught her. She must have blacked out because the next thing she knew, Shiloh was straddling a food tray on a short stand in front of her.

"Vegetable stew with applesauce," Shiloh announced, adding a cold bottle of water to the stand. "I'll bring you up-to-date while you eat. I figure you're wanting to know."

"You bet I do," Jem said, picking up a spoon.

"As you can guess, things went to hell." She sat on the foot of the bed and twisted the top off her water. "There was a brawl between Henning's crew and the mercs."

And she missed it. "Who won?" she asked, before taking a large bite of potato and carrot.

"Who do you think?" Shiloh said on a chuckle. "Our ruckus brought the two mercs from the other table, plus a couple more of Henning's crew and Martin. You went down and the asshole bouncing you against the walls was about to kick you in the ribs. A merc threatened him if he did. The brawl started when the idiot tried to punch the merc instead. By the time Rolfe and Henning got there, the two mercenaries had Henning's entire crew laid out on the deck. And Martin," she added gleefully.

Mouth full, Jem gave her a thumbs-up.

Shiloh took several swallows. "The crew was spoiling for a fight. Between the frustration of this diversion and strained relations with Rolfe's team, I'm surprised there hadn't been one before then. It made things even more strained, though, and I think Henning cussed the whole way here. Good thing we were about ten hours out from Palmyra Two."

Jem stopped chewing. "Did you really say 'offspring of an infected bitch?'"

"Among other things, yes," she said, her cheeks turning pink. "Don't tell

Mom."

"Are you kidding me? Your whole family will be proud. Have you heard some of them? Heard Thane?"

"Well, yes. Anyway..." Shiloh waved her bottle dismissively. "The mercs got paid and left. Henning had a doctor come and examine you. Since nothing was broken, he wouldn't let him take you to a MedCenter. It's been quiet since then." She stared off for a moment. "The crew has been given leave and told to work it off. Only Henning and Myers are currently on board."

Perfect. "Do you think you can make it out? Get help?"

"From whom, Jem?" Shiloh asked somberly. "We're on a world where mercenary-ism is a way of life. Would their version of Law Enforcement care? Would they, or the nearest person, take a quicky contract to return me? And even if I could get past the locked hatch, I will not leave you behind. You are in no shape to go anywhere. Which is why Henning hasn't bothered with the tracker."

Jem glanced at her bare wrist. "Do you know where we're going from here?"

"That remains to be determined," she said. "They're waiting for Reginald Kurzvall. According to Henning, he should be here in a week or so."

Chapter 18

Thane and Boyd were eating supper when Markowitz climbed up and out of the stairwell.

"That smells good," he declared, heading straight for the food carousel. "I worked up an appetite."

"Yeah? How many?" Boyd asked.

"Three," Markowitz said, grabbing a tray.

"Ha! They aimed five at me."

Markowitz grinned over his shoulder. "Three. Twice."

Boyd glowered and shoved a forkful of meat in his mouth.

Thane shook his head. The two had made a game of it. After recognizing Boyd as a heavy-worlder, the Borlands had piled more on him. After today, they'd realize their error and do the same for Markowitz. Not that it'd make much difference in the outcome.

"While you two were playing, I've been in touch with Captain Atkins. He's confirmed the *Ode* hasn't been to Tylander—or anywhere in this System—for over a year, but it was on Hermes Four about three months ago."

"Getting orders, you think?" Markowitz said, leaning against the counter.

"Possibly. Or doing a normal cargo run. Dammit," Thane grunted in frustration. "I wish we knew for frigging sure we aren't wasting time. They're out there. Somewhere." Experiencing who knew what. Fire and Ice? Beatings? Rape? He stabbed a chunk of beef, barely restraining the urge to sling it across the room.

Markowitz claimed his meal from the micro and plopped down across from Thane. "Assuming Atkins finds no trace of the *Ode*, where do we go next?"

Thane chewed and thought it over. "There's that private spaceport of Kurzvall's."

"Not any longer," Markowitz said, chuckling. "Word is, Kurzvall told Admiral Gleason to do what he wanted to with the debris. So, he did. Anderson Station is now a well-established, fully outfitted, and heavily manned Naval-slash-Marine base."

"On the edge of Sector Three," Boyd said, giving a satisfied smirk.

"Close to the Consortium's neighborhood," Markowitz added, a hint of glee in his tone.

"Could he have set up another secret base? Something smaller?" Boyd suggested. "Maybe nothing more than an outpost."

"I hope not," Thane said. "Really no need to, now that he can position it somewhere inside Consortium space."

"Two messages received from Tylander Port Control for Thane Baron," Thor's disembodied voice announced.

"Type and sender of the first one?" Both he and Markowitz had sent 'forward' requests to their permanent postboxes yesterday.

"Text message from Assistant Director Rafael Goldstein Reis of Midgard, Wotan Two."

Thane's gloom dissipated. "Sounds like an update. Read it," he instructed.

"The Argainn Science Station reported *Transom Ode* dropped off their equipment as scheduled. Calculating the time from Midgard to there to Euphrates, there was no deviation. We've heard from the last three ships on our list. All arrived at their destinations within normal transit times. Again, no deviation and no kidnappers. *Transom Ode* has to be our culprit. No reported sightings of it yet. Good luck in your hunt. End."

"Feel better, Thane?" Boyd asked.

Thane's feral smile spoke for itself. "Second message?"

There was an unusual pause. "Text message with no name or origination."

Oh? "Read it."

"Palmyra Two. End."

Silence. The men exchanged glances.

"A tip?" Boyd said.

"A trap?" Markowitz warned.

Thane shook his head. "Doesn't matter. I'll get us an exit time."

"Not yet," Markowitz said firmly, halting Thane's rise. "We give Captain Atkins time for those last replies."

"We need to check it out." Thane's voice rose, along with his aggravation.

"Agreed, but this could be a ruse. We haven't hidden our search and you and your ship are well known. Think like a Tracker, Thane, not an emotional sig-ner," he snapped.

Damn. Getting dressed down by a commando. Which he deserved. The cool, calculating him of two years ago wouldn't recognize the him of today. *And he wouldn't change it.*

Thane took a deep breath, let it out slowly. "You're right. The anonymity of the message makes it suspect. Kurzvall or one of his minions could be trying to distract us. We give Captain Atkins another day. Then go. Agreed?"

Both men echoed "agreed."

Thane stared at the wall as his brain sorted and evaluated. "Toulouse. Mercenary capital. Kurzvall can have his pick of contractors to kidnap one or all of us. Or frame us for something. Wouldn't be the first time," he grumbled.

"More likely, they'll kidnap you and kill us." Boyd snarked.

"Think he'd risk killing you?" Thane asked Markowitz. "With his spies, he has to know who you are."

"No telling, but the bastard does seem to believe he's untouchable. Then there's always the 'accident' scenario. I'll alert General Kowalski."

"I'll forward the message to Reis. See if he can trace it back. I'll also let Granddad know that we might need a—*crap*. Will his lawyer license be as dead there as my Tracker one is?"

Boyd and Markowitz shrugged in unison.

***

Thane stared at the bulkhead behind the table comp, half-listening to the conversation around him. While his two passengers had been out for a final browsing of idiots to pound, he'd been getting the ship prepped and ready to go. So far, Hermes Four was the only planet in the Consortium the *Transom Ode* had visited in years. They were waiting now for the Tamarian System's report, which was the last one and should arrive today. He wanted to leave as soon as Captain Atkins got it.

Engines fueled, waste emptied, water and food stocked. All set. Hmmm. Maybe he should order some additional trays for the lower freezer bin. Boyd and Markowitz had large appetites.

"Receiving video call from Tylander Port Security for Thane Baron," Thor announced.

"Display on main viewscreen, lower left quadrant." As expected, the screen lit up with Captain Atkins's face.

"Captain Atkins, what do you have for us?" Thane asked, sliding into the pilot's chair.

"The Tamarian System report. *Transom Ode's* last visit there was over two years ago."

Thane rubbed his chin. "That would put it about when the Consortium seceded."

"Yes, and irrelevant to current issues."

"Agreed. Thank you for your help. You saved us a lot of time. If there's anything we can do for you, send word."

Captain Atkins said "Thanks" and disconnected.

Thane contacted Port Control and requested a slot in the next outbound window.

***

"Receiving video call from Adam Igel Atkins for Thane Baron."

Markowitz eyed Thane from the co-pilot's seat. "A private call does not bode well."

No, it didn't. "Display on main viewscreen."

The captain's grim expression proved them right.

"Your exit window starts in twenty-four minutes," Atkins said curtly. "Call Control and request permission to leave as soon as the ship in front of you clears."

A ship's takeoff had an exit window with a minus-or-plus leeway of five minutes. Technically, the next ship could leave after the one prior to it cleared the air lanes.

"Why the extra minutes?" Thane asked, shoulders tense. Boyd came to stand behind him.

"Trey Mosley, CEO of Burkhart-Devney Security Services of Tricast, has messaged my office, requesting we 'hold' the *Lone Tracker* and its occupants until his arrival. He has 'questions' on an unspecified topic and an unspecified time of arrival." He flashed a grin. "I'm currently out of the office and unavailable to authorize that action."

Thane's jaw set. "Thank you. I'll contact Control."

Atkins held up a hand. "Also, *Cassie* left Hermes Four yesterday. It's Reginald Kurzvall's private cruiser that he uses when he wants to travel incognito. Officially, its destination is restricted. Unofficially, it's headed for Palmyra Two."

Publicly restricted destinations were reserved for military and law enforcement ships. Trust Kurzvall to finagle it somehow.

"You know that how?" Markowitz demanded.

"I asked an old classmate of mine who works in Port Security there to keep me posted about him. *Cassie* is a Class Two Drone, eighteen meters. It'll take about a week to get there. Maybe he has a need for more mercenaries."

Thane's thoughts flashed to the anonymous message. *Or to pick up someone.*

"I can't stay unavailable for too long," Atkins warned. "Blast when you can and I'll send my regrets to Mosley. Good luck and safe travel."

Thane thanked him and contacted Port Control as soon as they disconnected. Then he asked Thor to confirm the transit time to Palmyra Two from Hermes Four for that size ship.

"Six days, ten hours, eight minutes, Midgard time," Thor replied.

Crap. It'd take them five days from here and Kurzvall had a day's start.

"We may still beat him," Markowitz said, his thoughts evidently aligning with Thane's. "*Lone Tracker* has the size advantage."

Thane glanced at the clock. Twenty minutes minus whatever. "Wonder why the captain had Kurzvall being watched?"

Boyd snorted, walked back to his seat at the table. "Because his family was close friends with Sys-Senator Roberto Stevenson's wife's family. That talk we had earlier? I included a number of things we know about Kurzvall's tactics and victims. I could almost hear his teeth grinding."

Reginald Kurzvall had spearheaded the conspiracy that led to the Consortium's secession. By hook, crook, and assassination, he arranged to have 'their' people filling crucial Senatorial seats and other affluent positions across the Republic. Stevenson was a victim of the last method. Tragically, his wife and three small children also died in the engineered rockslide.

The CEO of Burkhart-Devney Security Services had been one of his co-conspirators.

Seventeen minutes.

"Think this means the anonymous tipster can be trusted?" Thane asked. "It's certainly not an entrapment if we were to be held here."

Markowitz looked thoughtful. "My trust meter isn't pegged, but it's not in the green either."

Twelve minutes.

Thane ordered the ion engines brought on line. The low rumble of standby was comforting.

"Receiving audio call from Port Control," Thor announced.

"Accept." Seven and a half minutes. They'd gotten an extra two-plus minutes.

"*Lone Tracker*, *Balls Glory* has reached altitude and you are cleared to launch."

Thane managed to choke out an understandable reply of "Affirmative."

"Who names their ship *Balls Glory*?" Boyd said, snickering.

"Receiving video call from Port Security."

"Refuse call. Engage engines, thirty-five percent thrust."

The *Lone Tracker* lifted smoothly into its assigned flight path.

Hang on Jem. I'm on my way.

Chapter 19

Jem watched what was probably the fortieth fight scene in a very boring movie. But it was better than the ones with just as many sex scenes. The crew really needed to expand their repertoire. Suddenly the door slammed open on its tracks and Shiloh was shoved in hard enough she needed several dance steps to keep from falling. The door slammed shut.

Jem had shot to her feet. "What's happened?"

"I was getting our drinks when Henning bolted out of his room to the flight deck. I heard plenty before he ordered me brought back. You'll never guess who's inbound."

From Shiloh's grin, it wasn't Kurzvall. Henning had kept someone listening on Port Control's primary frequency since they landed. He'd even made Myers take a shift.

"Admiral Gleason and a fleet?" she said, more in jest than belief.

"The *Lone Tracker*."

Jem gaped for a moment. How—the mercs. He must be tracking them. "I'm going to see what's up."

"You can't teleport into the hall. Someone might see you before you can switch to invisible."

Right. She still hadn't explained the phasing part yet. "I'll be careful," was all she said before shifting to ghost-mode. Leaving Shiloh staring worriedly, she phased through the wall and jogged down the hallway. She passed several of Henning's crew, huddled in the lounge and casting nervous glances toward the flight deck. She found it crowded with Henning, Myers, and two more crewmen.

"…another twenty-two minutes before the inbound window closes," Henning was saying. "Davis, how many in the inbound queue?"

"Wasn't told to keep track of that," one of the crewmen said, scowling. "But at least five or six."

"He probably won't make this window then. Next one won't open for ninety minutes."

"Nope," said the other one, which Jem recognized as the pilot. "You're forgetting Baron's ship is a Globe. They'll bring him in on a beacon through their vertical air slot. Unless there's another Globe in front of him, he'll be down in about fifteen minutes."

Henning spewed out a couple of curse words.

"I don't like this," Myers snapped. "How did he find us?"

"Didn't," Henning replied, listening to the comm's chatter. "He's coming for the mercenaries and whatever information he can get from them. Although," he turned a furious gaze to him, "it seems they already know most of it. If he finds and questions them, he'll get the rest. There's no reason for them not to mention this ship or anything they overheard, including names."

Wow. If looks could incinerate, Myers would be blackened charcoal.

Henning grabbed Myers by his shirt and slammed him against a console.

"Nothing was supposed to track back to me, the *Ode*, or Reginald Kurzvall. Now, thanks to your bumbling, I can't take my ship into any major Republic port and the authorities will know Kurzvall is involved."

"Thane probably was already suspicious of him anyway." Myers shoved Henning away. "You know what?" he sneered. "It doesn't matter. Kurzvall has diplomatic protection and we're outside the Republic's jurisdiction. So, yeah. Let the Great Tracker learn everything. I'll enjoy watching my oh-so-noble cousin's face when he realizes he can't touch us. Can't do a damn thing," he said in an unmistakably gleeful voice.

Jem was seething.

"Except hire some mercs of his own," Davis said sourly.

Henning shook his head. "They can't take an in-system contract."

"*Keosauqua Port Control to* Lone Tracker."

"Lone Tracker *here. Go ahead Port Control.*"

Jem listened as they eavesdropped on Control giving Thane his landing instructions and coordinates. Soon. He'd be here soon. Had Boyd come with him? Surely he wouldn't have come here alone.

"Where is V-16?" Henning snapped.

The pilot displayed a map of the spaceport on the viewscreen. He pointed to a spot. "There." His finger moved to the left. "We're here, on B-24."

"Good."

Jem leaned in to see better, dismayed to find Thane would be parked over a kilometer away. At least they were on the same side of the spaceport. She was turning away when the pilot let out an exclamation.

"The *Cassie* is inbound!"

Who?

"Talk about bad timing. Will it make this window?" Henning snapped.

It had to be Kurzvall. Cassandra is his daughter.

Jem could almost see the pilot's mental calculation: *Cassie's* distance vs queued ships vs time the inbound window had left. Otherwise, the ship would have to orbit or hold position until the next one.

"It'll be close," he finally said.

"Comm the *Cassie's* pilot. Tell him to burn ions."

Shit, damn, crap.

Jem hurried to their room. "Things are about to get interesting," she said, telling an astonished Shiloh what she'd learned.

"How..." Shiloh started, then changed to, "Are you okay? You're bleached out."

"I'm fine," Jem lied, getting an 'oh, really' look from her. "Be right back." She shifted and went quickly to appropriate a few items she'd discovered on a previous recon. Leaving the ship's storeroom, she spotted their door standing open. *No!* Jem zipped into the room, phasing recklessly through one of his goons, past Shiloh and on into the bathroom. Its door was kept shut for this kind of emergency.

"Where's Wilmont?" came Henning's demanding voice.

Jem *poofed* back and pressed the flush switch, then hid the backpack in the shower stall. Ignoring the pounding pain, she calmly washed her hands before sliding the door open. She assessed the room as she stepped out. Shiloh gave her an enigmatic look from her chair. Martin had a death glare aimed at Henning.

Henning acknowledged Jem's presence with a grunt. "You'll both be transferring to Kurzvall's ship as soon as it lands."

"She said it was Thane arriving," Jem said.

"She was mistaken," Henning lied brusquely.

"Shiloh is staying with me," Martin said, stalking over to her.

Jem pressed her lips to hide a smile when Shiloh crossed her legs.

"*Baron* was to stay with you. You've screwed our plans for the last time. Mr. Kurzvall will decide what happens next—with her *and* you," Henning told him in a hard voice.

"No. She comes with me." He reached for Shiloh's arm.

Shiloh's leg flashed out in an arc ending in Martin's crotch.

He let out a whimper and folded in on himself.

Henning motioned to the snickering guards. "Drag him back to his room."

They each grabbed him under an arm and, literally, dragged him out.

Henning snorted. "Good move." Then he walked out.

Jem managed to restrain her laughter until the door closed. "I was hoping you'd do that."

"How'd you know I was thinking about it?"

"You don't normally sit with your legs crossed," Jem said drily, heading for the bedroom. She snatched up the bottle on the small night stand. The pain pills the doctor had left had done little for her headaches. Jem swallowed three this time, hoping they would at least dim the current skull-thumping one. She hurried back out to the main room. How much time had passed? Thane could be landing anytime now.

"I'm going to do a quick check." Jem shifted, and was halfway down the hallway when she heard Henning's voice in the kitchen. She froze. He was going to put the wrist tracker back on her. She bolted back to their room.

"We need to leave. *Now.*" She ran into the bathroom, grabbed the backpack and raced back out. Apologetic, Jem said, "Shiloh, I planned to give you an explanation about phasing but, for now, you'll have to trust me."

Jem pulled out a TACEXM from the backpack. The Tactical Explosive Munition was basically an oversized grenade.

Shiloh's eyes widened. "Bomb?"

"Don't panic," Jem said, rotating the top 180 degrees.

Shiloh went white. *What did you expect?* she chided herself. Dropping it back in the bag, she took a firm hold of Shiloh's arm and shifted, phasing's stasis halting the countdown.

The door slid open behind them.

Without giving Shiloh time to adjust—or panic more—Jem phased them through the side of the ship. Shiloh's open-mouthed expression was to be expected when someone found themselves hanging in mid-air, in the dark, after going through a supposedly solid hull. Jem gave her a wan, apologetic smile as she lowered them down to the tarmac, her months of practice now paying off.

Hurrying to the rear of the *Transom Ode*, she slung her bag of bombs into the main engine cowling. Materializing as soon as it left her hand, it landed with a thud. Verifying it was in place, Jem took off in the direction of V-16 at a run, Shiloh firmly in tow.

They were several meters away when the night lit up behind them with an enormous *boom-swoosh*. Jem hoped Shiloh didn't notice the shrapnel that flew 'through' their phased bodies. Subdued lighting behind the parking spots and along the taxi way guided her. Two ships they passed were apparently getting prepped for launch, though all activity around them had ceased as everyone faced toward the inferno behind them. Sirens sounded.

They crossed two well-lit runways, their emergency lights flashing. Jem was now thankful the vertical landing-slash-parking area was so far away from the chaos she'd caused. Regular traffic was undoubtedly suspended, but were the verticals?

Jem paused in front of V-2, holding a baby Class I Globe. Shiloh tried to say something, then grabbed her throat when she realized nothing was coming out. Jem gave the panicking woman an everything-is-okay thumbs-up and smile. Neither seemed to help much. Boy, did she have some apologizing to do. Jem looked up, a distant roaring sound accompanying the bright, flaring star growing bigger by the second. *Thane!* If her heart was working it would have beat faster.

They watched until it settled down somewhere behind the line of ships.

The tarmac around the *Lone Tracker* still glowed when they arrived. No impediment to them, nor was either hatch. Jem didn't stop until they were in the ship's plazo, then shifted them back. Shiloh dropped the arm she'd flung up out of reflex and stared at Jem. Dazed.

"We went through…that." She waved a hand at the closed hatch. "And the other ship…I couldn't talk…" she sank down into a huddle.

Jem ignored the pounding in her head, her eyes on Thane as he dropped past the last two stairwell rungs. She took a step forward and found herself enfolded in his arms. Warmth. *Safety*. She dimly heard someone else coming down the stairwell.

"I couldn't believe it when Thor said you were here. You wouldn't know anything about the emergency on B-ramp, would you?" Thane asked, a dry grin in his voice.

Her reply of "Maybe" was muffled by his shoulder.

"I think we might need the med-room," came Boyd's voice.

Turning added nausea to the throbbing. He was squatting in front of Shiloh. Her expression shocky, her breathing fast—nearly hyperventilating.

"I am so sorry," Jem whispered.

"Are there any other bruises? Injuries?" Boyd asked, stone-faced.

Right. That side of Shiloh's face had mellowed to a greenish-yellow. "No."

"What about you?" Thane asked in a hard voice as Boyd helped Shiloh up.

"One bruise, on my back," Jem admitted. She watched the lift take the two of them upwards. She leaned back against Thane's comforting bulk. "I've traumatized her."

"I take it she got the full treatment without prior warning?" Thane chuckled. He kissed the top of her head. "My first exposure was a small sample and it still rocked me. After she's had it explained and time to absorb it, she'll be fine." His tone changed. "How did you get the bruises?"

"A disagreement between us and a couple of crewmen." She closed her eyes. The nausea was morphing into vertigo. "You know about the *Transom Ode*?"

"Yes. And Kurzvall is on his way here."

"He's here. His ship is inbound," she whispered. She felt herself scooped up; dimly heard him saying something, losing all but the last word: *later*.

At least there'll be a later, Jem thought happily before the dark took her.

*****

Jem found herself looking up at the med-bed's scanner when consciousness returned. Gratefully, she found her headache was down to a low throb. Would it go back up if she moved? Turning her head slowly toward the door didn't cause an increase in pain. Great. She was debating whether to try standing when Thane came in.

He took her hand. "How do you feel?"

"Not too bad," she said, returning his smile. "Good drugs."

"Dr. Blackwood's special blend. He gave me a supply to keep handy. Just in case."

Dr. Blackwood was her specialist. He'd attended her extremely painful teleporting trials and had devised a special blend of painkiller and suppressant that worked fabulously on her screwed-up system.

"Bless him," Jem said on a sigh. "How long have I been out?"

"About an hour." Angry, he then said, "Shiloh filled us in on events, including bruises and your concussion. Med-scans don't show any other damage."

"How is she?"

"Settled. We gave her Phasing 1-0-1 and a glass of Aspric whisky."

Jem winced. The second probably helped the first go down. With Thane supporting her shoulders, Jem sat up carefully. No change in the headache department. Yay. "Where did they park Kurzvall?" She slid slowly to her feet. Thane slid a supportive arm around her waist.

"In orbit," Thane replied smugly. "*Cassie*'s pilot tried to get them moved up in the queue. Port Control not only declined, they moved two Palmyra-registered ships in front of him. The comments and snickering on the port frequency from the other ships were entertaining. It's another thirty minutes to the next inbound window.”

Jem snickered herself. Leaning against Thane, she walked out into the main command deck where the local news was playing on the main viewscreen. She stopped in surprise on seeing Markowitz.

“Major? I didn't realize you were here.” She gave Thane a what-the-hell look.

“He got the lecture, too,” Thane deadpanned.

“Along with two glasses of excellent whisky,” Markowitz said, giving Jem a wink.

Oh, well. Given the circumstances, it'd been unavoidable. “Why is the major here?” She aimed the question at Thane, but it was Markowitz who answered.

“General Kowalski suspected these two might have need of a calm head,” he said, moving over to the pilot's chair so Jem could sit down. The *Lone Tracker*'s dining table, the fat leg of the L-shaped counter that divided the command area from the compact kitchen, only sat four around it.

Boyd's cough from the table's backside sounded suspiciously like 'bullshit.'

“I've got something for you warming in the micro,” Thane told Jem as he settled her next to Shiloh on the fat end.

“I'm sorry,” Jem said, carefully looking her friend over. Her breathing and color were better. “I shouldn't have procrastinated in telling you about the phasing but…well...”

“It's something you have to experience to understand,” Shiloh said dryly. “I apologize, too. I don't normally—that was my first ever panic attack.”

Jem rubbed her nose. “Not like you get yanked through walls and such on a normal basis. Then there were the bombs.” Thane placed a pasta-filled food tray in front of her. The aroma had her realizing how hungry she was. She said “excuse me” to everyone and dug in.

“They're reporting on the *Transom Ode*,” Markowitz called out, then ordered increased audio.

“*...port's mystery fire on the B parking ramp is of main concern to the authorities,*” the solemn reporter stated. A visual display of the ship's charred remains—the nose section and one wingtip—filled the screen except for the lower quadrant the reporter's image had shrunk down to. *"Were the explosives somehow hidden in the ship at its last port call? Did one of those onboard plant them for whatever reason? Or worse, someone from here?"* droned the reporter. *"Authorities are combing the wreckage for clues and hope to have an answer soon. Anyone with any relevant information is encouraged to contact Law Enforcement or Keosauqua Port Security."*

"Viewscreen off." Thane scratched his chin. "Henning and Martin are staying mum about you and Shiloh. They've got to be worried. With the two of you loose in the breeze, Henning is now as open to kidnapping charges in Republic space as my asshole cousin already is."

"Fools, both, if they set foot back there," Boyd grunted.

"I'm surprised Henning hasn't blamed me for his ship's explosion," Jem said.

"He can't be positive it was you. He'd also have to admit you were on board, which would tie him to your kidnapping," Thane replied. "An official report would be proof Henning can't lie away."

"Even if someone did make an accusation—merc or crewmember—they'd still have to prove you did it," Boyd said.

"Would they?" Jem asked, worried. "This is Mercenary Capital. Could they go with just reputation and 'it had to be her'?" She'd faced that type of accusation once before.

"I think you're safe. Otherwise, they'd be opening themselves up to feuds among the various mercenary teams and a deterioration of their entire legal system." Thane paused. "With the social structure collapsing right behind it most likely. This would become a very dangerous place."

"As if it's not that already." Boyd crossed his arms. "What do we do about the assholes?"

"Nothing," Thane said. "We'll let their soon-to-be very unhappy employer deal with them."

Jem flashed a wicked grin as Shiloh asked if they could file charges against Henning and Martin here on Toulouse.

"Nope," Thane said, the other two men chiming in with "Uh-uh" and

"Useless."

"It didn't happen here," Thane clarified. "As far as the Palmyra authorities are concerned, what happens in the Republic, stays in the Republic."

"What about the mercs that were involved?" Jem said.

"By Palmyra's messed up laws, they haven't done anything wrong. They took a job and completed their contractual obligations. Did you ever interact with them?"

Jem shook her head. "Only in passing."

"And when they stopped that bastard from kicking Jem after she went down," Shiloh added angrily.

"They typically hung out in the lounge or down in the plazo," Jem said. "We didn't go farther than the kitchen. Ate and went back to our room, trying to avoid what eventually did happen. I do know they didn't care much for either Henning or Myers."

Thor spoke, announcing the *Cassie* had received clearance for landing and was assigned to short term C-8. Thane must have ordered it to track the ship.

"Kurzvall has to guess we're here, on the *Lone Tracker*," Shiloh said. "We're safe for now but…what's to keep him from hiring another group of mercenaries in a couple of months?"

"I intend to ensure that won't happen," Jem said firmly.

Thane's gaze locked on her. "Jem?"

"The *Transom Ode* is a turning point for me. I've been restrained. I've ignored and let slide all the threats—"

"What threats?"

"—all the posturing, all the inconvenience," she continued, ignoring his outburst. "No more. No more being seen as a passive weakling. I'm tired, Thane. Tired of the constant barrage of requests or outright demands and assaults." Her voice steady, she said, "I've been branded as a dangerous wildcard. So be it." She should have done this before now.

"I am going to make it abundantly clear that there will be consequences for those that piss me off," she said, her tone implacable. "Whether it's annoying demands to me or threatening those I care about. Otherwise, none of our family and friends will ever be safe." Jem gestured toward Shiloh for emphasis. "Starting now, with the Palmyra's mercenaries. I intend to show them, beyond any doubt, that *they* aren't safe. That I can get past their security and deal with them as they deserve."

"And how do you plan on that?"

Jem winced internally at his hostile tone, then shored up her resolve. "I figure a few well-placed bombs will—"

"*Bombs?* You plan on blowing up ships? Buildings? Injuring or killing any occupants?"

"I'll send an anonymous warning in advance."

"Then what? Have the networks broadcast your message of stay-away-or-else? Where will you get bombs?"

Matching Thane's hard tone, she said, "Yes, to the message and," her index finger made several circles in the air, "there's undoubtedly numerous places around here that has oodles of bombs of all shapes and sizes."

"It's a stupid, ill-considered plan," Thane snapped.

Jem's back stiffened.

"First, your target may not get cleared in time and someone dies. You were lucky no one on the *Transom Ode* did."

Her chin jutted out. "I knew the cargo hold would buffer the living area, giving them time to get out. That's why I targeted the rear engine. Otherwise, I could have just tossed the damn bag at Henning's feet."

Unappeased, Thane glowered at her. "Second, blatantly admitting to it will get you charged and arrested by Toulouse's Enforcers. If you've already left the system, they have plenty of mercenaries to go after you. Third, what happens when your warning is disregarded and someone else is kidnapped? Count on it, Jem. Until you actually *do* respond, and violently, they'll call your bluff."

"Who says I'm bluffing?" Jem said, holding his gaze. If that's what it took to—

"You're not a killer, Jem." Shiloh placed her hand on hers. "Don't turn yourself into one."

"Do you consider Major Markowitz a killer?" Jem asked tartly. Stunned, Shiloh's hand dropped away. "Or is he simply someone who does what's necessary to protect others? As I—and others—have done." Jem turned back to Thane. "I was once told that being forced to kill in self-defense or in defense of others was not the same as *being* a killer." Did he remember that long-ago conversation? Apparently so.

Thane laced his fingers through hers. "The key there is *forced* into it," he admonished gently, "not wielded indiscriminately as a club."

Jem's anger collapsed. He was right. And, truly, could she do as she threatened? Deliberately take that step? She managed a small smile. "We have to do something, Thane, or we'll keep going through this. If we can take Palmyra's mercenaries off the battlefield, we'll at least eliminate our most dangerous adversaries."

There came a loud throat clearing.

"After the military," Jem corrected, her eyes cutting sharply to Markowitz. "Although, I expect General Kowalski and Admiral Gleason will keep them in line."

"They'll be happy to know you hold them in such high esteem. Unfortunately," he said with a head shake, "there's only so much they can do. There are a number of factions that normally operate independently of their influence."

Jem shuddered at the thought of facing a military branch and all its resources. The fiasco with the now-retired Admiral Hawthorne, operating on his own authority to have her drugged and expedited to Military Command Headquarters, had been bad enough.

Thane drummed his fingers on the tabletop. "Okay, any other ideas on pacifying the mercs?"

"I like Jem's original plan," Boyd said.

Shiloh blinked. Jem snickered.

"You're kidding, right?" Thane retorted.

"Not really; they're mercenaries," Boyd growled. "But it could be modified."

It'd be a while before Boyd got over them kidnapping her. "Modify it how?"

"Instead of blowing up a building, mess with its security. That, more than anything else, will make the strongest impression. They'll get the message. As for consequences? If it comes to it, I'm sure you can find other alternatives than death. Depending on what you implement," Boyd added, "some might even end up wishing you had just killed them."

Thane and Jem locked gazes. His eyebrow asked a question. Her grin was the answer.

Chapter 20

Reginald Kurzvall didn't hide his displeasure as Martin Myers strode into his quarters and plopped unbidden into the seat across from him. Henning had stood, properly deferential, as he'd given his report and answered his questions.

"This is a fucking mess," Myers said.

"Most of which is your doing," Kurzvall snapped.

"You accusing me of blowing up the *Ode* last night?"

"No, but your unapproved actions led to it."

"Unapproved? I got Jem Wilmont. Something you hadn't been able to do."

Insolent asshole. A true Stohlass, Kurzvall sneered inwardly, *even if he didn't use the name*. "Neither did you. The team *I paid for* did that. You were to provide local information for them. What you didn't get was Thane Baron. You left him free to do exactly what he did: come after Wilmont."

The asshole frowned. "How did he do that? Know to come here?"

That was a very good question. He could understand Baron suspecting him to be behind Jem Wilmont's disappearance. Baron's recent visit to his home system was proof of that. How had they linked the *Transom Ode* to it? And how had he known to follow him to Toulouse? And within a day, at least, for that ship of his to beat him here. Trey Mosley should have had him stuck on Tylander for at least a week.

"Thane Baron is a *Tracker*," Kurzvall finally said. "He can follow leads and clues better than anyone else. Hell, I think he sniffs them out of the ether. Besides being cousins, you'd know that if you hadn't been sitting in a Fed-Pen cell for the last six years," he added sarcastically.

Myers had the audacity to glare at him.

"Which supports my decision," Myers said. "Jem Wilmont and Thane Baron make a great team. Holding a third person they both cared about would have them following whatever orders you give."

Kurzvall digested that for a heartbeat. True, except for one very telling point. "Then you would have taken his sister. Not his cousin. From Henning's report, you took the woman for your own personal reasons."

Myers's insolent shrug left him seething. No more. "You are dismissed."

"Fine. It won't take me long to check out of my hotel."

"I don't care if it takes all day."

"What?"

"Did you expect me to retain your impertinent, substandard services? You've cost me time, money, and opportunity. Wilmont and her friends will not be caught so off-guard again. Plus, you're now wanted by the Republic authorities for kidnapping."

"It's Henning's fault we lost Wilmont," Myers snapped. "If he hadn't taken off Wilmont's tracker, they wouldn't have been able to sneak out. One of the crew had to have helped them."

No, she'd used that invisible trick of hers. "Her wrist tracker was removed for repair as it appeared to be malfunctioning," Kurzvall deigned to reply.

"Wilmont knew she couldn't run with it on. Whoever helped her escape must have also messed with the computer sensors for that exact reason," Myers argued.

Myers was half right but…had the sensors been messed with? Henning *did* say they couldn't find anything wrong with the tracker. And they *did* disappear when he was about to put it back on her. His brow creased. What if…what if her invisibility somehow blocked the signal? Could Wilmont have fooled them, using short episodes to simulate a malfunction? He nodded to himself. Yes, that had to be it. That's why the Myerstone folks had used zap bands instead of simple trackers.

Kurzvall became aware of Myers's watchful scrutiny. "Get off my ship."

"I have a plan that—"

"Fund what will undoubtedly be another spectacular failure yourself," he said brusquely. He activated his comm. "Basso, my guest needs an escort off the ship."

Myers stood slowly. Kurzvall did not miss the malice in the man's expression. A large-sized guard opened the door, a hand resting warningly on his stunner.

"You will regret this," Myers said before stalking out.

Kurzvall leaned back in his seat. At least this fiasco hadn't been a total waste, as it had provided him with new insights. Myers was right in his assessment. If he could find some way to manage it, Wilmont, Baron, and his ship combined would be great assets. And that was a pretty damn big *if* after Myers's screwup. Still, it would make some of the plans he was contemplating more feasible.

He needed to verify with Henning that none of the tracker "malfunctions" occurred when Wilmont was in view of anyone else. Which he was willing to bet on. Unfortunately, Henning would now have to go, too. He couldn't maintain ties with him, linked as he was to their kidnapping.

As for Wilmont? There were too many gaps and conflicting details in the information he'd acquired over the past year. How much more extensive were her capabilities? He needed more information. He needed higher-placed resources. He needed to re-examine what he did have on everything that had happened this past year. No, since Pappia.

And he needed to acquire a zap band or two.

Chapter 21

They found Trystan Rolfe enjoying a quiet meal and drink at his favorite barrill—localism for a bar and grill combo. He didn't even stop chewing when she and Thane settled in the chairs across from him. He'd undoubtedly spotted them as soon as they entered the place.

Rolfe finished chewing, swallowed. "Thought you would have taken off by now."

"My first trip here was all business. I decided to play tourist this time…view some of Toulouse's fine sights. That smells good," Jem said, leaning forward. "What is it?"

"Drantorn stew. A native meat source," he clarified.

"Is that the only size?" Jem asked, eyeing the very large bowl.

"No." He forked up another bite.

The silence stretched, broken by a server coming to their table. Jem ordered a small bowl of the stew and moon ale. Thane asked for a glass of whisky.

"So. What kind of sights interest you?" Rolfe asked, reaching for his glass.

"*Ohhh*—the Weatherall Armory and Toulouse National Bank sound interesting," Jem replied.

Rolfe's gaze sharpened over his glass. His voice remained indifferent as he asked, "Thinking to make a deposit?" After a beat, he added, "Or withdrawal?"

"Maybe a little bit of both," she said, giving him a bland smile. She heard an amused huff on her right. Thane shook his head when she glanced over.

Yes, I'm having fun, her eyebrows said, bobbing at him.

The server returned, depositing their orders in front of them before heading off to another table. The bowl in front of Jem was the same size as Rolfe's.

"This is small?"

The merc grinned and waved his spoon. "There are several gyms nearby. Keeping in shape burns a lot of calories. The *Strangler* provides plenty of replacement calories for refueling, and they're open 22/9."

Jem's first bite was…interesting. It wasn't bad, but… "Tastes like a beefy turnip."

Thane blew whisky out his nose. "Sorry," he managed between coughs and wiping the table.

A minute and several bites later, Jem asked, "Heard anything about Henning?"

"Lots of LE questions. They're still trying to figure out what happened to the *Ode*." Rolfe gave her a knowing look. "It's a good thing the explosion happened on the rear engine," he said mildly. "Everyone managed to bail before it spread to the center of the ship."

"That was fortunate, wasn't it," Jem agreed, taking a sip of ale. Rolfe didn't know how she managed it or their escape, but the mercenary was sure she was responsible. Good instincts.

"Henning's crew has been job hunting, taking local jobs or ship berths. I heard Henning was involved in a dustup on C-8 this morning."

"Oh?" Thane said, curious. "Did you hear what about?"

"Seems he was pounding on the ship's hatch, demanding to be let on board. Port Security hauled him to jail. The ship—*Cassie*—left in the next exit window."

No ship. Wanted. And Henning still expected Kurzvall to take him with him?

"Is Myers job hunting, too?" Jem asked after several more bites. Rolfe was evidently tuned into the merc's gossip network.

"Not that I've heard." Rolfe pushed his empty bowl aside. "He's being a rude, overbearing, obnoxious asshole in my cousin's hotel. If he's not careful, he'll find himself stuffed in a UPMS pod and mailed to the nearest Republic

LE office."

"Yeah?" Thane perked up. "The Wotan System isn't the closest. However, if a certain individual does end up in a mail pod, the Midgard authorities would be very interested. I'll personally reimburse the expense."

Rolfe's expression turned contemplative. "I'll pass it on."

Enough dancing. Jem pushed her half-empty bowl toward Thane. He pushed it back. She crinkled her nose at him, gave a near imperceptible nod, and drank the last of her ale. Thane paid their bill. They'd decided to give a kind of forewarning, else they risked her future claims being brushed off as taking advantage of events caused by others or natural circumstances.

"If you'll excuse us, we'll be going." Jem smiled. Stood. "Need to get started on that tour." They clasped hands and walked out.

* * * * *

It was a quiet night at the Weatherall Armory, a massive two-story building on the city's southern edge. The two nightshift technicians flirted in their basement office as the security guards lounged in theirs on the second floor. Computer screens lined the walls in both offices.

Half of the technician's comp screens went black.

A third of Security's comp screens blanked.

Chairs scraped. Hands flew over keyboards.

A technician raced down a hallway toward the main server room.

Lights flickered, steadied, then all the remaining comp screens blanked.

Chaos ensued. Calls were placed. Swearing was rampant.

Security personnel raced into the corridors, weapons in hand. Searching.

Exits were locked. No intruders found.

Law Enforcers arrived. Management arrived. A nosy reporter arrived.

Nothing appeared disturbed. Then an enforcer tugged on Vault No. 4's door.

Swearing resumed when it swung open.

Within fifteen minutes they knew twelve high-yield TACEXMs were missing.

Chapter 22

Jem stumbled from bedroom to bathroom to main area. Thane sat in front of the navigation panel, arms crossed and watching a local news channel on the viewscreen. A serious-faced reporter was apparently grilling an equally serious-faced woman in front of a building. The audio was either muted or Thane had on an ear receiver. Not that she needed to hear it to guess the content.

She squinted at the Midgard chronometer above Thane's head. Three hours? That was all? She was tempted to go back to bed. It'd been almost dawn before she and Thane got back to the ship. He'd dragged her to the med-room, given her another shot of the doctor's fabulous concoction, and curled around her in their bed.

Momentarily bypassing a thankfully ready pot of coffee, Jem selected a meal from the food carousal and popped it into the lower micro. The top one was busily counting down on what had to be Thane's breakfast; Boyd and Shiloh's were in front of them. No sign of Markowitz. Surprising, since she'd figured him for an early riser. Military and all that.

The top micro dinged. Leaving the viewscreen on, Thane retrieved his meal.

Jem's stomach rumbled at the smell wafting from it as he sat next to her. Still a couple of minutes to go for hers.

Thane pulled the cover off. "I'm curious about one of the details Shiloh gave of your escape."

"We all are," Boyd grunted from his usual spot. He preferred sitting on the inside of the "L" as it gave him full view of the command area.

"It was after you exited the ship's hull. Shiloh described it as 'drifting' down to the ground. That's new." He forked up a bite.

"I've been practicing, mostly when you're gone. I wanted to surprise you," she added, cheeks turning pink when Thane stopped chewing. "According to Andi, my brain was stuck in two-dimensional mode. When I shifted, I always stayed on the same, uh, level at the point I shifted from and then 'walked' up or down by whatever means was visually available back here. Stairs and such."

"You visually linked your shifted…position to what you saw here?" Shiloh said.

Jem pointed a finger at her. "Perfect description. Thanks."

"That's why you don't sink through floors," Boyd said.

"Floors, chairs, whatever. Andi figured it out, after a lot of chair-bouncing, hand-waving conversations. Just watching her was tiring," Jem said to several chuckles. "She postulated that an Otanak Engine has to maintain some kind of a connection to the universe *here* when it's running *there* to keep itself orientated. Don't ask; even Andi doesn't understand dimensional physics. Ergo—yes, she said that—since an O-field had caused my mutation, I must have the same type of connection."

"Which explains why you can still see and hear when shifted," Thane said.

Jem nodded, took a sip of coffee. "I can now move downward from my initial level, but I have to be careful. While I have no problem picturing me drifting *down*, my brain just can't grasp the idea of floating *up*. It could create a dangerous situation." Jem snorted. "Andi told me to think like a balloon."

"Dangerous how?" Thane asked, his fork paused in mid-air.

"Imagine sinking below ground level. Or halfway through a floor. As long as I'm shifted, no problem."

"Which you can only hold for so long before—" Thane grimaced. So did Boyd.

Shiloh looked between them. "What's the problem?"

"Rematerializing in the same physical space occupied by something solid can get, uh, messy. Now I've traumatized you again," Jem said, disheartened as Shiloh blanched. The micro dinged and she retrieved her meal. Reseated, she said, "I'm sorry, Shiloh. I never wanted you exposed to this."

To her credit, Shiloh managed a small smile. "Not your fault. You've evidently been doing this for some time. This connection is pretty solid, right?"

"Mostly." Jem poked at her stew.

"Jem?" Thane laid his hand on hers.

It seems today was confessional day. "I once shifted so far that my connection faded to almost nothing—just a white blob in a black sea." It had been necessary to force her way through an electromagnetic field. The frigging things were evidently interdimensional. One of her arms had been numb for hours afterward.

"What would happen if you shifted far enough to lose the white blob?" Boyd asked.

"Probably means I lost my connection to this universe. What happens then?" Jem shrugged. Not even Andi had hazarded a guess. Would she be able to unshift? Stuck *there* forever? Was that what had happened to the ships that have vanished, like Thane's father's Survey ship?

Jem took advantage of the silence that followed to dig in to her meal.

"Something's happening," Boyd said, looking over Thane's head at the viewscreen.

Everyone turned. "Resume viewscreen audio," Thane ordered.

"...not fully disclosed all that happened at your armory, Miss Weatherall. You said it was a security failure caused by two shorted computer nodes. Now, we're getting reports of the Toulouse National Bank at 163rd Avenue and Lotus Street being evacuated due to a bomb on the CEO's desk. Quite a coincidence, wouldn't you say?" the reporter finished in a suspicious voice.

Rachel Weatherall's face went blank. *"Until we get further word, that's exactly what it is."* She turned and walked away.

"For those just tuning in, we're reporting live from the Weatherall Amory where an unprecedented security breach has occurred. It's—"

"It has not been declared a breach!" someone yelled off camera.

The reporter's face briefly twisted into a sour expression, then continued. *"Not only was last night's unexplained* occurrence *unprecedented, another one is currently underway. Please stay tuned as we will be covering both in detail and—"*

"Viewscreen off," Thane ordered.

Absently, Jem said, "Guess they haven't found the one in the first-floor bathroom yet."

Shiloh gave her a weird look. "Why there?"

"Why not?" Jem asked, giving her an innocent look.

Markowitz bounded out of the stairwell as they finished eating. "Morning all. What'd I miss?" he said, leaning against the kitchen counter.

"Just Jem's drifting explanation, which we'll fill you in on later," Thane said. "Have you got anything?"

"Yep. Speculation is rampant. The *Transom Ode*, the armory, and now the bank."

Oh, he'd been out nosing around. Gathering intel, as he'd put it.

"What are they saying?" Thane asked, satisfaction evident.

"That it's mighty peculiar," Markowitz drawled, "that Jem Wilmont, who was on the *Ode*—courtesy of a very shook-up crewmember—vanished *mysteriously* along with one unnamed other before the ship *mysteriously* exploded and is now on the *Tracker*. Which, coincidently, happened to be landing as the *Ode* burned. No one is *saying* she's responsible, but they're all wondering."

Boyd gave a derisive snort. "What about last night's *other* mysterious events?"

"Speculation is that it's someone advertising their services."

"Kind of is," Shiloh said, amused.

"True. I doubt Rolfe has told anyone about yesterday's conversation. He'll keep his suspicions to himself, at least for now," Markowitz added.

Shiloh crossed her arms and said firmly, "Well, while you plan your next mystery, Jem and I need to go shopping."

Mouth full, Jem nodded vigorously. Since they'd only had what they were kidnapped in, and the *Ode's* laundry facility had been minimal, they'd been wearing the crew's handouts when they escaped. Still were.

"I'll repay whatever I use from your cash card," Shiloh added.

"You'll do no such thing," Thane replied before Jem could. "You are in this mess because of us, buying a few clothes is the least I can do."

"Shopping sounds good. Especially having them see me out and about." Jem rubbed her hands together. "I'm going to put all those pesky rumors and speculation to use."

***

Jem and Shiloh stretched their outing into early afternoon. They wandered through stores, bought clothes, toiletries, and a few mementos. Everyone was polite; no one approached them. Of course, having a silent shadow named Boyd as bodyguard might have had something to do with it. After enjoying a hearty and non-frozen meal, they returned to the *Lone Tracker*. Jem dropped her packages on her bed as her friend disappeared into the med-room, aka Shiloh's bedroom. Boyd and the major were bunking in Thane's holding room on the lower deck.

Her headache had dimmed to a dull, easily ignored throb, but she still tired way too soon. Jem was tempted to take a nap, but tonight's activities needed to be discussed. The men should have come up with several options while they were gone. Giving the bed a wistful look, she wandered back out to the kitchen to get a drink from the cooler and joined Boyd at the table.

"Where's Thane and the major?"

"Thane is down in the workshop—not sure doing what. Markowitz is still out. He's going to nose about some more, act like he's looking for employment. We *think* he's not yet been associated with us."

Shiloh joined them as the soft humming sound of the lift preceded Thane's arrival.

"I've permanently disabled the remaining TACEXMs," he announced. "No chance they'll go off now."

Jem breathed a sigh of relief. That had been their one fear. That the ones they'd left in the bank would be accidently set off.

They sat around the table, talking, waiting for Markowitz to get back. Shiloh selected a bottle of juice from the cooler while Thane warmed up a tray of beef cubes swimming in a Barwotz sauce. The ultra-spicy dish was one of his favorites. Jem informed him, to the others' laugher, he'd need to wash up and rinse his mouth before she kissed him again.

Markowitz arrived about an hour later, rotating the pilot's chair around to face them.

"How did you do?" Thane asked.

"Not bad. I've got eleven employment offers and two propositions." He waited until they stopped laughing. "Seven of the eleven are for mercenary positions, the others for local bouncers and/or security. In fact, I learned something very interesting. They're branching out."

"Yeah, they've added kidnapping," Jem said.

"I imagine there will always be the mercenary soldier-for-hire aspect," Markowitz agreed, "but they have added a security branch offering external services. The Mercenary Guild is heavily promoting it. One of those offered jobs? It was on a team recently contracted as security escorts for Jaguide gem shipments."

Thane let out a low whistle, which accurately reflected the astonishment on all their faces.

Jaguide crystals, named for their home system, had revolutionized the laser and construction industries. Cut and polished, the crystals powered everything from medical scalpels to large military weapons. Ground and melted, they increased the tensile strength of any material they bonded with. Each one was worth a small fortune.

"That does make sense," Shiloh said. "Especially in those systems that have broken away. Palmyra's people have skills and training that can be used in a number of different avenues."

"I'm more worried about it being extended to intersystem fighting," Markowitz said.

"Republic commandos might have a real job to do then," she fired back.

Markowitz leveled an unreadable stare at her.

Jem twisted around in the silence to look at her friend. Shiloh's gaze jerked to her, then down. Spots of pink bloomed on her cheeks. *Hmmm.* She shook her head at Thane when he started to say something. She'd broach the subject with Shiloh. Find out what was bothering her.

"The Guild is still relatively small," Markowitz continued after a brief silence. "Many I spoke with are wary of it, wary of the whole new political order. They're in wait-and-see mode. Then there are the ones that prefer being loners or, like the psychopath I spoke with, don't want to be curtailed from *any* type of job." His voice turned cold. "I'll be turning that bastard's name into our watch list."

They have a watch list?

Thane's head angled slightly, and Jem could practically see the calculations whirling about in it.

"I've got a list of agencies and law firms that handle merc contracts," Thane said. "We should add some high-profile places to our list of potentials."

"Well, while you get that, I'm going to take a shower," Markowitz said, rising to his feet. In a disgusted voice, he said, "I still feel dirty from that psycho guy."

Jem waited until he had finished showering and had gone down to the lower deck. Thane and Boyd were researching the city, looking for those high-profile sites. She motioned to Shiloh, led her into the med-room and pulled the door down. She much preferred the *Tracker's* roller-style than the *Ode's* pocket-style doors. She turned, put her hands on her hips.

Sternly, she asked, "All right, what was that commando comment about?"

Shiloh matched her stance. "I'm irritated. Major Markowitz and his commandos weren't stationed on Midgard for 'strategic placement.' They're there to keep an eye on you. That's why *he* is here now. Like they expect you to suddenly go on a thieving campaign or…" a hand flapped, "or something. Military Command has to know those rumors about you are bullshit, Jem. You'd never do things like that."

"Unless forced into it," Jem replied evenly, "to prevent harm to someone else."

Shiloh's expression shifted from angry to sullen.

"Major Markowitz, Captain Tagawa, and their teams *have* been strategically placed." On an unused Sea Patrol base on a mid-sized island southeast of Azusa to be exact. "Admiral Gleason initiated the program after more of the Republic began breaking away. Unlike teams elsewhere, they are under the direct command of Admiral Gleason, through the Planetary Defense Office, with orders to watch *over* me. Protect me. By extension, that includes Thane and his family. You. For the exact reason we've just gone through."

Shiloh mulled that over for several seconds. "This was an *oops*, then?"

"Nope. It's an embarrassment. Trystan Rolfe being a former and highly rated commando himself is what's salvaging their pride. If Martin Myers had hired a less experienced team, the commandos—hell, all of us—would have been alerted and on guard."

She turned and grabbed the door handle. Shiloh stopped her before she could raise it.

"Jem, why are they under the admiral's command?"

She would have to catch that. Jem walked over to the bed. Sat, and patted it for Shiloh to do likewise. Might as well sit for the rest of this conversation.

"Because Military Command is worried about the potential harm I could do to the Republic, either through coercion or going rogue. There are those among them who already feel I am too dangerous a threat to live…and they only know about my teleporting. What might they do when they learn about my extra-dimensional invisibility or phasing?"

Shiloh paled. "Oh, my, God. You have a target on your back."

"Back, chest, head, ass," Jem said with a wan smile. "Fortunately, Admiral Gleason and General Kowalski have deemed that information as need-to-know to keep the zealots at bay."

Shiloh's gaze held hers. "Military Command can't override *Supreme* Admiral Gleason's orders."

Jem waited. Shiloh was too smart not to figure it out.

"But they could order others to…" Her voice rose, agitated. "…those independent factions…the major and his team would have to fight their own people?"

People they may have trained with. Friends even. "We're hoping it never comes to that," Jem said somberly. Did the paranoids have contingency plans already drawn up?

"Do you think this might have triggered something?" Shiloh's voice shook.

"No," Jem told her reassuringly. "I'm sure Kurzvall's goals are aligned more on the financial spectrum." She waggled her head a couple of times. "Maybe some Consortium politics he's not adverse to supporting and helping along.”

“You deal with this a lot, don’t you? Because of all those stupid, nasty, *wrong* rumors.” Shiloh straightened. “We teach these mercenaries a good lesson, others might get the frigging hint.”

Jem’s grin widened.

“What about the family? Who can I talk with that’s aware of the phasing? Avoid any oops myself?”

Jem curled her nose. “We need to start a scorecard on who knows what. Let’s see…GG, Andi, Nicholas, Stuart, Seth…Kowalski, Gleason and their aides…I think that’s it.”

Suddenly feeling in need of that nap, she excused herself. It might also relieve the headache that had wound back up. This post-concuss headachy-drain was getting old.

***

The evening went better than the morning. The tense atmosphere evaporated with Shiloh’s apology to Markowitz and they spent several hours debating the items on their lists, including the names of the team leaders the major had spoken with. Shiloh successfully argued against the high-profile places, as she said they didn’t align with their ‘mercenary agenda.’ The bank, she said, had made their point in that circle. She even came up with a new page for their lesson plan in dealing with the team leaders.

They watched the news. The two explosives found in the Toulouse National Bank had been verified to have come from the Weatherall Armory. There was no mention of Jem, Thane, or the *Lone Tracker*.

“I’m kind of surprised,” Boyd said, listening as another interviewee gave their ‘expert’ opinion. “With all the rumbling in the Circle, I would have expected an enterprising reporter to have heard the speculation about us and come sniffing around.”

“Professional courtesy, most likely,” Markowitz said. “They’d shut out reporters.”

“It’s the Enforcers I’ve been expecting,” Thane groused. “The ‘just a few questions if you don’t mind’ routine. Wonder what they’d say if I told them I did?”

Shiloh frowned. "I thought we hadn't been linked to the bombs?"

"Not about those. About the *Transom Ode*," Thane said.

"Why? You hadn't even landed when it blew up."

"But you and Jem were."

"Oh." She paused. "Wonder what Martin is doing?"

"Being a pain, most likely. Anyone?" Thane said, looking around.

"Nope."

"No idea."

"He knows better than to come anywhere near me," Jem snapped.

Chapter 23

Jem levered herself to the side of the bed, shaking off the last dregs of sleep. She had no recollection of when Thane got up, but he'd left the room dark and the door pulled down so she'd remain undisturbed. She'd slept hard and deep and felt…good. No headache. *Yay.*

She stretched, enjoying the quiet moment. Today would be busy. Finalizing plans. Setting them in motion. Prepping to leave. Yep. Busy, busy. Last night they'd rented bikes and toured the city, although, in the major's vernacular, they'd reconnoitered it. They'd wanted to visually inspect their potential targets and their surrounding areas. She'd had to go into ghost-mode only once, to get Trystan Rolfe's address and contact information from the Guild's files. Unlike the others on their list, his information wasn't publicly available.

Thane figured it was probably more about letting the Guild filter job requests than paranoia. Considering the man's reputation, he probably got a lot of them. Hah! Maybe she should start forwarding all *her* requests to LE. Bet that'd stop them.

Ordering the lights on dim, she dressed, combed out her night braid, and pulled it into a ponytail. After a brief visit to the bathroom, she sauntered out onto the main deck. She did a double take at the local-time clock.

1334?

She'd slept almost half their day away. She squinted at Thane, sitting in front of the table comp. "Did you slip me something?"

"Nope," he said, amused. "Your body took what it needed."

True. Fifteen minutes later, she was sitting next to Shiloh and forking up an omelet with cubed potatoes as Thane detailed their final targets. Murphey's Security Services, A-1 Specialists, Paulison & Pelz, Inc, Baljevic & Associates, Tomich Legal Services, and the Mercenary Guild would all receive late-night gifts. So would Trystan Rolfe, Adam Hurt, Barbara Whitehill, and Peter Simms, plus a breakfast invitation.

"What about Hamhurst Liquidators and Freyer Equipment?" Jem asked, swallowing.

"Freyer Equipment is nixed; they're open round the clock," Thane said. "Hamhurst is a bit far out. I don't think we'll have time to get to them."

"I vote for doing them first," Shiloh said, "with fully armed bombs on timers. Work your way back from there."

Jem couldn't blame her. They were assassins: first, last, and only. "I'd have to get new—"

"No," Thane interrupted.

"It'd just be the building," Jem wheedled.

"No," Thane repeated firmly.

"Spoilsport," Jem muttered. Giving Shiloh an I-wish shrug, she reminded Thane they had made the loop last night.

"We also started early in the evening and, except for that one time, didn't hide. We're not going to start tonight until full dark. Plus, we'll need time for avoiding patrols and ghost-mode trips into targets that, hopefully, shut down or go to bed at a decent hour. And the night is frigging short as it is," Thane said with a frustrated growl.

Yeah, not as convenient as Midgard's twenty-six-hour cycle. A *thump* echoed up the stairwell.

"That would be Boyd and Markowitz sparring," Thane said, lips twitching.

Oh, boy. "Will the plazo survive?"

"The *Tracker* is pretty sturdy," Thane said laughing. "I did tell them they'd be repairing any dented lockers."

A loud *clang* had his expression morphing into a slightly worried look.

Snickering, Shiloh asked, "They do know we're leaving tomorrow, right?"

Jem waved her fork. "Boyd's an old supply troop. He'll know where to source—" *thump, thump, clang, thump-thump*, "…stuff."

"Are you sure they're just sparring?" Shiloh asked, looking toward the stairwell.

Thane's worried expression deepened.

***

An hour later, Jem switched the table comp to comm mode and inputted Trystan Rolfe's contact number. He answered on the third ring. Sorta. Jem said "Hello," and smiled politely at what to her was a blank screen. She was calling with full video. Cautious, huh?

"Jem Wilmont," his voice said. "Should I ask how you got this number?"

Nope. "I'm calling to invite you to a breakfast meeting tomorrow morning at the *Strangler*. I have a proposition for you and…" *Oh, my.*

One of the best chests she'd ever seen was suddenly on display. Bronzed, wide, corded with muscle, it filled the comp screen. He'd taken the call standing as the view now shifted, changing to Rolfe's face as he sat. That wasn't so bad either, especially with that amused glint in his eyes.

"Proposition?"

She cleared her throat. "I have a *proposal*," she restarted, "for you and several others."

His expression turned cautious. "To do what?"

"The *Strangler*. 0600 tomorrow. All will be explained then. I look forward to seeing you." Jem flashed a smile and disconnected. Blowing out a breath, she couldn't help wondering if the rest of him had been bare too. That would account for the initial video block. Good thing she loved Thane's chest. And the rest of him. She smiled inwardly at the memories that invoked.

Yanking her libido back to the present, she made the same call and offer to the other three mercenary team leads, minus the discomfort. They were counting on curiosity for them to show up. She glanced at the viewscreen clock. The others should be back soon. Boyd and his split lip were escorting Shiloh to pick up some last-minute food supplies. Markowitz and his puffy left eye were browsing the Port Circle. Thane was at the Port Services office. Being a non-citizen with no local bank account, he had to provide a cash pre-payment for his requested ship services.

The plazo had indeed held up, only needing a few locker dings undented.

Jem peeked at the clock again. Nervous. So much rode on tonight, her stomach was already twisting into knots. *I really needed to work on my badassery.*

***

Jem halted inside the *Strangler's* entrance and surveyed the room. Was it always this full at six in the morning? How many were here as backups to the four she'd called? That was okay. Her own backups were here. Boyd and Markowitz might appear to be focused on the large food platters in front of them, but they would have been aware of her as soon as she stepped in.

Her targets were in a booth against the right wall, undoubtedly chosen because they expected to be discussing business. They were. Just not what they expected. The guy behind the counter watched her warily as she crossed the room. She pulled a chair from a nearby table and settled down at the booth's edge, returning the occupants' scrutiny. Barbara Whitehill and Peter Simms had the two inside seats. Trystan Rolfe and Adam Hurt the outside ones.

When a waiter sidled up cautiously, Jem realized the room's low murmur of conversation had died away. Instincts, she figured, sensing something out of the ordinary was happening.

"Do you have Slovinka tea blend?" Jem inquired politely. "Great. I'll have a large cup, hot. Has everyone else ordered?" she asked checking the table. They all had drinks and silverware, but no sign of food.

"We didn't get here as early as your associates," Rolfe said, flicking a glance over her shoulder.

Ah. "Just so you all know, I'm only paying for your breakfasts." She made a thumb-over-shoulder gesture. "Your associates are on their own." *Yes, I am aware of yours, too.*

The server materialized with a steaming cup of tea. Behind him, two more servers carried laden trays. Jem cradled her cup and leaned out of the way. Wow. Even Whitehill's platter was heaped with more than she would have wanted to try. Did they always eat like this? *Probably did*, remembering the earlier conversation with Rolfe.

"Anything else I can get for you?" the last server asked nervously. Getting head shades, he gave a watery smile and scuttled away. *Hmmm.* Guess having the four top mercs together was a nervous situation.

Jem told them to "eat while it's hot," and proceeded to follow suit with her tea. Naturally, she finished first and motioned for a refill. She needed it, having been up since yesterday. She and Thane had barely finished in time for her to make this meeting. He should be back at the *Tracker* by now. Lucky him. But no one would get any sleep until all were safely on board.

"You look a bit…tired," Rolfe said, studying her.

"Long night," she replied candidly. Three sets of eyes narrowed; Rolfe's calm study remained unchanged. Wondering, huh? They'd know soon enough. The city was waking up, so *annnny* time now. Too bad the viewscreen over the back wall was off.

Peter Simms laid his fork down. "Okay, we're here. We've eaten. What's your proposal?"

Jem took a sip of tea. "You leave me and mine alone, I leave you alone."

The silence lasted several seconds. Even Rolfe looked nonplussed.

"What kind of proposal is that?" snorted Adam Hurt.

"A fairly simple one," she replied as Rolfe and Whitehill's phones went off with a pulsating tone. More sounded behind her. *Yesss.*

"Mercenary Guild being evacuated," Rolfe read from his text. "TACEXM found in President's office." He looked up at Jem, his face unreadable.

"Enforcers on the way. Stay advised," Whitehill finished reading from hers.

Oh. She's a Guild member, too. Probably why she was seated next to Rolfe.

"Just one?" Jem asked innocently. "The last place had two, if I remember the news report correctly." Except it was in the men's bathroom this time. Equal opportunity.

Whitehill bit out a curse and started texting, her fingers flying over the keys.

Adam Hurt's phone sounded, again echoed by others around the room. He read the text, laid it on the table. Tonelessly he said, "Murphey's Security Services is being evacuated due to a TACEXM in their server room. Are there two?"

Jem blinked. He didn't look like a Murphey man. "Hard telling."

Simms suddenly leaned sideways and stared past Jem. Everyone turned to see the viewscreen that was now on.

"...chaos at the moment. Bomb reports are coming in from all over the city and the specialized units are having to split up."

Jem recognized the Mercenary Guild behind the reporter.

"For those just now tuning in, we're having a repeat of two days ago, except more. The Mercenary Guild behind me reported the first bomb and—excuse me?" She put her hand to her ear for a second, dropped it. *"Correction, the Guild is now reporting two bombs on their premises. So far, Murphey's Security Services, Baljevic & Associates, and Tomich Legal Services are reporting one each."* She made a face. *"So far."*

The bartender muted the viewscreen, but didn't turn it off.

"Wow, isn't that something," Jem said, turning back. Four blank expressions faced her. "Where were we? Oh, right, my proposal. The why-for is because my reputation, fueled by both rumor and speculation, has been spreading for over a year. I've refused numerous job offers, both long-term and short, because I'm not a thief or a spy or an assassin. Unfortunately, there are those who won't take *no* for an answer and use other methods to acquire my services."

She looked directly at Rolfe, saw his slight nod. As did the others.

"You four are among Palmyra's elite: the most experienced, the best trained, the most respected, and the most likely to be approached." Her gaze wandered over her listeners. "I highly recommend you give them a strong *no*. In fact, avoid anything that touches me or mine somewhere in the mix, however remotely it may appear. Because I. Am. Tired. Of it," she enunciated in a low, hard voice. "Otherwise, there will be consequences for the offending individuals. Consequences they will not be able to escape, regardless of any form of security you can dream up."

Hurt pointed. The screen now listed A-1 Specialists and the Palmyra Federal Building as having a bomb report. Jem smirked at that last one. They'd had one TACEXM left, and she couldn't resist leaving it in the Director's office when they passed the Fed Building on their way back.

All eight eyes returned to her. She could feel more on her back. "If there's nothing else?" Jem said. Pulling out Thane's cash card, she handed it to Simms. "Mr. Simms? If you would be so kind as to pay the bill?" He plugged it into the menu box and selected *All*.

Rolfe held up a hand. "One question, if you don't mind?"

Jem tilted her head, waiting.

"Have you ever heard of a whisky brand called 'Pounding J'?"

Jem kept her smile vague. *Thank you.* She'd been wondering how to broach it.

"Of course. It's an excellent brand. Thane's favorite, in fact." He'd hated giving up four bottles, but Shiloh's suggestion had been deemed a good one. From the covert glances Rolfe's question had sparked, none of them had mentioned to the others on finding a bottle of it in their homes this morning.

"Do they sell it here?" she continued blandly. "We're running a bit low at the moment."

"No," Whitehill said slowly, "I've only found it in one place."

Oh, good innuendo.

All four were suddenly trading glances. Hurt made a small hand movement; Whitehill's thumb lifted briefly. Some kind of merc-code? "Card?" Jem said, seeing the flashing green acceptance light. Simms pulled it out and handed it to her.

"Please take heed of my warn—proposal. I'll only be an enemy if you make me one," Jem said tiredly. She pushed away from the table, almost too exhausted to stand. She needed the *Lone Tracker*, Thane, and a bed. In that order. She had tapped into her last nugget of energy for this meeting and it was about to bottom out.

"Miss Wilmont?" Rolfe said, his tone respectful. "You ever change your mind about branching out, give me a call."

It took a couple of seconds for her fogged brain to realize he was offering her a job. Oh, well. Turning, she found herself the room's focus in a silence that was almost thick enough to earn an atmospheric rating. Jem let her gaze wander for a moment, then walked unhurriedly out the door. Without admitting to anything, she'd made her point.

Boyd and Markowitz fell into step beside her.

Jem didn't remember much of their silent trip back to the spaceport. The fog in her head drifted down her neck and shrouded the rest of her body. It took concentration to put one foot in front of the other. Again. And again. Somewhere along the trip to V-16, Boyd took hold of her arm.

Right foot. Left foot. Right…left…

Stairs. Boyd pulling, tugging her up them. Then Thane's arms were around her. *Home*, she thought contentedly.

* * * * *

"She's pretty well wiped out," Boyd told Thane. "I almost had to carry her the last bit."

Thane smiled tiredly over Jem's head. "Not surprised. We kept her shifting times down to a minimum, but it added up. And she's not slept since yesterday." Looking down, he found her asleep on her feet. Shaking his head, he gently scooped her up.

"I'll put her to bed, then you and the major can tell us how it went."

When Thane rejoined them on the main deck, they were focused on the news playing on the viewscreen. "Looks chaotic," he commented, seeing all the activity going on behind the reporter and his interviewee.

"That's putting it mildly," Shiloh said, grinning. "Especially after they found the one in the Federal Director's office. We unmuted it long enough to hear his rant."

Thane walked over to claim another cup of coffee. The stout beverage would have to keep him upright until he could climb in next to his sig-ner. Something he planned to do as soon as they were safely in space. *Which would be in…*he glanced at the local clock…*one hour and eight minutes.* He had more-or-less collapsed into a seat when Shiloh let out a squeal, causing him to slosh coffee on the tabletop.

"You did it!" she said, pointing.

The screen now displayed another line under Paulison & Pelz, Inc: Hamhurst Liquidators, two bombs reported.

"Sorry, not armed," Thane said with a tired smile. A quick swipe with his sleeve took care of the coffee. He gave her back a quick pat as she hugged him. He didn't tell her it was the reason Jem was almost late for the breakfast meeting. Or that she had exhausted herself, pushing hard to add it. Eyeballing the list again, something in the reporter's face had Thane ordering the viewscreen audio back on.

"...report brings a total of twelve bombs over the last three days. It's the exact number and type missing from the Weatherall Amory: TACEXMs, which stands for Tactical Explosive Munition. Coincidental? No one believes that. Nor does anyone know who these perpetrators are. This is too extensive to be just a sick prank, even though they're finding all except the first two bank TACEXMs have been rendered inert. Is this a demonstration of some new equipment? Or of a flaw in our security systems? A powerplay warning? Is this the beginning of an internecine struggle for dominance in our newly acquired Independent status?

"What we do know," the reporter's somber voice took on an even more serious undertone, *"is that each and every incursion—each security breach was made undetected. Security protocols were still active and in place when personnel arrived. Nothing on sensors or video; no alarms. It's as if the culprits simply strolled in and back out again, ignored by all electronics."*

Boyd barked out a loud "*Ha.*"

"This has generated an uproar, not only at the affected facilities, but at all levels of the government. Law Enforcement is taking this very seriously and is determined to find the ones behind these events, learn the why and how, and make them accountable. To that end, I've been authorized to announce that, until further notice, all of Keosauqua Spaceport's outbound windows are closed.

Thane's cup made a hard landing on the tabletop.

"Port Control has issued an alert," Thor announced barely two seconds later. "Exit windows are closed until further notice."

"The comptroller's finger must have been hovering over the button, waiting for the announcement," Markowitz said sourly.

This was an unexpected and draconian turn of events. As the reporter continued to drone on, Thane asked if anybody was interested in hearing more.

He ordered the viewscreen off after getting noes and headshakes.

"What do we do now?" Shiloh asked, looking around uncertainly.

"Read. Play cards. Go shopping. Do pushups," Thane said, shrugging tiredly. He pushed up from the table, his head throbbing. "I'm going to bed. Don't wake me for anything less than an emergency."

Chapter 24

Jem lay content in the pitch-black darkness. Thane's arm, wrapped around her waist, snuggled her into his chest. There was no better way to wake up. She listened to his deep breathing for several minutes. He must have been worn out. He would have waited until—she frowned. No tell-tell throbbing at the base of her skull. The O-engine wasn't running.

Were they still on Toulouse? What had happened?

Gently, she started sliding out from under Thane's arm. She didn't get far before his arm tightened, drawing her back.

"Where going?" he asked, drowsily.

"At the moment, nowhere," she said chuckling. "Morning."

"Is it?"

"Since we're waking up, yeah."

"Thor, lights on dim," Thane said. He shifted her back far enough to see her. "Headache? Vertigo?"

Her heart gave a small tug at the sleepy gray eyes staring into hers. "No. No throbbing, either." He'd know what she meant. "I'm guessing there was a complication?"

"Just a slight one," Thane replied, proceeding to tell her about it.

Jem was stunned. "Shutting down a planet is *not* a slight complication."

"They're worried, wondering what's next," he said, yawning. "The shutdown is inconvenient and not just for us. I imagine the authorities are getting inundated with complaints and threats. It won't last long—it's mostly for show."

"Show?"

"Uh-huh. Well, threat more likely. 'You mess with us; we mess with you.'"

"They're copying us?"

Thane gave her a crooked smile. "Unintentionally, I'm sure. Think about it. If the general populace is inconvenienced and businessmen are faced with the potential loss of income or contract defaults, what will happen?"

Jem didn't have to think about it. General Kowalski had done it on Midgard when Richardson had kidnapped her. The one-day shutdown had caused a one-week disruption.

"They'd be stomping all over each other to find and turn in the one responsible." She paused. "Do you think we've been reported?" she asked in a worried voice

"No. Even if Rolfe or one of the others had, they'd still have to prove it was us. We left no fingerprints. No security footprints."

Us. In a woebegone voice, she said, "I've corrupted you. When we first met, you were a by-the-rules Tracker. Do you regret it?"

Thane's gaze drifted over her shoulder. After several moments he said, "Keeping things simply as black or white did just that: it kept things simple. No debating. No questioning. Living in the gray zone can be…difficult. There are times when decisions may be tempered more by human factors than legalities. Is that choice more right than wrong?"

Was he remembering what happened on Pappia? Something else?

His attention swung back. "Honestly, Jem, I am a bit uncomfortable with this. We've committed theft and, technically, breaking and entering. Except we've, technically, returned what we took."

"Borrowed," Jem corrected.

"Technically," Thane chuckled. "We didn't plan to hurt anyone or enrich ourselves in some manner. The goal is to protect our family and friends from a repeat of what's happened with Shiloh. The best way to keep Palmyra mercenaries away is to, uh, intimidate? Educate? For this, the end does justify the means and I can live with it."

"Let's hope others get the same message," Jem said firmly.

He kissed the top of her head. "While you and I may never have a, quote-unquote, 'normal' life, we can try to ensure that others have one as much as possible."

Yes, they would. No matter what it cost her. Them. She looked up. He was no longer sleepy. With a push of her elbow, she rolled them over. Now she was looking down. His smile lazy, his gaze hot.

Yep, perfect way to start a day.

*　*　*　*　*

They eventually wandered out to the main area, Thane's arm slung around Jem's shoulders. Shiloh was in his usual seat with the chair rotated around to access the table comp on the narrow counter. The clock told him it was late afternoon, Toulouse time.

They each got a drink from the cooler and joined Shiloh at the table. Wondering where the others were, Thane asked about Boyd and Markowitz.

"They're out and about," Shiloh said. "According to the major, they were going to 'canvas the area' while we were stuck here. I've been browsing the legal and financial info sites. Do you know, it's illegal for them to take a contract in the Palmyra System itself?"

Thane nodded. "It was that way even before they seceded. To do so would make them as legally liable as the criminal element. Any further word on the lockdown?"

"Officially, no." Shiloh grinned, "The newscast and community networks sure have plenty to say, though."

Thane was still chuckling when he asked Thor if there were any messages.

"Affirmative. Five for Thane Baron. Two for Jem Wilmont. One for Elijah Markowitz."

He'd let Markowitz know. Probably an update from the general. "Access—"

"Wait!" Shiloh interrupted. "Before you do that, there's something you need to see. I caught the live broadcast, then had Thor record it off of their news link. Thor, display file 'Stupid Editorial' on main viewscreen."

The viewscreen lit up with the banner, 'Something to Think About.' The banner vanished, replaced by a man sitting in an executive chair behind a large desk. The shifty eyes and fake smile had Thane taking an instant dislike to him.

"The past few days have been filled with extraordinary events, of which the shutdown of the spaceport is the most egregious of all. One of the ships grounded is the Lone Tracker, *the private ship of Thane Baron. Evidently, he and a small crew have been here for several days. One can't help but wonder why the Republic's premier Tracker is here. Afterall, his Republic-issued license isn't valid in our space."*

Okay, add condescending arrogance to the dislike list.

"If he is visiting our wonderful city of Keosauqua as a private citizen, why does his crew consist of a couple of enforcer types and the Ghost?"

Thane stiffened. Jem voiced her favorite cuss phrase.

"That's right, my fellow citizens, Miss Jem Wilmont is onboard the Lone Tracker. *A ship with an unusual crew that arrived just prior to the start of those extraordinary events I mentioned. Coincidence?"* He paused, flashed a mocking smile. *"Something to think about."* The viewscreen blanked.

Thane voiced a few cuss words of his own. "No one's come banging on the hatch?" he asked Shiloh with barely suppressed anger.

She shook her head.

"What the hell is he trying to stir up? Guess we'll get to test that need-proof policy you mentioned," Jem said, flushed cheeks showing her own anger. "Bet at least one of those messages is 'let's talk.'"

"Thor, access messages for Thane Baron. Type and sender of first message."

"Video message from Stacy LePalma Singer."

Local and not LE. Thane waved her back down when Shiloh started to rise. No sense using the table comp. She was involved in this mess, too.

"Play message on main viewscreen."

Thane judged the image of the smiling brunette to be late twenties.

"Mr. Baron, please allow me to introduce myself," she said in a throaty purr.

Thane gave an exasperated grunt. Not another one. Then she said, *"I'm Stacy Singer and I'm with the Toulouse National Herald."* Well, crap. Worse. A reporter.

"I'd like to feature you in an upcoming newscast. I'm interested in hearing how your life differs now as head of Baron Financials versus your previous as a Tracker. I'm sure it will be interesting. Please contact me. Whenever you're available, I'll be available." She closed out the video with a coquettish smile.

"She's stroking your ego," Jem said.

"Stroking something," Shiloh commented dryly.

One corner of his mouth kicked up. "You've been around my sister too long. Type and sender of second message," Thane said.

"Video message from Charles Durand Jones."

Who? "Display on viewscreen." He eyed the resulting image curiously.

"Mr. Baron, allow me to introduce myself," the man said in a brisk tone. *"My name is Charles Durand Jones, and I'm the CEO of Patton's Banking and Financial Services. I apologize for not realizing you were here sooner. You are undoubtedly in need of a local account to facilitate any transactions you may need to make whenever you are here. Our institution can meet any of your requirements. Perhaps we could discuss it over dinner this evening? Please contact me at your earliest convenience. I look forward to doing business with you."*

"Huh," Jem said, scratching her nose. "That allow-me-to-introduce-myself must be a local standard."

Thane's next message was much the same as the previous one, except from the Senior VP of Marketing at a different financial institution. The shifty commentator's broadcast had definitely stirred up interest.

The fourth one was the 'let's talk' from Law Enforcement. A Captain Booker made the very polite request for both him and Miss Wilmont to come to their office. Having a reputation wasn't all bad, Jem conceded.

The last one was again from Miss Stacy Singer. Same message, her tone sounding a bit miffed this time.

"My turn. Access messages for Jem Wilmont. Type and sender of first message."

"Audio message from Martin Myers Stohlass."

The bastard, Thane fumed as Jem's cheeks flashed hot again.

"Play it," she snapped out.

"Hello, Jem. Things have not gone like I expected, thanks to you. Somehow. But I'm not one to hold a grudge." A lie they could all hear. *"I have information to sell. Would you like to know what Reginald Kurzvall has planned for—sorry, no freebies. I'll be at the* Spook's Roost *tonight at 1900 if you do."* The laugh held a vicious edge. *"Appropriate, wouldn't you say? Leave your bodyguards at home or you'll get nothing. Although, I won't object to you bringing Shiloh. I'd love to see her again."*

"End of message," Thor said.

Thane stared, mesmerized. Jem's flush had spread as the message played out. Down her neck and then her arms. This, on top of the insinuating newscaster? She had gone way past pissed, maybe even past livid. He'd never seen her so—did anger even describe what he could feel coming off her in waves?

Jem stood up abruptly. "Excuse me."

Thane watched until she disappeared into the bathroom. The door slammed down sharply. He turned back to Shiloh, her eyes as big as saucers.

"Wow," she said.

"Double wow," he agreed. "I've never seen her so pissed."

"I've never seen *anyone* that pissed," she said. "Not even when Janice accidently deleted all of Dad's finance records. She can't go." Shiloh gestured. "It's a trap. He'll have hired locals to grab her."

"Can't. In-system contracts are forbidden, remember?" Thane said. "And after last night, who'd dare?"

She leaned forward. "Someone who doesn't care, and having a cash card waved under your nose isn't a contract."

Shit, she was right. "That's assuming Martin has the funds. The way Kurzvall dumped all of them here…still, it could be a ploy," Thane said, nodding. He could see it. He could also see the bastard needing funds if Kurzvall had cast him adrift and without whatever payment he was promised. Still, a ploy would require planning…a way off planet…

"Thor, how many ships have landed since the outbound windows were closed?"

Technically, the spaceport wasn't closed. Ships could still land, but they wouldn't be able to leave until the closure was relaxed. Palmyra Two's orbit was filling up with ships choosing to wait.

"Four," Thor provided, after a brief pause to access the port's records.

"How many of those four have Consortium registrations?"

"Two."

Not conclusive, but the possibility was there. His stomach growled.

When Jem finally returned, Thane had a steaming tray of her preferred breakfast waiting. He dug into his. Without a word, she picked up her fork and started eating. He studied her cautiously. Her color had returned to normal, but she still exuded…danger. Knowing how dangerous she could be was one thing he realized. Now he could feel it. His bones felt it. He didn't like it.

Their meal was eaten in silence. Thane dumped their empty trays in the recycler and started a pot of coffee before setting back down.

"It's most likely a trap," Jem said without preamble.

"Or he does need the funds," Thane said. "Odds are 50-50 for either one."

"Thor, access second message for Jem Wilmont. Type and sender?"

"Text message from Trystan Whitmore Rolfe."

"Read it."

"Miss Wilmont, I hope this morning's ill-advised editorial hasn't caused you problems. Also, there's a termination contract with your name on it circulating. No idiots, so far. End."

What the hell? At least it appeared Jem's message had been received, loud and clear. Thane did not like that unfocused look on her face as she stared toward the ceiling. It was a full minute before Jem broke the tense silence.

"Thor, record reply to Trystan Rolfe message."

Uh-oh. Thane eyed her warily.

"Text mode. Begin. Mr. Rolfe. Thank you for both your concern and your warning. Could you meet me at the *Strangler…*" her gaze flashed to the clock, "at 1430? I have a small favor to ask that will benefit us both. Thank you. End."

Two hours. "What are you planning?" Thane asked.

"Duplicity, same as Myers. You and I will meet with the SOB tonight."

"If his offer is genuine, he won't tell you anything," Thane warned.

"I don't give a damn," Jem said, the venom in her voice startling Thane.

"I'm not paying him a single credit. If anything, he owes us. If Rolfe's willing—bet he will be—he and his men will be there to cart his ass to the nearest UPMS center as soon as this shutdown ends."

"Express to Midgard?" Thane said, grinning. Shiloh wore an even bigger one.

"Bet your bottom credit. If you'll excuse me, again, I need to shower." She reached the corner of the hallway, turned. "After we drop the others off at Midgard, our next stop is Hebros. I'm going on the offensive," she announced, before continuing on.

Thane sat, stunned. She was going after Kurzvall on his home world? How far…how far would his sig-ner go? He found the same worried question in his cousin's eyes.

* * * * *

Their meeting with Rolfe went well. He was more than happy to assist Martin Myers off Toulouse. He was not happy to hear where their meeting was to take place.

"*That's a dangerous part of town*," Rolfe had told them. "*No one goes into the* Spook's Roost *by themselves, much less walk its streets alone at night.*"

The odds of Myers up to no good zipped to an almost certainty.

They went straight to the Law Enforcement Center after leaving the *Strangler*. Captain Booker's questions were polite, for the most part. They responded politely, for the most part, and without managing to lie. Mostly. It did get a bit testy toward the end.

…aware my license is invalid…here on personal business…friends accompanied me to help…can't help how things look…no, I can't say…

…working with my sig-ner…traveling with his cousin…she's part of that personal business…insinuations like that lend themselves to lawsuits…do you have proof…yes, we'll leave as soon as they're opened…

They headed straight for the *Lone Tracker* after leaving Captain Booker's irritated presence. Boyd and Markowitz should be back, waiting. They had plans to make.

* * * * *

The sun's glow was long gone when they walked into the *Spook's Roost* at 1858.

Jem looked around, curious. Definitely different from most of the bars she had worked in. It was well lit, tables had plenty of space around them, and no booths. The bartender worked behind a transparent shield and there were no bar stools. Understandable. Who would put their back to this room? The whole place was designed around access, egress, or fighting.

Martin sat at a table located in the center of the room. Alone. *Interesting*, she mused, sitting down on his left. Thane sat on his right, ready to react if he pulled a weapon. Shiloh took the seat across from him. She had insisted on coming, refusing to miss his comeuppance.

There was a *Lone Tracker* pool on whether or not she'd knee him if given half a chance.

Jem and Thane angled their chairs to better face the SOB. He gave Shiloh a way too-familiar smile. He got a cold stare back.

"So," Jem said, "where's your escort?"

Martin's smile faltered. "Escort?"

"We're told no one comes here alone." Jem smiled at his blank look. "Did you expect us to come here without checking out this place first? Especially with a top-notch research analyst available?" They had, after Rolfe warned them.

Shiloh flashed a smile that didn't warm the cold light in her eyes.

Martin looked briefly to his left. Jem glanced sideways at Thane, whose attention was over her shoulders. Yep, he'd seen it and was currently assessing the individual indicated. The resulting curl of his lip said 'no problem.'

"I didn't figure you'd come alone, anyway," Martin said, shrugging.

"Which means you never intended to sell me any information," Jem said. "So, what do you want?" *Let's get this farce over with.*

"Tell you what, I'll still provide the information." He gave her a bland smile. "For a price and a ride off this crazy planet."

A server came up to them. Everyone declined, except for Martin, who ordered a beer. He handed a cash card to the server, who registered his pre-payment on a mobile payer. A smart method if the tables and their occupants were constantly being trashed. Or worse.

Thane's gaze met hers. *Stalling*, he mouthed.

Chapter 25

"Hello, Tanner."

All four of the men lounging against a storefront opposite the *Spook's Roost* turned. One straightened and took a step forward. The other three watched silently. Alert.

"Rolfe," Tanner acknowledged. "Aren't you a bit far from your usual haunts?"

"I could say the same for you," Rolfe replied, both voice and stance relaxed. Adams, his second, stood silently beside him, arms crossed and not so relaxed.

"Yeah, well, you know how it goes. Sometimes there's this urge to experience something different."

Rolfe wasn't fooled by his attitude. The man was a snake and would strike at the first opportunity. "I heard there might be a bit of excitement tonight. Thought we'd watch, see how it played out."

Tanner's men adjusted their positions slightly, effectively fanning out behind their boss. Adams nonchalantly took a step sideways, dropping his arms. A door slammed shut somewhere behind them.

"Nothing to see here, Rolfe," Tanner snapped. "Unless you're looking for a bit of excitement yourself?"

Rolfe raised his hand. The rest of his team materialized behind him. Five to four. "How much excitement do *you* want, Tanner?" His eyes narrowed when Tanner grinned. Not good.

Tanner raised his voice and called out, "Anyone up for extra credits?"

Shadows began detaching themselves along the street and forming a semicircle around them. *Six, eight...ten*, Rolfe counted silently. Basic street weapons—except for the guy with a shepherd. That hook would be nasty, its edges honed to a razor-sharpness. Did the handle telescope? His men spread out, facing the new threats.

Rolfe stared impassively at Tanner, plotting the best attack scenario. Wondering how he had known that tidbit of street etiquette.

"'Palmyra's best mercenary' my ass," Tanner mocked. "I'm knocking you off that pedestal they've put you on."

"Not tonight you aren't," said an unexpected female voice.

Tanner's head whipped around.

Rolfe spared a quick glance as Barbara Whitehill stepped out of the alley opposite them. She wasn't alone. Nine others flowed into positions on either side of her.

The rattle and slam of doors echoed up and down the street.

"MedCenter or morgue, your choice," Barb said loudly. Tanner's impromptu helpers decided on a third choice: leaving.

She strode over to Rolfe.

"Good to see you, Barb, albeit unexpected."

"Can't let you have all the fun," she said, flashing a grin. "I happened to overhear about tonight's excitement, too."

Interesting. Rolfe stared down a stiff and seething Tanner. "Take whatever you received upfront and go. There won't be any more." He took a step forward, his voice dropping to a menacing growl. "I look forward to our next meeting."

Tanner and his men were gone. Barb made a hand motion and the ones with her melted away. A head nod later, so had his men. Rolfe knew none of them had gone far, watching from the shadows.

"Taking cash constitutes an under-the-table contract," Barb said. "We could turn him in."

"Not worth it and no proof."

"No proof?"

Rolfe grinned. "Martin Myers won't be here to verify our statement."

"Ah. Got it." She studied the *Roost's* door. "She couldn't have done what she did—not in one night. Her friends had to have helped."

He'd pondered that himself. "Thinking of asking one of them?"

She grinned. "Well, if that large hunk of maleness goes wandering again, I might."

With a shot of something conducive to questioning? He shook his head. "The man has extensive military training, probably an ex-commando." He'd recognized himself in the younger man. "Besides, Miss Wilmont might take that as a move against her."

Barb's lips pursed. "Shame."

"Since you're here, Miss Whitehill, would you care for a drink?" He gestured toward the bar.

"Dealing with morons does work up a bit of thirst."

Chapter 26

"You expect us to take you aboard the *Lone Tracker*? Seriously?" Thane said.

Martin curled his hand around his beer. "Kurzvall dumped me here. Emptied my account before he left. I can't afford a ticket."

"Too bad and not true," Jem snapped. That's how Kurzvall was funneling funds to him, since Palmyra banks had the same anonymous policies as their postboxes. "I don't know how much Shiloh's cash card held, but mine was substantial. Since I doubt you plan on returning them, you have plenty."

"It's all gone." His tone was a bit sulky.

All? Hiring ambushers became a certainty. Thane's set jaw told Jem he was thinking the same.

"Damn, Martin, you have some expensive tastes. Guess you'll need to get a job like Henning and his crew," Jem said tartly. "Cleaning toilets and working warehouses doesn't require a skill set." His face flushed. "Beneath you, huh?" she taunted. "How do you expect to live now? Go back to Midgard and climb in your family's pockets?"

"You know I can't return to Midgard," he snapped.

"Well, we're certainly not sailing into the Consortium." *At least, not for you,* Jem amended silently.

"Fine. Euphrates, then." Taking a sip of beer, Martin shot a worried look over his glass rim.

Turning her head, Jem spotted Trystan Rolfe coming in, accompanied by Barbara Whitehill. She waved as they settled at a nearby table. Jem's eyes did a quick *take a look* flick over Thane's shoulder. He did. His barely perceptible shrug then said *oh well*.

"Say, Thane. Why *don't* we take your cousin aboard the *Lone Tracker*?" Jem's smile was coy. Thane's answering smile was wolfish.

"Hell, no. Not till I've got your word—from both of you—that you'll take me where I want to go."

Jem glowered at him. "The man with no honor insists others hold to theirs?"

Martin smirked and started to reply, then cast a startled look to the side.

"Your escort appears to be leaving," Thane said, as a middle-aged man hurried past them. "Looks like that phone call he received wasn't good news."

Jem smiled. "Think Rolfe and Whitehill's presence has something to do with it?"

"I'll ask." Thane winked, got up and took a seat at their table.

"You're a degenerate-spash-of-a-disease-ridden-bastard," Shiloh spat out.

Jem's jaw dropped. Thane taught her that?

"You are a blight on the family, on the entire Universe," she continued, her glare locked on Martin. "If I had my way, I'd kick your ass into the nearest black hole so as to remove you from both. The only good adjective to describe you is *gone*."

Wow.

Thane strolled back to their table. Surveyed their faces. "What did I miss?"

"Later," Jem said. "What did you learn?"

"As we suspected, the red-faced bastard here had no intention of dealing with you straight. He had hired a merc team to waylay you when you left. I'm assuming you then intended to leave aboard one of the two Consortium ships that's landed," he said, giving Martin a dark look. "That's no longer happening, thanks to Rolfe and Whitehill."

Martin's jaw tightened and he downed a large swallow of beer. "I do have information about Kurzvall's plans," he said sourly. "We can negotiate."

"Uh-uh. It's probably all lies," Jem said contemptuously. "Kurzvall doesn't divulge his plans to underlings."

"Fine. Go. Enjoy your lives."

"We intend to. We've also arranged an escort for you out of this lovely area. Finish your beer," Thane said coldly. "It'll be your last one," Martin paled, "for a long time. You *are* going back to Midgard."

Martin's shoulders tightened. Bunched.

"Don't even think about it," Thane told him. "Assuming you make it out of here, there are trained mercenaries all around this building. None of whom who likes you."

He picked up his glass and drained its contents. Still standing, Thane easily dodged its violent sling in his direction. "Let's go." The words dripped with hate.

Rolfe and Whitehill followed them out. A few feet away from the door, Rolfe's men materialized. Two took hold of Martin's arms.

"Looks like the fun is over for the evening," Whitehill said. "See you at the Guild tomorrow?" she asked Rolfe.

He nodded. "We'll have that drink. I owe you one, Barb."

"You do, indeed." She waved. Several other men stepped out to join her and then they were gone.

Martin and his escorts left too. He would be taken to a safe place and kept there under guard until the exit windows reopened.

"A UPMS courier pod for two has been reserved under your name," Thane said, handing Rolfe a cash card he'd transferred money to. "This will cover your expenses and your man's passage back. If there's any left, consider it a bonus and a thank you. Have you heard any more about that contract on Jem?"

"Still circulating, despite the amount being offered." Rolfe's teeth flashed in the dim streetlight. "I do believe that's set a new record."

"Can it be traced back?" Thane asked. "Find out who issued it?"

"Rarely. In this case, not at all. The firm handling it keeps all its transactions anonymous, even internally."

"How can they ensure they'll be paid, then?" Jem asked.

Rolfe's smile flashed again. "Because the full amount must be deposited into the account they establish specifically for that contract before they'll even begin circulating it. Half given on acceptance. Contract completed, they pay out and close the account."

"Meaning the issuer is never in contact again and anonymity is maintained." Jem said. A perfect setup, darn it.

Nodding, Rolfe added, "Scuttlebutt says the lockdown will end sometime tonight. Rumor also says UPMS will have priority and to expect them to take most, if not all, of the first two exit windows. Is Myers really a Stohlass and your cousin?"

Thane made a sour face. "To my family's embarrassment, yes."

Rolfe gave a hearty laugh and melted away into the night.

"Come on, let's go." Jem took Thane's arm.

He offered the other elbow to Shiloh and gave her a lopsided grin. "I can't wait to hear what I missed."

* * * * *

Thane was in a good mood as they rode the lift up to the main deck, depositing them at the end of the short hallway between the med-room and a supply room. When they stepped into the main command area, Boyd and Markowitz started clapping.

Thane waved. "Yep, it's done. Martin should be on his way to Midgard some time tomorrow."

"That's good to hear," Markowitz said, "but we weren't clapping for you. Way to go, Shiloh," he said grinning.

Shiloh blushed. "Thank you." Her arm swept out in a short bow. "You have all been an inspiration."

Jem winked. "Especially Thane."

Thane propped his hands on his hips. "Okay, now I have got to hear whatever it is. Thor, replay audio recorded from Jem Wilmont's comm unit." They'd both been wearing one. His mouth hung open when it got to Shiloh's degenerate-spash comment and stayed open for her whole fiery speech.

"Shiloh Taft Stohlass," he sputtered. "Where did you hear that?"

Wearing an impish grin, she said, "From Andi, who got it from Nicholas, who got it from Stuart. Evidently you impressed the detectives on Milania with it last year."

"Don't you dare let your mother know that," he said, his ears turning warm as the others laughed. "By the way, you cost me and Jem a hundred credits. Each."

Shiloh's brow furrowed.

"That's right," Boyd said. "They bet you'd knee the bastard before he was taken away. Me and the major figured you were too reserved for that. However, after hearing *that*…" Boyd's head was shaking, but his eyes were laughing.

Shiloh's chin came up. "Like Jem, I believe in dealing with situations with whatever level of finesse is required. Right, Jem?"

"Uh-huh. Right now," she yawned, "I'm going to deal with exhaustion. You guys can collect your ten dollars from me tomorrow. 'Night all."

"Ditto," Shiloh said and headed for the med-room.

Boyd looked to Thane. "So. How soon can you request an exit from Port Control?"

Thane rubbed the back of his neck tiredly. "I'm going to wait until tomorrow afternoon. Let UPMS and any other priorities clear first. Not like we're in any big hurry."

"Are you really going to Hebros?" Markowitz asked, his voice flat.

Thane slid into his seat at the table. "I'm not happy about it. I don't know what Jem is planning, or even if she has a concrete idea. But, unfortunately, she's right. Something has to be done about Reginald Kurzvall. He'll keep coming after her otherwise and we're a bit short on legal options."

"You don't think what happened here will make him back off?" Boyd asked.

"No," Thane said bluntly. "He'll know how she did it."

"But he doesn't know it all."

"Thank the Universe for that," Thane muttered. He blew out a breath. "The man is not going to quit until he's made to. Which is Jem's whole point."

"Then I'm going with you," Boyd said stoutly, crossing his arms.

"I…we'll all need to go," Markowitz said, hesitating and looking down the hallway.

Thane's brow furrowed in puzzlement. "Why?"

"Jem being off-planet now doesn't violate her contract because she was forcibly *taken* off. If you land us on Midgard and then take off again…"

Thane sucked in a breath. "She's leaving voluntarily and that will violate it. He could say the circumstances warren—"

The major's head shook vigorously, stopping Thane in mid-word.

"General Kowalski is under a microscope when it comes to Jem Wilmont," Markowitz warned. "There are several high-ranking members in Military Command that are looking for any reason to terminate their contract. If he can't justify a breach *and* doesn't act on it, they would force it. They could also force General Kowalski's removal from Planetary Command for failure to perform his duty properly, probably citing conflict of interest."

Crap. Whoever replaced him would not be a friend.

"While I understand Jem's frustration, going there to throw down the gauntlet isn't the safest thing to do. And I don't like the idea of taking a civilian there, but…" he glanced down the hallway again, "it's going to have to be all of us going, or not at all."

Huh. Thane had a sneaking hunch the major and his cousin's flirting wasn't a light pass-the-time thing anymore. He held up a hand when Boyd's mouth opened. It closed.

"Whatever it is, it can wait till morning. Which I guess will be decision time. Let's all get some sleep." Hopefully, curling around Jem would unwind the knots in his muscles.

***

The conversation next morning deteriorated rapidly. Boyd and Markowitz refused adamantly to let Jem go without them. Shiloh refused to be 'dumped' on Toulouse to take the next transport going to Midgard.

"*Fine!*" Jem growled.

Thane put his hand on hers. "I know it's not what you wanted, but going home to Midgard works for the best. We can make plans there."

She gave him a level look. "I'm going to Hebros." His hand dropped away. "The resolution is for me to hitch a ride on one of the Consortium ships, or the next transport going Kurzvall's way."

"The hell you are," Thane said sharply.

"They won't even know I'm there. I'll check the scheduled departures," Jem said, starting to rise.

"*Park your ass!*" the major roared.

Jem's butt dropped, so did her jaw.

"You mind?" Markowitz asked Thane.

Thane's hand gesture toward Jem said "go for it."

"When did your switch get flipped to stupid?" Markowitz asked in a hard voice. "You've got three professionals telling you this is crazy. Risky. And you still want to launch an operation that has no guarantee of succeeding. The man is fixated on you. Ask Shiloh about that." He leaned his forearm on the table. "Yes, you have an amazing arsenal, but it comes with some serious limitations. Even the best laid plans can go fubar in a heartbeat, leaving you in enemy territory without backup and without resources."

"You once accused my family of grandstanding because we reacted without thinking," Thane said. "Is this any different? Doing the chest-pounding thing? You are re-*acting*, Jem, not thinking. And, for the record," his eyes flashed, "you are not going anywhere near the Consortium, much less Kurzvall, without me."

"Or me," Boyd said loudly from the pilot's chair.

Shiloh's hand shot up. "I'm in."

"General Kowalski would have my rank otherwise. Do you even *have* a plan?"

Jem scowled, first at Markowitz then Thane. "Kinda, sorta. Figured I'd pop in, show him there's no way he could hold me—" She winced at their loud chorus of "*NO!*"

"Fixated wouldn't begin to describe his reaction," Thane said grimly. "He'll drop everything else."

"He's already figured out an effective way to ensure your cooperation," Shiloh said. "Me, or someone else, kept somewhere you can't find."

Thane watched her flickering emotions as Jem slowly deflated. She gave her braid a couple of tugs. "You win," she finally said in a small voice. "We'll head home. But we have to come up with something, sooner or later. We *have* to."

Thane shot her a crooked smile, his expression slipping to sympathy.

"How about sooner?" Shiloh said, breaking the silence that had fallen.

They all stared at her.

"Modify it," she said, shooting Boyd a smirk.

"You have our attention," Thane said cautiously.

"Kurzvall had four partners in the succession conspiracy. Two were a security and legal firm, both on Tarragona in the Tricast System. Right?"

"Uh-huh. It was one of their lawyers that visited my cousin on Skewed," Thane said darkly. "And the security guy was the one that tried to hold us on Tylander. That means they're still working together."

"Perfect," she replied. "Jem. You could visit them instead of Kurzvall, which should be safer. Happen to mention Kurzvall's past engine problems…maybe hint about a few other things you could do. Like their clients finding their legal and-or security information posted publicly. Suggest the Consortium—them—and their various enterprises would benefit from Reginald Kurzvall modifying his behavior toward you. Even recommend they inquire about Palmyra Two's recent problems. Then give them a great big, tooth-filled smile." Which she demonstrated.

Jem blinked. "That's a wonderful, devious idea. Force Kurzvall's partners to restrain him."

"Shiloh, you are truly a credit to the Stohlass family," Thane said.

"It could also blow up in our faces," Markowitz cautioned.

Jem scrunched her nose at him. "Negative noggin'."

"Cautious commando. Do you know enough about them to evaluate how they'll respond? Anyone?"

"Short of blowing his ass up, it's the next best idea," Boyd said brusquely. "You got one?"

Markowitz gave it a moment's thought. "We blow up his ass."

There was a short silence before everyone burst out laughing. Thane wasn't sure if he was serious or not, but it definitely broke the tension. "So, everyone for going to Tarragona?" he asked. He got *yeps* and raised hands. "Thor, what is the transit time from current location to Tricast Three?"

The comp brain's reply was "Thirteen days, nine hours and three seconds."

Unhappy, but not unexpected news. Thane rubbed the back of his neck. They'd be traveling from Sector Six almost to the bottom of the galactic arm.

"Okay," Thane drawled. "Can everyone make nice for two weeks? The *Lone Tracker* is a bit crowded with this group."

"That'll give me time to win back my pride," Boyd said.

"Ditto," Markowitz said, crossing his arms. "Did you know your cousin is a card shark?"

Shiloh pointed to herself. "Analysist."

Jem laughed. "We need to analyze the pantry. Bored people have a tendency to munch." She waggled a finger between Boyd and the major. "You two already eat about twice what the rest of us do."

"I'll request a departure for this afternoon." Thane said. "Everyone take care of their errands by noon."

"I need to get a message off to General Kowalski about our upcoming detour. No, stay put," Markowitz said when Thane started to rise. "I'll use the table comp downstairs." He swung into the stairwell and dropped down it.

"I better let Granddad know, too. If things do go fubar, we might be needing his legal expertise. Plus, I'll alert him to his dear nephew's pending arrival."

"The way they were launching UPMS pods this morning," Boyd chuckled, "he's halfway there."

Silence. Jem cast several glances at Thane.

Shiloh cleared her throat. "Boyd, will you help me check the lower freezer compartment? See how much room we have?" she said, standing. He gave her a puzzled look for a moment, then mouthed an 'O.' They took the lift down.

Thane's lips quirked. "Privacy is already at a premium."

"The bedroom has a stout door," Jem said, slipping her hand in his. He squeezed it. "I'm sorry."

"For?"

"Being an unthinking, muleheaded idiot."

"Been that myself, more times than I care to mention," he said, giving a derisive snort. Teasing, he said, "I'll forgive you this time." Gradually his expression slid into a more serious one, thinking of what lay ahead.

The rest of the morning was spent prepping.

Thane coordinated port services while Jem and Shiloh left for shopping. They picked up fresh fruit and salad fixings, two dozen entertainment videos, several comfortable outfits, and a dozen TACEXMs at one of the specialty shops. They were on sale, six for the price of five. Jem defended their purchase as "just in case they ran into stubborn mules."

All of which depleted Thane's cash card.

Boyd and Markowitz were late, barely making it back before Thane was forced to request a later window. He'd already switched their original slot with the last one available in this exit window. They watched on the viewscreen as the two men raced across the tarmac, dodged around a waste hauler, and bolted up the *Tracker's* staircase. Both balanced several packages in their arms.

Hatches clanged. Boyd's head popped up in the stairwell and said they'd stay below, ducking back out of sight before Thane could bless him with a few choice words.

At precisely 1455, local time, the *Lone Tracker* thundered upward. For good or bad, they were headed for Tricast.

Chapter 27

The *Lone Tracker* settled gently onto V-38, its assigned parking spot. The ion engines shut down. The large viewscreen above the command console displayed the panoramic view of their immediate surroundings.

"Wow," Jem marveled from the co-pilot seat. "We landed in the middle of a mushroom field."

Globes spread around them, more could be seen through the evenly spaced safety intervals. Most were Class Twos, like the *Tracker*. Smaller Class Ones were dotted here and there.

"Tirana is Tarragona's capital," Shiloh said from the table.

"Another T?" Jem grumped. "Did the Survey cartographer have a fixation?"

"It's one of the largest cities in the Consortium," Shiloh continued, ignoring her. "I read that the spaceport alone covers 398 square kilometers. That's almost as large as Azusa."

"I've never seen this many Globes in one spot before," Thane marveled from the pilot's seat.

"Makes you wonder why the Consortium needs this many land-anywhere ships," Markowitz commented. He was studying the display intently.

Globes didn't need established spaceports, as their vertical aspects allowed them to operate from nearly any solid, mostly flat spot. Perfect for supplying newly established colonies and places with extremely rugged terrain. Or delivering military troops.

"I doubt they're all Consortium ships," Shiloh said, though her tone held a shade of doubt. "There's bound to be others, like ourselves, stopping in for one reason or another. And personally," she said on a sigh, "I can't wait to get out and about."

Jem sympathized with her. At least on Henning's ship they'd had a hotel-style suite to themselves. Despite all the card games, movies, exercising and/or sparring, the *Lone Tracker's* tight quarters had worn on all their good natures. Even Thane had gotten a bit testy. But in all fairness, he usually had the *Tracker* to himself. Boyd and Markowitz had been with him since leaving Midgard.

"I'm sure that goes for all of us," Thane said, confirming her assessment. "As soon as the heat radiates off, Jem and I are headed to the nearest bank to set up a transfer account. It'll take a day or more for the funds to arrive, but it doesn't cost anything to wander and browse."

"Not sure that'd be safe," Markowitz said. "Certain offices have probably already been notified of the *Tracker's* arrival."

"True," Thane said, frowning. "We can assume we'll be watched, although I doubt they will try anything overt."

"We're in their neck of the universe," Boyd said curtly. "All they have to do is send enforcers to hold any or all of us for any number of trumped-up reasons."

Thane rubbed the scar above his ear. "Right. Okay. As soon as we get funds, those of us with phones will get a kiosk number. No one leaves the ship by themselves, and at least one of you better be carrying one."

Jem planned on buying one. She and Shiloh had been phoneless since their kidnapping.

"I recommend sticking with the *Tracker's* comm units," the major said. "Phones can be blocked."

Thane pursed his lips. "Good point."

Jem nodded, dumping the phone-buying idea.

"Two incoming messages from Tirana Port Control," Thor announced.

"Identify messages."

"One audio message for Thane Baron from Gordon Larrs Stohlass of Midgard, Wotan Two. One text message for Elijah Markowitz from Sergi Harmon Kowalski, of Midgard, Wotan Two."

"I'll take mine downstairs," Markowitz said, striding toward the stairwell.

Jem frowned after him. "Think he and the general have something going on?"

Thane splayed his hands. "General Kowalski may be using our adventure as a means of information gathering. I would. No mention of rank kept it under the radar. Thor, play message for Thane Baron."

"*Have you all lost your frigging minds?*" Gordon's voice thundered out of Thor's speakers. "*Which one of you concocted this demented, hair-brained, ill-conceived, idiotic idea?*"

Shiloh's flaming face was doing a good impression of Betelgeuse, a red star.

Gordon's tone dropped to an irritated normal. "*That said, Seth and I are on standby. Send word if it comes to it. There should be a package waiting for you at the UPMS Tirana port office. Cash cards in a transfer box, including one provided by Kowalski for Markowitz. Figure you're all running low by now. Code is A43750HQ444, usual security. This is dangerous, Thane, Jem. Potentially catastrophic.*" There was a long pause, then in a low voice he said, "*And might be what's needed. Don't tell the general or your grandmother I said that. Be careful, all of you. Tell Shiloh her mom sends a hug.*"

"End of audio message," Thor said.

Boyd snorted. "That wasn't aimed at me and my ears still feel pinned."

"Yep, Granddad's special talent." Thane huffed out a breath. "At least we've got funds now. When Markowitz—here he comes."

Markowitz bounded up and out of the stairwell.

"Did you get your ears pinned, too?" Jem asked.

"No. He knows I couldn't have prevented you from going if you were dead set on it. And my orders are to stay with you. Mr. Stohlass fumed about us tackling Kurzvall's partners?"

"He wasn't happy about it," Jem admitted. He'd be absolutely appalled if he knew how it had changed.

"Uh-huh. By the way, Kowalski says I have a cash card coming?"

"We all do," Thane confirmed. "Care to go with me to get it? Great. Thor, how long until the tarmac heat drops within tolerable limits?"

"Approximately five point three minutes."

"I'll call for a shuttle. It'll take at least that long to get here," Thane said.

They studied the port schematic displayed on the viewscreen. The UPMS port office was way over on the other side of the spaceport, next to the cargo terminals.

Worry set in when Thane and the major hadn't returned after an hour. After another half hour, Jem and Boyd were ready to go looking for them when Thor announced a shuttle stopping in front of the ship. Relief hit Jem hard when the viewscreen showed Thane and Markowitz climbing out of it and up the staircase.

"Sorry," Thane said, when the two men joined them at the table. "It was a long line, even with two service-reps working non-stop." He set a square metal box in front of him, about the right size to hold two bars of soap. "Thor, convert Gordon Stohlass audio message to text. Display on table unit."

"Your grandfather took a risk," Jem said. "If someone had hacked into the message and gotten that code, the box would be empty. Or gone."

"Wouldn't have done them any good," Thane said with a smirk. "We have a code of our own." The comp terminal lit up, displaying the appropriate text.

"They're not in the proper sequence. Smart," Boyd said, nodding.

"Uh-huh. It was Grandmother's idea." Holding the box, Thane activated the access chip on the side. Referencing the text, he carefully entered HQ44405A437 in the small, recessed panel. *Click, click-click-click-click-click.* Thane popped the top open and took out a sheet of paper. Glanced at it then handed it to Jem.

It had four numbers next to each of their names. Jem rolled her eyes at the detailed instructions at the top: *match them.*

Thane pulled out a handful of cash cards. Holding one up to the light, he squinted at the tiny serial number on one side. "Last four are 7211."

"Boyd," Jem replied, checking the list.

Boyd looked surprised as Thane handed it to him. "Not expected. I'll reimburse your granddad."

"As far as I'm concerned, you're earning it. This one is 9005."

"Markowitz."

"3446."

"Shiloh."

"0014."

"Huh. Not on the list. An extra? Wait. That looks like a regular T-drive."

"Updates or personal messages, most likely," he said, putting it back in the box. Umm, 7210."

"You."

Thane handed the last one to Jem.

"Okay, we've got funds. What's the next step?" Boyd asked.

"I'll arrange to have the *Tracker* fully serviced tomorrow—make that as soon as possible. There's probably a long line for that, too. I want to be ready to take off on short notice. In the meantime, if anyone wants to go out, partner up with somebody and at least one of you wear a comm unit. No solitary excursions—that includes you, Jem," Thane said firmly.

Yeah, she'd planned a walk on the ghost-side this evening. She aimed a nose-scrunch in his direction. Oh, well. She had a meeting to arrange.

***

Two highly irritating days passed. The *Lone Tracker* was still waiting for servicing, and Jem was still waiting for call-backs several secretaries had promised. When Shiloh and the major made a trip out for food, several unidentified 'security' men had blocked their way.

Thane called for a strategy meeting.

"This is nothing more than a damn power play," Thane growled out, "and I'm fed up with it. Starting tomorrow, I'm pushing back. Ideas?" he said, looking around. He'd rigged a temporary seat so they would all fit into the kitchen area.

"I can sneak me and Shiloh out for food tonight," Jem said. "The surprise at spotting us coming back should give them heartburn."

Shiloh vigorously nodded an agreement.

"More like a migraine," Markowitz said. "Getting past their security will be a big red flag. It'll also tip them off that we're going to be a problem."

"Isn't that the whole point of coming here?" Jem said, eyebrow cocked rakishly.

He flashed a grin "Consider it a warning shot across their bow, then."

***

Trey Mosley shoved the door open to his executive office hard enough it bounced off the wall, nearly smacking the aide trotting in behind him. "Get DeVille on the phone." He slammed his briefcase down on the grandiose desk. "I want to know how those two women got off the *Lone Tracker* and past all our top-of-the-line and totally-worthless surveillance last night."

"I suppose I could answer that," Jem said, stepping out of the executive bathroom. Both Mosley and the aide froze.

Markowitz slid past her to the door, shutting it. He leaned against it with crossed arms, his attention locked on Mosley. Not saying a word, not making any gestures, yet exuding menace with a promise of intense pain.

Exactly why she'd brought him. Plus, that left Thane free to get help if things went wrong.

Jem stopped halfway across the room and motioned Mosley away from his desk. He was bound to have a alarm switch of some sort and she didn't want to be interrupted. He stopped next to his aide, gave Markowitz a single glance, then focused back on her.

They studied each other. According to Thane's information, the CEO of Burkhart-Devney Security Services was a tad over six feet, an expert marksman, a ruthless boss, and the grandson of Lillian Burkhart, one of the founding partners. She wondered if his granny would approve of what he had done with her legacy.

"Miss Jem Wilmont." Cold, razor-sharp eyes swept over her again. "I've read numerous reports about you. Seeing it in action is quite…impressive. Frustrating, actually."

"I get that a lot."

"No doubt. Isn't Thane Baron your usual sidekick?"

Jem jerked a thumb over her shoulder. "He was more appropriate for this outing."

"I see." Pause. "You were going to illuminate me?"

"Nope. Said that I *could*, not that I would."

Anger glittered in his eyes, quickly snuffed out by a frigid watchfulness.

Nor did she miss the slight shift in his balance. *Uh-huh. Getting grabby thoughts?*

"I've been trying—politely—to arrange a meeting with you and your conspiracy cohorts. None of you appear interested. I strongly recommend you get with Abrahams, Hier and etcetera, and ramp up that interest. Our little excursion last night," Jem's voice turned hard, "was both warning and demonstration. It directly relates to what I will be discussing."

Mosley's marble-statue expression told her nothing.

"A closed conference room at one of your offices will suffice. Attendees will be you and at least three of your legal sharks, but no more than six total. You can contact us on the *Lone Tracker*."

Jem backed toward Markowitz. "You have one day to make arrangements, then we're leaving and you'll be stuck with any consequences. If you try something stupid, you will not like the results."

The major's low chuckle briefly drew their attention. Mosley remained impassive, but his aide showed a hint of worry.

"You," Jem crooked her finger at Mosley, "are going to escort us safely out of the building. Anyone trying to detain us will count as stupid."

"Pass the word. No one approaches us," Mosley told his aide. He stepped forward. Scrutinized Markowitz for a second, then made a *shooing* gesture.

Markowitz stepped aside and they followed him out silently.

The elevator dropped them from the sixtieth floor in a near free fall that had Jem's inner ear protesting. The multiple gauntlets of hallways they passed through were silent. Mosley faced them once they were outside a fancy set of double-doors.

"I look forward to our upcoming meeting," he said curtly before re-entering the building.

Jem waved at the angry-faced guards watching through the glass, then she and Markowitz ambled down the sidewalk toward the subway station three blocks away. It was eerily quiet, with only a few pedestrians and a handful of cargo and service vehicles passing them. The city's public transport was largely underground. With most of the work in the surrounding office buildings done electronically, there'd be very little foot traffic during the day.

The major activated his comm unit and reported they were on their way back. He'd kept it off to prevent accidently transmitting in a building they assumed would have sensors 'sniffing' for unauthorized ones.

"That has to be the universe's fastest elevator. What do you think about Mosley?" she added.

"You've got him spooked. Pun intended." She laughed. "Mosley wants your secrets. He won't try anything until after, or maybe during, the meeting. And…" he blew out a breath, "that phasing is something else. I can't believe how easy…the potential…" he shook his head.

Like Shiloh, this had been his first exposure to ghost-mode. They'd arrived early that morning, riding the elevator upward with morning workers that got off on various floors. Then they'd walked past the aide primping at his desk and through the closed door into Mosley's office.

Markowitz shot her a sideways look. "You're scary, Jem. Do me a favor? If you ever do go rogue, don't do it on my watch. We won't stand a chance."

Jem stared straight ahead. At least he was being honest.

***

It took less than two hours for Mosley's terse message to arrive after Jem and Markowitz's return.

"My office building. 1000 tomorrow. Conference room 58B. Jem Wilmont only. No weapons."

By dinner time, the silence permeating the ship had become suffocating. *Screw this.* Jem tossed down the fork she'd been poking her food with. Thane gave her a moody look and Shiloh ignored her.

"Thor," Jem called out, "locate Boyd and Markowitz. Tell them to get their asses up here. Wait," she said, stopping whatever Thane was about to say with a furious look.

She dumped her food tray in the recycler, leaning back against it as the two men clambered out of the stairwell. She pointed at the table and said "Sit."

Arms crossed, fingers drumming, she scowled at the four wary expressions. "We all agreed to come here and do this. So, whatever's bothering you, spit it out. Thane, you first."

"We can't trust people who consider assassination as normal business. My gut says they're going to pull something. Stunners, maybe gas or drugged darts. It's obvious Kurzvall is still keeping your secret to himself, but he had to have told them how to keep you from sneaky-footing it away."

The others were nodding.

"Same worry," Boyd said, "especially since they specified only you and no weapons."

"We can't count on regular Law Enforcement," Markowitz said. "Mosley and his group will block them and feign innocence. That's assuming they don't already own them."

"Think we should go ahead and send for Gordon and Seth?" Shiloh asked tentatively.

Markowitz shook his head. "Any message we try to send won't make it past the UPMS office. In fact, we only got those initial messages because they were an automatic disbursal once Port Control entered us into their database. Now, we're being blocked. I should have received at least one additional update before now."

"The assholes *are* planning to screw us," Boyd growled.

"No way to prevent that unless we have the meeting here," Markowitz said.

"I don't want the SOBs on my ship," Thane stated firmly.

Boyd snorted. "They wouldn't come anyway. They'd expect us to employ the same underhanded tactics as them."

"What do we do?" Shiloh asked. They all looked toward Jem.

Jem gazed back calmly. Having taken their enemies' duplicitous nature in to account, they wouldn't be happy with her answer. "I understand and agree with your assessments. Not surprised by the UPMS block, either. Whatever they have planned, if things do go fubar—like drugged darts—they won't hold me for long. At the first opportunity, I will take whatever steps are needed to get away."

"What kind of steps?" Markowitz asked cautiously.

"Not the kind you're imagining," Jem replied. "More like shifting and running like hell. But, Thane, how far is Mosley's Security building from here?"

"No. Hell, no," Thane said, arm slashing in emphasis. "Teleporting is out."

"That will expose you," Markowitz said in a harsh voice. "Rip the lid off everything."

"You might as well make a video and post in on all the news networks," Thane snapped.

"So what? It doesn't matter."

The three men gaped at Shiloh. Jem raised an eyebrow.

"Once the meeting is over," Shiloh continued, "with or without mayhem, they will be contacting Kurzvall and demanding everything he knows. How long before it spreads outside their circle? It's already out there—remember? Vanderbilt and the Jaguide Enforcers. Hawthorne, Military Command, and the commandos," she said, gesturing toward Markowitz. "Not to mention, all of us who witnessed her teleporting to our island vacation home."

Shiloh gave the men an exasperated look. "Seriously? Sooner or later, under the influence of bribes, alcohol, drugs, or the age of ten, it's going to be spilled."

Jem gave Shiloh a thank-you nod. "Anything I do, per my contract or otherwise, also increases my exposure. We're learning to live with it..." her gaze locked with Thane's, "and its risks." She knew what lay behind the fear she saw deep within his eyes.

"Your mutation isn't natural, Jem. Your body was never meant to handle dimensional shifting. One day it will simply say 'I quit' or your brain will explode."

She'd only told Thane about Dr. Blackwood's warning. Teleporting put the greatest strain on her system; she'd use it as little as possible. Unfortunately, there would be times when it would be the best, or only, option. Jem reached over and took his hand. With a gentle squeeze and a soft smile, she said, "It'll be alright."

After a moment, Thane grudgingly nodded. "You and my analytical cousin are right. We'll do what we have to. I suppose that means winging it some days."

Markowitz snorted. "Military hates that."

The responding chuckles drained most of the strain from the room. Jem knew it wouldn't dissipate entirely until after tomorrow and they were off this frigging planet.

"At least you can keep the phasing aspect hidden," Boyd said. "Right?"

"Count on it." No way did she want that revealed.

Markowitz cleared his throat. "There may be another way to neutralize their plans, or at least have them stand down. According to General Kowalski's last message, Admiral Gleason was enroute to Anderson Station with a contingent of both navy and marine troops. Six ships worth," he added, his gaze sliding toward Jem then away.

"That's a frigging fleet," Jem exclaimed, remembering how she'd jested about it.

"The admiral was to update me upon his arrival, the base's status, and any orders. I'm going to assume he's there and primed for battle. Attacking Tarragona would be tantamount to declaring war, which none of us want. But if the situation deteriorates enough…" He shrugged, not looking at any of them.

"Mosley and cohorts are not going to want war either," Jem said. "We threaten them with a fleet that's practically on their doorstep and they'll back down. Ungracefully, most likely."

"Do you have the coordinates for Anderson Station?" Thane asked.

"Yes. It was in the general's message. We're supposed to go there after leaving here for a full debrief."

"You're just now telling us?" Thane asked a bit sharply.

"I was waiting for any additional information in the admiral's message. Which is how I know we're being blocked."

"Huh. The ship still hasn't been fully serviced, either. Only the waste has been, and that's because I told Port Services I was opening the external drain tube the next time someone flushed."

Laughter and a few crude comments ringed the table.

"We're not staying here a minute longer than necessary," Thane continued. "At this point, I also don't want them messing around the ship. The *Lone Tracker* has enough fuel to hop to the nearest non-Consortium system. We'll get serviced there then launch to Anderson."

Jem pushed away from the counter. "Everyone get a good night's rest. No telling what's going to happen tomorrow."

Chapter 28

Shiloh stepped off the last rung and faced Markowitz. He was on a bench, doing arm curls with weights from Thane's exercise locker. Perfect. Boyd was on the upper deck, talking with Jem and her cousin. Nobody but the two of them.

She paused, the up and down motion of his right arm almost mesmerizing. So was the huge bicep that kept popping up.

"Major, you didn't tell us everything earlier, did you?" Not from the way his eyes kept shifting around. So different from the way he normally looked at you straight on.

"What do you mean?" He switched the weight to his left arm. Kept his focus off in the distance somewhere.

Up, down, up, down...

"About why Admiral Gleason brought so much military might with him."

"It will take a lot of firepower to breach their defensives if he has to attack."

"Which he'll do if Jem is taken and, for whatever reason, cannot free herself?"

Up, down, up, down...

"Elijah?" Shiloh said softly. "Will they try to rescue her first?"

Up, down, up. The weight paused. "The admiral will wing it." He shifted it to the other arm.

Up, down, up, down...

She walked past him to get to the lift. It would deposit her on the main deck outside her room. Climbing back up the ladder meant passing by the others. She couldn't handle seeing them right now. Didn't want them to see her. She was not that good of an actress.

"Shiloh, you understand why?"

The quiet question stopped her. Turning, his gaze finally met hers. The depth of emotion she found there made her wish it hadn't. She swallowed, nodded. Jem had been very candid in one of their conversations, describing all the ways she could be used against the Republic, against her family and friends. Something she never wanted to happen.

And it couldn't, wouldn't, be allowed.

Chapter 29

"Well, where is she?" an irritated voice demanded.

"We need to get this over and done." The second voice was male, snarly, and contemptuous.

Jem cocked her head, listening to the comments floating out of the hallway. There were a couple more she couldn't quite hear. Then came a voice she recognized.

"She's coming," Mosley said impatiently. "Wilmont thinks she's got us by the nose. She'll arrive in some grandiose manner. For now, I want to go over our plans to—" His voice snapped off and he froze one step inside the doorway.

Plans? That did not sound good. Maybe she should have arrived sooner and eavesdropped on a few offices.

They'd debated on the best way for Jem to make her appearance. Politely show up at the front door and be escorted, or be waiting for them in the conference room? The unanimous vote had been for a mind-blowing, heartburn-inducing performance. The better to demonstrate their vulnerability, with the added benefit of knocking them off balance.

"Would this be considered grandiose?" Jem asked innocently. She'd positioned herself center-table, with her back to the wall and facing the door.

Mosley recovered and barked "Get Carlsson" at someone she couldn't see. Heard the pounding of boots, though. He stepped all the way in and took the seat across from her. Avarice flared as he took in the hand comp her hands were folded on top of.

Nope, that is not my super-secret thingamajig. But they were counting on them thinking that.

Four more wearing expressions of wary disbelief had filed in behind him. They also took seats opposite her, leaving the one immediately on Mosley's left side open.

"I assume we're waiting for this Carlsson?" Jem said.

"Your escort up from the lobby."

"Oops," Jem said.

They waited in silence. A couple of youngish faces did hit-and-run peeks around the doorframe. Her hand comp was getting a lot of interest. Finally, there came the sound of a heavy, purposeful stride.

Oh, my, God.

Jem's eyes widened as a behemoth wearing the Burkhart-Devney uniform stepped in, ducking under the door lintel to do so. He stood at least a foot taller than Nicholas O'Daniel and wider proportionally. He closed the door before taking the open seat next to Mosley. Despite the chairs being on the larger size—undoubtedly why this room was picked—the woman next to him scooted hers slightly to make more room. Or get more distance. He was head *and* shoulders taller than all of them. Even Mosley barely topped his armpit.

"My Senior Vice President," Mosley said with a snide smile. "Tragg Perilo Carlsson."

"Would that be of Marketing? Public Relations? Assassinations?" Jem asked politely.

Mosley's smile disappeared. Carlsson remained impassive, his attention never wavering.

"I'm Horatio Byron Abrahams and I resent being summoned here like some intern," said the man furthest from her.

Ah. The senior partner was the snarly one.

The nose-in-the-air woman next to Carlsson said, "Dolores Rivendal Gaspers and I concur."

"Naviere VanDyke Taylor, and I'm curious as to what you expect to achieve."

Taylor was between Abrahams and the man seated next to Mosley. When Jem looked at him, he simply said, "Hier." It was the guarded introduction one expected in a Port Circle. Here, it was highly rude.

According to their public news site, Gerald Kawamoto Hier was the other senior partner. He'd been the last to enter the room, yet the others had left Mosley's right-hand seat open. Unless her guts were wrong, he was someone she needed to be wary of.

Hier continued with, "Your obviously deserved reputation precedes you, Miss Wilmont. It will be interesting to hear how you got past all of Mosley's security, electronic or otherwise."

Covetous looks dropped to her hand comp.

"You all know who I am and, for the record, I have even less respect for you than you do for that intern you maligned." That certainly set them on their entitled ears. "What I expect to achieve, Mr. Taylor, is to put the Consortium—namely those that control it—in their place. Shall we begin?"

Eyebrows went up in an almost synchronized movement.

Jem pressed the button on her hand comp. Instead of recording, she had activated a very strong jammer. Boyd had handed it to her before she left the ship. He'd gotten it on Toulouse and why they'd been late getting back to the ship.

Carlsson's eyes suddenly sharpened. "Jammer," he said in a deep baritone.

"Yep," Jem said cheerfully. The receiver hidden under that hair would be generating a low hiss in his ear. No sign of a mic, though. "Cameras, phones, comms. You got it, I blocked it. Now, down to business."

There was a knock on the door. Jem huffed out a "really?"

Mosley got up, cracked it. There was a brief murmur. "Yes, we know. Move everyone into position." Closed it and returned to his seat. Gave a brief head nod to Hier.

Unease flickered in her stomach. They'd implemented something. Those plans? She folded her hands back on top of her comp. *A winging it we go.*

"Your two companies, along with three others, were part of a decades-long conspiracy to break your individual systems away from the Republic and form your own kingdoms."

"Our people voted to decide their own future," Dolores Gaspers said.

"That was very pompous of you, Miss Gaspers. Especially since it was the manipulation and deceit of your handpicked or bought lackeys that engineered that vote."

"You can't prove that," Horatio Abrahams said.

"Actually, I can." Great poker faces. "I've recently learned you are back at your old games in the Vangaria System next door. You're suborning people through bribery, blackmail, or extortion. Fortunately, assassination isn't as viable an option this time—it'd be too noticeable due to the smaller population spread. Unfortunately, you're replacing it with Palmyra mercenaries. They are being hired by contractors that are funded, discreetly, through an account kept stocked by Burkhart-Devney Security, Abrahams and etcetera, and Kurzvall Industries. Add a little sabotage, a little mayhem, a little manufactured civil unrest, and those mouthpieces will convince the people that the Consortium is the safest place to be."

From the tic in Miss Gaspers cheek, the information had been accurate.

The message from their anonymous ally had arrived on Toulouse in the nick of time with that interesting and worrisome information. In fact, if they hadn't been delayed by their two tardy passengers, it would have missed them. Its contents had changed the focus of their plans significantly and generated a heated argument with Major Markowitz. He had wanted to head directly to Anderson Station and the admiral with it. The rest of them had argued that while the scope was larger, Jem's plan could apply to it as well as the original one and stop the SOBs' meddling. He had grumpily acquiesced, after warning that the admiral would have a humdinger of a hissy-fit when he found out.

"In the spirit of moving things along, let's say you are right," Abrahams said. "Let's also say someone with your obvious skill and accessories," another glance at her comp, "would make an excellent addition to our portfolio."

"With an excellent compensation package, of course," Hier added.

"Sorry. I'm not for sale." Their blatant attitude worried her. They were too sure of themselves.

"We'll even make room for your friends. The ones that currently have three mobile rocket launchers around them."

Eyes on Hier, Jem turned the jammer off and her comm unit on. "Thane, status?"

"Got three tanks pointing missiles at us," Thane replied harshly.

"Not tanks," came Markowitz's calm voice. *"They're heavy-duty armored vehicles, AV-74s carrying a 6-cannon ALM system to be exact. They came in on a military transport that landed late last night."*

"How do you know that?" Jem asked, watching Hier watch her.

"I had Thor link into the spaceport's database and satellite feed after you left," Thane answered. *"They didn't off-load until shortly after you went silent, so I couldn't warn you."*

That explained Mosley's comment.

"That's why we've been stonewalled," Markowitz said, in that same calm voice. *"They were waiting for them. Us forcing a meeting wasn't necessary; they would have contacted us, probably today. If their military is aligned with them and their expansion agenda, as it appears, we have a problem."*

A chill snaked down Jem's spine. We, meaning the Republic. It also put new light on their hiring of mercenaries.

"Do whatever you have to, Jem. We need to get this information to Admiral Gleason." The grim undertone in Markowitz's voice told her all she needed to know. FUBAR.

Jem was aware Mosley had been taking advantage of the moment, texting on his phone. The door opened to admit another man. A general, from the rank insignia. He took a seat at the end of the table.

"Standby," she told the *Lone Tracker*. She re-activated jamming. This would require extra-careful winging.

"Allow me to introduce General Michael Li Nesbitt," Hier said.

She flipped a cool look from Nesbitt to Mosley and back to Hier. Interesting. Her guts had been right. Hier was the main power broker of the Tricast group, not Mosley as they'd surmised. From the sudden furrowing of his forehead, he'd realized he had shown his hand.

Like to operate from the background, don't you?

"Miss Wilmont, I've been looking forward to meeting you," General Nesbitt said. "The reports on you make for very interesting reading. Especially the one by Major Elijah Markowitz."

"That report does seem to be getting around," Jem replied coolly.

"So does he. We've identified Major Markowitz as the one who accompanied you when you, ah, visited Mr. Mosley's office yesterday."

"The major is not here in an official capacity. He's here as a friend, assisting in a kidnapping resolution that involved myself and one other."

"Then I'm sure you don't want anything to happen to him or any of your friends."

Jem sat silent, contemplating each opposing face. Arrogance, satisfaction, and shark smiles on most of them. Carlsson's remained blank and Mosley wore wary caution. The man had good instincts.

"Don't know what to make of me, do you?" she said to Mosley. Carlsson's left eye twitched minutely. Addressing Hier, she coldly said, "This misguided attempt at extortion does demonstrate the reasons I'm here. First, the attacks on my family and friends are to stop by any and all of you. Especially Reginald Kurzvall. Otherwise, I will target you and *your* families. That military hardware around the *Tracker* had better roll back to the barn before something happens that all of you will seriously regret."

"I can't believe this," Gaspers burst out. "You are threatening *us*?"

"Nope. I'm making a promise. It also applies to the second reason I'm here."

"And what is that?" General Nesbitt said, disdainfully.

"To tell you to cease and desist all your shenanigans," Jem said. "Cajoling other systems to join you is par for the course, politically and economically. And militarily," she added, glancing down the table. "However, you are to leave out all the underhanded, illegal, immoral and just plain dirty tactics. You are to withdraw your hands from throats and fingers from the various pies you've got them stuck in. And you'll start immediately."

The general burst out laughing. Several others joined him.

"My dear child," gray-haired Hier said patronizingly. "What makes you think you are in any position to tell us what to do?"

Jem leaned forward on her arms and channeled one of Thane's most-fiercest expressions. She must have got it right, because Dolores Gaspers drew back.

"I will destroy the Consortium," she told Hier, ratcheting her voice even colder. Addressing the whole table, she continued, "I will slip into your installations, factories, mines, buildings, homes. You won't know where I am, only where I've been by the destruction I leave behind. Undetected. Unstoppable. Like an avenging angel…or ghost. If you have any doubts, you might want to have a conversation with your contacts on Palmyra Two."

Silent, frozen statues stared at her.

"I will expose every deep, dark secret. Briberies, extortions, testimony from those who were hired to assassinate their friends and family. I will show the people how they've been lied to and deceived—manipulated individually and collectively. You and your corrupted institutions will burn in the resulting implosion."

Shock. Disbelief. Fury.

"I fail to see how you expect to follow through on that," Nesbitt said with a scorching look. "You will be taken from here to a secure facility, where a tracking chip will be surgically implanted and then briefed on your new duties and *loyalties*. Your friends will be sequestered at a different facility, except for the major. He will be taken into military custody and tried on charges of espionage.

"Thane Baron and his friends' status will depend on you. Afterall, espionage charges can be brought at any time," he said, a nasty smile flashing across his features. "I look forward to working with you and learning more about your methods."

"I don't and I'm not going anywhere with you." Unfortunately, it appeared they were about to get a firsthand sample of her method.

The general's smile slipped.

Mosley angled forward. "I have men positioned outside this room. You won't get past us. Your friends are locked down. What makes you think you have a choice?"

She had one final shot at maintaining leverage. "You're all aware of Anderson Station? Reginald Kurzvall's old shipyard?"

"Of course," Nesbitt said. "It was appropriated from Kurzvall and turned into a Republic Naval base. I intend to demand it back."

Good luck with that, especially now.

"Well, Kurzvall did tell the admiral to do what he wanted to with the debris Beckett left behind—which included all the bodies, by the way. Admiral Gleason is currently in residence on Anderson. He's expecting to hear from us. Which we've been unable to do since you've been obstructing our messages, along with everything else since the *Lone Tracker* landed. I'm not sure how long he'll wait before he comes looking for us…along with the six frigates he brought with him. Tell me, does those long-term plans of yours include war? Are you prepped for it? I certainly hope so, because it's on your doorstep." Would the threat work?

There were multiple pale expressions.

Hier whipped around to the general. "We're not prepared for that large a scale yet."

Yet reverberated in Jem's mind. "So, you idiots planned on nipping at the edges, counting on a general aversion to war to hold off any major Republic response?"

"Which is why Admiral Gleason's response will be limited," Nesbitt said haughtily. "Extremely aggressive tactics on his part will be detrimental to his career and very unpopular with the civilian population. He can bluster and threaten all he wants."

Bluster and threaten? Jem snickered. She couldn't help it. They certainly didn't know the admiral.

"I wouldn't count on that," Mosley said slowly, staring at Jem. "Would you want someone with Miss Wilmont's skill and resources used against you?"

Jem tipped her head in a "points to you" gesture.

"We sure as hell don't want them used against us," Hier said sharply. "We'll deal with Gleason *if* he comes and *if* he has a fleet. We only have her word for both. General, Mosley, please proceed."

It'd been worth a try. Jem switched off the jamming. "Thane—"

Carlsson lunged.

Jem *poofed*.

Curses and pandemonium erupted.

Armed men barreled in as someone screamed "*shut the fucking door.*"

Jem dropped faster than she'd ever tried before. She phased through floors, desks, cabinets, toilets—*yuk*—a vault, and a couple of people—*double yuk!* She slowed her descent as she neared her target…and phased right through it before she could stop. Dammit. Now she was in a subfloor. Stairs. Stairs. *There*. Jem ran up them, found herself in the lobby, now in an uproar and Carlsson standing in front of the entrance.

Damn express elevator.

Hands on hips, narrowed gaze raking the room, the human boulder blocked the double doors. She maneuvered around a couple of lost-looking security types and paused in front of Carlsson. An impish urge for a now-you-see-me-now-you-don't prank nearly got the best of her. But his lunge upstairs had showed how fast the man-mountain could move.

Jem slid around him and outside. Finding the sidewalk once again empty, she thought, *"Why not?"* and dropped the shift. Tapping on the glass, Carlsson got her biggest grin when he whipped around. *Now you see me, now—*

A woman and two children came around the corner.

Jem bolted.

She was barely two running steps into the service way abutting Mosley's building when a hand grabbed her braid. Yanked back against a hard chest, a hand wrapped around her throat. Carlsson squeezed. Desperate, unable to breathe, Jem grabbed his wrist and shifted.

Carlsson staggered, his hand dropping away from her hair. *Yeah, first time is a bitch.* Jem pushed his hand away from her throat. Turned. He stared in disbelief. At her. Holding his wrist. *Welcome to nothing-land. No weight, no mass, nothing—*

Carlsson yanked his wrist free as he stepped backward and materialized— in a wall. At least, part of him did.

Jem's eyes flew wide with horror before jerking around. Bent over double. She could feel herself gagging, but there was nothing. *Nothing-land*, her hindbrain reminded her. Regardless, she rubbed non-existing puke off her chin and straightened. Head averted, Jem staggered out of the alley as several Burkhart-Devney employees and a military type ran in. She flinched at the sound of choked off yells and retching. The military guy was hoarsely updating someone by comm.

Thankfully, the civilians were nowhere to be seen, probably spooked by Carlsson barreling down the sidewalk. The kids did not need to see what was behind her. *No one did.*

She needed to get to the ship. It was twenty-nine-point-four kilometers away, according to Thor. A lot less than the previous distances that had put her in the hospital. Still... Jem swallowed, steeled herself, and pictured the *Lone Tracker's* main deck. Pictured the command console with the viewscreen above it and...reached. Black. Pain. Searing agony blazed down her spine and into her limbs. Wrenching pain wove through her skull, trying to rip it open.

The blackness cleared abruptly. Thane and Markowitz were watching the viewscreen, Boyd standing between their chairs. Shiloh watched from the table.

Jem dropped the shift. Dropped the comp. Dropped to her knees. Seconds later, alerted by Shiloh's yell, Thane's arms were going around her.

He pulled her to her feet, then spit out a curse. "Your throat." He started to pull her toward the med-room.

"No. No time. Need meds," Jem managed to croak out. Barely able to stand, Thane helped her to the pilot's chair then bolted. She blinked twice, forcing her eyes to focus. "Major. The AVs. How damage without killing..." His head was shaking.

"Anything you try on one, risks the others launching their missiles." His expression turned calculating. He straightened. "Boyd, I need three TACEXMs. Thor, display external image of an AV-74, side view."

Jem stared at it, dimly aware of Thane returning. He pulled down the neck of her tunic and administered a shot in the curve of her shoulder, the area Dr. Blackwood said was the most effective spot. Half of her brain listened to Markowitz, the other half reveled in the spreading relief.

He pointed to the missile rack. "The small space under here is where the TACEXMs need to detonate. That will detonate the missiles' ordnance and take out the AVs."

Thane frowned. "The others will fire as soon as the first one goes up. That spot is almost two meters high. No way that can be climbed without being seen."

Jem shook her head slowly. "I don't think...I can manage it."

"You don't have to," Markowitz said, his expression locked solidly in military mode. "You get me there and I'll do the rest." He laid out his plan.

It was a good one, especially on short notice. *Hell, no notice.*

Thane squatted down beside her, worry wrinkling his forehead. "Jem, are you up to it?"

"I have to be," she replied. The pain had lessened to a bearable level. Which was good, since intense pain could inhibit a shift. Still, the pounding in her head made it hard to concentrate.

"How many crew?" she asked the major. Three was Markowitz's reply. Nine. Nine more souls staining hers.

They congregated in the plazo, the tension thick. It had been almost thirty minutes since pandemonium broke loose at Burkhart-Devney. How much longer before the bastards made the irrevocable decision that risked war?

Markowitz cradled the explosives against him, their timers set to 62, 32, and 4 seconds, respectively. Jem's arm was wrapped firmly around his bicep. At Markowitz's signal, Thane and Boyd twisted the TACEXM caps, arming them. They stepped back and Jem shifted them into the stasis safety of ghost-mode. Markowitz took off, dragging her through the ship's hull.

Just along for the ride was Jem's whimsical thought.

They ran toward the first AV, their feet pounding away on an invisible 'floor.' The major had Jem keep them at the same level as the *Tracker's* lower deck. No climbing needed now as they were at the right height. Reaching the AV, Markowitz carefully placed the longest timed explosive in place.

Without waiting to watch it rematerialize, Markowitz almost yanked Jem off her feet as he raced to the next target. Left the next bomb. He was placing the last one when the other two bombs went off, almost simultaneously. Markowitz jerked them away.

The last AV exploded around them. Jem kept her eyes closed, not wanting to see what he was dragging them through. She opened them when he tugged on her arm. The plazo. They shifted back. Markowitz steadied her when Jem staggered.

"Meds," she told him, the word a bare whisper. The throbbing in her throat almost matched the one in her head.

They rode the lift up, the sound of General Nesbitt screaming from the viewscreen making them bypass the med-room. The general immediately went silent when he spotted them. His gaze tracked them as Thane quickly stood so Markowitz could lower her into the pilot's seat.

She gestured toward the screen.

"He's complaining about his AVs," Thane said in a hard voice. "I told him he'd have to take it up with Admiral Gleason."

Nesbitt kept staring at Jem. She met his hot glare with a cold one. He was thinking something up. Figuring it was best to head it off, she motioned for Thane to lean down. Whispered into his ear.

After giving her a slightly puzzled look, Thane turned to the screen. "As you can see," he pointed to Jem's throat, "she's having difficulty talking. She has asked me to pass a message to you. Quote. 'Any more stupid shit and there'll be more Carlssons.' End quote. And end of conversation. Terminate call."

Thor blanked the viewscreen.

*　*　*　*　*

Thane and Markowitz both grabbed for Jem as she slumped sideways.

"Med-room," Thane snapped. "Syringes are set out. Use one with a red cap. They're the strongest and include a sedative."

"Got it." Markowitz scooped her up, Shiloh hot on his heels down the hallway.

Thane watched them go before turning back to the viewscreen. "Thor, connect to Port Control," he ordered.

After more than a minute passed, it appeared that they were going refuse it. Or forced to by General Nesbitt. He ordered the ion engines brought on standby. Launching without authority would be the least of their problems, and he wasn't waiting around for them to bring in more firepower. Suddenly, a worried looking middle-aged woman's image popped up.

"Ma'am, Thane Baron on the *Lone Tracker*," he said needlessly. "Are there any V-inbound transports?"

"Uh...no, sir," she said. "Nothing. Everything has been...temporarily suspended."

No surprise. "Then the *Lone Tracker* will be launching within the next ten minutes. I'm sure you won't mind us leaving." He gave her a polite smile.

She gave him a weak one. "Not at all. *Lone Tracker* is cleared for immediate launch." The screen blanked.

"Thor, calculate closest transit point to Vangaria One, minimum safety factor." The less fuel used, the better. He glanced over as Markowitz came striding back. "Jem?"

"Out. Strapped in. Shiloh is locking down the med-cabinet."

Didn't want to lose that. Especially Jem's meds. "Everyone needs to strap in. General Nesbitt might actually try something stupid."

Markowitz plopped down at the table. The deck vibrated faintly beneath their feet.

"Any idea about what that Carlsson warning was about?" Boyd asked from the co-pilot's seat.

"Nope," Thane said. But he had an unpleasant hunch.

"Engines reaching standby," Thor announced.

Shiloh came hurrying in and joined Markowitz at the table. Thane waited till she was ready, then gave Thor the order to launch. The deck's vibration intensified as the engines' roar increased and the *Lone Tracker* rose gracefully out of the smoking debris around them.

They had survived Tarragona. Now, Thane mused as they passed through the stratosphere, they just needed to survive Admiral Gleason, General Kowalski, GG, and his mom.

Chapter 30

Conscious returned slowly. *Still alive*. Groggy, sluggish, she started a self-assessment. Head—achy but manageable. No O-throb at its base—which was either good or bad, depending on how long she'd been out. Throat? Jem swallowed. *Oowwww*. Hope there's still soup in the carousel. Her body felt heavy, an overall lethargy she didn't like. Teleport hangover?

Her eyes opened as her brain slowly de-fuzzed. Yay, the *Lone Tracker's* med-room. She sat up slowly, sliding her legs over the edge. She was still waiting for her head to quit protesting the change in altitude when Shiloh came breezing in.

"Oh, good. You're awake. How do you feel?"

Jem tried to answer, but ended up giving her a thumbs-up followed by a so-so hand waggle.

Shiloh smiled. "I'm going to assume that means everything is good except your throat. Thane plans to have you checked out at a MedCenter after we land on Vangaria One, which is about another fifteen minutes. I was going to strap you down in case we hit turbulence or crash."

Jem's eyes widened.

"Fuel tanks are almost empty. Are you up to sitting with us?"

Jem nodded and slid off the bed. Shiloh took her arm when her legs proved to be a bit wobbly. As soon as they were in the hallway, Jem pointed to the bathroom.

"Want me to wait—I'll meet you at the table then."

Jem didn't bother looking into the mirror until after she'd relieved herself.

Oh, my. No wonder it hurt so bad. Carlsson's hand had encompassed her whole throat. Her neck was a dark blueish-purple from one ear to the other and, from the looks of it, probably on around. She did see a few pinkish slivers on one side that had probably been between his fingers.

Jem returned Thane's hug on reaching the command deck. Her throat got winces and angry looks from Boyd and Markowitz. Thane set her in front of the table comp and told her to type anything she wanted to tell them.

The landing went smoothly and hilariously. Relaxed, arms crossed loosely and his feet stretched under the command console, the major kept a constant stream of 'advice' from the co-pilot seat on how to land a ship on fumes. The fact that Thor was handling their descent seemed irrelevant to him. As did Thane's dagger-glares and snarky comments. Jem would have snickered along with Shiloh if it hadn't involved throat muscles.

Venice, Vangaria One's capital, sat high and dry on a wide plain. Nothing like its namesake on Earth, Jem observed.

Since Thane wanted to expedite everything with the port services, Jem hopped on a surface transport with Boyd to a MedCenter four blocks north of the spaceport. The receptionist took one look at Jem, asked if she had her medical records, and then ushered them back into one of the exam rooms. A few minutes later, a nurse and a portly, grandfatherly type that reminded her of Dr. Blackwood entered. The nurse took a seat at a short counter and plugged Jem's T-drive into the table comp.

"Miss Jem Seaborne Wilmont of Midgard, Wotan Two. No allergies listed," the nurse said, scanning the main bio section of her medical file. Her lips pursed. "Indicates high tolerance of and sometimes unusual reaction to medications."

"Genetics," Jem managed to whisper after the doctor's *uh-huh* look.

"And a lab explosion that adversely affected her system," Boyd added.

Well, that was true.

"I don't see it listed," the nurse said, scanning Jem's file.

Jem gave Boyd a look that said, "You brought it up."

"They kept it quiet and took care of Jem themselves."

"Private lab? Figures," the doctor said, shaking his head. "But they should have at least made some annotations in her file. I'm Doctor O'Neill. Any other injuries besides the very obvious throat?"

The doctor's hands were gentle, but Jem still winced at several points in his examination. The nurse typed as he dictated his findings.

…severe bruising…suspected tracheal…

Finally, he scooted his roller-seat back. "The larynx itself doesn't appear damaged, thank goodness. Any coughing or trouble breathing?"

"Just pain and trouble talking," Boyd said, Jem nodding in agreement.

"Not surprising, from the amount of damage to the soft tissue. You probably have a tracheal deviation, Miss Wilmont. A slight one, since there's no noticeable symptoms. We'll do an imaging to verify."

"What's that?" Boyd asked for both of them.

"It's where the trachea has been pushed sideways. In this case, caused by the pressure from the Cyclops's hand. I'll have—"

"Cyclops?" Boyd said, his confusion mirroring Jem's. "Isn't that a one-eyed monster from old Earth tales?"

Doctor and nurse both chuckled.

"Tourek is a planet-sized moon around Tricast Five, a gas giant. It's lightly populated," O'Neill told them. "Mostly farmers and ranchers as there's no minerals worth mining. They also grow tall kids. Average is about seven-foot, with a good chunk of them between eight and nine feet. From the size of the handprint, your attacker was at least an eight-footer."

Boyd's startled eyes met hers. Jem nodded. *Yep, sounded right.*

"No record of who started it, but the Cyclops tag has stuck," the doctor continued. "They haven't found whether the cause is something on the planet or emanating off the gas giant. Research teams have been investigating the phenomena for years—or they were," he said gruffly. "They left when the Consortium split off a couple of years ago and, from what I've heard, it hasn't ginned up any of their interest."

"I hear the Consortium systems are still getting themselves sorted out," the nurse said.

"Most likely," the doctor agreed, frowning. "Cyclops don't usually travel outside the Tricast System. Did the Enforcers get the one that attacked you?"

"He's been dealt with," Boyd said without inflection.

The doctor gave him a sharp look but wisely decided not to press further. "Anyway, I'll have a technician come get you for the scan. Your father can wait for you here." He and the nurse left.

The corner of Jem's mouth turned up at the weird expression on Boyd's face. Given their age differences and his hovering, that would have been a logical assumption.

***

The imaging did confirm a mild tracheal deviation, which Dr. O'Neill said should recover on its own. The doctor recommended rest, a soft-food diet for the next week, gentle neck stretches, and the liberal application of the numbing lotion he handed her. He also cautioned her to seek immediate medical care if breathing did become difficult or uncomfortable.

The nurse entered the test results and Dr. O'Neill's recommendations into Jem's file before exchanging Jem's T-drive for her cash card. She blinked on seeing its balance. After deducting the charges due, she handed it back and then left them in the lobby with "take care."

Jem felt a whole lot better on returning to the *Lone Tracker*. Her headache was gone and the lotion worked as promised: she'd applied it in the MedCenter's restroom. Which was good. Doctor Blackwood's medications needed to be saved for extreme needs. Like teleporting.

They found the area around the ship bustling. The Venice Waste Retrieval truck was pulling away and a water service employee was snaking its tanker hose up to the connection on the *Tracker's* side. Weaving around them, they got onboard and climbed to the upper deck. Thane was conversing with a perky youngish female on the viewscreen. No sign of Markowitz or Shiloh. They settled at the table and Thane joined them after a minute.

"Fuel bowser will be here as soon as the others clear out," he said. "Food delivery is on hold until they leave. I had to promise everyone double pay to get things expedited. I want us headed to Anderson Station as quickly as possible."

Jem reached into her pocket and held up her cash card.

With a weary sigh, he nodded. "Yeah, we might need it."

Jem understood his drive. They needed to get their information to Admiral Gleason. She listened as Boyd related Dr. O'Neill's information. Thane was as flabbergasted as they'd been on hearing about the Cyclops.

"Well, they've certainly managed to keep that information quiet. Think they're hoarding them for security and military purposes?"

"Would give them an advantage. It'd also be kind of hard to attract new settlers if they thought their kids would get mutated."

Thane grunted his agreement and wondered aloud if the major had heard of them.

"Where'd he get off to, anyway?" Boyd asked.

"No idea; he just up and vanished. Shiloh is shopping for fresh stuff for the cooler."

Jem held up a hand. "Soups." Her voice was raspy, but the numbness let her talk.

Thane swiveled his seat around to the table comp. He linked into the spaceport's network, selected Food Service and scrolled to the listings. Jem stood at his shoulder, Thane annotating three for each item she pointed to. She also selected a few simple pasta dishes that she could graduate up to.

Thane hit "Update Order" and then rotated back around. "Can you talk well enough to tell us what happened?"

Haltingly, between sips of water, she told them. Her glass began shaking as she got to the scene in the alley. She wouldn't—couldn't—provide the final grisly details, but she did manage to tell them what happened before bolting to the bathroom. She huddled on the floor afterwards, the tears she couldn't shed then now streaming down her cheeks.

Thane stepped in and squatted beside her.

"Carlsson attacked you," he said in a quiet, even tone. "You shifted to keep your throat from being crushed. Basic survival, Jem. What happened next was bad luck on his part. Horrible, yes, but don't you dare blame yourself for it."

"I shouldn't have stopped. It was stupid," she whispered miserably. A childish impulse that had cost them both. "I should have shifted there, on the sidewalk, not run. Didn't matter at that point."

"Reflex. Habit," Thane replied. "You're used to hiding it." He tugged on her braid. "Come on. Wash up. There's a thin stew in the carrousel. I'll heat it up, even mash the vegetables for you."

It was several minutes before Jem climbed to her feet and scrubbed her face. Taking a deep breath, she finally looked into the mirror. Haunted, shadow-filled eyes stared back. *Actions have consequences. Remember that,* she told the image.

Her stomach rumbled at the smell drifting in from the hallway. She went to feed it and to give her sig-ner a hug.

* * * * *

Thane kept an eye on Jem as she scraped up the last of the stew. She looked more like herself, if a bit pale. And not counting her throat. He sensed a subdued air, a deep-seated quietness that hadn't been there before. Not surprising, considering what she was dealing with. *Fubar.* It was the only way to describe it. There was nothing he could do to help, other than be there for her.

The lift locked into place and Shiloh and Markowitz walked off it. She had an armful of fresh fruit and he had news.

"We've got watchers around the ship," Markowitz said. "At least three groupings, eight people total that I saw."

"Consortium?" Thane asked sharply. "We know their agents are here."

"Could be. The nine hours it took us to transit was more than enough time for a military express pod. I'm sure General Nesbitt has one."

"I didn't post a flight plan."

"Didn't have to. Not getting resupplied, the general would know we'd head for the nearest system. They could also be the usual port riffraff. Word that you're throwing out a lot of credits has already made the rounds."

Thane made a sour face. "Anyone need to leave for anything? Good. Fuel is on its way. Food Service is last. With no issues, we'll be gone in a couple of hours."

There were issues.

Westhaven Fuel Suppliers was an independent contractor to the Vangaria Spaceport. When the tanker driver pulled up, Thane was informed he needed to contact his office about payment before he could begin pumping.

"That's triple and not what was agreed to," Thane stormed at the non-perky fifty-something man who answered Thane's irate call.

"Miss McCutcheon is a new employee and is unaware of all our guidelines," Mr. Hamlin replied.

"Like your *gouging* guidelines?"

He ignored that. "The amount of your request, as well as the expediting of it, is *very* inconvenient. We will have to resupply from our *off-site* depot before we can service any other ships."

"I'm surprised the Vangaria Spaceport utilizes you, given your limited capability," Thane snapped.

Hamlin ignored that, too. "Of course, you can choose to be added to our normal refueling schedule. Rather lengthy at the moment, I'm afraid." He wore a triumphant, I-got-you smirk.

Uh-huh, Thane reflected sourly. *He'd heard about that spending spree.* Jem walked up behind him and laid a hand on his shoulder. She leveled a cold stare at the viewscreen and Thane had the pleasure of seeing the smirk slide off the SOB's face. She wasn't wearing contacts and very few port workers wouldn't recognize her. Not after all those FLEA flyers.

Jem handed Thane her cash card, gave Hamlin another cold look, and returned to the kitchen area.

"You'll get your payment. But the *Lone Tracker's* fuel cells had better be fully topped off." Thane took the satisfaction of manually cutting off the transmission.

He made the additional payment to Westhaven Fuel Suppliers. And then one to Murdock's Food Service. They were also an independent service and, apparently, in cahoots with Westhaven. Thane didn't even bother arguing with them. He paid and then filed a complaint with the Port Authority Office against both of them. Fortunately, Port Control didn't work on the greed system and they received a slot in the next exit window.

Two hours later, the *Lone Tracker's* Otanak drive took over from the ion engines. Anderson Station was three days transit, on the upper edge of Sector Three's boundary. Turning from the darkened viewscreen, Thane observed the others' contemplative expressions. Were they, like him, wondering how their recent events would affect the future? Affect them?

He gazed at Jem. What would that future demand of her?

Chapter 31

Thane jerked awake, battered by Jem's flailing arms. "Lights on," he called out loudly. Rolling her over him to the bed's edge, she made it to the trashcan at the foot of the bed.

"Sorry. Myerstone," she mumbled.

The nightmare must have hit really hard tonight. It still visited her occasionally, but it hadn't been this bad in a while. He made a mental note to toss the top he'd left on the chair in the laundry when Jem wiped her face with it before collapsing back down on the bed. Thane scooted over and put his arm around her.

"It was different this time," she said in a shaky voice.

His arm tightened protectively.

"When I looked over…it wasn't Dana's hand…it was Carlsson."

Thane's muscles tighten. That would have been a horrible scene. Blood and other fluids leaking from the parts sticking out? Parts sheared off? Both?

"His eyes…he must have had a second or two…" She stopped, swallowed. Ugh. Worse.

Thane pulled her onto his lap and wrapped both arms around her. He felt the rapid thudding of her heart and the tremors that racked her arms. Felt so frigging helpless. Only time would dim this newest nightmare.

* * * * *

"Mind if I join you?"

Jem looked up from her seat on the plazo bench. Markowitz stood in front of her in loose clothing. "Not at all," she said, her speech still raspy but coming easier.

She resumed doing arm curls, using a lighter set than the one the major used. Her attention focused downward at her feet, it took several moments before she realized he was sitting cross-legged on the deck. Studying her.

"You can't let what happened on Tarragona eat at you," he said.

She froze, her arm mid-curl.

"If you do, it will end up ruining everything in your life and hating yourself."

"How did…?" she whispered.

"How did I know?" He snorted. "You've been down here doing reps more times for the past two days than during the whole transit from Toulouse."

Jem flushed, laid the weight down beside her. "Carlsson was an accident. The AVs…weren't." Intellectually, she'd known it would happen one day and, intellectually, believed herself prepared. Never had she been so wrong.

"We had three options: surrender, die, or escape," he said flatly. "The first would have been the absolutely worst for all of us, and nobody wanted the second. That left escape, which meant we had to take out the AVs." He leaned forward. "No. Choice. Accept that." He straightened, looked away for a moment. "It doesn't mean you have to like it. And it will always be here," he tapped the side of his head, "but it does make it livable." He fell silent.

Guilt assailed her. "A choice that wouldn't have needed to be made if I hadn't been so arrogant." A harsh laugh escaped as bitterness swamped her. "Did I really believe I could intimidate them? A whole government, basically? I should never have gone there. We should have gone straight to Anderson Station like you wanted."

"If we had," he replied evenly, "we wouldn't have learned the full scope of the Consortium's intentions. It's the ass-kicking wake-up call we needed. We've been too complacent about these breakaways. As for you? The others must have believed in you. *They* voted to go to Tarragona and implement *Shiloh's* idea. Who, if you haven't noticed," his jaw flexed, "is now blaming herself—saying it's all her fault."

"No!"

"Everything you told those assholes was true." His eyes bored into hers. "Because you are. That. Dangerous. You could wage a one-person war and bring an entire organization—or government—to its knees. You've always thought in singularity: individual, self-contained events with little to no ripple effect. Even on Toulouse, the 'lessons' were to strengthen an already well-known reputation, with reprisals aimed at *individuals* failing to heed your warning. Tarragona was the first time you applied the *totality* of what your combined actions could achieve. To be honest, Jem, I don't think you could be stopped except by sheer luck and a lot of causalities."

She flinched.

"*That* is why the Military Council has turned into a hotbed of paranoia." He paused, then added. "And why Admiral Gleason brought six frigates with him." He gave a single nod, rolled to his stomach and started doing pushups.

Jem sat motionless, her thoughts elsewhere.

Chapter 32

The Catawampus System was a failed system and undoubtedly named by an exasperated cartographer as they dodged the rocks that filled it. There were two rocky planetoids and several wide asteroid bands that couldn't get their act together for even that much. The patrol ship that had challenged them seconds after dropping out of O-space had advised approach from a high inclination to the solar ecliptic plane to avoid the worst of the mess.

Anderson Station orbited above the larger planetoid, humorously called Rock-One by the patrol captain. It was a huge construct that grew even larger the closer they got to it. Built on a linear design, wheeled spokes and open-end docks angled in every direction from a central core. Ships of all sizes filled the surrounding space, some at docking arms and others parked at various points around it. Everyone gathered around the command chairs, gawking at the viewscreen.

Thane let out a low whistle. "What's the core length? Two kilometers?"

"Closer to three," the major replied.

"Damn, Kurzvall was one ambitious SOB," Boyd remarked.

"Nope," Markowitz said. "Half of it has been added since the admiral claimed it for the Republic."

Thane glanced at him sharply. That much in two years? They must be more worried about the Consortium than they officially let on.

Following Control's instructions, the *Lone Tracker* closed in on docking arm Six carefully. Thor was in the—figurative—pilot's chair while Thane sat tensely in the physical one.

Space docking was one of a Globe's few disadvantages. Because of its configuration and the hatch location, standard docking arms couldn't latch on properly. They usually had to park nearby and personnel jetted over in spacesuits. As a military base, Anderson had several docking arms modified to accommodate Globe troop carriers. Their pincher-style arms 'snuggled' around a ship, locking it into place and deployed a specially designed access tube.

"You either trust Thor's navigation or you don't," Boyd chuckled.

"Can't help it," Thane admitted. "This is his first time. With a military dock," Thane added when laughter broke out.

"Wouldn't expect anything less," Markowitz said with a wide grin.

A few more comments had even Thane snickering.

"Docking complete. Access tube extending," Thor announced.

"See. Not even a thump," Boyd said.

"Access tube attached. Pressurizing now. Receiving video call from Anderson Station Control."

"Accept," Thane said, and found himself looking at Lieutenant Commander Terrance Johnson, the admiral's aide. He took the lack of a welcoming smile as a bad sign.

"Mr. Baron, glad you could finally make it." His scrutiny shifted. "Major Markowitz. You are to report to Admiral Gleason's office as soon as docking is completed."

"Yes, sir," Markowitz said from the chair next to Thane.

Jem stepped forward between them.

The Lt. Commander's eyes widened.

"*We* will report to the admiral's office," she rasped out.

"I will let him know." The viewscreen blanked.

"Maybe you should wait until—"

Jem pivoted sharply to Markowitz. "No."

"Think there's been scuttlebutt coming out of the Tricast System?" Boyd asked.

"If so, it'd be their version," Thane said darkly.

Silence.

"Pressurization complete. Warning, no gravity inside access tube," Thor informed them.

* * * * *

The trip through the access tube was embarrassing. Not used to zero gravity, Jem had flailed and bounced off a couple of ribs until Thane and Markowitz—*laughing!*—each grabbed an arm and hauled her to the base hatch. Two escorts waited inside to navigate them through the warren of corridors to the admiral's office.

Both men shot to their feet when they entered.

"At ease, Major. Miss Wilmont. Do you need to go to the infirmary?" Admiral Gleason asked.

Johnson had reported her throat condition. It had acquired a lovely palette of yellow and green during their transit. "Thank you, no. I saw a doctor when we stopped to resupply on Vangaria One."

"Sit," Gleason ordered brusquely. He followed suit behind his desk.

Jem exchanged a quick glance with Thane. The admiral's tone might have been unreadable, but the anger coming off him wasn't. The major had accurately predicted his pissed-level.

"I was planning on speaking with you and Mr. Baron later. I wanted to hear Major Markowitz's report first."

"About Palmyra or Tricast?" Jem asked, hesitant.

"While there's interesting rumors coming out of Palmyra, we'll start with Tarragona, Tricast Three," he snapped.

"Uh, parts would fall under classified," Thane said glancing sideways.

The admiral reached over and pressed a button. There was a distinct click from the door.

"The room is secured. Commander Johnson is fully briefed and will be recording this meeting. First," the anger he'd been controlling slipped out, "I'd like to know why the bloody hell you all thought it a good idea to go into a potentially hostile territory and threaten their citizens."

Markowitz coughed.

"Have you heard anything from Tarragona?" Thane asked cautiously.

"No. Should I have?"

"Three AV-74s getting blown up should have made the news," Markowitz said neutrally.

Admiral Gleason froze.

"Not to mention the mess at the spaceport and…elsewhere," Thane said.

Jem blanched. Pulled a bottle of water from her jacket pocket and took a long swallow.

"Means they're blocking all outbound UPMS mail now," Boyd said, rubbing his chin.

"All outbound traffic as well," the major agreed, "or someone would have blasted the news at the nearest port."

The admiral finally unfroze himself and leaned forward. "Back it up. What AV-74s and who blew them up?" When all he got was silence, he pinched his nose. "I'm going to assume you had a damn good reason *other* than intimidation."

"My original goal was superseded," Jem rasped, "when we received a message from an unknown informant."

Thane detailed what that information consisted of to save her voice.

Furious, again, the admiral said it should have been brought immediately to him.

"I tried, sir," Markowitz said, "but I was outvoted."

"Out. *Voted*?" he choked.

"The *Lone Tracker* is a civilian ship, sir. Manned by, uh, headstrong civilians. Sir."

"Headstrong is not the proper term in this case," Gleason said brusquely.

"It's a good thing we did go," Thane replied in the same tone. "Want to hear it or not?"

Gleason glared. Jem held her breath. He finally gave a 'go ahead' gesture.

"At that point, sir," Jem said, "we believed we could use the intimidation tactics we'd originally planned to stop their *political* shenanigans. At least for the immediate future."

"Things did not go as planned," Thane said.

"Not fucking surprised," Gleason snapped.

Jem exchanged a worried look with Thane. They couldn't afford to alienate him.

"Sir, you need to hear them out," Markowitz said quietly.

Gleason met Markowitz's unflinching gaze for several seconds, then took a deep breath. "Continue."

Thane told him about the obstruction of port support. Then Markowitz told him about the obstruction of messages, in or out.

"A stranglehold on UPMS would be a first," Commander Johnson said. "Wonder if their HQ is aware of it."

Then Jem began. Her story unfolded haltingly, paused occasionally to sip water. The admiral's expression turned impassive when General Nesbitt entered it. She carefully summarized her threatened intimidation tactics, leaving out the "I will destroy the Consortium" declaration. Markowitz's words from the other night still reverberated. She stopped completely when she got to the part they were going to hate.

"There's only one way you could have gotten out of that room."

The admiral's noncommittal tone was a relief, signaling they'd past the hissy-fit stage. Thane reached over. With his hand firmly in hers, she told the rest of it.

Shifting, dropping through the building. Carlsson and the alley. Teleporting to the ship.

Markowitz took over at that point. Detailing his actions and taking full responsibility for the AVs and their crews' deaths. Thane finished up with their trip to the Vangaria System.

The room fell silent.

Finally, Admiral Gleason stirred. "Major, your assessment?"

"Sir. They have to know their aggressive expansion program will eventually draw Republic reaction. The fact that their military leadership is already on board...the question becomes, how far are they planning—and willing—to go?"

"A very big question, indeed. We have to assume the recent kidnapping of Miss Wilmont was not for Reginald Kurzvall's benefit alone, but for the Consortium as a whole. General Nesbitt's attempt to add her to his inventory on Tarragona, as well as the AV threat, validates your actions, Major. Well done."

Gleason leaned back in his chair and studied Jem for a moment. Breaking out in a wry grin, he said, "When word of this gets to Military Command, the brown stuff will really hit the fan."

Jem gave a rueful laugh. "Sir, I think I buried it."

He barked out a laugh. "Truly." His expression turned serious. "Exposing your abilities, which was bound to happen sooner or later, has now made you a target. You have to be even more careful, Jem, going forward."

She noted he didn't say from whom. Earth's Military Command was not her friend.

"I would appreciate you visiting our infirmary, Jem. An official medical evaluation and report will assist in a response to any Consortium claim of unprovoked mayhem. Cyclops, huh? I had heard rumors of giants, but nothing substantiated or to that height. Commander Johnson will escort you to Dr. McFadden's office. Major, please remain. I require a more formal debriefing."

***

Anderson Station ran on Earth time, and they'd arrived about mid-morning. Admiral Gleason invited them to have supper with him on the station. A real dining room, freshly prepared food, fresh faces, and room to stretch your legs? They'd all enthusiastically accepted. Even Thane welcomed a break from the *Lone Tracker*.

Drawing out the evening, they sat now in a lounge two hallways away from the dining room. Or was it three, Jem pondered, sipping her Moon Ale. The place was a maze. She and Thane were sitting with Adm. Gleason, while Maj. Markowitz, Boyd, and Lt. Cmdr. Johnson made another grouping. She couldn't help noting Markowitz's glances—and occasional scowl—aimed toward the group across the room that Shiloh was happily chatting with.

That was good to see.

Wrapped up in her own misery, she hadn't seen Shiloh's. She'd gone to Shiloh after the major's revelation, assuring her friend that she bore no responsibility for the resulting chaos. They'd been expecting amoral assholes and got militaristic hardliners. They'd talked, sniffled through a few tears, then talked some more late into the night. It'd been good for both of them.

Jem glanced over again. *Oh, my*. Shiloh was *flirting*.

She hoped Shiloh knew what she was doing because something was about to break. Like, someone's nose? *Aaannnd*, there he went. The major strode across the room, barked something at the four guys, grabbed Shiloh by the arm, and pulled her out of the lounge. Looking over, she saw matching grins on Boyd and Johnson.

With their backs to the room, Thane and the admiral were totally oblivious, although they were both giving her wary looks now. Oops.

"What's that smirk for?" Thane asked.

"Oh, remembering…things," she said.

"Wouldn't be about Palmyra Two, would it?" Gleason asked. "That was you playing pranks with the mercenaries, wasn't it?"

"I'm afraid I don't know what you're talking about," Jem said airily.

Thane hid his grin in his whisky glass.

"Right. I've got a whole directory filled with reports from Toulouse. Makes for very interesting reading. I believe we can safely drop them to the bottom of your threat list. *Hmmm*. Is that what gave you the idea to try and cower the Consortium?"

"Well, my original intent was to cower Kurzvall," Jem said, rubbing her nose.

Thane held up a finger. "Which we talked her out of because going to Hebros was too dangerous."

Gleason gave him a disbelieving look. "So you took on the Consortium instead?"

"Shiloh suggested targeting Kurzvall's partners rather than him directly, thereby forcing *them* to restrict him or else," Jem said. "Since two of them were based in the Tricast System, they won." And ten others lost. *Consequences.* "Receiving the informant's information didn't change our objective, sir, only the level of it," she finished quietly.

Gleason *harrumphed* and turned to Thane. "Shiloh Stohlass is the one that came up with the idea? You've got some family there."

"Proud of it, too." Thane craned his neck around. "Where did she get off to?"

Jem gave him an innocent look. "Might be wandering. It has been pretty cramped on the *Tracker* for the last while." Definitely not much room for romance.

"Can't say I blame her," Thane said.

Boyd and Johnson wandered over to join them.

"Admiral, if I may ask, what happens now?" Jem asked in her raspy voice.

"The *Lone Tracker* and crew will head back to Midgard. No side trips. Then brief General Kowalski on arrival. I will provide an encrypted copy of this morning's recording to take with you." He swirled his glass contents for a moment, then lowered his voice.

"Everyone *here* knows Military Command is only cognizant of Jem's teleporting ability. Therefore, a modified text-only copy of the same report was dispatched to MC by express pod before dinner. It has you, Jem, teleporting from Mosley's conference room directly to the *Lone Tracker*. Your stealth and Major Markowitz's expertise combined took out the AVs. That needs to be your official story."

All true, from a summary viewpoint. It left out anything related to her phasing.

"What about…" Jem took a steadying breath, "…about Carlsson's death?"

"We'll deal with that when and if it becomes an issue. In the meantime, you don't know a damn thing about it. As for what happens next? I don't even want to guess." Gleason shook his head. "As my grandpa would say, 'Hope for the best, expect the worse, and shot-puck their asses to hell.'" He raised his glass. "Go Grandpa."

With broad grins, the others raised their glasses.

"I'll drink to that."

"No problem."

"Absolutely."

"Hell, yeah."

Chapter 33

Everyone was busy the next morning and looking forward to getting home. Thane had declined the admiral's offer for any restocking. They had more than enough fuel and supplies to make the six-day transit to Midgard. Commander Johnston had popped in earlier to drop off the video file for General Kowalski. Both hatches were sealed on his departure.

"Access tube disengaging. Receiving video call from Anderson Station Control."

"Accept," Thane said. He had the docking arm displayed on the screen.

A female wearing captain's bars smiled out of the viewscreen's lower corner. "Anderson to *Lone Tracker*. Dock Six airspace is clear. Is everything a go for release?"

"Yes, ma'am. Launch when ready. We've enjoyed our stay but eager to get home."

"Copy that. Standby for release and have a safe journey." Her image vanished.

Thane watched as the dock's arms began to slowly open. Once the ship was de-snuggled, they began sliding to the sides, leaving the *Tracker* hanging in space.

"Thor, initiate dock withdrawal, five-percent thrust."

The dock's image began to slowly recede. Thor continued to back them until they were a hundred meters away and Anderson Station hung beneath them. Giving it one final look, Thane ordered Thor to put them on course for their transit point at ten percent thrust. He'd up it to two-thirds once they cleared the last of the parked ships.

He cut the viewscreen off and joined the others at the table. Except for Markowitz. He'd elected to stay in the lower level during launch, claiming "seen one space dock launch, seen them all." Uh-huh. The major and his cousin were pretending to ignore each other. Just as they'd all ignored both of them coming in late last night.

Boyd stood, stretched. "Markowitz wants to spar this morning. Work off some energy, I guess." He flashed a wink at Shiloh before heading toward the stairwell.

Thane bit his lips together. Okay, maybe not.

Cheeks pink, Shiloh excused herself to watch a documentary on the hand comp she'd purchased from Anderson's base supply.

"Think we should tell her that 'dreamy smile' is a dead giveaway?" Jem said, amused.

"No, let them have their moment," he said, his gaze drifting to the stairwell.

"Moment? You believe it's a fling?"

"I…don't know what to think," he admitted. "He's a soldier, stationed on Midgard. He'll eventually leave. Nothing wrong with spending time with someone you like, but I don't want to see her hurt."

Jem reached over and took his hand. "However it's meant to be, they'll figure it out. You and I did. So did your mom and Lee."

True. Even though they had eventually returned to live on Midgard, his mom had followed Lee to Earth. "Katrina will be unhappy if she leaves." They were more like sisters than cousins.

"For herself, yes, but happy for Shiloh."

Thane agreed and then asked Thor how long to the transit point.

"Forty-three minutes, nineteen seconds."

Otanak engines didn't work well in gravity fields. The stronger the field, the more likely, and violently, an engine would explode on activation. Experimentation had determined the minimum field strength for safe operation and gave it a safety factor of fifty percent. Because, as one engineer commented dryly, it gave 50/50 odds on what happened. Ship size would be a factor. Most pilots prudently applied an additional safety factor when setting their transition points. Here, they were climbing out of an ecliptic plane full of gravity-inducing rocks.

They were chatting, drinking coffee when Thor suddenly announced an unidentified ship detected, its trajectory on an interception course with them.

"Viewscreen on," Thane ordered as he and Jem hurried over to the command chairs. All he saw was empty space with a large grouping of rocks in the distance. "Magnify. Ship description?" *There.*

"Class One drone, approximately ten meters length. No ID broadcast."

Dammit. "Time to intersection?" Its ion engine was a growing blaze of light.

"Two minutes, two seconds."

"It's going to ram us," Jem said, her voice tight. "Laz-cannon?"

"Disabled," Thane said grimly. "Thor, can we transition to O-drive in sixty seconds?"

"Negative. Safety factor at thirty-nine-point six percent."

They'd explode. Thane swore and hit the All-Ship comm switch. "Brace for impact and wild-ass maneuvering," he yelled, as he and Jem belted themselves in. "Bogey intending to ram us." *Where the hell's that patrol ship?*

The screen changed to a dark purple background as Thane ordered it switched to radar mode. The *Lone Tracker* was a solid blue dot in the center with a red dot too frigging close for comfort.

"Thor, full burn." Not enough time to bring the auxiliaries up and outrun it, like they had at Magnus. This ambush had been well planned. The ship surged forward. The bogey's angle altered.

"Impact in fifty seconds," Thor's unemotional voice said.

Thane stared at the screen. Calculating. Waiting.

"Impact in twenty seconds."

"Engines off, full thruster reverse," Thane yelled.

Lone Tracker's gravity field buckled for a moment as acceleration and deceleration collided. If not for their safety belts, he and Jem would have been smashed into the navigation panel. Thane had a moment to hope it had missed them before there came the grating, squealing sound of tortured metal.

Everything stopped. His brain. His lungs. Time.

"Hull Breach in Section E1. Significant damage."

Thane took a deep breath and everything restarted. It'd hit the electronic module. It was located in the ship's dome top and sealed from the rest of the ship. His laser cannon was—had been—located up there, too.

"Sensors degraded, working at eighteen percent," Thor said.

Explained why the viewscreen was off. The ship suddenly lurched sideways, and they heard muffled *thunks*, bangs, and clangs. *Shit, shit.* Now what?

"Detonation detected twenty-eight meters distance. Damage in Section E2. Minor punctures in outer hull. Inner hull intact."

Thane breathed a sigh of relief. Then Thor continued.

"Unidentified ship detected, approximately one hundred kilometers. Class Two frigate configuration, no ID broadcast."

Thane swore. The drone's control ship.

"Laser fir—" Thor went silent as the deck beneath their feet gave a sharp jerk.

Everything around them died. Lights. Command console. Gravity. There came another loud clang, this one from the direction of the stairwell.

"Thane?"

He understood the dread in her voice. "Automatic pressure seal," Thane confirmed calmly. "Lower deck's been breached. The laser probably went clean through, took out the computer core." Plus a lot of other things. Boyd and Markowitz were dead or dying. Nothing he could do to keep them from being next. They were blind and helpless.

Jem whispered, "Shiloh."

They should have heard a scream, yelling—something. That they hadn't didn't bode well for her, either.

Something nudged his ear; he head-bumped it away. He groped for Jem's hand in the dark. "Love you."

"Love you," Jem returned softly, squeezing his hand.

They waited.

After what felt like an eon, Thane said, "They should have finished us off by now."

"You're going to complain?" Jem asked, sounding strained.

A flicker of amusement went through him, followed by a surge of hope. "No, but it means they weren't given time. That patrol ship must have spotted what was happening and came at full burn. Help is on the way. There should be enough air for at least five, six hours, but it's going to get cold. I'm going to check on Shiloh," he said, unbuckling his straps.

Using his chair as leverage, he sailed across to the other side, arms outstretched to—yep, found the lockers directly behind them. He pulled himself over to and then down the hallway. He found the med-room's doorway by feel. He took a deep breath before swinging in.

Crap, crap, can't see a thing. He floated gently with arms and legs spread wide. His left thigh brushed against something and he grabbed for it. Cloth. Shiloh's torso. He ran a hand upward to her neck where he found a weak but working pulse. *Thank you, Universe.* He carefully maneuvered them around until he found the med-bed, then fumbled with the straps until Shiloh was safely tucked in.

My next ship is going to have a few more extras.

Thane stilled, drifted. A tidal wave of emotion swept through him as the realization fully sunk in. The *Lone Tracker*. Thor. Gone. He took a few moments to curse the Consortium—who else would it be—before heading back to Jem.

"Shiloh's alive but injured. I've got her—" he broke off at the sound of pounding from the stairwell. He shot toward it, muttered a couple of expletives when he slammed into the hull, then grabbed a rung to steady himself. He banged on the cover.

Someone banged back three times, paused, then three more.

Thane pounded three times. When the silence stretched out, he floated back to his seat. "Okay, they know there's survivors and I'm going to assume they're friendlies," he told Jem as he strapped himself in.

"I'll check," Jem's voice said in the darkness.

By the time he grasped her meaning, she was gone. At least on this plane as he couldn't feel anything in her seat. He bit his lip, worried. How did phasing work in space? She'd said she hadn't mastered moving upward, which she'd need to do to get back up here.

After what seemed like forever, he jumped when a hand gripped his shoulder. He grabbed it, pulled her to him.

"It's the patrol ship, *Nero*. Heard them say they've got a salvage crane coming to tow us back to Anderson." There was a pause. "It's a mess," she said. "Literally. The laser beam went through the waste and water tanks as well as the memory core. I didn't…see anything else."

There were several seconds of silence, remembering their two friends. The *Nero's* crew would have removed their bodies. Thane ignored what sounded suspiciously like a sniffle.

"I'm worried about Shiloh," Jem said.

"We don't know how badly she's hurt," Thane agreed, "and the temperature is starting to drop. You can get us across space to the *Nero*? Okay, then. Let's go get Shiloh, then bedazzle the *Nero's* crew and give Admiral Gleason another headache."

Thane worked his way back toward the med-room. "We need to get you familiar with zero gravity," he told Jem, as she hung on to his foot.

"Remember when I teleported in front of the Azusa Enforcers to your family's vacation island?" Her voice sounded contemplative. "General Kowalski had to do a lot of in-briefings then, too."

He remembered that it had nearly killed her. "From the way things are going, it won't be the last for either of them."

Once in the med-room, he drew Jem's hand to one of the bed straps. "Take her first. The infirmary is usually located—oh, crap. Admiral Gleason will definitely not like this."

"What? Why?"

"Officially, you can only teleport to places you've been to. How do we explain you teleporting to their infirmary? If Thor was still working, we could have them display a visual of it and pretend that sufficed."

"But I did get a visual. I was watching when you spoke to Captain Barnes. The viewscreen captured quite a bit of the bridge behind her. We'll go there."

"*Will* a visual work for teleporting?" He felt her shrug.

"Don't see why not. We ought to try it one day when no one's watching.

And that's not what we'll be doing now, anyway."

Yeah, as if that wouldn't open a whole new slew of possibilities. He got the upper strap undone. He knew Jem had undone the other when Shiloh stared to drift upward. He kept a hand on her arm.

"Hang on for a minute," she said. "I need to check something."

Check what? "Jem? ... Jem?"

"We have a slight problem," her worried voice suddenly speared out of the dark. "Positionally, the Nero is hanging above us."

She must have phased outside the hull and back. "How'd you get back from the lower deck?"

"Didn't. Just stuck my head and shoulders through the floor."

Thane choked back a laugh. "We can do this," he said with more confidence than he felt. "If we can't figure out how to move upward, we'll come back here and wrap up." There were emergency blankets—*dammit*. Store room, lower deck. Definitely need to replan things.

"You're right. Do you have Shiloh?" she asked.

"Yes." He bumped against the med-table.

"Snuggle her tight to your chest. That should ensure she'll shift with us."

"You're going to take us both at the same time?" Her hands were sliding over his. Confirming his hold?

"Uh-huh. Less traumatic for the *Nero's* bridge crew."

She's worried about getting us across. How much time had she already spent shifted? Jem's hand worked its way between him and Shiloh, until her arm locked tight around his bicep. He heard several deep breaths.

"I've never tried shifting people this way," she said in a low voice. "Stacked, kind of."

"You weren't sure you could shift anyone else at all," he reminded her, "until you had me press your hands against my chest." On Pappia, when he was helping her escape from Kurzvall's men. It had been his first shocking exposure to shifting.

"True," she said, sounding a bit more upbeat. "Ready?"

He grasped Shiloh in a tighter grip. "Ready."

The familiar tingle told him they were shifting. It didn't affect him now, as it had the first few times. *Human adaptability is just plain amazing*. He was surprised to find he could see around him now. Dimly and in the usual shades of gray, but he could see. Huh? Did this whatever place have its own light source?

He couldn't help the moment of panic as they approached the wall, his brain going *stop, stop*. Then, they were outside. Hanging in space next to the *Lone Tracker* and with the *Nero* off to the side. Wow. He stared, mesmerized, until Jem tugged. Right. He took a step. Then another, amazed. It was like walking on, well, nothing. This was great. Spooky, too. He checked their position and, yeah, they were below the *Nero*.

Without thinking, he mentally pictured a staircase. On his next step, he pictured his 'left' foot on the first 'step' and brought his other foot up to join it. Then he took another one, Jem moving up with him. Looking over, her wide-eyed grin said she had the answer to her "up" problem. *Just have to fool your brain.*

Finally, they were inside and on the *Nero's* main deck. Thane discovered phasing's really creepy effect of walking 'through' people, or vice versa if they couldn't dodge in time. They found the bridge humming with activity and moved carefully to an open area that was devoid of equipment and people. Jem smiled up at him…then he was blinking in bright light.

There was a choking sound, followed by *"Captain!"*

Captain Barnes turned from her viewscreen, her expression morphing into shock at seeing them. He'd be shocked too, having three people materialize in the middle of his bridge. Him giving her a goofy grin probably didn't help.

"Oh, well, this simplifies things. Hi, Admiral Gleason," Jem said, stepping away from him and waving.

Thane squinted at the viewscreen. Admiral Gleason, with a resigned look on his face.

"Sorry about this, but we don't know how bad Shiloh is hurt. And, well, we figured you would, ah, handle it afterwards," Jem finished a bit weakly.

"Uh-huh," the admiral said. "Captain Barnes, please have your *guests* escorted to the infirmary where they will *all* undergo an examination." He gave Jem a don't-try-me look. "In the meantime, there will be a complete blackout of any information pertaining to your guests and their presence on the *Nero*. You will return to Anderson Station immediately, where you and your entire crew will be in-briefed. Congratulations. Your security clearances have shot to the top. Gleason out."

Silence, and a lot of stares.

"Lieutenant Loux, please alert Doctor Swoboda she has more patients inbound. Commander Hunnington, three-quarter burn back to Anderson Station." Captain Barnes gestured to them. "Please follow me." She paused at the door. "Everyone heard the admiral. No discussion."

Thane heard "no one would believe me" before it slid closed behind them.

A surprise awaited them in the *Nero's* infirmary. Boyd and Markowitz surged out of chairs as they entered.

"How bad?" Markowitz asked, darting to Thane's side.

Thane shook his head. "Couldn't tell in the dark. Doctor?"

Jem gave Boyd a warm hug as Thane followed the middle-aged doctor through a doorway. "We thought you were dead," she said.

"Came close," Boyd replied.

Thane popped back in. "We're to wait our turn," he said. "It's frigging good to see you. What happened?" he asked as everyone took a seat.

"We were sparring in the plazo when your warning sounded," Markowitz said. "We headed for the environment lockers. Fortunately, the *Lone Tracker* had two suits."

"We made them fit," Boyd added dryly.

Jem snickered. Boyd had a thick, high-gravity body and Markowitz was a couple of inches taller than Thane. Good thing suit joints worked like accordions.

"We'd barely gotten them on when that wild-ass part started. What did you do?" Markowitz merely shook his head when Thane told him. "Anyway, Boyd and I had barely scraped ourselves off the hull when a narrow laser beam came through. We scrambled to get helmets and O2 tanks on before full depressurization."

Boyd grunted. "I can still taste crap."

Markowitz grimaced. "Yeah, it was nasty. I'm surprised they didn't use a wide beam, cutting the ship open."

"They fired at an extreme range," Thane told him.

"Ah. Had to ensure enough power to punch through. That gave us time to dress out." The major jerked his thumb at Boyd. "And Bonehead here had grabbed a high-powered light from another locker right before we pancaked."

"Next time, Jarhead, I'll leave you to flounder in the dark," Boyd snarked.

Markowitz ignored him. "We figured you two were okay when the seal activated. Not too long after that, the *Nero* people lasered their way through the hatch. They brought us over and did a quick med-check. What happened to Shiloh?"

"I'm guessing she didn't get strapped down in time. I found her floating in the med-room."

Boyd looked sideways at Jem. "Should we ask how you got off the *Lone Tracker*?"

"Ah, no."

"Admiral Gleason is not going to be happy when he finds out," Markowitz said.

Jem made a face. "He wasn't. He happened to be having a video conversation with Captain Barnes when we materialized on the bridge."

Boyd and the major gave identical snorts.

"We didn't know how bad my cousin was injured," Thane said, his chin lifted defensively.

Markowitz held his hand up, palm out. "Understood. So will Admiral Gleason. The rest of Military Command won't. Expect flak."

"That seems to be all I get from them," Jem said sourly.

Doctor Swoboda bustled in several minutes later. She confirmed a mild concussion for Miss Stohlass, who was sleeping after briefly regaining consciousness.

"Now, which of you two wants to be first?" Dr. Swoboda asked. "I've already examined these other two. Fine specimens, both of them," she added cheerily.

Jem waved her hand and followed the doctor out.

Chapter 34

The four of them were escorted to Admiral Gleason's office immediately upon arriving back at Anderson. Jem found herself perched on the edge of her chair, her back ramrod straight. His earlier fury at their antics paled in comparison to his current state. *At least it's not aimed at us this time.*

"Report," the admiral snapped.

Thane immediately launched into speech. Jem was mildly shocked at how short a time it required to tell it. It had felt a lot longer.

"I have Captain Barnes's report," Gleason said after he finished. "The *Nero* was in another section but, fortunately, the radar officer was monitoring your flight path. He spotted the bogey as soon as it went active. They immediately headed toward your position but were too far away to get there in time. They witnessed the strike, followed by its explosion no more than thirty meters from you. A second bogey, undoubtedly the drone's controller, bolted out from the clump of rocks that'd hidden them. They managed to get off two laser shots—"

"*Two?*" Thane and Markowitz chorused.

"Yes, two. The depressurization from the first one acted like thrusters, which you can thank the Universe for. They spun the *Lone Tracker* away in another direction and the second shot fell short as the ambushing sons-of-bitches were barely in range."

So close, Jem shuddered.

"Anyway, the SOBs turned tail and ran. Captain Barnes stopped to render aid instead of giving chase. Her radar officer tracked the bogey until it transitioned into O-space."

Gleason spotted Jem's stiff posture. "Relax, Miss Wilmont," he said brusquely.

"Yes, sir. As soon as you come out of ultra-admiral admiral-mode," she replied.

He blinked. Looked at the others, then pinched his nose bridge. "Ultra-admiral mode," he muttered, slumping back in his chair. "I'll have to remember that. Everyone at ease, please. I am so damn pissed at the Consortium. To think, they'd do something like this and right under our nose."

"Can we prove it was them?" Thane asked in clipped tones. "No IDs, and I doubt there's enough left of the drone to identify it."

"Correct. However, given your recent problems, suspicion will weigh heavily in this instance. None of the other Independent Systems have the wherewithal—or the balls—to mount this level of operation."

"What about the Palmyra mercenaries?" Boyd asked.

Markowitz shook his head. "Far as I know, they don't own frigates of any class. And if they did, they wouldn't take the risk. If anything, they have a lot of respect for Jem and her, uh, capability."

"One of them even offered me a job." Jem found herself the center of intense stares. "Sheesh. Not like I'm going to take him up on it."

The admiral drummed his fingers for a moment. "Nothing more we can do at the moment, and I need to debrief the *Nero's* crew. Your ship is being brought back here, Thane. I've requested a preliminary report on its condition by morning. We'll reconvene then. What happened to your laser cannon?"

"The Hermes authorities," he said, explaining their ultimatum. "I planned on having it undone on return to Midgard." His jaw flexed. "I should have asked to have one of your techs do it, but I didn't think about it and we paid the price."

"Thane, we weren't expecting to get in a firefight," Jem said, patting his leg.

"*Nobody* expected anything like this or I'd have had ships plastered all around the system," the admiral said. "Which is something I'll be looking into. Now, you will undoubtedly want to visit Miss Stohlass in the infirmary. I'm told her condition is mild. Commander Johnson is arranging quarters for your use and will page you when they're ready. In the meantime…hell, go have a drink. I could sure use one." He speared Thane with a hopeful look. "You wouldn't happen to have that strong stuff Kowalski pranked me with on board, would you?"

Jem couldn't help laughing when Thane shot him a wink.

General Kowalski and Admiral Gleason had been friends since serving aboard the same trainer during their cadet years. The general had tricked the admiral into taking a large swallow of Pounding J's Aspric whisky "to get past the bite and to the flavor." Two of the Republic's highest-ranking men had regressed into ear-burning, insult-hurling teenagers right in front of them. It'd been hilarious.

Several hours later, Jem found Thane where she expected: watching the *Lone Tracker's* arrival from the large observation window overlooking maintenance dock Eleven. The salvage crane had already withdrawn several of its spidery network of arms that wrapped around the *Tracker*. The remainder slowly slid away as the dock's arms telescoped out and gently attached to the damaged ship. Jem slid her hand into his and stared as the ship was gently tugged into place.

The dome top had been all but ripped off, miraculously leaving the seal to the main deck intact. The blackened hole in the lower section stood out starkly, the matching one somewhere on the backside. The damaged engine section was barely visible from their viewpoint, so the hull perforations would also be on that side. A black streak diagonally across the main body said the second shot hadn't fallen short completely. Luckily, it hadn't had enough power to penetrate the hull. From the outside, the ship looked repairable. Jem's memories of the inside said differently.

"They intended to breach the main section, then detonate the pod," Thane said woodenly.

"It didn't happen, thanks to your quick thinking." Jem squeezed his hand.

"I'm told it's only a ship. A hunk of metal, cabling and circuits. Replaceable." His gaze never left the technicians swarming over the hull. "But it was more than that. It was a home…a companion for half my life. It was the last link to my father."

The misery in his voice tore at her. "Not the last link, Thane."

Jem moved to face him and quoted the last two lines from Midgard's *The Liturgy of Passing*. "'A part of you will live in us, and continue on till all is dust.'" She touched his chest with her free hand. "You and your sister *are* your father's link and will carry him with you into the future. I agree that, while you will undoubtedly get a new ship, the *Lone Tracker* itself is irreplaceable."

She, too, had felt the sense of 'home' when aboard it.

He finally looked away from the window. She gave him a sympathetic smile, right before he folded her into his arms. Jem hugged him tightly, comforting him as he so often had her. Finally, she raised her head and tugged at him.

"Shiloh's awake. Why don't we go visit?" The reason she'd come searching for him.

Thane gave one final look out the window then, hand in hand, they walked away.

* * * * *

Noon-ish the next day found them back in his office as Admiral Gleason went over the maintenance report on the *Tracker*. The four expressions across from him were various shades of glum. Especially Thane's. He sympathized with the young man. Accepting his ship's loss was one thing, hearing the details of it would be depressing.

Finished, Gleason sat back from his computer. "The attack has all the earmarks of a military operation. We may not be able to prove it was the Consortium but, as I said yesterday, suspicion will lean heavily against them. Think that anonymous informant of yours might send us some proof?"

"We can hope," Thane replied.

"The *Nero* is being prepped and leaves for Midgard tomorrow morning. Your first stop on arrival is Odinheim to debrief General Kowalski—the video file."

"It should be okay," Thane assured him. "It's in a drawer in my bedroom. Uh, would it be possible to rent one of your troop ships to go home? Or a scout ship?"

A small smile quirked the Admiral's lips. "You're turning down a two-week worry-free cruise?" The *Nero's* size would more than double what they'd expected time-wise on the *Tracker*.

"Two weeks of nothing except worrying," Thane groused. "I'm going to need a new ship."

"We need to get Shiloh home as soon as possible," Jem added.

Gleason folded his hands on his desktop and stared at them for several seconds. Did they not realize—no, guess not. Then he'd best make sure they did. That unpleasant reply from Military Command this morning was a start, and it only dealt with his report about what happened on Tricast Three.

"Your lives have entered a new stage—we'll call it the fubar stage. It's unknown how well, or long, the Tarragona authorities will be able to contain your demonstration there."

"Sir, I'm sor…" Jem stopped in mid-word when his hand snapped up.

"Your actions both there and here were legitimate responses to the situations you found yourselves in. All this has done is accelerate what would have happened eventually, especially in pursuant of any Military Command tasks." *Which the snots should realize.* "That target on your head has quadrupled in size. You are a wanted woman, either for gain or elimination."

"With all due respect sir," Jem said sourly, "that's not exactly new."

"In actuality, no. In level of effort, yes." Gleason leaned forward. "Whatever plans the Consortium—or anyone else may have, you will be a major, inhibiting pain-in-their-ass. They will need to either circumvent or neutralize you first."

"So we're back to where this started?" Thane said, giving a humorless laugh. "Me or any member of my family used against her?"

"Yes," Gleason said bluntly. "While most mercenaries won't go near you now, there's always a few who can't resist any challenge—especially well-paid ones. Then there's privately-financed teams or military operations."

"From which military?" Boyd growled, followed by a tense silence.

Gleason couldn't fault him for that. A number of his own high-ranking peers had already questioned if Jem Wilmont was too dangerous to remain free, or even living. Her contract with Midgard's Planetary Defense Office had been General Kowalski's attempt to placate them. Now? When Military Command learns about this fiasco? He wouldn't put it pass some asshole general to make a 'what's best for the Republic' decision.

Drumming his fingers in thought, Gleason finally said. "The Consortium won't try anything so overt again anytime soon. If the doctor clears Miss Stohlass for travel outside the *Nero's* infirmary, I'll see about arranging faster transport. You'll be allowed back on the *Lone Tracker* to collect your personal things and anything else you need off the ship. If the video drive isn't found—which will be a security nightmare—or appears damaged, let me know. I'll secure you another copy. After the Midgard debrief, General Kowalski should release you to go home."

"It's going to be bad, isn't it, Admiral?" Jem said quietly.

Well, Wilmont wasn't completely clueless. "It depends on where the leaks happen and by whom. Remember, there's still that breach on Jaguide Three last year that Vanderbilt caused. No telling how well they'll contain it, especially since they're now an independent system." In fact, Gleason mused, they should get agents into the system to learn exactly that.

"Once leaks start, they'll bloom. Exponentially, unfortunately, due to the nature of the content. Eventually, the news media will—I quite agree," Gleason said when Jem and Thane both groaned. "Once they start blasting the information out, any expectation of anonymity is gone."

"It'll be a circus," Jem said bitterly. "Everyone will want to see the freak."

"Miss Wilmont." His voice was a whip. "I do not want to hear that word again. You have a unique and unusual ability. That is all. Do I make myself clear?"

Jem snapped her gaping mouth closed. "Y-yes, sir."

"We will do what we can to minimize the effects of all this because," he continued with a more normal tone, "that unusual ability does make you a valuable military asset. To that extend, and for the foreseeable future, the *Nero* will be stationed in the Wotan System and patrol alongside Wotan resources."

"You expect them to attack Midgard? Azusa?" Thane said, alarmed.

"No, that would definitely incite a war. Another ambush similar to yesterday is more likely. Or they'll try to sneak agents on-planet to do whatever. Vigilance will be our theme."

"That's not new either," Thane muttered.

"Major Markowitz. General Kowalski will update your orders as necessary as additional safeguards are put in place. By the way, you are receiving a commendation for that quick thinking on Tarragona."

His "Thank you, sir," was followed by a round of congratulations.

"If nothing else, I have a lot to do. Dismissed." At least he got a salute from the major.

* * * * *

They congregated in the hall outside the admiral's office. Thane asked Markowitz to help him retrieve their things from the *Tracker*.

"Jem is unskilled in zero gravity and the maintenance chief will go ballistic when I try to bring TACEXMs on board," he told him.

Markowitz nodded. "I'll get the admiral to authorize it. Hang on for a minute." He zipped back into the office.

"I'll go, too," Boyd said. "See what I can salvage from the lower deck. The extra O2 tanks at least should be good."

"Well, I guess I'm off to sit with Shiloh. We'll rendezvous…somewhere." She gave Thane a quick kiss and disappeared around a corner.

Markowitz popped back out and the three of them headed off to dock Eleven.

"Major, how sure is the admiral that he can use those 'earmarks' to point at the Consortium?" Thane asked, curious.

"It's the sequence of actions," Markowitz said. "The drone was the opening gambit, which had been kept deactivated to avoid detection until the last minute. When it failed, they were forced to take direct action. The first shot was to the lower level to take out the computer memory core and, if lucky, hit the oxygen recycler. Big boom, go home. No boom, so second shot on the upper level meant to cause depressurization and, possibly, take out the command/navigation console."

"Looks like they would have gone for the upper deck first," Thane said, thinking it over. "That's where we would be expected to be."

"And that would be *civilian* thinking. Which makes it more likely a military mind was behind it," Markowitz said, pushing open the door to

Eleven's locker room. "A ship's computer would override the pressure seal, keep it open until all personnel were safely below deck. Unless there's significantly more damage, the ship is still functional and headed for the nearest port."

"Which makes the memory core even more vital a target."

"Yep. Hi, there." Markowitz flashed a smile at the technician behind the counter. "Major Markowitz and friends. We need to sign out three suits and a sled."

"How big?"

"Three meters?" Markowitz replied, getting Thane's nod of agreement.

The salvage sled was a cargo-type container they'd anchor next to the *Lone Tracker's* hatch. Bags and netting accompanying it would be used to collect the items, then empty them into the enclosed sled. Thane wondered if the first sleds had been some kind of open container and the name had just hung on. The same way spaceport support areas were always called Circles, regardless of whatever terrain configuration they were built around.

History, Thane decided as he followed the tech into a locker room, could be very interesting. Or weird.

***

They gathered that evening in Jem and Thane's assigned quarters, it being the largest. They'd given Shiloh, newly released from the infirmary, the most comfy chair. Major Markowitz had given up all pretense and hovered in a nearby chair. Discussion had naturally turned to home.

Shiloh wondered how Martin 'the Myers' Stohlass had fared. Thane said he didn't give a damn except that he'd better be sitting in a cell. Jem wondered if Captain Kelding and Detective Bristol had cleaned up Danford's mess. Boyd said he hoped so and that Midgard's jail cells were overflowing. Markowitz looked forward to reintegrating with his team. He had no doubt Captain Tagawa was handling things well and said the command experience would look good on her record.

"By the way, I spoke with Admiral Gleason a short while ago," Markowitz said. "He's arranging for a small troop carrier to shuttle us to Midgard. Nothing fancy and even less privacy than on the *Tracker*, but transit time will be under four days.”

“That’s good, that’s good.” Thane sighed. “Not sure what I’ll do once we get back. No ship, remember.”

“Majority of Trackers don’t have one,” Boyd said dryly, “especially when starting out. They depend on public transport and the occasional courier pod. Being gifted with your parents’ old ship put you ahead of them.”

“Of course, you can always change careers. Put your name on that big office at Baron Financials,” Jem said blandly. “I know Gwen would love to have your counsel at all those meetings she goes to.”

The room filled with laughter as Thane’s woebegone expression morphed into horror.

“Aunt Gilida has been after Thane to join her Valhallass Dance troupe for years.” Shiloh’s eyes twinkled. “From what I hear, besides being an excellent free-gravity dancer, he was a pretty one. There were a lot of *late* dinner invitations.”

The horror had been replaced with embarrassment. “I was nineteen and it lasted one season,” Thane said, his cheeks gaining a reddish hue. “I filled in for one of the dancers who’d broken a leg.”

“Free-grav dancer, huh?” Boyd said, smirking. “I wondered where you’d gotten your zero-g experience. Some of those pirouettes were pretty artistic.”

Thane shot him a dirty look.

Jem patted his arm. “See? You do have options.”

“I’m buying a ship,” Thane stated loudly and firmly.

Laughter rang out again.

Chapter 35

Their landing at Odinheim Spaceport was quiet and uneventful. One of Markowitz's commandos, in civilian clothes, met them outside the main concourse and escorted them through a more private entrance. He led them to a closed van and they all climbed in. The driver was another commando.

"Status?" Markowitz asked as they pulled away from the curb.

Their escort looked over his shoulder. "The others are in a side parking lot. Two vehicles. Schwartz will pull in front as we come up to it, Timberline and McGee behind us. General Kowalski is waiting for you in his office."

Despite the office of Planetary Defense being next to the spaceport, it still took over thirty minutes to weave through the heavy traffic. The general's aide ushered them into the office and pressed a panel next to the door after closing it.

"Locked and secured," Lieutenant Lisa Corrigan said.

A tenseness Jem hadn't been aware of melted away. The room was now a physical and electronic vault. They settled in the chairs lined up in front of the general's desk. Jem's once-colorful neck had aged to a dull brown, but still drew a worried look from both of them.

"Well, you certainly stirred up a hornet's nest," General Kowalski commented.

"Not deliberately," Jem replied. "I'll admit things did not go as planned."

"Admiral Gleason's message did indicate events on Tricast Three went 'fubar' and that I'd get a full report on your arrival."

The five of them exchanged glances. "Just Tricast?" Thane asked.

"Nothing since?"

Kowalski's brow lifted. "Yes, and that Military Command was going ballistic. I take it something else has occurred?"

"Yes, sir." Thane pulled out the T-drive with the video he'd rescued from their bedroom. Handing it across the desk, he said, "I recommend the Tricast video first, then the *Nero's* report before ours." Those and several other reports had been added to the T-drive.

Motioning his aide to watch over his shoulder, Gleason plugged it into his desk comp. Lt. Corrigan flicked a couple of glances Jem's way as the video progressed, but the general's attention never left the screen. When Jem heard herself detailing her escape, she stared at the floor. The outline of Carlsson's image briefly wavering into view.

Then it was Major Markowitz's voice and his report on the AVs.

The general studied them after it finished. For a moment, it looked like he was going to say something, instead he activated the *Nero* report. He stiffened and Corrigan's hand flew to her mouth about five seconds into Captain Barnes's terse detailing of events. He turned a smoldering look to them as soon as it was over.

"I had assumed the troop carrier was an attempt to sneak you home quietly. How bad?"

"The maintenance report has the full list of damages," Thane said. "Admiral Gleason will arrange for a salvage yard to take it, minus the memory core. They will dispose of that."

They wouldn't want some tech genius to tweak out something they shouldn't know.

"Give me a verbal of your report."

Again, it didn't take long to describe getting rammed, side-swiped, lasered, and rescued.

Markowitz then added, "Admiral Gleason is assigning the *Nero* to patrol Wotan System—it should be in transit. He will be contacting you further about it." He frowned. "I'm surprised he hasn't already."

"Probably because he has his hands full with Military Command. If they had a meltdown on just his Tricast report... Dammit, there's a limit to how much Anton can mitigate the fallout." Kowalski taped his desktop a couple of times. "Major, you and your team are dismissed back to base but remain alert."

"Yes, sir."

"Lieutenant Corrigan will arrange a private shuttle—is the troop ship to remain here?"

"No, sir. It's expected to return to Anderson Station on your release. It also has a salvage sled with everything we recovered from the *Lone Tracker*."

"One of our small cargo transports then, Lieutenant. I'll inform the trooper he's released as soon as everything's off-loaded."

General Kowalski stood along with them. "Safe trip home. I recommend you batten your hatches tight when you get there."

***

The plane taxied to Cargo Dock One, where a limousine and a large truck waited. Fifteen minutes later, the limo pulled away. Late afternoon traffic was heavy and it took almost forty minutes to reach the Stohlass estate. The gates closed protectively behind them. Family poured out of the house, hugs and handshakes and questions bombarding them.

"It's a good thing Dad said to keep it quiet when he called or I'd have been shouting it all over the place," Reyna said, giving her son another tight hug.

"True," Gordon said with a wide grin. "Lieutenant Corrigan said you were coming 'incognito,' so I personally alerted a few of the family."

"A few?" Jem said with a laugh.

"Okay," Andi said, Dante draped across a shoulder, "you have to tell us what all happened."

Jem's smile died and she shared a look Thane. They both looked over at Shiloh, nestled in her mom's arm.

Gwen clapped her hands. "Everyone inside. Merle has refreshments waiting."

Stuart sidled up to them. "The truck bringing the salvage container will be here shortly. I'll have them park it next to one of the garages for the time being."

Jem waited till he was out of earshot then whispered, "Should we tell him about the case of TACEXMs?"

"Nope," Thane replied as they started to follow the rest inward.

"Hope there's something stronger than tea," Boyd muttered.

Chapter 36

"There is no way," Admiral Gleason said, fuming as they brought up that ridiculous idea for the hundredth time, "that Miss Wilmont will take up residence under military guard here on Earth." He'd spent the last three days reining in their demands. Of all the paranoid, egotistical, close-minded *idiots*.

He and his aide had rushed to Earth in a Class One Scout, a short eight hours transit from Anderson Station. His Class II flagship, *Solar Wind*, wouldn't arrive for at least another week.

Thank God he had done so. The high brass making up Military Command had been on the verge of issuing that abysmally dumb order. Dumb because it was unenforceable. After he related the attack on the *Lone Tracker*, there'd been nothing but frantic, paranoid rounds of suggestions on how to 'deal' with Jem Wilmont. What they needed to deal with was the Consortium.

He and the other five members of the Senior Council had been arguing all morning. "She doesn't need guards," Gleason continued. "She doesn't need to be dealt with. Miss Wilmont is a dedicated Republic citizen—"

"Whose rogue behavior is going to precipitate a war!" Army General Joseph Crantorri yelled.

"You have to agree," Admiral Linda Burgasov said, "her trip to Tricast Three was ill-advisable."

Beside the point now. "Have any of you *not* acted on information that was later found to be incomplete? Or wrong?" That earned him a bunch of sour looks. "Wilmont and friends expected to confront and, yes, intimidate a bunch of businessmen. They certainly did not expect AV-74 missiles pointed at them."

"If nothing else," Marine General Stephen Arita said, "we are now aware of several aspects of the Consortium's plans, including military involvement."

"Precisely," Gleason stressed. "We should be addressing what is potentially a hostile enemy, not trying to make one in Miss Wilmont."

They actually appeared to be mulling that. Had he finally gotten through to them?

Army General Katherine Pillen leaned forward. "All the more reason Miss Wilmont should be brought to Earth, her behavior moderated."

Evidently not. "That is being accomplished through her contract with Midgard's Planetary Defense Office," Gleason said through clenched teeth.

"Insufficient," Crantorri all but snarled. "What's to keep her from doing whatever the hell she wants, as evidenced by recent events? The woman needs to be *controlled*. By *us*."

"Just how do you expect to control a teleporter, General Cranky?" Admiral Gleason said, so exasperated he slipped and used his private nickname for the man.

The general reared back, affronted, before snapping, "Medical substances will render her compliant."

"Seriously?" Gleason responded with a derisive snort. "That will work exactly once. When you let the drugs lapse, for whatever task you want performed, she will vanish. Literally. Have you forgotten her reputation? Her nickname? Your paranoid idiocy will have cost the Republic one of its most valuable resources."

"Not if we use Nuralathenolate."

"Like hell," General Arita burst out. "I will not agree to that."

Gleason stared at Crantorri, unable to believe he'd even suggest using a drug that effectively turned people into automatons. Long term? The condition became permanent, even with the drug discontinued. "You want to turn Jem Wilmont into a zombie?" he spit out. "That makes no sense. She'll be totally unfit to perform any task."

Crantorri gave him a gleeful smile. "She doesn't need to."

"The operatives she'll transport to their objective will do that," General Pillen said.

"Or simply deliver explosives or other equipment to designated targets. Whatever is required," Marine General Colbert Cook added.

The *assholes*. They'd actively been discussing it.

In his hardest voice, Gleason said, "We are not destroying the will, the personality, and the mind of a young woman in the 'best interest' of the Republic." A phrase he'd come to hate. He evaluated the expressions around him. From the look of it, stone-faced Arita was the only other sane person in the room. *Shit, damn, crap*. Jem's favorite phrase seemed appropriate as he recognized their greed for the perfect tool. And weapon.

Not on his watch.

Admiral Gleason slowly pushed himself upright and took a deep breath. He spoke clearly and precisely so there'd be no ambiguity. "I, Admiral Anton StClair Gleason, Supreme Military Commander, hereby order all members of Military Command to stand down from any and all plans concerning Jem Wilmont. I will personally arrest and order the confinement of any one of you who thinks you know better than me."

Jaws dropped in shock.

Gleason stormed out of the council chamber. Furious at them, angry at himself. He should have found some way to avoid taking this step. Although, honestly, he didn't think there was one. This had been building since his arrival from Anderson Station. Hell, longer. Ever since the first news about Wilmont's ability slapped Military Command out of their complacency.

He skipped the elevator. Pounded down three flights of stairs, marched down a short hallway to a lounge and turned into the enclosed skywalk that joined Headquarters to the upper floors of its residency building. He stalked rapidly through it, people instinctively melting out of his path. Another hallway, then he strong-armed the door to his quarters open as soon as the lock released. He stopped in the middle of the room, trying to wrestle down his emotions.

Cmdr. Johnson, who'd maintained a silent presence behind him, closed the door.

"Paranoid, egotistical, close-minded assholes!" Gleason fumed. "I just clubbed MC into submission."

"They pushed you into a corner," Johnson pointed out. "For all we know, there's an OPs team either in transit to Midgard or being prepped to go."

"Agreed," Gleason said, kneading the back of his neck. Dammit, he hated losing control of his temper. Last time was hearing Hawthorne scream *shoot them* at General Kowalski. Which reminded him… "I need to get a message off to Sergi, brief him on the *Nero*." And MC.

"I'm sure Major Markowitz will let him know. They should be completing transit to Midgard any time now."

"I still need to formalize it," he said, dropping into the well-worn chair behind his desk.

Gleason's gaze rested for a few moments on the glass statue housekeeping had apparently tried to spruce up his quarters with. The swirling shades of blue were soothing. Meditative. However, the thing took up too much desk space, so he'd moved the statue to the bookcase behind him. He swiveled his chair around.

"Contact Senator President Alisha Dupont's office. Request another meeting as soon as possible." He needed to know of any upcoming Fed-Senate rulings that might affect patrol realignments. He'd outlined the Consortium's plans and tactics in a private meeting two days ago. 'Incensed' was the best description of her reaction.

All full-fledged Systems, regardless of size or population, had five Federal Senators to represent them equally in the combined Federal Senate on Earth. She'd promised to have a 'chat' with Vangaria's five. Both to warn them and to determine if any of them were in collusion with the Consortium.

"I also need appointments with Planetary Defense and Fleet Acquisitions," he said. "And get a copy of today's council recording."

Johnson's breath caught. "I'll do that immediately," he said before bustling out.

Gleason activated his computer. Reaching into a desk drawer, he pulled out the bottle of Aspric whisky Thane had gifted him. He didn't bother with a glass, just took two probably-not-wise swallows before returning the cap. As the burn worked its way down his throat, he had to admit he no longer trusted his fellow officers. Except Arita. He made a mental note to have a private conversation with the man.

He'd sent his encrypted file for General Kowalski to UPMS for overnight delivery when Johnson returned.

"You have appointments with Defense and Acquisitions tomorrow, sir. 0945 and 1300, respectively. Senator Dupont will be in committee until 1930. She will be happy to meet with you tonight at 2000 if that's amenable," he said.

"Excellent."

***

It was after midnight when Admiral Gleason returned from the Federal Senate building, a bit more upbeat than when he left HQ. Besides agreeing with his action in regards to Jem Wilmont, Senator Dupont informed him the Fed-Senate would be voting on several resolutions over the next few days that would directly affect relations with the Consortium.

"We didn't know what to make of all these new entities when it started," she'd told him. *"How to deal with them. Well, the days of hands-off are over. We will stand firm and make our position known, now and for any future pain-in-the-asses."*

"Think the Fed-Senate's resolutions will make a difference?" Cmdr. Johnson asked as they rode the elevator up from the underground parking area.

"Depends on a number of things," Gleason admitted. "If we're lucky, it will make them stop and think. Maybe reconsider a few things." He could always hope.

The elevator doors dinged open and they walked down the hallway. This late at night, their footsteps echoed eerily in the quiet. Gleason slid his key card into its slot, heard the lock disengage.

"If you don't need me, sir?" Johnson said, trying to hide a yawn.

"Sorry, but I'd like to go over something with you." He pushed the door open and activated the lights. "I'll compensate you with a glass of Thane's whisky."

"Won't turn that down, sir." Johnson closed the door behind them.

Nine seconds later, the explosion blew it off its hinges.

Chapter 37

General Kowalski worked his way down his morning's correspondence. Several he forwarded to be handled by Lt. Corrigan. Two notices of retirement ceremonies he put on his calendar. He'd definitely attend one, but had to think on the other one.

His brows drew in at the next two files' identifiers. Dupont? Not one of Midgard's Federal Senators. He activated the video file. Nope, he didn't recognize the stern-faced woman on his screen. Her short white hair had the roughshod-hand look.

"General Kowalski, I am Federal Senator President Alisha Dupont. A little over fifteen hours ago there was an assassination attempt on Admiral Anton Gleason."

Kowalski stiffened.

"Admiral Gleason was badly injured but survived. His aide, Lieutenant Commander Johnson, did not. I knew he was worried at our meeting last night when he asked me to contact you if anything happened to him. According to Admiral Gleason, the Military Command meetings have been extremely hostile lately. But this?" Her lips pressed tightly for a moment. *"Unacceptable. I will personally lead a Senatorial inquiry into how an explosive made its way into a supposedly secure government facility.*

"Anyway, he wanted you to know what happened and left me a copy of a recording to send to you. I don't know what's on it as it's encrypted. Still, I bet my next reelection it's from one of those MC council meetings."

She drew a deep breath. *"I don't know what's happening to us, General.*

The Republic appears to be falling apart, in more ways than one. You and Miss Wilmont watch your backs. Good luck." The video ended.

Kowalski stared at the blank screen for several minutes, processing what she'd said. What she'd implied. How it correlated with the information he'd received from his friend just yesterday. The attack must have happened soon after Anton sent his message. Two days, now. His chest knotted. Was he still alive?

He decrypted and activated the second video file.

* * * * *

Jem and Thane relaxed on the narrow terrace outside their fjord home, where they'd retreated to after a night at Thane's grandparents. Nestled inside one of the tree-lined slopes, it provided a much needed and secure getaway from the turbulent reality of their lives. Windows in all the main rooms eliminated any sense of claustrophobia, looking out over the fjord's waters and the cove holding their home's entrance and dock.

The family had found the Tarragona events disquieting. The attack disabling the *Lone Tracker* had changed that to a cold fury. In return, they'd learned that Martin Myers Stohlass was indeed in an Odinheim prison cell. His lawyer was claiming the recorded but non-sworn testimony provided by Jem Wilmont and Shiloh Stohlass was insufficient and a prejudiced collaboration against his client. He had managed to win a trial-stay until the women were available to testify in person, despite additional evidence provided by the Enforcers.

Jem had liked the way Gordon phrased it. *"Martin's boat is sunk and the moron is clinging to the mast hoping someone will come along and save him."* The roomful of snorts and comments that followed indicated what odds the family gave that.

Boyd had called this morning to let her know Thom Danford's organization had been taken down, all the way to its rotten roots. With all the charges pending, he and his senior thugs were most likely going to spend life on Hellspawn. He'd signed off with a cryptic comment about looking into the off-world organization called Dragonfly.

It was so nice, Jem thought stretching lazily, to bask in the sun and do nothing. No watching everything and everyone around them. The last of the past weeks' stress had finally melted away sometime during the night. She'd awakened refreshed. As had Thane. So they'd had a refreshingly good morning. Her eyelids drooped slightly at the memory.

She looked over, grateful to see the worry lines in her partner's forehead had smoothed out. He needed this respite as much as she did. They'd tackle reality later, say in a week or two. If nothing else, being kidnapped off-planet meant she had avoided the worse of Midgard's foggy winter. In fact, this nice, warm March spring day called for a swim.

About to make the suggestion to Thane, Freya's voice spoke from a hidden speaker.

"Jetter entering two-kilometer perimeter. Trajectory indicates Fjord as destination."

The comp brain's sensors were set to track anything within three kilometers, simply monitoring if it appeared to be passing through and alerting them if it wasn't.

They exchanged frowns. Visitors were rare, as a video call sufficed for most needs. Jetting was better than the usual hour-long boat trip, but no one had called to ensure they were home. They were waiting outside on the flagstone walkway when the jetter settled down with a blast of heated air.

"Damn."

Jem silently echoed Thane's sentiment. Not only was it General Kowalski's face underneath the helmet, it wasn't smiling.

"Well," Jem said, resigned, "at least we got two days."

"I know," Kowalski said, walking up to them. "I wouldn't have come if it wasn't important."

"Come on in and tell us about it," Thane grumbled, helping him out of his gear. Leaving it inside the entrance, they climbed the steps to the living area.

The general declined a drink and got straight to his reason. He told them about the assassination attempt, then played the council's audio recording. The silence afterward lasted about a minute.

"You believe it's one of them—the Military Council," Thane stated.

"I do," Kowalski said. "If not directly, then ordered by him, her—hell, could be any number of them behind it. They're all used to being in command, giving the orders, and can't see past their own agendas—all of which forced Anton to issue *his* order. Being slapped down like that would have rankled."

The anger-coated words told them just how furious the general was.

"You once said there were those who would do whatever they believed had to be done to ensure the Republic's safety. Still, having one of them go so far as assassinating one of their own?" Jem shook her head in disbelief. "And this drug, Nural-whatever?"

"Nuralathenolate. It's primarily reserved for violently psychotic patients."

"Are they that afraid of me, General?" Thane had inhaled sharply on hearing the drug's effects, while all she'd felt was resignation.

Kowalski sighed. "I honestly don't know what to think anymore, Jem. Worry…fear that you could be weaponized against us. Hearing this, I think it's grown into a control issue due to full-blown paranoia."

Jem bit her lip. *You are that dangerous.*

"They want a new toy to play with," Thane said, his tone sharp.

"That, too. From the way several of them spoke, they're already making plans. Makes me wonder what and against whom," Kowalski said darkly.

Jem gazed around her home, instinct telling her it would be a while before she was back. "What do you need, General?"

"Help," he said bluntly. "I need to go to Earth and I need to do it quickly. No telling what the MC has put into motion, especially now that the admiral is…indisposed. Lieutenant Corrigan will remain here, as my representative and eyes-and-ears. Markowitz and Tagawa will be her backup." He flashed a sharp-toothed grin. "With Anton alive, they are still under his—and my—direct chain of command and our orders cannot be countermanded.

"I tapped your mother, Thane. She is putting in a request through the Foundation to UPMS for a two-person pod leaving tomorrow morning. We will arrive as unnamed couriers at the Madrid Spaceport and take a shuttle to Military Command Headquarters in Brussels. Thane, you'll have to sit this one out," Kowalski said candidly. "Security will be even tighter now, and I intend to keep Jem's presence hidden as long as possible."

Thane's jaw flexed. "Understood."

"My *task* in this?" Jem asked, head tilted.

Kowalski gave a dry laugh. "Contract, right. Miss Wilmont, I formally request that you accompany me to Earth as my secret weapon to watch my back and investigate, as needed, the individuals who may be responsible for the attack on Admiral Gleason."

"I accept. Tomorrow morning, you said? Where should I meet you?"

They arranged a time and place and then the general jetted off.

Jem watched Thane watch Kowalski's dwindling figure through the terrace glass doors. She walked over, put her arms around his waist and her forehead against his back.

"I know, I'm not happy either," she said.

"We knew there would be fallout, but nothing like this. Fubar," he said on a sigh. He turned, her head now pressed against his chest and he put his arms around her. Rested his chin on her hair.

"I knew there would be times I couldn't go with you. But, dammit, this is bad, Jem. This stinks all the way to the Core. Betrayed by your own people. How do you know who to trust?"

Chapter 38

"I like Kuala Construction on Euphrates Five," Andi said as she accessed her engineering program. "The shipwright usually has a few basic frames ready to go and will customize the remainder per design. Cheaper, too, since they smelt ore from their own mines."

"There's nothing cheap about buying a spaceship," Thane muttered from his seat across from her. "Especially when you start adding non-standard things."

Andi's office was in the house behind GG's home. As Head of Security, Nicholas was on call 26/7, so they had moved into the guest cottage after their marriage. Located about a hundred meters away, it afforded them privacy yet accessibility. Stuart, his Second-in-Command, had happily moved into his old set of rooms inside the house.

Andi flashed him a grin. "You're a trillionaire now, you can afford it."

Not completely. Most of it was tied up in Baron Financial assets. Still, it had put a lot of zeros in his bank account.

"Okay, I've made a copy of the *Lone Tracker's* schematics, figuring you'd want to go with that size and style again."

"Definitely. It's perfect for mine and Jem's needs."

"Hmmm. Let's see…you want to keep the auxiliary ion engines?"

"And the laser canon," he added. Both had saved his butt at Magnus. He was not ever letting it be disabled again.

"I'll need a copy of your license to get that installation approved."

"I'll get one from the issuer tomorrow. Can you make the cooler a bit larger? Jem likes fresh fruits and vegetables.”

“There is a larger size available,” Andi said after a brief pause to check the options list. “You’ll lose the overhead cabinet.”

“Fine by me. Also, a multi-selector coffeemaker like on the larger ships. I had to keep bringing out the standalone to augment my small one.” Be nice if they didn’t need to use its highest setting very often. Thane stared off thoughtfully for a moment. “How hard would it be to add backup electronics? When the dome got smashed, we were all but blind.”

Andi sent an enigmatic look over her terminal. “You expecting a repeat?”

His laugh was humorless. “I wouldn’t bet against it.” Not with the volatile turn their lives had taken.

Andi pursed her lips and studied her screen. “That bank of lockers, top deck, between the hallway and stairwell. You use them for anything specific? Then we’ll use one or two of those spots. Got some ideas on that. Anything else?”

Thane sat back and ran several ideas past his brain. Brain. “Do you know how Dad managed to get a comp brain in the *Lone Tracker*? I’m going to get a basic computer in this new one, right?”

“Uh-huh. An Altus Five-Six with a rated Navigational module is the current model. Your dad had the computer core extended.”

“Where?” The ship didn’t have much in spare room.

Andi crooked her finger and Thane went to stand behind her.

“See here? This small wall section at the end of the hallway? Normally it’s thinner, standard width. Your dad had it widened and enclosed with a hollow core instead. That’s why your kitchen was about a third-meter narrower than it should’ve been.”

“Still not very big. It’s what? A meter in length?” Thane said, estimating how far down the hallway the core had stretched. Certainly not past the bathroom door.

Andi reached around and bopped him in the forehead. “A one-meter by third-meter shaft connected from the primary computer core on the lower deck all the way up to the dome electronics and chock-full of circuitry.”

Thane’s jaw dropped. That would do it. It would double the computing power.

"They'll need the Altus for the transit here. I'll have Kuala frame-in the kitchen, leaving the shaft seam open and handle the upgrade myself, here, at the Bocharova Shipyard. In fact, let's have Bocharova handle the rest of the interior. That way you can answer questions, make any changes, do spot checks and such."

Spot checks? The shipyard was located on the north coast of Stockholm—an hour-plus shuttle flight. "Can you do the upgrade? I mean…" he trailed off weakly at her glare.

"Just who do you think did all the work installing and programming Freya?" she demanded. "Did you forget about those special sensors I added to the *Lone Tracker* for you?"

"All thoroughly fantastic jobs, too," he said hastily, hurrying back to the safety of his chair. She was still shooting hot looks and muttering under her breath when Nicholas walked in.

He took one look and shook his head. "What'd you do, Thane?"

"Made a stupid comment."

Nicholas grinned "Really? Jem's only been gone a day and your brain's turned to mush?"

"Ha, ha," Thane retorted without any heat as the man walked over to check on Dante, sleeping in his daybed. Evidently not, as his father picked him up, a wide grin on his face. The man was totally gone over his son. Lucky guy.

"Anything else?" Thane asked, turning back.

"Yes, that license copy as soon as you can get it. Nick, are we cleared?"

"Leave is approved and ready to go when we are. BC shuttle *Argos Maiden* leaves tomorrow night, second stop is Euphrates Three. We'll take an inter-system shuttle to Five. Is that doable? Too soon?" He juggled Dante a couple of times. "I imagine most of our packing will be for this guy."

"That's plenty," she assured him.

"I'll confirm the reservations then."

"You're going physically?" Thane asked, surprised. "I thought you'd send them schematics and notes."

"I could, but then it'd be weeks of back-and-forth. Them asking questions, confirming design, then dickering over deposit or final cost. Being on-the-spot saves a lot of time and argument. Unless you don't mind waiting?" she added, head cocked.

"No, no. Personal works great."

"I'm going to make sure she doesn't go climbing over ship frames. Which you have no business doing," he admonished when Andi rolled her eyes. "By the way, Thane," Nicholas said, "Gwen asked for you to come up to the main house. She wants to talk to you about something."

"Baron Financials?" Thane asked, his expression pained.

"Didn't say."

"See you at supper?"

"Uh-huh. There's going to be a lot of Dante-cuddling before we leave."

Forty-five minutes later, Thane was making a reservation on the *Argos Maiden* himself. His grandmother had decided that, with the expansions planned for both Baron Financials and Stohlass Enterprises, they needed their own business class shuttle. Thane had agreed to the eventual need, though not now. He did offer to go assess the available models. It mollified his grandmother and allowed him to personally pick out his next ship. Dodging a lot of BF drudgery was a bonus.

Chapter 39

General Kowalski checked in at the front desk of Belgique Earth Force Residency. Tired and grumpy, he rode the elevator to the thirty-seventh floor. It had been a long time since he'd used commercial transportation. His ears were still ringing from the unhappy twin toddlers two rows back. He sincerely hoped the room's minibar was stocked.

The door unlocked and he marched in. Dropping his bag in a chair he headed straight for the bar. Hallelujah, there was whisky. He was taking his third sip when Jem suddenly materialized. His hand jerked, sloshing drink on his chin.

"Oops, sorry."

That twinkle she sported said different. "I'll get used to it," he said, wiping his chin with his shirt sleeve.

"Cameras in lobby, elevators, and hallways, like you said. Took a quick look around before popping in. Didn't see any in here," Jem said, pulling off her short blond wig.

"That would be illegal, even for military quarters."

"We know someone's ignoring the rules," Jem said, scratching her head.

Kowalski saw the automatic reach for her braid; saw the quickly hidden wince. Regrettable, but there'd been no way to fit all that beautiful, hip-length hair under a wig. *It'll grow back*, she'd assured everyone, even as she avoided looking at the pile behind her. Their insistence that the shoulder-length style Merle's niece had given her looked good had helped…somewhat.

He finished off his drink. "I'm going to contact Senator Dupont, find out where Anton is and who I need to yell at for authorization."

"Huh?"

"Botched assassination on an Admiral? He'll be under maximum guard with an authorized-only access list." And hope the responsible party isn't on it.

"I'll visit the security office while you're gone. Basement? Great. I'll check for any gaps in their monitoring. Then I'll pay a visit to Admiral Gleason's room."

"Top floor, suite 4210." Kowalski tapped his glass. "It's been his assigned quarters since he first made admiral."

"Well, that certainly made it easy. He doesn't have a home of his own?"

"He didn't see a reason for one. Anton's had a few short-term relationships over the years, but he's never settled down. The military is his life."

"Is that why he was selected to be Supreme Admiral?"

Kowalski leaned against a desk. "That, and the fact he's a highly respected leader. Most never return to space duty once they make admiral rank. They sit in cushy command offices somewhere and send others out. Anton? He's happiest when sitting on a bridge issuing orders. Earth Force lost an outstanding captain when he was promoted, but thank Odin they did. Could you imagine Hawthorne as a Supreme Admiral?"

"Oh, my God, no."

The now-retired admiral had tried to trap her. He'd nearly come to blows with the egotistic bastard himself.

"We need Anton, Jem," he said somberly. "We need his expertise and his wisdom and his compassion. Mostly, we need his leadership through whatever mess the Republic is heading into."

Jem stepped forward and laid a hand on his arm. "Go visit your friend, General. I'll see what I can find." She vanished.

Poofed, as she called it. He shook his head. Maybe he'd get used to it. He moved behind the desk, activated the computer, and switched it to communication mode.

***

General Kowalski strode into General Arita's office ahead of the protesting lieutenant trying to stop him.

"I'm sorry, sir. I couldn't stop him. He says he's—"

"General Sergi Kowalski of Wotan Two," Arita said brusquely.

The young man's mouth snapped shut.

"It's quite alright, Jenkins. Close the door behind you."

The two generals eyed each other as Jenkins hastily complied.

"General Kowalski, please take a seat," was delivered with polite irritation.

"You know me?"

"The man who brokered a contract with Jem Wilmont? The man who's protected her from various FLEA and military offices? Do you think I wouldn't have investigated you?"

I, not we.

"I also know you're a good friend of Admiral Gleason, which I'm assuming is why you are here…unofficially," he added, glancing at Kowalski's civilian clothes. "I'd be interested in knowing how you heard, since we've kept it quiet."

"Senator Dupont. Would it surprise you to learn Anton expected something to happen to him?" Apparently, it did. "He asked her to contact me in that case. He'd already sent me a long message concerning MC's paranoia toward Miss Wilmont and growing hostility toward him. I also received a copy of that last meeting's recording. It wasn't hostile, General, it was malignant." He leaned forward. "Someone here, in Military Command, is behind the assassination attempt. You know it and I intend to prove it."

Arita's stone-faced expression gave him no inkling of how he'd respond. He was taking a risk, but his guts and research made him believe the Marine general wouldn't be a party to assassination. Of course, it wouldn't be the first time he'd miscalculated either.

After a moment, the man nodded.

"You're right. It couldn't have been done otherwise. The question is still *how*. I've gone over sensor data, the reports, the video recordings I don't know how many times. No one entered the suite between the times he and Commander Johnson left and their return. There is absolutely *nothing* to show how an explosive was placed in the admiral's suite. Is there another fucking ghost out there?”

The frustration and anger coating Arita’s tirade couldn’t be faked. Okay, then. One down, four more to go. At least one on the Senior Council had to be involved.

“Don’t think so. You know Wilmont’s ability isn’t natural. You didn’t?” Kowalski said, surprised. Oh, right. He’d left that out of his reports. “The Myerstone Lab, here on Earth, was trying to create an instantaneous transfer system based on the same Otanak principles the O-drives use. An experiment went haywire, she was caught up in it with resulting DNA-slash-cellular mutated changes. The lab was later sabotaged and destroyed, so it’s unlikely to ever to be duplicated,” Kowalski finished. Few knew that Jem had a copy of their notes safely hidden away.

Arita mulled his information for a moment. “While it’s possible someone else could have evolved a teleport ability naturally, it’s a bit extreme and, for sanity’s sake, we’ll pass on that idea for now.”

That was an interesting stance. “Which puts us back to how.”

“A full investigation is on-going. As a matter of fact, I was studying a number of reports when you barged in. No security breaches, no sensor blackouts, nothing.” Arita paused, leaned back in his chair. “Kind of reminds me of recent reports from Palmyra Two.”

Kowalski snorted. “You know very well Jem was on Midgard when it happened.”

Arita nodded slowly. “But she would make an excellent scapegoat. It will also justify their plans toward Miss Wilmont.”

Their, not our. Second time he’d separated himself from the others. “Sounds as if you’re not in complete agreement with the others,” he probed cautiously.

“We have our differences of opinion,” he replied.

“Especially about Nuralathenolate.”

“I would never agree to use that on anyone,” he said in frosty tones.

Kowalski tapped his leg. “Can you get me copies of all those reports? Fresh eyes and all that.”

“No need. I’ll have my aide set you up with a desk here.”

"Thank you, but I'd rather have the copies so I can study them as I get time. I'm staying next door. The computers in the rooms there are secure, yes?" he asked blandly.

"They are," Arita said slowly, his gaze holding Kowalski's. "That would allow for independent review. You have…help?"

He wasn't about to confirm Arita's suspicion. Without a twitch in voice or expression, Kowalski told him he'd left his aide on Midgard to keep the office running and that Senator Dupont had offered her staff's help as needed.

"By the way, can you get me in to see Anton? Admiral Burgasov has refused to allow me visitation. Considering I couldn't have planted the bomb in his quarters, she has no grounds to."

"She is undoubtedly being extra careful due to the unusual circumstances. We all are." Standing, Arita flashed him a sharp-edged smile. "Which is why two of *my* Marine guards are posted at Admiral Gleason's hospital door and one on each end of the corridor. The private facility he was taken to is two blocks away. We can walk."

***

"Anton, you look like shit," Kowalski said, trying for lightness and hoping his dismay didn't show. Burns and lacerations. Concussion. An oxygen tube draped among the lines hooked to him.

"Better than Johnson. Dammit, Sergi." He stopped to take a couple of shallow breaths.

"Lieutenant Commander Johnson was a good man," Kowalski said quietly. "Has his family been notified?" he asked Arita.

Arita shook his head. "The whole incident is being kept quiet for the time being. Admiral Gleason, I know it may be difficult, but what do you remember?"

Anton's unbandaged eye closed. Remembering? Unconscious? It opened again.

"I'd gone to a meeting with Senator Dupont. Johnson drove."

Kowalski frowned at one of the displays over Anton's head. Its squiggle had gotten larger.

"I was going to discuss…something with him when we got back to my quarters. Don't remember what now."

"Easy, Anton, don't worry about it," Kowalski cautioned as the squiggle got larger and a soft beeping started. "You're doing great as it is."

"Going to have drinks." Pause. "Johnson went to get…bottle…from desk." Shallow breaths. "I was getting glasses…" The beeping suddenly got louder. He raised his head off the pillow. "Find the bastards," he demanded, fire in the eye glaring at them.

A doctor came scurrying into the room. "I specified the patient was *not* to be agitated." He moved to the head of the bed and made an adjustment. The beeping stopped. He made a second adjustment to the I-V, and the admiral's eye closed.

Just as well, Kowalski thought grimly. His friend needed his rest and he'd given them all he could.

"What are you doing here anyway?" the doctor said, glaring.

"My question, exactly," Admiral Burgasov said from the doorway. Both generals turned as she strode into the room. "I gave explicit instructions that I alone was to be informed as soon as Admiral Gleason regained consciousness."

"And what makes you think you have exclusivity over Admiral Gleason?" General Arita asked coldly.

"Because I am his peer," she said haughtily.

Kowalski's lip curled. *Not even close.*

"Last time I checked, we were all equally one step *below* him," Arita responded icily. "Is that belief why your name is the single one on the access list?"

"Which begs the question of how you got in."

Arita pointed to himself. "Senior member, Earth Military Council. All the Senior Council should be on it."

"We both know why not."

"Yes," Kowalski snapped. "One of you is responsible for his condition and the death of his aide." That got her attention.

"Who the hell are you?" she demanded.

"General Kowalski." It was rude. Not that he cared.

"Of Wotan Two? Who has a contract with Jem Wilmont?"

"Who is a long-time friend of Admiral Gleason. I came as soon as I heard, figuring he needed at least one friend here." He didn't even try to keep the hostility out of his voice.

"You're insubordinate."

"Don't think so. My four stars equal yours." Kowalski didn't miss the gleam in Arita's eyes. *Don't laugh, you'll ruin my moment.*

Burgasov decided to ignore him. "Doctor Inness? What is the admiral's status?"

"Stable, for the moment. The lung and liver damage due to the pressure wave is the most serious. He will—"

"Can he be brought back to consciousness?" Burgasov interrupted.

"Why?" Kowalski and Arita both said.

"His memories may contain a clue to how and who perpetrated this crime."

"I don't recommend it," Doctor Inness said firmly. "His condition requires—"

"The decision is not yours," Burgasov said, cutting in again.

"It sure as hell isn't yours," Kowalski said hotly.

"You shouldn't be here," she snapped back.

"None of you should be here," said a cold voice.

Spinning, Kowalski found a tall, hard-eyed man filling half the hospital's large doorway. The guy's muscles must have muscles, which he found more impressive than the two stars on the Marine's shoulder lapels.

"I have not authorized any outside visitors," Burgasov said frostily.

"You aren't authorizing anything, Admiral Burgasov," he replied brusquely. "Major General Ian Morelli, Inspector, Earth Force Office of Special Investigations."

Burgasov's mouth snapped shut, swallowing whatever she'd been about to say.

The equally hard-eyed woman following him in wore silver eagles on an Army uniform.

"My associate, Colonel MaryJean Shannon. We are taking over this investigation, which should have been brought to EFOSI moments after it happened. Whose benighted idea was it to not do so?"

"It was our decision as Senior Council," she said stiffly. "We wanted to keep the investigation quiet and inhouse."

"Of course," General Morelli said, his voice losing a few more degrees. "It'd be embarrassing for people to learn their military leaders are blowing each other up."

Kowalski pressed his lips together to hide a grin. Must not have worked, as Morelli aimed a piercing glare at him. Anticipating the Inspector General, he said, "General Sergi Harmon Kowalski of Midgard, Wotan Two."

"And your presence here?"

Kowalski looked at the still figure on the bed. Met the man's gaze. "To find out who tried to kill my friend."

Chapter 40

Click. Jem shifted as the door lock disengaged. Seeing it was Kowalski, alone, she shifted back after the door closed behind him. Once again, the general headed straight for the whisky. Ouch. Not a good sign. Filling a glass, he plopped down in a chair and leaned his head against the headrest. Jem slipped onto the small couch opposite and waited.

"Anton has second- and third-degree burns, a mid-grade concussion, blown eardrums, damaged liver and lung, numerous cuts and gouges that also took out his right eye. But he's alive." He took a large swallow then gave Jem a weak smile. "And pissed."

"He's conscious then?" she said, relief surging through her.

"Briefly and pumped up on meds but, yeah." Another smile came and went. He gave her a summary of what the admiral had told them, then the interchange that followed, concluding with the EFOSI's arrival and tossing everyone out, including the doctor.

"This Inspector General…is that going to cause trouble for us?" Jem asked.

"No, and I'm glad he's here. According to General Arita, Admiral Burgasov has gotten full of herself lately. I'm also pretty sure Arita is the one who tipped off the EFOSI. They *should* have been involved from the beginning—hell, their HQ is on the other side of town. It's another black mark against the MC council. Morelli and Shannon are but the tip of the iceberg. There will be others behind them, digging into each and every one of the council members, their aides, staff…hell, everyone in Military Command or has access to the Residency."

He shook his head. "This is an unprecedented event, Jem, a supernova that is going to burn any number of careers. They *have* to resolve it, completely and openly, or else it'll erode trust right down to our foundations."

"Trust," she said quietly, "that those like you have striven so hard to earn." He'd certainly earned hers. He'd walked a thin line with his superiors, left certain information out of his reports. Negotiated a contract. All in an effort to prevent her exploitation.

Kowalski blinked, then gave her a wan smile of thanks. "What did you learn?"

"The building's security is tight. They're a bit rattled and a lot scared. Since nothing shows up in any of the sensor or video scans, they know it's a logical assumption that someone must have altered one or both. That puts them in the hot seat."

"It's going to get even hotter now with OSI involved because that's exactly what they'll look at first," Kowalski said, sipping on his whisky.

"The front room of the admiral's suite is pretty much demolished. The master bedroom is pretty bad too, but that's because of the large hole in the wall between them. The remaining rooms were singed, I guess you could say, but mostly okay."

"Minimized destruction," Kowalski summed up. "Which is why Anton is alive. He was across the room from the blast epicenter. Arita said it was somewhere around the desk, probably close to that hole in the wall. I know I spend a lot of my time at my desk and Anton undoubtedly did too. It was a good—if bastardly plan, which had to have taken more than one person to put together. Unfortunately, it was Commander Johnson who tripped it when he went to get the whisky bottle from the desk drawer."

In the silence that followed, Jem reflected on the fickleness of fate and the difference one small act could make.

***

Jem's scouting trips the next morning started with the Security Office where, yep, Colonel Shannon was grilling the Security Chief. He candidly admitted he was at a loss to how it was done, and vehemently denied their data had been tampered with. Then she asked about the protocols for unauthorized building access. He insisted they covered all contingencies.

"For instance, Colonel, when we lost power two weeks ago, teams were immediately dispatched and all building accesses were secured within five minutes."

"They climbed forty-two flights of stairs under five minutes?"

"Uh, no, ma'am. Two teams from the HQ building covered the skywalks at the forty-second and twentieth floors."

"HQ still had power?" she asked sharply.

"Yes, ma'am. Only our building was affected by two blown circuit breakers due to a power surge. There was a thunderstorm at the time; lightning must have struck nearby. Power was reestablished in fifteen minutes and an immediate sweep of the entire building was performed. No intruders, no unexpected findings."

"Why is there no backup to the power system?"

"I have recommended that, Colonel," the chief said in a neutral tone. *"It keeps getting denied as redundant. It's deemed the city has sufficient fail-safes and backups."*

Kowalski had laughed when she repeated that last part, saying the facility manager would be standing tall in front of someone's desk for that.

Jem sprawled on the couch now, drained. Her second trip had lasted only about seventy minutes, instead of her usual ninety. Still, she'd managed to browse through most of the administrative offices before hurrying back to the room.

"Providing General Morelli with an office for his use and questioning of personnel is standard," Kowalski said after she relayed her information. "HQ keeps several offices just for visitors."

"From what little I observed," Jem said dryly, "it was more interrogation than questioning. Also, he's not happy with his guest account. He wants full access to all MC records. Says he can't properly investigate without knowing all the 'motivational' factors."

Kowalski shrugged. "He's not wrong, but he's also not getting it. I'm sure he's already heard about the main subject of contention—you. That would be considered sufficient.”

“That’s more or less what General Crantorri told him.” Jem chuckled. “Cranky does describe him. He wasn’t pleased at being escorted in by two security guards. To quote him, ‘hauled in like some errant ensign.’” Remarkably similar to that Tarragona lawyer.

Kowalski tapped his chair arm. “Strategy, I think. Senior rank is usually handled with more finesse. Not getting it will throw them off and perhaps cause something to inadvertently slip out. Are you alright?”

Jem’s eyelids flew up. Her head had fallen back against a cushion. “Yes, just tired. This is the first time I’ve tried doing two full shifts so close together.”

Kowalski pursed his lips thoughtfully. “You had a two-hour break between them. The second one was shorter? Thought so,” he muttered when she nodded. “Multiple shifting and endurance are something we should have tested.”

“I’m sorry, sir. Looks like I’m not going to be as much help as you expected.”

The General’s eyebrows winged up. “Are you kidding? You’ll just need to do it in smaller chunks so as not to overextend yourself.”

“Well, then I’m going to take a nap. Wake me in…forty-five minutes.”

***

Jem managed two more short trips to ‘peek’ over the IG’s shoulder. Then she and General Kowalski went over the reports and video General Arita had provided. They even watched the hallway security video showing Admiral Gleason’s quarters in slow motion.

Two people Kowalski identified as aides walked past Gleason’s door. Then a guy running at breakneck speed came from the opposite direction. They briefly debated the reason: late for a meeting? A flag officer needing something yesterday? Jem snickered at several incidents Kowalski reminisced about from his younger, lower-ranking days.

Resuming the video, Admiral Burgasov stopped and knocked on the door several times. Getting no answer, she proceeded on out of view. General Crantorri started to pass by, then reversed and pounded on the door. Two looky-loos stopped to gawk until driven off by his aide’s scowl. Crantorri finally stomped off.

"He really is the cranky type, isn't he," Kowalski remarked.

They watched at least a dozen others passing in either direction as the timestamp clicked toward midnight.

"Fairly busy hallway," Jem commented.

"Anton's quarters are around the corner from the skywalk."

Ugh. At least he didn't have to listen to an annoying ding like she had, the last time she'd roomed close to an elevator.

Then nothing, until the admiral and his aide appeared and entered his quarters. Then came the blast. The video stopped on smoke seeping out of the damaged doorway. There were no blips, no sudden shifts, nothing to indicate a portion had been deleted or overwritten. They stared at the frozen image grimly.

Later that night, Jem returned to Morelli's assigned office. Plugging a T-drive into the desk computer, she downloaded a copy of his day's files. His password had been fairly simple to memorize. She added two files Colonel Shannon had forwarded to him.

Kowalski was frowning when she returned. "I don't like this."

"I can't spend all day in ghost-mode, so this is the only way we're going to learn what questions Morelli is asking and what they're telling him. If we can't narrow it down to the most likely, we'll never have a chance to solve this," Jem told him bluntly.

"Yeah, well, I still don't like it."

Chapter 41

General Morelli crossed his arms and leaned back in his chair. Looking at his partner busily typing away on her keyboard, he said, "We have a problem, MJ."

"Too many frigging suspects with entitled attitudes?" she said without looking up.

"Somebody accessed this computer, from here, last night at 2310." It's a good thing he'd loaded that hidden program into memory.

Shannon's head jerked up and she spat a cuss word.

"Using the password I created yesterday," he continued, "and performed several copy commands. We can assume someone has all of our reports."

"I'll check the security feed," she said, shooting out of her chair.

Morelli stared at his comp screen, pissed, yet intrigued. How did they get the password? His sneaky program reported a single entry, no fumbling or repeated tries. Craning his neck around, he verified there were no cameras discreetly, and illegally, placed behind or above his desk.

MJ returned, fuming. "Timestamps appear uninterrupted with no sign of anyone entering between when we left at 2240 and our arrival this morning. Someone in security is dirty."

He shook his head. "If they were in the network, they would have logged in remotely to retrieve the information then scoured the record. Whoever it was, they had to physically access the computer *here* while employing whatever means to keep from being seen."

"Well, they certainly did that," she said, frustrated.

"I revise my statement," Morelli said. "Military Command has a problem."

Chapter 42

Kowalski fumbled his phone when Jem suddenly popped in, right in front of him. "Dammit, Jem."

"We have a problem," she said.

"What's one more?" he said, exasperated.

"Both General Morelli and Colonel Shannon are reviewing Military Command's files on me."

"And that surprises you?" he said, relaxing. "Controversy about you has dominated MC discussions for months. To *not* research it, or consider it as a possible motive behind Anton's attack, would be dereliction approaching deliberate blindness. Don't worry. Your teleport ability is not mentioned in the general files. Those few who do know about it have been briefed separately under a different classification category."

"Those files are pretty in-depth. Like General Arita said, I'd be the perfect scapegoat if they—we—can't figure it out."

"They can't do that, Jem. You have an unshakeable alibi. Military Command might try to run roughshod over you, but General Morelli and EFOSI won't."

Jem chewed her lip for a second. "I hope so."

Considering her past experiences, she was entitled to pessimism. "Doctor Inness called, says Anton has asked to see me. I'm going to see Morelli about getting access. I'll bring back food. Oh! Arita sent a file, names with pictures, listing everyone in the hallway video."

"I'll review it again while you're gone. Maybe I'll spot something new."

* * * * *

Jem browsed the HQ corridors after giving up on the video, hoping to see or hear something worthwhile there. She passed a couple of small huddled groups conversing in low tones and continually casting worried looks around. *Wouldn't do to be caught debating who tried to kill Admiral Gleason.* She was mildly surprised to overhear references to Consortium spies. Guess that would be a logical assumption. Had Admiral Gleason's Anderson Station reports made the rounds yet?

Admiral Burgasov exited an office and speed-walked down the hall. Curious, Jem trailed along behind. The admiral's phone rang. She pulled it out of her purse, glanced at it, and put it back without missing a step as she turned a corner. Boy, the woman had that down to an art. Burgasov turned down another hallway then into a conference room. The door closing behind her was no deterrent, as Jem phased through it to find the room full of brass. The other four Senior Council members were there, along with about a dozen lower-ranked admirals and generals.

Jem listened for a half hour where she was the main topic of discussion. Surprisingly, there was very little said about the assassination attempt. Well, maybe not. They had to know that at least one of them was responsible and was probably sitting in the room. That would account for all the sideway glances and tense atmosphere.

Her eyes narrowed on hearing there was a Special Operations team on standby that Generals Pillen and Crantorri wanted to deploy to Midgard. General Arita reminded them that was impossible unless Admiral Gleason either rescinded his order or died-slash-retired and someone else then countered it. The way Burgasov's eyes lit up, Jem had a hunch she was fishing for the Supreme Admiral promotion. Especially when she launched into a fairly aggressive debate with the others about dealing with the Consortium.

Feeling a tug of tiredness, Jem hurried back to their room. Kowalski was waiting with a bag that emitted a wonderful odor. She munched while he talked. His visit with Admiral Gleason had been brief, due to both his injuries and tests the doctors had scheduled. Nor had his friend remembered anything new to help resolve the attack.

Jem swallowed. "I'm surprised General Morelli allowed the visit."

"No reason not to. I'm probably one of the few he knows for sure isn't guilty, including Senator Dupont." He chuckled. "Spotted her arguing with the receptionist on my way out so I took her to lunch. I updated her about Anton's condition, she updated me on the Fed-Senate. They've passed several diplomatic resolutions."

"I thought they were already in place."

"So did I. Secession has caught everyone off-guard. Senator Dupont says they dredged up those old Earth traditions to deal with it, then people stood around 'flapping their gums and making noise' as she put it. As of now, those traditions have been converted to a set of protocols that have legal standing."

"Well, it seems Military Command may be adopting some new protocols, too." Jem then told him what she'd overheard. The wall was getting a good frowning from Kowalski by the time she finished. She ate the last of her sandwich and dragged a couple of fries through ketchup while he pondered.

"What is your overall impression?" he finally asked.

"Shock. Disbelief. Denial. Did it really happen here, at HQ, and by one of them? Everyone is looking sideways at everyone else. Was it them? Was it Consortium subversion agents seeking to weaken our military leadership?"

Kowalski's brows drew down. "I suppose that last is a vague possibility, given what we now know."

"Most are in a wait-and-see mode," Jem continued, "waiting for the OSI to finish its investigation and, quite frankly, worried at what they'll find. Oh. I think Admiral Burgasov is thinking she'll be the next Supreme Commander."

Kowalski shook his head. "That rank was established for wartime conditions. Anton was the very first, promoted up to deal with Beckett's pirates. He'll keep it for life, but there won't be another unless…" he trailed off.

"Unless there's another, similar reason," Jem finished for him. Was the attack on the *Lone Tracker* a prelude? Was war with the Consortium in their future?

* * * * *

Kowalski rubbed his neck. "Let's hope there's not. If General Morelli doesn't find—" He cut off sharply at the loud knock on the door.

Jem bolted up.

They did a quick scan for anything pointing to her presence. Nothing. She disappeared into the bedroom as he sauntered to the door. General Morelli stood on the other side.

"May I come in?"

Kowalski opened the door wider and stepped back. "I take it you have questions for me," he said, closing the door.

"More like clarification. Late dinner?"

"Yes, I was out and about earlier, as you well know. Give me a moment."

Kowalski popped the last fries in his mouth, sans the detested ketchup. He wadded up all the wrappings, stuffed them in the bag, and deposited it in the recycle bin. "Would you like something to drink while I'm over here?" he asked politely.

"Thank you, no." Morelli sat down in the chair Kowalski had been warming.

Kowalski took the couch opposite, sliding Jem's hand comp to the side as if he'd been reviewing something on it.

"I asked you once, and I'll ask again. Why are you here?"

Kowalski gave him a puzzled look. "To learn what happened to my friend, as I said."

Morelli gave him a hard look. "You are Wotan Two's Planetary Defense Commander. You up and left your post to come to Earth to perform an investigation you have no authority to conduct?"

"Yes." That took the wind out of his sails. "And I'm on leave, not AWOL."

"How close of a friend are the two of you?"

Kowalski chuckled. "Not *that* close. I have a wife and two sons." He leaned forward, arms resting on thighs. "Anton needs someone to watch over him. Someone he can trust and, yes, I planned on doing some snooping. Your arrival superseded that. They *have* to talk to you." All he was getting was scowls and cold shoulders. They saw him as an outsider, something he hadn't expected and highly resented.

Morelli's phone rang. He answered it, listening for two minutes with his eyes never leaving Kowalski. "Thank you. Please join us."

Kowalski watched him put away his phone, getting a distinct 'oh, shit' feeling.

"Where is Jem Wilmont?" Morelli said without preamble.

Kowalski blinked. "She should be on Midgard—Wotan Two."

"That was Colonel Shannon. She has verified that you and an unknown woman arrived via UPMS pod at the Madrid Spaceport. You both traveled to Brussels on public transport, paid by cash card. The blue-eyed blond—whose other features are remarkably similar to Jem Wilmont—has disappeared."

Kowalski remained silent. The 'oh shit' feeling morphed into something stronger.

His voice hard and tightly controlled, Morelli continued. "'Should be' is a prevarication because you know damn well she isn't on Midgard. What I think, General Kowalski, is that you brought Miss Wilmont, in disguise, to do the snooping. A woman with a proven reputation of getting past level seven security in all its forms. That it was she who accessed my computer last night and copied a number of files. You are complicit in an unauthorized civilian accessing military facilities and classified military files. Is there a reason you should not be court-martialed and stripped of rank?"

They'd been caught by a monitoring program of some sort. Okay, fine.

"Jem Wilmont is not entirely a civilian," Kowalski responded in clipped tones. "She is listed as a military asset under the Midgard Planetary Defense Office and, due to circumstances, has a fairly high security clearance. I have a five-year contract with her to perform tasks that meet certain criteria and on an as-needed basis. I have tasked her, under that contract, to investigate the attempted assassination of Admiral Gleason that also resulted in the death of his aide." *Thank Odin she had insisted.*

Morelli leaned back in his chair and studied him. "All right," he said after a moment, "I'll accept that."

But you don't like it. "How much do you know about Jem Wilmont?"

"Not as much as I should. There's damn little in the files I can view, and I've been refused access to other files despite having the clearance for them. I'm investigating a murder and attempted murder at Military Command Headquarters. And they tell me I don't have the need to know?" Morelli's voice thickened with irritation.

Kowalski briefly sympathized with him. He'd experienced the same frustration of having information withheld and for the same reason.

"I'm assuming you are keeping her presence secret to keep the culprits off-guard and from destroying any incriminating evidence," Morelli continued. "There are too many safeguards for just one person to have accomplished this. That, or we have a very wily troop that should be in a Commando Unit and not sitting behind a desk." He let out an exasperated huff. "We both want the same thing and, honestly, I'm not getting very far. Can we work together?"

"Yes," Jem said, walking around the corner from the bedroom. "As long as you understand I work for General Kowalski and, by extension, Admiral Gleason."

Before he could reply, there was another knock on the door. Colonel Shannon went straight to Morelli, who proceeded to give her a condensed summary of their conversation. She took the other chair on Morelli's left and Jem sat beside Kowalski.

"Have you learned anything helpful in your snooping?" Morelli asked, eyeing Jem.

"This has been planned for a while," she replied, "and were waiting for the right time to implement it. I believe the bomb was put in place about two weeks ago, during a fifteen-minute blackout caused by a power surge from, supposedly, a lightning strike."

Shannon looked at Morelli, got a head nod.

"Agreed," the colonel said. "Forensics found numerous blue glass-slivers radiating outward from the area around the desk and embedded in Commander Johnson. I've spoken with the person responsible for that floor in housekeeping. He remembers seeing a blue glass sculpture on the admiral's desk, then later on the bookshelf behind it. He doesn't remember exactly when it first appeared, but he's sure it was there *before* Admiral Gleason returned from his last trip.

"Besides getting room access, using a timer would be too unpredictable: was target in the room, sitting at the desk, etc. Therefore, we're assuming the explosive was triggered by proximity. Admiral Gleason and his aide were in, out, and around that desk for several days prior to the explosion. Not to mention, physically moving the damn thing. So, when and how was it activated?"

If they knew that, Kowalski grumped silently, they'd know who was responsible.

"This is a premediated act of at least two people," Morelli said. "That makes it highly unlikely it's a personal grudge, unless someone talked an idiot into helping them. That leaves career." He studied Jem for a moment. "There seems to be a lot of discussion about you though, again, I can't get any substance as to why. I have to admit, after seeing—or not seeing—how you accessed my computer last night, it would be a legitimate concern. If the methods you utilize fell into the wrong hands it would be a security nightmare." He made a face. "Would that still be worth assassinating an admiral?"

"In this case, General Morelli, it is," Jem told him. "It's fear of others coercing me. It's paranoia over what I might choose to do. And it's greed. They want to control me, utilize me themselves for their own purposes. For the good of the Republic, of course," she added with a touch of sarcasm.

"That's the other reason I didn't want them to know Jem is here and within their reach. Do you know what Nuralathenolate is?" When Morelli nodded warily, Kowalski said bluntly, "that's what they want to use on Jem."

The general recoiled and the colonel's face paled.

"They want to turn Jem into a zombie taxi, under their complete control and utilizing her ability to deliver military operatives and/or ordinance to their targets. Anton—General Gleason has been blocking them. Jem, that recording on your hand comp…fast forward it to where they bring up the drug."

Jem scooped it up. Pausing the recording right after the admiral's teleport question, she handed it to Morelli, saying, "This occurred hours before the explosion."

Morelli angled it so Shannon could see it and started it. They watched it silently to the end. Their expressions remained impassive, even when Morelli replayed Admiral Gleason's order a second time.

"That," General Morelli said darkly, "is one hell of a motive."

Jem held out her hand. After a moment's hesitation, he handed the comp back. "What's the reference to delivering operatives or explosives—zombie taxi? What the hell is going on here?" His scrutiny switched back and forth between Jem and Kowalski.

"From a meeting I, uh, overheard this morning, there are some militaristic hawks spouting very aggressive ideas. Primarily toward the Consortium…for the moment. Personally," Jem shrugged, "I think it's a limited coup. The number involved? Who knows, but they wanted Admiral Gleason out of the way so they can move forward with whatever their plans are."

"Which means they'll strike at anyone else getting in their way," Morelli said, disgusted.

"Not just them—it's set a precedent," Colonel Shannon said grimly. "If someone doesn't like their orders, or how they believe things should be progressing—*boom* or a laser zap."

Kowalski looked at Jem. "They need to know fully what's at stake, Jem. They can't continue to work blind. Reports first or demo?"

She stood, said "demo," and walked into the bedroom.

Kowalski turned to their two visitors. "You both have the security level and I've decided you have a need to know due to the threat level."

"At least you won't have to do all that paperwork," Jem called out.

"Thank you, and we're definitely curious as to Miss Wilmont's methods," Morelli said, watching the bedroom entrance.

"We've debated a couple of ideas, but none seemed sufficiently plausible," Shannon added. "Especially when sensors didn't show any indications of disruption."

Kowalski chuckled. "Well then, hold on to your sanity. Jem?"

Jem materialized beside him from ghost-mode. She finger-waived at the two gaping officers and sat down.

"Allow me to formally introduce you to Jem Seaborne Wilmont, the Republic's only known teleporter," Kowalski said.

* * * * *

Once the OSI officers got over their shock, the afternoon moved quickly. General Morelli arranged to have a table computer rolled into Admiral Gleason's hospital room. Propped up in his bed and ignoring the fuming doctor, Gleason spent a half hour giving out orders in short bursts of speech. Morelli,

Shannon, and Kowalski were to be provided access to all Military Command files and directories. The Security office was also to provide any and all assistance the three of them requested.

Morelli and Shannon dug into the files as soon as their access had been unblocked. Kowalski and Jem, in ghost-mode, went to visit the admiral, worried about how much the calls had cost him. A lot, an irate Dr. Inness informed General Kowalski, to the point he'd placed his patient in a healing coma. Returning to his room, Kowalski started on the files and Jem went snooping.

She snooped on and off all the next day, too, as her energy allowed. By dinner time, she was barely able to hold a shift for five minutes. "Enough time," she told Kowalski tiredly, "to make one useless pass down the hallway and back."

He told her a meal cart from the ground floor cafeteria was on its way up with enough dishes "that they'll think I'm a pig." Jem laughed and grabbed a plate from the small kitchenette. They'd finished and was setting the cart outside the door when Morelli and Shannon arrived to compare notes. They lounged in the chairs, everyone's hand comps turned on.

"I've come up with six names I believe deserve a deeper look," Kowalski said, reviewing his list. "I based my selection on their level of displayed aggression. Keep in mind, they may be hawks, but not necessarily involved in the assassination attempt."

"Understood. We've got thirteen and ditto on the reasoning," Morelli said. At their surprised looks he added, "There's two of us. MJ and I split the reports between us."

"Perfect. We'll let you come up with the names, then, and we'll do the snooping," Kowalski said.

Jem rolled her eyes. "*We'll* do the snooping?"

Ignoring her, Kowalski read his list. "Generals Crantorri, Pillen, Cook, and Admiral Burgasov from the Senior Council. Lieutenant General—"

"How about skipping the ranks," Jem said waving a hand. "Everyone in Military Command is a general or admiral of some level. Excluding the aides."

One corner of Kowalski's mouth kicked up. "Be quicker, too.

Okay…Danziger and Hammad. Army and Navy, respectively."

"We've got all of those, too," Morelli said, checking his list. "Plus Lyon and Fritzsch—Army. Ankenbrand, Naval. Marines Doleman, Burrell, Hensley and Hensley—brothers. You have a kiosk number?"

Kowalski gave him his temp number and said he'd forward what they sent him on to Jem.

"I have Barlow, Burgasov's aide, on my list," Jem said. "Heard her bragging to another aide. Seems she's anticipating a promotion and a ship captaincy to go after those 'traitorous Consortium scum.'"

"Scum?" Morelli echoed.

"That's…intriguing," Shannon said.

"Uh-huh. Especially when the other aide came back with, and I quote, 'Not with that reprimand in your jacket.' Interesting enough, Barlow didn't appear worried. Then I also have Jamila McGauley."

"Why? I reviewed the Commodore's file; nothing stood out," Shannon said.

"I think she's a hawk in sheep clothing," Jem said. "Caught sight of her and Barlow with their heads together yesterday, but couldn't get close enough to hear." She'd been short on time, barely making it back to the room before her shift failed, dropping her back into the same universe as everyone else. "They seemed awful chummy."

The silence lasted while three sets of fingers updated their lists.

"We haven't looked at any of the aides, yet," Morelli admitted. "MJ, if you'll review the aides' files—starting with Barlow, I'll go deeper into Admiral Burgasov's file. I'm also going to call the office and have Lieutenant Widmark and his team start running a deep search on our list of suspects. Thank you, Miss Wilmont," he said, standing. "If you learn anything else, please let one of us know."

They exchanged good-nights and left.

"Well," Kowalski said, stroking his chin. "It would appear Admiral Burgasov and her aide have moved to the top of our list."

About time somebody did. *Hmmm*, Burgasov and Barlow. Jem rummaged through her memories of the past few days. She'd observed the haughty admiral several times, either in meetings, her office, or walking down the hallway. Sometimes with Barlow, sometimes with others, sometimes alone…except for that phone. She wondered idly how many Burgasov went through in a year. It was never outside her reach. The admiral rarely went more than ten minutes without either calling or being called and/or texted. Even in front of Admiral Gleason's door on the hallway video.

Something teased, just out of reach. *Something…*

"…you okay?"

Realizing he'd called her name several times, she gave him a wry smile. "Thinking too hard. I'm wondering what we missed." As soon as the words left her, instinct spiked. That was it. Missed or overlooked.

"I'm going to review more files," he said. "Want to pull up a chair and share the boredom?"

Jem patted him on the arm. "Uh-uh. I want to check out the hallway video again." She settled on the couch after downloading a copy to her hand comp. Feet propped on the coffee table, she watched the video. Ran it a second time in slow motion. It was on the third pass when she finally saw it. She stopped it, backed it up several seconds then played it forward. Very slowly. Froze the video. Stared for several seconds as her brain confirmed what she was seeing.

"General Kowalski?" she drawled. Her tone must have alerted him.

His head popped up sharply. "Jem?"

"I know who activated the bomb."

Chapter 43

For five days, the tension grew steadily throughout Military Command's corridors. General Morelli continued his questioning of members and staff while the rest of them dug furiously into records and followed leads. On Morelli's authorization, Jem snooped through the private quarters of those emerging as prime suspects. In one, she found a beautiful, green-glass figurine. On a hunch, she took a picture of the small statue and its manufacturer and sent it to Colonel Shannon.

Lieutenant Widmark's team found several interesting items, such as four of their suspects meeting at a resort in Spain three months ago. General Lyon was supposedly enjoying a fishing vacation off the coast of Norway.

"Must have boarded the wrong shuttle," had been Kowalski's sarcastic comment.

The Earth Force Office of Special Investigations was located across town next to the well-maintained Centre of Fine Arts building. They gathered there on the sixth day in a conference room to outline their case for the OSI Commander. General Alistar Estrada, another hard-eyed Marine, listened to Morelli's high-level summary without interruption. Then he demanded to know their exact reasoning for why high-ranking officers would even conceive risking their careers "for these kind of charges."

The video of Admiral Gleason's last MC meeting was played. The whole video. Afterwards, Jem gave him the same demonstration—*poofing* in, supposedly from the bathroom down the hall. The General's response? Two raised eyebrows, two blinks, and a "well, that's damn handy." ·

Jem liked Estrada. He reminded her of Stuart.

Estrada leaned back in his chair and ran a hand through the snow-white stubble he called a haircut. "This sucks. You're sure Admiral Burgasov is involved?"

"Past her eyeballs," Morelli responded. "She's the one that activated the bomb."

"How sure are you?"

"One hundred percent," Jem replied. "That military purse of hers isn't very large and she's always carrying it. Primarily to keep her phone handy, evidently. I observed her several times and, even while walking, she'll reach in and pull it out in one smooth move without even looking. Yet, standing in front of the admiral's door, she not only *looks* down, she *fumbles* getting it out. In slow motion and enhanced on a computer, you can see her hand moving around inside the purse before bringing the phone out. She's pressing some kind of trigger."

"That's speculation," Estrada said, fixing her with a level stare. "Defense will rip that apart."

"Then they'll also have to explain the two rooftop sensors that registered a spike at the exact same timestamp," Shannon said, smirking. "Admiral Gleason's quarters are on the top floor and within their radiant distance."

Estrada grunted. "And it was her aide—Barlow?—who purchased it?"

"Commander Barlow purchased the glass statue," Morelli clarified. "Miss Wilmont found a similar one during a search of Barlow's quarters, which Colonel Shannon then traced to a specialty shop in Paris. The artist picked out Barlow's picture as commissioning—six weeks prior to the explosion—a customized blue statue with a hollow center and a false bottom."

Estrada gave him a hard stare for several seconds before demanding documentation.

Morelli produced both the artist's and Jem's affidavit of discovery.

"Who put it in Gleason's room?"

"I'm thinking it was Admiral Burgasov—her quarters are three doors down the hallway. Barlow and Lyons have electronic and engineering career fields, respectively, in their history; both would know how to generate the power surge. Fifteen minutes would be more than enough time to zip down the hallway with a small light or night goggles, open the door, leave the statue, and zip back to her rooms. And, no sir, we haven't determined how and where a master key was acquired. Housekeeping isn't missing one."

"Better find that key, Morelli, because defense will use it as a weak point in proving access which leads to knowing it's there to blow it up."

"Yes, sir."

Estrada went back to his who-got-the-bomb question. That they had to admit was guess work. General Doleman had unexpectedly attended a joint exercise a month earlier, supposedly to observe. Among other things, it had utilized proximity TACEXMs. They were the exact size to fit in that hollow statue. The ordnance supervisor wouldn't be able to tell if one went missing instead of utilized, or question a wandering general. Morelli further strengthened that by saying the bomb exploding in the admiral's quarters hadn't been at full strength. Low-powered explosives were commonly used in exercise/training scenarios for obvious reasons.

"Which also limited the scope of the hotel damage," Kowalski added. "Especially as Admiral Burgasov's rooms were just down the hall."

General Estrada scowled at them, hard enough that his bushy eyebrows almost hid his eyes. "A glass stature with a TACEXM's dimensions was ordered weeks before the exercise they supposedly got the bomb from? You're telling me that they planned…they actively conspired to kill Admiral Gleason for *months*?"

"Not like they could pull this together overnight," Jem snarked.

"It does appear that way, sir," Morelli said, noncommittal. "Exercise details are planned months, sometimes a year in advance. General Doleman was an attendee at the Spain meeting. We can assume the exercise was discussed and may even have been the…inspiration for their plans. I fully believe, sir, it would have happened in the near future anyway. Admiral Gleason stood in opposition on a number of issues they are rather adamant about. They were simply waiting for the right catalyst."

Jem pointed to herself.

More silence. "I'd prefer you narrow down the bomb's acquisition more,"

Estrada finally said, "but I guess the where-from doesn't matter as long as you can prove Admiral Burgasov knew it was there *and* that she activated it."

"I expect a number of issues and/or gaps will be clarified once they're arrested and start jockeying for deals."

Estrada leaned forward. "How do you plan to proceed, Morelli? You can't just slap on cuffs and haul them to the brig."

"Why not?" Morelli replied hotly, before belatedly adding, "Sir. They have abused their rank and privileges, actively worked to subvert Republic laws, and given all of us a black eye."

"Agreed. However, until they are *convicted* on those charges, they will be treated accordingly to their rank. Wipe that sour look off your face, Kowalski. Prosecuting them in full accordance with the Uniform Code of Military Justice will maintain confidence within our ranks. Doing so publicly will maintain trust within the civilian communities and help mitigate that black eye."

"Publicly, sir?" Morelli asked, straightening.

"You bet your ass. They are not escaping the embarrassment they've caused."

Oh, wow. Morelli had expected closed trials for all of them to avoid exactly that.

"Well then, sir," Morelli said with a full-face grin, "in two days the full Military Council will be holding their bimonthly meeting. Arresting them there, per protocol, will start both the publicity and the embarrassment."

"Speaking of protocol," Estrada crossed his arms and leaned back, "I see two UCMJ issues. General Morelli, you authorized searches of private quarters without judicial or command approval?"

All three of Jem's military cohorts stiffened. *Uh-oh.*

"Sir. Those quarters are in a government facility that has the expectation of being searched—with or without notice—at any given time. I also felt it was in keeping with the necessity of both speed and secrecy as some of them are Senior Council members. Nor do we know how far this conspiracy goes or who all is involved. Miss Wilmont's searches were limited in scope and only on the individuals' quarters I specified."

Morelli swallowed. "Sir."

General Estrada nodded slowly. "Let's hope, then, it doesn't get several critical pieces of evidence thrown out. Speaking of authority, that brings us to the second issue."

Chapter 44

"I vehemently protest this," Dr. Inness said. "He should still be in a healing coma. He can barely sit up and—"

"Then strap me into the frigging chair," Admiral Gleason ordered hoarsely. "Sergi, move that idiot aside and help me. I intend to look those bastards in the eye."

* * * * *

All conversation ceased when Major General Morelli and Colonel Shannon strode through the double doors of the Military Command chamber. They stopped in the center of a squared-U arrangement, the individual seats arranged on two tiers. The Senior Council members and an empty seat were in the flat part, with the rest filling both "wings."

They slowly surveyed the room. So did Jem, who, unbeknownst, was beside them in ghost-mode.

"General Morelli and Colonel Shannon, this is a bit inappropriate," General Crantorri said. "You should have requested to address this meeting if you wished to do so."

"Would you like to hear the results of our investigation?" Morelli asked.

Admiral Burgasov frowned. "Well, yes. But we expected it to be presented to the Senior Council first."

"Afraid of what the others might hear?" Shannon said coolly.

Her tone haughty, Burgasov said, "You will address me as Admiral."

You're not going to like it when she does, Jem mused.

"I assume you've identified and removed any and all Consortium actors?" General Cook said.

"No. Because there are none. The failed assassination attempt on *Supreme Admiral*," Burgasov's cheek twitched, "Anton Gleason was perpetrated by members of this council."

"That's absurd," General Pillen declared loudly.

"I'd say the room's silence says different." Morelli motioned with his hand. "They knew, despite the false rumors. Rumors that were spread to validate a hawkish need for aggressiveness, readiness, and, of course, increased military buildup." He swiveled the arm on his comm unit down into position. "Now."

A line of Security Policeman entered and fanned out in front of the doors. Jem was sure she'd have heard that proverbial pin-drop if it'd happened.

"The following individuals are under arrest on the charges of, but not limited to, conspiracy in the attempted assassination of Admiral Anton Gleason. You will be escorted to EFOSI and held pending court-martial."

He pivoted on his heel to the right. "Lieutenant General Johnathon Greenbowe Lyon."

Two SPs marched to the man turning white.

"Th-This is, is preposterous!" Lyon sputtered as the guards flanked him. Taking an arm each, they escorted him to the floor's center.

"You can argue that at your trial," Morelli told him brusquely.

Shannon wheeled to the left. "Brigadier General Ryan Holland Doleman, Commodore Jamila Smithe McGauley."

They were each flanked by two more SPs and joined Lyon.

The two OSI officers turned to face the Senior Council. Jem was sure she heard several sharp inhales. *Yep, them too.*

"The following individuals are under arrest on the charges of, but not limited to, conspiracy in the planning and implementation of the assassination of Lieutenant Commander Terrence Ellington Johnson and the attempted assassination of Supreme Admiral Anton StClair Gleason. You will be escorted to EFOSI and held pending court-martial."

Morelli paused, and Jem would swear the whole room was holding its breath. Then, in ringing tones, he said, "Admiral Linda Sawyer Burgasov and General Katherine Loschen Pillen."

Crantorri jerked sideways away from Pillen, gaping at her.

"Keep your hands off me," Burgasov snapped, as the SPs approached her.

"*Admiral* Burgasov," Shannon said sarcastically, "they are authorized to stun and carry you out bodily if you fail to cooperate. By the way, your aide, Commander Angela Knier Barlow, has already been taken into custody."

Burgasov was nearly purple with indignation by the time she halted in front of Morelli. "I will see you charged and demoted for insubordination. You have no authority over me. I am the next Supreme Admiral."

Jem glared at her. *Was that her real reason for getting rid of the admiral?*

"You will *never* carry that rank, or any other for much longer," Morelli said coldly. "As for having authority…bring him in, General Kowalski," he said into his comm.

The doors opened again and the murmurs died as Admiral Gleason entered, pushed in a wheelchair by General Kowalski. An oxygen bottle was strapped on the back and an I-V hung from a small, attached hook. The burns visible on his neck and face stood out starkly, as did the covered eye socket. His spine was straight and his left eye held determination and fury.

Jem bit her lip, worried. None of them had liked this. They'd planned on having him do a recording. Once he'd been brought to consciousness this morning and the situation explained, he had insisted on performing it personally.

Gleason rolled to a stop. Morelli and Shannon took up parade-rest stances on either side of him. His scrutiny ran over the officers in front of him. Lyon and McGauley looked down, unable to meet his gaze.

"You have betrayed your oath, betrayed your fellow officers." The voice was hoarse, but the contempt came through. "You do not deserve the uniforms you wear, much less the rank you hold." He paused. All but a glaring Burgasov were studying the floor. He didn't bother giving them that abused rank when he continued. "By my authority, Burgasov, Pillen, Lyon, Doleman, McGauley, and Barlow, are hereby relieved of their command positions and all military duties. Dismissed." He coughed. "Get them out of my sight."

Even Burgasov was silent as the prisoners and their guards filed out of the room.

"For the rest of you…" Gleason raked his glare around the room. "This is your reality check. We are here to protect and serve our worlds and our people. Not to garner power or prestige or whatever else you think you deserve." He paused for several shallow breaths. "The Republic is changing, as Earth did when her children went off to start new lives on those worlds. We, the Republic's *guardians,* must address those changes. I look forward to working with each of you as we face the coming challenges."

At Gleason's signal, Kowalski turned the wheelchair around.

General Arita rose to his feet. "Room, a-tent-*HUT!*" he barked loudly.

As one, they stood and everyone—including Jem—gave their silent respect. Arita gave the "at ease" command after the doors closed behind them. Clothing rustled as people sat back down. Exchanged whispers.

Jem's gaze lingered on the closed doors. Dr. Inness would be whisking Admiral Gleason back to the hospital. Refusing to leave his patient in the care of "non-professionals," he had been practically bouncing on his toes outside the chamber, glaring at everyone as he waited.

"Are we free to leave?" Arita asked, still standing.

"In a moment," Morelli said. "There's another who wants to address this assembly."

Jem tensed. She'd have taken a couple of deep breaths if ghost-mode allowed it.

"Miss Wilmont?"

Jem waited several seconds before materializing. Morelli and Shannon would believe she teleported from the room they'd left her in. The stares and open mouths were not unexpected. Even for those that had read the reports, seeing it for the first time was a jolt, not to mention having one or two of the uninitiated nearly falling out of their chairs. Jem reached up and slid the not-really needed comm unit off and handed it to Colonel Shannon.

Both Kowalski and Gleason had initially protested when she'd told them her plans on the way here, arguing she could walk in normally. Fortunately, they'd recognized the logic after she'd quoted Shiloh's reasoning verbatim.

"It's time to raft the rapids," Kowalski had said, expressing his acceptance with a Midgard idiom. *"I call dibs on the steering rudder,"* had been Gleason's dry reply.

"For the record," she said, her eyes roaming as she spoke, "I am Jem Seaborne Wilmont, of Midgard. Late of Earth," she added impulsively. "Ever since my abilities…emerged, I've been hunted. I've been kidnapped. I've been damn near killed a couple of times. All because I was seen, not as a person, but as a tool to use or a threat to eliminate." Yep, her claim to fame. "Do you see those who serve below you that way? Would you want yourself to be?"

Would putting it in military terms help?

"I was alone. No backup. No resources. Always on guard, always fearing the next betrayal. No one stood between me and the hawks who'd swoop in, grabbing a choice morsel for their use. I learned to live in the shadows, hiding from hawks and opportunists alike." She paused. "If you can call that living."

Kowalski had slipped back in and came to stand beside her.

"Despite all that, despite the malicious rumors, Miss Wilmont has not turned to criminal or other nefarious pursuits. She actively discourages them, in fact." Kowalski grinned, then let it slide away. "She has, instead, assisted people in trouble and worked to help others in various ways. She has offered her services to Midgard's Planetary Defense and, by extension, Military Command. That's you, you morons. So why in the frigging Universe are you messing with her?"

"This is my reality check. Staying in the shadows is no longer possible. And too costly," she said quietly, studying the near-empty senior section for several moments. "As I move forward, as my skills are called upon by you or others, awareness will spread even more that it already has. Inevitable and unstoppable. I have accepted that. Will there be difficulties? Sure. I have to walk a fine line between not scaring people and being scary enough to be left alone."

"Walk softly but carry a big stick," a general on the left said, then added, "That's a very old saying" when Jem gave him a quizzical look.

"Sounds like good advice," Jem said, comprehending the intent behind it. "Today, I have friends and allies. I have a family. I'm asking you, now, to become part of that support. Be a knot on that stick. I understand your wariness—I have my own toward you," she added bluntly. "Please, put aside your fears and accept me as someone who, like you, wants a better, safer future for everyone."

"Just so you know," Kowalski said, folding his arms across his chest, "if Military Command can't, or won't, accept Miss Wilmont as a *person*, not some damn tool, the Wotan System will be seceding."

Jem's head jerked around. Her "What?" joined the crowd of exclamations.

"I've spoken with Wotan's five Fed-Senators. They, and I, do not want to be part of any body that is not only continuously harassing one of our citizens, but would deliberately use Nuralathenolate on someone for the sole purpose of creating a mindless 'tool' to exploit however they want."

"Who the hell wanted that?" demanded a man in a Marine uniform.

"Take a guess," Arita replied coolly, looking at General Crantorri.

"That's despicable."

"Hell, no I don't agree."

Comments, questions, and angry looks raced around the room, a number of them aimed at a tight-lipped Army general.

"Really?" Jem asked out of the corner of her mouth.

"Bet your ass," Kowalski responded in a like manner.

"Is that what Admiral Gleason was so mad about?" someone yelled.

The room quieted as General Arita retook his feet. "Yes, it was the last straw. Admiral Gleason's cease-and-desist order was given because of the drug and because of the repeated attempts…" Arita paused, as if wondering how best to phrase it.

A female in naval regalia snorted. "Just spit it out, Stephen. Kill or capture. Right?"

"Right as always, Agatha," Arita said over the burst of laughter.

He waited until the chuckles died away. "Admiral Gleason is correct: the Republic is changing. *We* are changing. I firmly believe we are evolving as determined by our new worlds and environments. We've all seen how the bodies of those from high-gravity planets have compensated. Anyone care to arm-wrestle General Gustin?" he asked to more laughter.

Jem grinned as a man looking a lot like Boyd stood and flexed his arm.

"I know an individual who comes from a subterrain city, fifth generation," Arita continued. "He can see in the dark. Literally. He was an outstanding night-time scout and sniper, a valued member of his unit. But this accomplished, decorated soldier rarely spoke of it within the ranks. Still doesn't as a civilian. Why? The reactions of others both in and out of uniform." He paused to scan the room. "While Miss Wilmont may be an extreme case, she does not deserve to be ostracized, ridiculed, used or abused…any more than my son does."

Ooooh, that was interesting. How good was Arita's vision? Judging from the reactions around the room, others were curious about that too. She gave Kowalski a quick look on hearing his muttered, "Well, that explains that."

Ignoring the expressions around him, Arita pressed on. "We, the leaders of today, must pave the way for the ones to come. We must learn to work with those changes, whatever they may be. In that respect, Military Command can expect changes, too. We must—we will—adapt."

Arita turned to them.

"General Kowalski, the people of Midgard do not need to worry. We will not be using that drug, ever. We will adhere to, and I second, Supreme Admiral Gleason's command concerning Miss Wilmont."

Kowalski's chin dipped in acknowledgment.

"Miss Wilmont, please accept my apology, on behalf of Military Command, for any adverse encounters you have experienced originating from us. I, personally, look forward to working with you in the future."

"Thank you, sir, and likewise," Jem replied with a grateful smile.

"Thank you, General Arita," Morelli said. "The EFOSI office will keep Military Command appraised of charges and any other findings as we complete our investigation. Good day to you all."

Morelli and Shannon executed a crisp salute before pivoting to leave. Kowalski simply gave Arita another nod while Jem gave the room a wave.

Outside the double doors, Jem sagged in relief. "That went better than expected. I am so done. Can we go home now?" she whined.

"Not without checking on Anton," Kowalski said.

"Go ahead, both of you," Morelli told them. "We appreciate your help; it was invaluable. We may not have been able to bring charges for months—if at all—without it." His phone rang. After several "yes, sirs" and "no, sirs," he hung up. "General Estrada has requested you stop in and speak with him."

Jem and Kowalski shared a look.

"I don't suppose one of those *nopes* was if we were with you?" Jem asked. Then they could pretend ignorance. Afterall, they weren't in Estrada's scope of command.

"Uh, no. That was actually the first 'yep'," Morelli replied with a rueful grin.

"All right. Let him know we'll be there *after* we visit the hospital," Kowalski said.

Chapter 45

They had been back from Euphrates for about four hours, and that included over three dreary hours on a shuttle from Odinheim's spaceport. Andi had immediately headed home with Dante, while he and Nicholas had opted for comfy chairs in the family room. Expecting his grandmother to quiz him about the BC models he'd viewed, Thane was surprised when she announced that Boyd had left Midgard during their absence. He'd left behind three boxes of belongings, asking for him and Jem to store them until he returned.

They were debating what could have drawn him away when Thane was called away for a video-call. Finding Miss Lexington on the other end dampened his good mood. Having her invite him to her hotel room for 'some news' completely ruined it.

"I'm just back from a tiring business trip, Miss Lexington," Thane said coldly. "If you have something to say to me, then do so."

"It concerns Jem Wilmont," Tia said haughtily, "and if you want to hear it, you'll come to suite 2011, Oberlander Garden Suites." The screen blanked.

Thane swore under his breath.

"Interesting that she knew we were back," Nicholas said from behind him.

Turning, he found his grandmother frowning at him. "I don't like it," she said.

"I don't either. Whatever she's got on Jem is undoubtedly circumstantial." Which he wouldn't put past Tia to manipulate like Kurzvall had. He'd made it look like Jem was an assassin so the authorities would hunt her down.

"Ever since Tia blew back in a week ago, she's done nothing but hint at *impending* news every chance she gets. Naturally," Gwen said, disgusted, "she doesn't say about what, just simpers and smiles when Baron Financials or you are mentioned. She's setting the stage."

"I'd recommend not going," Nicholas chipped in, "but she's dangled bait she knows you won't ignore."

No, he couldn't, which was why he was knocking loudly on her door almost two hours later.

Tia opened the door wearing…not much. A loose wrap of some kind that stopped at her thighs and was slit down past her breasts. He had yet to see her in anything that didn't.

"Why, Thane," she purred, "I'd begun to think you weren't coming."

He halted in the middle of the room. Short on patience, he said, "All right, I'm here. Let's hear it."

"So grouchy. A drink should fix that," she said, moving toward the bar.

"No," he said forcefully. "I don't want a drink. I want to hear whatever you have about Jem."

"Fine." She faced him, a hand on a hip and her breasts thrust out. "Midgard has been growing in prominence. With the recent additions of Baron Financials HQ and Hands of Hope Foundation, it is even more so. In certain circles, speculation puts Midgard on course to eventually eclipse Earth as the financial powerhouse. Which means you and your family will be at the center of that growth."

Really? "My family will be thrilled to hear that. What does it have to do with Jem?"

"Jem Wilmont is a nobody with a, let's say, murky reputation. I've amassed details on numerous occurrences involving her. Not someone you want to align your family's future or business interests with."

Thane snorted and shoved his hands in his pockets. "Those 'details' are coincidences and rumors and lies. Nothing new. You wouldn't be the first to try and use them against Jem, *my sig-ner*."

She ignored that. "By merging our businesses, we'll dominate the financial markets. Won't anything happen we don't allow to happen," she said, a predatory gloat in her voice.

"No merger." Was she even listening?

"I've already spoken with Father. He's agreed to bring in Baron Financials as a subsidiary, keeping the name and you as its head. I've even had it included in our prenup to make you more comfortable. As soon as we file—"

Thane reared back. "I'm not marrying you."

"Of course you are. It makes perfect sense."

"You've evidently lost yours, along with your hearing." Hands fisted, he snarled, "No merger. No marriage. I'm leaving."

In one smooth motion, she dropped the wrap. Her full breasts bobbed as she sashayed toward him. She slid her hands slowly up his chest. "I'm sure you're not thinking the matter through thoroughly. Why don't we—" Tia broke off with a laugh when Thane grabbed her by the waist and lifted her off her feet.

He strode to the couch. Her smug smile changed to a shocked squeak when he dropped her on it and stepped back. "I want nothing to do with you," he said, glaring down at her. He turned on his heel.

"Walk out that door and there will be repercussions."

It wasn't the words that made Thane stop halfway to the door and turn around, it was the self-assured tone they were delivered in.

"As I said, I've collected quite a bit of information about your assassin *signer*," she said. "Information that will cause quite a stir if it becomes known, especially among Law Enforcement. The legal issues could be...serious."

"Jem is not, and never has been, an assassin," Thane said coldly as she redonned that scrap of cloth. "You have rumors and lies that were specifically designed to blacken her name. She—we have survived." Thane's lip curled. "What makes you believe you'll succeed where they failed?"

"An autopsy report."

He watched Tia walk to the bar through narrowed eyes. "Autopsy report?" he repeated carefully as she poured herself a glass of wine.

Tia waited until she was settled on the couch before answering. "Katherine Baron, your cousin." She took a sip, then motioned with her glass. "Have a seat."

Wary, he sat opposite her. He did not like the confidence she exuded.

Autopsy? Katherine? What the hell?

"Her death was suspiciously sudden, wouldn't you say? Naturally, an autopsy was performed immediately after she died. Tissue samples taken…the usual procedures."

"Her family has a history of blood disorders," Thane replied. "And?"

"All her organ samples showed a minute trace of an exotic poison."

Thane stiffened. "If she was poisoned, it was by her lover, Ahrymani Carpenter."

"I'm assuming that same belief is why Law Enforcement never pursued it. However, Ahrymani had ten million reasons not to," Tia said, her lips curling upward. "That was to be her pay-off from Katherine as soon as they returned to her home on Milania. I have her deposition stating that, as well as her suspicion Katherine had been poisoned by Jem Wilmont. Their hotel had an excellent security system—physical and electronic, meaning it would have taken a very stealthy person to slip that poison into her room. Like a ghost, perhaps?"

Smug eyes watched him over the glass rim. She was so sure she'd won.

"Or a roommate," Thane retorted, wrestling down his anger. "Assuming we take the word of a psychopathic killer, others were in and out of that room. Housekeeping. Food Service. Any one of them could have done it."

"True, but what would their reason be? Other than being paid to do it? And by whom? Maybe it wasn't Jem. Maybe it was your grandmother—their meetings were contentious, I hear. Maybe it was someone else in your family."

She leaned forward and her voice turned hard. "Bottom line. The only ones profiting from Katherine Baron's death were you and your family. Jem Wilmont has the skills necessary to have done it for you. Circumstantial? Yes, but others have been convicted on it. Even if she isn't in court, she will be in public. And not just her. Your whole family will be tainted. Who knew? Who sanctioned it?" Cruelty laced her words. "Who wants to socialize or do business with that kind of people?"

Thane rose to his feet. "I need to verify this."

"Certainly." She leaned back. "But don't make me wait too long."

Thane stormed out of the room. Nicholas had the car waiting at the hotel's portico. He slid in and they started down the expansive driveway. He picked the hand comp up from the center console and waved it. "Can we get her for extortion?" Thane said, furious.

"You'd have to tell me about what," Nicholas said grimly. "You went silent as soon as you entered her room."

Thane bit out *"Jammer"* and yanked the transmitter off his belt. "Think she suspected?"

"I think she's played similar games before and is savvy enough to not get recorded."

"She says—"

"Wait." Nicholas interrupted. "Call Gordon and ask him to meet us at the house. Give it to all of us at one time."

Thane pulled out his phone. If Tia Lexington was right, his granddad's expertise might be all that stood between them and disaster.

***

The temperature in the secure conference room hovered slightly above glacial after Thane finished relating his visit to Tia. "Had any of you heard about an autopsy on Katherine? She sounded too confident to be making it up."

"And it's too easy to verify," Gordon said, drumming his fingers on the table. "Autopsy would indeed be standard procedure and it'd be assumed her lover did it after their falling out."

"The main sticking point would be Ahrymani Carpenter's deposition, if anyone would be crazy enough to believe her," Seth said, having accompanied Gordon from their law office. "We could rebuttal by claiming that she was getting back, not simply at Jem, but at the whole family for ruining her plans."

"Do you think…" Thane paused, "do you think Ahrymani told them anything else about Jem?" Like teleportation.

"If Tia didn't gloat about revealing a *secret*, then I'd say no," Gordon said. "She'd consider that a stronger lure, something you most assuredly wouldn't want out." He glanced at his wife. "The poison issue does need addressed."

Thane traded looks with Nicholas and Stuart. "You don't seem surprised by it," he said.

"No, because I'm sure the report is accurate," Gwen said calmly. "Helga

Baron all but admitted to it in a conversation I had with her at the hospital."

Thane stared, flummoxed. "Katherine was poisoned by her aunt?"

"Yes."

"Why? I mean, I know why one of us would, but Helga?"

Gwen cleared her throat. "I had inadvertently let it slip that we suspected her niece and Ahrymani of the attacks against us. She must have come to the same conclusion. She told me she'd gone to Katherine's suite and had a 'conciliatory drink' with her. That was just days before Katherine's collapse. She didn't come right out and say it, but the implication was clear."

"She'd rather kill her own niece than have her go to a Fed-Pen cell?" Nicholas said.

"No," Gwen replied tartly, "she didn't want the scandal to smudge the Baron name. With Katherine dead, all the blame could be—and has been—placed solely on Ahrymani Carpenter."

Unbelievable arrogance. And now it was going to bite them all in the ass. Resigned, already knowing the answer, Thane asked it anyway. "Don't suppose Helga would confess, do you? For the good of the family?"

He got disbelieving looks from both grandparents.

"Son, she killed her *niece* to protect the family name," Gordon said. "Since she doesn't consider Jem as part of the family, she'd have no compunction letting her take the blame."

Thane's teeth ground together. Helga Baron had spent over two decades ignoring them until his uncle's family had died and he and his sister became the last of her line. This was another strike against her, another reason why he'd never call his father's mother grandmother.

"Can we get Tia on extortion?" Thane asked.

Both Gordon and Seth considered it for several seconds.

Seth shrugged. "We could try, but it'd be a he-said, she-said case."

"Especially when she hands Carpenter's deposition to Law Enforcement,'" Gordon added. "She'll accuse Thane of trying to suppress the evidence."

Gwen sighed and rubbed a hand across her forehead. "This a mess."

Chapter 46

Breakfast the next morning was a conspiratorial flurry. Thane's granddad was going to visit Miss Lexington, as his legal representative, to verify and read Carpenter's deposition. Seth, as Jem's lawyer, would speak with Captain Kelding to verify the autopsy report and its contents. Thane was going to spend the day at Baron Financials with his grandmother, pretending to have an interest in it.

"Tia is obviously keeping tabs on you. This will make her think you are looking into BF's management and debating her proposal," Gwen said. "The longer we can postpone her backstabbing, the better chance we have to find something to block her. Or at least, offset the damage."

Thane jokingly replied, "I could take up Tia's—" The chorus of *No*s nearly deafened him, and the heat from Andi's glare radiated clear across the table.

"We will face this storm head-on, son, as we always have," Gordon said before striding out of the dining room.

***

"This is something you should have done before now," his grandmother gently chided as their driver pulled into BF's underground parking area. "You need to be able to converse intelligently about your own company. Not sound like some clueless twit that's never worked a day in their life."

Thane winced, recalling snippets of conversation overheard from Marissa and her booth buddies.

As the day progressed, he was surprised to find his BF tutoring interesting.

Not that he had any plans to push his grandmother out of her CEO position. Tracking was his calling and he couldn't wait to get his new ship. There had been several inquiries waiting in his email when he and Andi got back. He could have pursued one or two by commercial transport, but he'd politely declined.

When he mentioned that as they all relaxed that evening on the terrace after a fattening supper, Andi laughed and accused him of being spoiled.

"Uh-huh, guilty as charged."

"Think he can hold out until the new ship arrives?" Katrina asked, snickering.

"Won't be a problem, since he promised a hefty bonus if it was delivered in three weeks," Nicholas said dryly.

"Three weeks? Isn't that a bit demanding?" Gwen asked.

"Actually," Andi said, rocking a drowsy Dante, "it was two weeks plus a week transit to here."

All eyes turned to Thane.

"The basic ship was already completed," Thane said defensively. "All they have to do is add the auxiliary engines and the laser. Andi will do the computer and sensor upgrades at the Bocharova Shipyard while they build-out the interior."

"So, about two weeks to arrival plus whatever time it takes at Bocharova," Katrina said, her voice ruminative. "Planning on offering them a bonus, too? I knew it!" she laughed when Thane's cheeks turned pink.

"What's the good of having money if you don't spend it occasionally," he muttered. "Andi will need the longest time. She has to program the comp brain after installing the new circuitry."

"Nah. I'll just download the Altus and upload Thor."

"Thor's gone, Andi. They sent the salvage payment to my account."

"You ever heard of *backup*, cousin? When the *Tracker* was at Bocharova last fall for a maintenance refresh, I did a full download of Thor's memory banks. I used that as reference when programing Freya. I also copied all your past cases to Freya. I suggest you start backing them up regularly.

"I never expected to need backups," Thane said weakly. Changing the subject, he asked if his mom and Lee were coming over.

Gwen shook her head. "Sam's got a cold or something and they didn't want to bring it over to Dante."

"Excuse me," Van said from the doorway. "There's an individual at the gate. He's asking for Miss Wilmont and identifies himself as 'the Kid.' I wondered if you might want to see what he's about yourself."

"I do," Thane said straightening. "Have a guard escort him in."

"That's the one who helped Jem on the pirate ship—*Hidden Trove*, wasn't it?" Gordon said.

"Yes. The Kid helped swing the rest of the crew to her side against Daryl Richardson." Then had killed the psychopath when the man had attempted to kill them. And, according to Jem, he knew she had a special ability, if not what exactly. Nor had he been spreading his knowledge.

He stood when the young man was ushered into the room.

Thane estimated him to be in his early twenties, about an inch shorter than him and with reddish-blond hair. Impassive blue eyes returned his study. The Kid stood unmoving, yet Thane had the impression he could explode into violent motion with little warning. Nicholas must have, too, the way he was watching him from his place beside Andi.

He stepped forward and held out a hand. "Welcome to my grandparents' home. I'm Thane Baron and I'm glad to finally meet you. Jem has told us about you. Kaleb, right?" Thane introduced everyone and led him to a chair.

Kaleb glanced around, his expression unreadable. "I was told Jem wasn't here. Will she be back soon?"

"Jem is off-planet attending to a matter. We don't know how long it will take," Thane told him. "Is there something I can help you with?" He waved a hand. "You can speak freely. Those of us here know about you helping Jem." Few others did, as news of his association with the pirates could cause problems, legal or otherwise.

"I wanted to talk with her about something. It can wait."

He's lying. He needed something bad or he wouldn't have come.

When he started to rise, Gwen motioned him back down. "You're here now, so sit and visit for a spell. Jem mentioned you were on the *Hidden Trove*. We were wondering—"

"I never went on any raids. I did not participate in any of their games." The Kid's expression had gone ice cold.

Games? That sent a chill went down Thane's spine.

"What Grandmother meant to say, before you rudely interrupted," Katrina said briskly, "was that we're interested in what all you worked on. Jem told us you were their mechanic, with a naturally gifted talent to fix just about anything, often in a non-conventional manner. She also said," Katrina leaned forward, "that you were Beckett's youngest merc with the eyes of the oldest."

"Katrina!" Gwen admonished.

Katrina gave her grandmother an unrepentant look. "Jem was right about that. His whole demeanor is that of someone who's been to hell and back. Treating Kaleb with kid gloves—no pun intended—is a waste of time." She turned to face Kaleb. "As is you treating us as imbeciles. You wouldn't be here if you didn't need help badly."

Thane grinned at the enigmatic look Kaleb was giving his sister. Katrina's bluntness often threw people off their stride.

Kaleb studied Thane. "I once asked Jem for help in a future personal matter. She agreed."

"And it's coming due," Thane guessed.

"I will be returning home soon. To deal with it."

"Where's home?"

"Mandoria."

Well, that certainly fits the description of hell-and-back.

Mandoria, Klaxton One: the cesspit of the galaxy. Its single industry was mining for rare and heavy metals. Everyone lived on an orbiting habitat as the planet had a toxic atmosphere and 5-Eg gravitation. Work that couldn't be automated had to be done in specially adapted equipment. Due to the difficulty of the work, only the hardest, toughest, and undoubtedly the meanest, lasted long. To keep them happy, more like pacified, they were allowed all sorts of…entertainment. Thane had heard that it wasn't uncommon for fights to end with a dead body or two.

"No wonder you joined the pirates," Katrina said. "It was a step up in circumstances."

Kaleb's lips did a brief, slightly upturned shift. "I do need to discuss it with Jem first," he said to Thane, "but it will, most likely, include you and her coming on the *Lone Tracker*."

"Unfortunately, the *Lone Tracker* was heavily damaged in an asteroid field," Thane said. It just wasn't an asteroid that did the damage. "My new ship won't be ready for…" he looked at Andi, "five weeks?"

"At least. You'll definitely need all my sensors if you're going to Mandoria. And things will slow down over Founding Week."

"Too bad you can't put some in the engine housing." He'd once had an enemy attach an explosive device to his O-engine. Fortunately, he'd found it before lift-off. Given recent events, they needed to upgrade all their security precautions.

"Why not?" the Kid asked.

Andi gave him a disbelieving look. "Because the ion engines would cook them in the first seconds."

Kaleb shrugged. "Not if you embed them." The entire room went still. "The plating is doubly thick between the housing and the lower deck, right? So, you embed the sensors in the plating with reinforced covers. Slide the panel open while the ship is sitting, close them prior to ignition."

Andi's gaping mouth snapped closed. For a second. "Oh, oh. It'll work. A rotating plate—no, individual in case of damage to one area. Oh, wow. Why didn't I ever think of that?"

Nicholas reached over and scooped the sleeping infant from the vibrating woman's arms.

Unencumbered, Andi was bouncing in place. "Jaguide-Four panels if I can get them. The best," she said, her hands in motion. "Probably will need annual replacement. No problem. Can Bocharova—yes, yes, they can handle it." She shot out of her chair, leaving "Got to get to my computer" echoing in her wake.

Silence reigned for several seconds, with Nicholas giving an affectionate head shake in his wife's direction.

"Does she do that often?" the Kid asked.

A spate of laughter was his answer.

"You gave her an engineering challenge," Nicholas said, rising. "I'll put this one to bed then be back. There's a couple of security additions I want to go over with you, Thane."

Thane shook his head. "You're off duty. Unless it's critical, we can do it tomorrow. Spend a quiet evening with your family."

"Oh, it'll be quiet all right," Nicholas said, throwing a grin over his shoulder. "One's sleeping, the other is glued to her computer." Reaching the doorway, he made a hasty sidestep when Andi barreled back through.

She pointed at Kaleb. "I need your full name."

"Why?" he asked, brows narrowed suspiciously.

"So we can file for a patent, of course. Once they build ours, they're going to want it as an option for others. This will bring in customers. The military will definitely be interested. You'll get rich from the licensing."

He blinked. "Me?"

"I'm drafting the design but the concept is yours. So, need both names."

When Kaleb still hesitated, Thane squinted at him. "Come on, Kaleb. How bad can the rest be?"

"Kaleb Izokaitis Despiegelaere."

Thane blinked. Gordon coughed. Katrina *woofed*.

"Great Aunt Astrid had a similar issue," Gwen said, tapping her chin.

Andi whipped around and pointed two fingers at her surprised husband. "Get that in writing," she ordered before rushing back out.

Chapter 47

Arthur McNeil, Kurzvall's aide, answered the knock on the hotel door. He expected it to be the local informant his boss was working with. It wasn't.

"Sir," McNeil said. "It's Federal Law Enforcement Agent Naoko Haswell. He insists on seeing you."

Kurzvall's brows narrowed. "What do those idiots want now?" He tossed his hand comp on the side table. "Let him in."

McNeil stepped back. The Enforcer stepped in, three others slipping in before he could close the door. Kurzvall's two guards immediately moved to flank his chair.

"I invited one of you in," Kurzvall said haughtily. "The rest of you get out."

"Not happening," Agent Haswell said as the three fanned out behind him. "You are Reginald Salazar Kurzvall of Hebros, Hermes Four, of the Consortium?"

"Are you as deaf as you are dumb? Out, all of you."

All four agents glowered.

"Are you Reginald Salazar Kurzvall of Hebros, Hermes Four?" he repeated.

"You don't know whose room you've invaded? Of course I am."

"You are under arrest for solicitation of murder-for-hire and complicity in the murder of numerous individuals, including four Republic Federal Senators and eleven of our System Senators."

Kurzvall threw back his head and laughed. "Even if you could prove it, you can't do a damn thing about it. I'm a Consortium Representative—one of the founders. I have diplomatic immunity while in your *space*," he sneered.

Haswell's gaze didn't waver. "We have unassailable proof in the form of communiques between you, those hired, their orders, and their payment."

Kurzvall stared at him for a moment. Then his head jerked toward McNeil, standing quietly to the side. "You!"

"I've hated you for years," McNeil replied, stone-faced. "But I knew you wouldn't let me just walk away. I waited, bided my time."

"Lives could have been saved if you'd come forward sooner," grumbled one of the agents behind Haswell.

"Who would I have trusted?" McNeil replied. "Information and reports from his spies came in anonymously and through false accounts. Even if I did find someone trustworthy, would the person they contacted be?"

The agents' expressions behind Haswell turned various shades of unhappy.

Kurzvall's web of spies and informants had infiltrated just about every level of government on and off Earth. They'd ranged from secretaries and chauffeurs to the Assistant FBI Director of Earth, who'd murdered FBI Director Thaxton when the man had become suspicious of him.

"Doesn't matter what he's told you," Kurzvall said, face turning red with anger. "Leave, and take that traitorous man with you. Don't bother sending for anything," he told McNeil. "I'll personally burn everything of yours when I get home."

"Kind of hard to do that from a federal jail cell," Haswell said, his attention focused solidly on Kurzvall.

"*Get out*," Kurzvall snarled. "This farce has gone on long enough." He motioned to his two guards.

Their hands dropped to their weapons but they exchanged uneasy looks. Drawing on Federal Agents was not going to have good results, especially since they didn't have any form of immunity.

"The diplomatic immunity you've been swaggering around the Republic with was based on Earth's archaic traditions. The Federal Senate recently decided to codify a number of them into legally binding laws. In the belief that no one, regardless of wealth, status, or political standing, should be immune to the law," Haswell's lips curled upward, "they have, unanimously, eliminated that aspect. *All* non-Republic individuals will be held accountable for their actions within our borders. Notification of our new laws were sent out to all the other…republics. I guess the Consortium didn't care enough to warn you."

McNeil held up a finger. "They did. I deleted it, then sent all the information I've collected over the years to the local FLEA Director. Your boss, I believe."

Kurzvall stared. Before he could say anything, Haswell stepped forward.

"I repeat, you are under arrest on the aforementioned charges." Haswell switched his attention to the guards. "If you persist in defending him and obstructing us in the performance of our orders, you will be charged as accomplices."

They simultaneously raised hands and stepped back from their stunned employer.

"You can't…this is ridiculous…I have immunity," Kurzvall sputtered as two agents pulled him out of his chair.

Haswell snapped cuffs on his wrists. "Nope. Already explained."

"I have my rights," Kurzvall yelled.

"That you do. You'll be allowed to arrange for legal representation from the Enforcement Center," Agent Haswell said, then began reading him those rights.

McNeil walked up to one of the other agents and held out his wrists. He didn't care what happened now. His soul was as stained as his hands. No punishment could be worse than the hell he'd been living in. He glanced over at his apoplectic ex-employer, now screaming obscenities over the agent's recital. The first real smile in years bloomed across his features.

Chapter 48

Tia Lexington forked up another bite of sautéed shard. If she didn't know better, she would think she was eating an Earth lobster. The mixture of butter, seasonings, and a light, spicy oil was delicious. *Jade Heights* had become her preferred dining spot since having her first meal in it. Even if a certain irritating person had shown up and ruined it.

As this one is about to be, she fumed as Gary Hagerty sat down across from her. Her father's watchdog and troubleshooter was the proverbial tall, dark, and handsome. He was also amoral, deadly, and totally loyal to her father.

She hated him. Almost as much as her father.

"Did Father send you to check up on me?" she asked, arching an eyebrow. Long practice kept her feelings from face and voice.

"He expected a more favorable progress report than what you sent," he said, waving off the server.

The one from three days ago, after her disastrous meeting with Thane.

"I would have expected you to have enthralled him with your charms by now," Hagerty said, giving her chest a brief glance.

How would he look with a fork in his eye?

"Thane Baron is not L-RAM's usual target. His Tracker reputation speaks for itself." Smart, tough, stubborn. Exactly what she needed to stand against Franklin Lexington. "He also has a sig-ner he cares about, so no, my charms aren't working." *Cold, gray eyes without a spark of interest.* She used two sips of coffee to regain her balance from the unexpected flare of emotion that was more envy than anger.

"The information I've collected is damaging not only to Miss Wilmont, but to Thane, his family, and their business interests. I've allowed his grandfather to verify Carpenter's deposition. Thane has a choice: my proposal or I provide it to Law Enforcement."

She'd expected to have heard from him before now.

"Would your charms be more effective if Miss Wilmont was out of the way?" he said in a low voice.

Something her father had undoubtedly considered and approved. "No, plus Thane and his family would immediately be suspicious. They could press LE into investigating me and L-RAM."

"Jem Wilmont has enemies. She was recently kidnapped by one. Circumstances around her return are…vague."

Oh, my. That has to be galling. "Leave Miss Wilmont alone for now. I'll let you know if that changes. I've identified several potentials for offices here in Azusa," she said, changing to the other subject she assumed he was here for. "Although, I believe L-RAM would be better suited in the capital, Odinheim."

"Perhaps later," Hagerty replied, "L-RAM will be taking over BF's offices here first."

She set her cup back in its saucer carefully. "My understanding was that Baron Financials would be a fully functional subsidiary, with Thane as CEO. It's even a condition in my prenup." A camouflaging condition she had never planned to implement.

"Your understanding is wrong. Once BF falls under L-RAM control, Mister Lexington intends to absorb its resources."

Invalidating the prenup with divorce soon to follow. *The bastard.* See how Mister Franklin Lexington liked it when he learned she had no intention of giving him BF. Baron Financials was *hers*. Anger made her reckless.

"It was also understood that I am to manage BF alongside Thane." Her bodyguards at a nearby table came to attention at her tone.

"As I said," Hagerty replied noncommittally, "your understanding is wrong. You can discuss it with your father when you return home. In the meantime, you need to complete your part in the acquisition. The sooner the better…for all," he said, eyes boring into hers.

Tia stiffened. "How long do you plan to be on Midgard?"

"Until all issues are resolved. Your father will be sending additional information that may help. He is also concerned."

"About what? That I won't make the acquisition?"

"What you'll do with it once you have it."

She blinked. Where did that suspicion come from? She'd kept her plans to break from L-RAM secret.

"Your father has noticed a change in your attitude."

Dammit. She'd slipped up somewhere. "I'm well aware of my place in my father's company," Tia said, barely restraining the impulse to throw her steak knife at him. As he stood to leave, she stopped him with a question. "How's Asa?"

"His studies are progressing well," he said before turning away.

Studies? Indoctrination, she seethed. Her father intended to turn her eleven-year-old brother into a copy of himself. Time was running out…for both of them.

***

Two hours later, Tia was still tossing curses at her bastard of a father when her phone rang. Thane's number. *Finally*.

"Hello, Thane," she purred. "I was beginning to wonder if I needed to stop by Law Enforcement."

"When you do," came his hard voice, "ask for Captain Kelding. She'll be the one to handle the case."

What?

"The answer is no. The family stands behind me on this. Half of them said to tell you 'Not ever.' I won't relay what the other half said. Is that clear enough for you?"

She stared at her phone. Speechless. He… They would really do this?

"Miss Lexington," he said sharply. "Is that clear?"

"You know what—*click*." He'd hung up on her.

She dropped into the nearest chair as her plans crashed around her. Watching him walk away, there in the lounge on Earth, she'd realized he and Baron Financials were the means to escape her father's grasp. To wrestle Asa away from him. She'd been so *sure*. He'd ruined *everything*. Tears threatened, and she swiped them away furiously. She hadn't cried in years and she wasn't going to now.

***

Mid-morning the next day found her ushered into a rather nondescript office. She'd expected better. At least the visitor's chair was comfortable. She gave the woman sitting ramrod straight behind her cluttered desk a gracious smile.

"Captain Kelding, I am Tia Rockefeller Lexington."

"Why did you ask to see me? I'm Homicide, not Robbery. As I have no intention of making a grab for those jewels, your guard can wait outside." Brown eyes stared steadily out of an impassive face.

Tia had dressed conservatively for this meeting. But aware the local enforcers were probably ignorant of who she was, she'd worn her favorite diamond jewelry—thickly encrusted necklace, earrings, and several bracelets—to ensure they knew she was someone to be taken seriously. Evidently, the woman was devoid of any social acumen.

Nonplused at the unexpected rudeness, she gestured for the guard standing behind her to leave. This was not going how she'd envisioned it, but she could adapt. She'd done it enough times with her father. Think diplomacy.

"I've been on Midgard long enough to have heard about the unfortunate happenings last year. As Thane Baron was involved, who my company is exploring business options with, I looked deeper into it. I was quite surprised to learn that Katherine Baron's death had never been investigated as a homicide, despite learning that the cause was an exotic poison."

No reaction.

"I have Ahrymani Carpenter's sworn deposition stating that she suspected Miss Baron's death wasn't natural and that Jem Wilmont was responsible, either on her own or at the behest of one or more members of the Stohlass family."

"You sent a lawyer to Hellspawn?"

"Yes, one of our corporate lawyers."

"Why?"

Tia's brow scrunched. "To get Miss Carpenter's statement, of course."

"Why?"

Exasperated, she retorted, "What do you mean, 'why'?"

"You sent some poor slob to the worst Federal Penitentiary planet to get a statement from a murderous psychopath concerning events that have been closed. That's a lot of effort for someone who's only a possible future business connection."

Screw diplomacy. "Someone had to do it," she snapped, "since it's obvious your office is turning a blind eye. I do realize the Stohlass family is rather prominent on Midgard, especially here in Azusa."

Kelding's eyes narrowed. "Ahrymani Carpenter and Katherine Baron had a major falling out, primarily over Carpenter's failure to kill Thane Baron. Despite that, the two ex-lovers were still sharing a suite and Carpenter has a well-known spiteful streak. Not to mention, her access to and previous use of poison. By the time the autopsy report came back, she was already sentenced to life on Hellspawn and we saw no reason to pursue it."

How convenient. "Miss Carpenter had every reason to keep Miss Baron alive," Tia said. "She stood to receive a ten million dollar settlement from Katherine on their return to Milania."

Kelding's eyebrow arched. "For what? Services rendered?"

"She refused to specify." She'd fired the lawyer for not getting it.

"Uh-huh. Do you have a copy of the deposition with you?"

Finally, she fumed, handing over a T-drive. She waited impatiently while the enforcer captain loaded it and scanned the file on her computer terminal.

"The date on this file is over two weeks old."

Tia's mind blanked for a moment. "Yes, well, I debated bringing it to you because of the Stohlass family's connections, but I felt the truth needed to come out."

Kelding folded her arms on her desktop and leaned forward. "Miss Lexington, I may have my reservations about Jem Wilmont, but she is not a killer. The Stohlass family damn well isn't. As for the ten million from Katherine Baron, you only have Carpenter's word about that. Strangely enough, that happens to be the amount she was trying to blackmail Miss Wilmont for. That's how we caught her."

Tia's eyes sharpened. Blackmailing? "What for?"

"Not relevant. Do you really expect me—and a host of others—to put any credence into the word of a spiteful, murderous bitch who will wreak vengeance in any manner possible for those that brought her down? She was willing to blow up *entire* Stohlass families."

Tia's jaw flexed.

"What I do find relevant," Kelding continued in clipped tones, "is that you went digging in the sewer looking for shit. Tell me, Miss L-RAM, is it to *extort* concessions for your side of those 'business options,' or to destroy Thane Baron and his family all together? Although, both strategies do go together, don't they?"

Stunned, she managed to choke out, "You're not going to do anything?"

"About reopening a closed case on worthless, highly-suspicious data? No. About how you managed to get a copy of Katherine Baron's official autopsy report?" She tapped the T-drive. "Yes. Will you be staying much longer on Midgard?"

Tia drew herself up. "I have arrangements to make—business to attend to."

"Uh-huh. If that includes spreading poisonous innuendos, I suggest you don't. Most people won't believe it, and Gordon Stohlass hasn't lost a lawsuit in decades. I also suggest you watch your ass while you're here. I certainly will be. You can go now."

Tia left the Enforcement Center in a disbelieving daze. She stared unseeing at the streets passing outside the sedan's rear passenger window. What was it about this frigging family that nothing went right? Were they *that* unassailable? Was Thane Baron really invulnerable? A hot flush of anger burned outward from her chest. *Maybe*, she seethed, *but he could be hurt.*

Waiting until she was alone in her suite, she dialed Gary Hagerty's number.

"You have a go," she told him.

Chapter 49

UPMS courier pod M34JUI920P23 landed at Eastport an hour after sunrise, Midgard time. Following the instructions sent to its electronic brain, it taxied to hanger U-3 and then powered down. Several humans took over, rolling steps to both compartments and unsealing the covers.

Jem climbed stiffly down from the front compartment and into Thane's waiting arms. Home, safety, and love wrapped around her tightly. She hugged him back just as fiercely. Anticipation of this moment was the only thing that had kept her sane and her temper in check while repeating herself for the umpteenth time.

"No general?" Thane asked, as packages were handed down from the rear compartment.

One final hug and she stepped back. "He's going with General Arita to take Commander Johnson's ashes to his family on Mars. Arita is representing Military Command and General Kowalski wanted to personally represent Admiral Gleason."

"How is the admiral?"

"Dr. Inness has him in a healing coma," she replied, then snickered. "He also banned us from the admiral's room. That's part of the story," she said, at Thane's 'say what' look. "I figure you want to hear all of it."

"You bet. I have us a private shuttle with food and drink."

Perfect. It would have a couple of couches instead of seats. They'd be able to cuddle.

They headed for the hanger exit. Shortly thereafter, their shuttle was climbing westward for the three-hour flight to Azusa.

"I definitely need this," Jem said, pulling out a sandwich and a bottle of water. She'd switch to coffee later in an effort to stay awake and adjust back to Midgard time. She yawned. *If I can.* It had been late-afternoon Earth-time when she'd climbed into the pod about six hours ago. Her body's internal cycle was saying "bedtime."

"All right, tell me all," Thane said, unwrapping a sandwich. "The official news of Admiral Gleason's attack didn't hit the networks until a couple of days ago. Reason given was to keep it quiet due to the sensitivity of the attack, the investigation, and his alleged attackers. Not to mention the repercussions."

Thane's expressions varied as her story unfolded, ending with two days of interviews by everybody and their commander. He was impressed with Admiral Gleason's tenacity, which had resulted in the hospital ban. The threat of Midgard's secession shocked him.

"I appreciate their support, Jem, but isn't that a bit extreme?"

"I asked him the same thing later. He said it was because of the implication. That like any weapon, once used, it becomes easier a second time. Or third, with the reasons becoming more slippery. Soldiers understand the risk of going into a battle where the odds for them may not be good. But, as General Kowalski emphasized, they're willing to do so because they believe their leaders will do their best to get them through it and back out."

"The assholes wouldn't even plan for backup or extraction. It would encourage them to go after more entrenched targets, multiple times if necessary. After all," General Kowalski had spat, *"the Republic has gazillions of people."*

Jem rubbed her bottle of water back-and-forth between her palms. "They could create automatons, Thane," she said bleakly, "people sent on missions with no expectation of them surviving."

"If they ever do such a thing, I'll vote with our Senators," Thane declared firmly.

Shaking off the depressive thoughts, Jem fished out another sandwich. "How's things at home?"

"Well, my new ship should be arriving at the Bocharova Shipyard any day.

Martin reversed sail and took a plea deal: he's getting fifteen years back on Skewed."

Jem though for a moment. "Shiloh?"

"Uh-huh. Her sworn deposition included his earlier stalking. The way Granddad heard it, life on Hellspawn was an option if they'd gone to trial. With Martin pulling this shit right after getting off Skewed, not to mention his history of judicial contempt, he was probably smart enough not to press his luck."

"That or he actually listened to his lawyer."

"First time for everything. The Kid showed up about a week ago and sent Andi in a tailspin," he told her, going on to describe Kaleb's answer to engine bay sensors.

"Sometimes it just takes a different perspective," she said around a bite of ham salad.

"Or a simple comment," Thane said dryly, then added, "Kaleb's been hanging around, waiting to talk to you."

"Yeah, about that," Jem said, sheepishly. "I promised to help him out with something. If I can. There's still six weeks left on that one-year clause."

Thane suddenly chuckled. "Oh. Want to know the Kid's full name?" He told her, to the best of his pronunciation.

Wide-eyed, Jem said, "Well, that explains him going by his initials."

Stuffing the last bite in her mouth, she tossed her wrappings back into the bag and rested her head against his shoulder. Sighed happily. "I'm assuming you heard about Reginald Kurzvall's arrest last week? The Earthers were throwing parties."

"Only someone totally off the network grids would miss it. From the news reports, Mister You-Can't-Touch-Me is still screaming." Thane's grin slid away. "Tia Lexington is here," he said, his voice devoid of expression.

Definitely not happy about it, either. "Don't think I know her. Who is she?" Thane's reply of 'pain-in-the-ass' had her eyes rolling. "Oh. Another fortune hunter."

"Not just any," he replied, before going into details.

Jem sat straight up, fury erasing all traces of sleep. "Miss Lexington is a bitch."

"Family consensus, that. I keep hoping granddad or Seth can come up with a countermove." Weary resignation hung from his words when he said, "They still haven't."

Jem reached for his hand. "Tell me you're not considering…"

He shook his head. "She would always hold that over my head, demanding that I sail on whatever course she set. I gave her my answer a couple of days ago." He flashed a wicked grin. "I believe it sent her into shock."

She bet it did. "For me, getting maligned is another so-what day. But the family?" Jem's expression hardened. "This has to be yanked out by the roots." Maybe with a lot of hair.

"Fine by me. Got a plan?"

"Not yet. Unless I'm mistaken, your mom and grandmother are keeping tabs on her, as well as an ear. Let me talk with them, see if they already have an idea."

***

Warm and relaxed, Jem drifted, her head on Thane's shoulder. The pleasant buzzing of voices around her grew fainter.

"*Jem!*"

She bolted upright. "I'm awake."

"Barely," Gwen said, chuckling.

Thane's arm slid around her. They were sitting on the love seat in the family room. Gwen and Reyna sat across from them, having taken the day off to be here when they arrived. Andi had popped in long enough to say "welcome home." Thane said she was in the middle of paperwork that had to do with his new ship.

"I know you're trying to cycle back around," Gwen said. "Honestly, I don't know how Thane does it, with all the time shifts he goes through when he's tracking."

"I ignore it. I keep Midgard time on board."

"Okay," Jem said, stifling a yawn, "From all I've heard, Tia Lexington has turned from pain-in-the-ass to full-blown-ass."

Reyna let out a derisive snort. "She's started showing up wherever she can expect an audience. Dining at restaurants, attending public functions—"

"Invited to a few private ones," Andi said derisively as she came back through the doorway. "Thane, Nick asked if you could come to Security for a few minutes." She plopped into his seat after he left and grabbed a pillow. Tucking it against her, she leaned forward. "What did I miss?"

"Nothing," Reyna said. "We still need to figure out what to do about the L-RAM bitch."

"Simply running her off Midgard isn't enough," Jem said, scooting to the couch edge. "We have to squash her *and* her insinuations. Has anyone heard from LE yet?"

"Captain Kelding called to let us know Miss Lexington paid her a visit. It did not go well for her," Gwen said, giving them a satisfied grin. "After Seth verified the autopsy report of poisoning, he alerted the captain to a possible extortion attempt. She likes that about as much as blackmail. Captain Kelding believes, like most would, that Ahrymani Carpenter is the one responsible for Katherine's death."

"Helga Baron really did it? I know the woman is cold," Jem said after Gwen nodded, "but that's hard to believe."

"I'm pretty sure she poisoned her brother, too, years ago," Gwen said calmly to the gaping expressions around her. "Same protect-the-family-name reason."

Reyna's mouth snapped shut. "I am *sooo* glad Greg was nothing like her."

From the stories Jem had heard, Thane's father had been a kind, even-tempered man.

Reyna's phone rang. "It's Katrina." She gave several "uh-huhs" then pursed her lips during a short stretch of silence. "I'll let the others know. Thanks, dear." Clicking the phone off, she gave them a long, thoughtful look.

"Well?" Andi said impatiently.

"Katrina has a friend who works at the courtesy desk where Tia Lexington is staying. She doesn't know the contents, of course, but she says they've forwarded an unusually high number of UPMS messages to Miss Lexington over the last few days."

Jem's eyes went flat. "Want to bet they're about me?"

"Probably. She also told Katrina that Miss Lexington has been asking a number of questions about Founding Week. Specifically, the Founders Ball. The banners and event advertising started last month."

"Founding Week?" Jem asked. She was still learning about her new home. "I gather there's a lot of celebrations for that?"

"Yep, all week, all across Midgard," Andi said. "Starts in two weeks."

"Each city holds their Ball on the last day, it being the official end of celebrations," Reyna said.

"*Hmmm*," Gwen said, her gaze unfocused. After a moment, she gave a sharp nod. "Perfect." She looked around at the puzzled faces. "Miss Lexington has been working toward a goal ever since she arrived. Thane was originally part of it, until he nixed it quite firmly. Since then, according to a friend, she's been talking us down and L-RAM up."

"As in future offices here?" Reyna drawled.

"Those frigging smear rumors?" Jem snapped.

"Yes, to both. Mostly stuff on Jem then splashing us with it. The viper has even found ways to insert her poisoning hints into a conversation. It's all insinuation and just plain trash. Unfortunately, as demonstrated in the past, that can be a very effective weapon. Want to bet she is counting on maximizing those effects by striking at us during one of our biggest venues?"

"That'd be a sucker bet," Andi said.

Gwen gave a smile that was all teeth. "Big mistake. By coming at us directly, *we* can use that same exposure to maximize *our* rebuttal. We'll stomp every lie she has with truth."

"Or as close to it as I can get," Jem said, holding up a finger.

"We'll show her for the conniving, muck-raking viper she is," Reyna said, the glint of battle lighting up her face.

"Not only that," Andi said, giving Jem a wink, "it gives us the opportunity to squash all the trash about you, once and for all."

"For this to work, Jem, you will have to drop the mystique. Speak about yourself—not *everything*, of course," Gwen added. "That near-truth thing."

Jem agreed with her friends and they began debating Tia's possible reveals. Plotting their responses. A small thrill coursed through her at what would be the first step in the new phase of her life.

Thane and Nicholas rejoined them a short time later, both men coming to a wary stop at the sight of the grinning women.

"Do I want to ask?" Thane said cautiously.

"Yes, you do," Jem said, beaming a bright smile.

"You'll love it, Nick," Andi said, bouncing up and over to hug her husband around the waist. "Excitement, scandal, revelations…it'll be the most exciting Founders Ball in Midgard history."

***

It was mid-afternoon and a short nap later before Jem and Thane settled into chairs in the Kid's room in a transit hotel outside Azusa's small Port Circle. Jem doubted he'd spent all the income from his share of Jaguide crystals. She figured it was an environment he was used to and most comfortable in.

They declined Kaleb's offer of beer.

The taciturn young man had never been much for the usual pleasantries, so she forged ahead. "What kind of help do you need, Kaleb?"

He took a swig of beer. "To rescue my mother on Mandoria."

Jem blinked. Shared another one with Thane. That was the last thing they'd expected. Technically, she would be on the Mandoria Habitat, which was in geosynchronous orbit above the planet. No one lived on that toxic surface.

"She's been kept in drugged isolation for the past fifteen years, ever since her *accident*."

Jem's attention sharpened at the stressed implication. "Why?"

"Because Aaron Leise, who married her eight months earlier, took over maintenance of the habitat due to her supposedly brain-impaired condition. By contract and inheritance, Mom is the rightful Habitat Manager."

"Your father?"

"Wyatt Despiegelaere was a miner. He died when I was a month old. They were on their way up from end-of-shift when, around 9000 meters, something failed on the shuttle and they crashed. There wasn't enough left to figure out what went wrong."

Not from that height and with a 5-Eg pull. "Okay, what happened to your mom?"

"Mom met Aaron Leise, another miner, when I was six. He played it slow, easing into a relationship. Then he talked her into upping their significant partnership to full marriage shortly after I turned eight. Eight months later, she's doing a standard inspection at an ore loading dock when an electrical malfunction—cause indeterminate—opens the carrier's doors and drops a ton of ore. The Ellison engineer with Mom was fast enough to push her out of the way of most of it, though he himself was killed."

"Where was Leise?" Thane asked sharply.

"Down on the surface—still working as a miner. Coincidently," Kaleb's voice went even colder, "a close friend of his who was on his three-day break happened to be *visiting* one dock over and at the same time. He became Aaron's Second once he took over management. At least, until he was found beaten to death three months later."

"Well, as if that's not suspicious," Jem said grimly. "It certainly eliminates any future liabilities or blackmail. How did he take over if your mother survived?"

"She was in a coma for almost six weeks. The doctors were worried about brain damage, which might be what gave him the idea. I was a minor, so he took guardianship of us both and slid into the manager's chair."

"And if she'd died, it would've been the same result: you as ward and him in the chair," Thane said.

"When my mother did wake up, she was disoriented, didn't know me at first, and there had been some initial indications of brain damage. The Ellison doctor treating her believed it was more of a bad bruise than actual damage and would repair itself eventually. He wanted to keep her in the MedCenter under supervision, but Aaron had her moved to a bedroom in our apartment and brought in a private, non-Ellison paid nurse. Elsa Yusuf, mom's long-time assistant, stayed on to help take care of her. She was let go after five months and replaced with another privately funded employee."

Kaleb's voice was ice cold, but his gaze held fire. Well, she'd always wondered what had shaped a young man into the hardened one she'd found on the *Hidden Trove*.

"You're sure about the drugging?" Thane asked.

"After we separated on Tigres, I went looking for Elsa. Took a couple of months to find her, but when I did, she told me much of what I've just told you. Elsa said she was let go after they found her bringing in food to replace what Aaron or the nurse were giving her."

"She'd gotten suspicious," Thane guessed.

"Uh-uh. Mom becoming alert and lucid enough to start asking questions is what tipped them off. Then, after Elsa was gone, she suddenly got that vacant stare and didn't recognize me again."

Jem massaged her chin, thinking. "If it was a simple matter of showing up and removing her, you already would have."

"Aaron Leise decrees who gets to see her, professionally or otherwise. The habitat enforcers are his private army," Kaleb said stiffly. "Nothing more than well-paid thugs who throw their fists around and help themselves to whatever they want. They play some pretty sick games among themselves at others' expense."

Jem made a face. "Yeah, they do. That was when I learned to start, uh, sneaking onto ships." Using ghost-mode to hide herself and her trail.

"You worked on Mandoria?" Thane stared at her in shock.

"Well, I wasn't aware of its reputation." Jem gave him an apologetic look. "It was my second stop after leaving Earth. Figured it out real quick that first night."

"How long were you there?"

"One night working, the next four spent dodging the thug-enforcers."

Thane glowered. "What happened?"

"I took a job as a waitress. Boss said to take orders, give them what they wanted, and be sure to get paid. Standard, right? I didn't realize his waitresses were included on the menu. It gave a whole new meaning to 'Hiring for all positions.'

"I was unprepared the first time I got pulled into some guy's lap. Took a minute and a hard thump with an empty beer glass to get free. By the fourth attempt I was savvy enough to keep out of their laps. Fifth cornered me outside the restrooms and said we could go to one of the private rooms since I was the shy type. He didn't like my 'no' and I hit something softer than his head."

Thane's face split in a wicked grin when Jem bobbed her eyebrows. "Yeah, I remember that knee move of yours."

"Someone complained. Boss pulled me aside and explained how things worked. I then explained how I worked. He sneered, I quit. When I went to buy passage the next day, I found my ex-boss had put a hold against me. Supposedly over some missing funds. From conversations I overheard later that day, security had bets on who would be the first," she cleared her throat, "to find me."

Thane's eyes hardened to gray steel.

"I slipped onto a supply ship prepping to leave and stayed hidden until we hit the first port," Jem finished.

"I remember that," Kaleb said. "The guy you kneed was Leon Threader, a senior enforcer. They were rather put out at never finding you and went on a find-who-helped-you-get-past-them spree. The beatings went on for several weeks," he said without any sign of censure.

Intuition's cold hand squeezed her chest. He'd been one of them.

"I've been hearing the gossip. I was right—you can teleport."

She neither denied nor acknowledged it. "Why are you so sure I didn't hack the *Hidden Trove's* computer?" She'd used that excuse to explain how she'd accessed the ship's vault.

"Because the last part of Beckett's order to change the password was to wipe it from the main computer memory, including overwriting the memory cells with garbage. Messing with the vault in any way would have blown the ship up. The only way left, was you going through the wall in some manner."

Well…damn. Definitely an outside-the-box thinker. "So…you want us to show up, get your mother out, and then what? Leave?" Jem said.

"Yes. We can be gone before they realize she's missing. We can get her real medical help. Once she's well, we'll go back with true Enforcers and throw the bastard into jail."

"That's assuming he's not grabbed everything he can and fled to one of the new areas our Enforcers have no jurisdiction in," Thane said.

"He'll be gone," Kaleb said coldly, "and out of our lives."

Jem studied him. The young man's facade had cracked, the anger and frustration he'd lived with for so long radiating out like a solar mass. Her heart bled for the years he and his mother had lost. A few months ago, she would have done it. She would have helped him spirit his mom away. And she would have been in the wrong. That should be a last-ditch step, when everything else had failed or his mother's life was in imminent danger.

Also, while she'd never apologize for spying on Reginald Kurzvall, she'd have to be careful in the future. More…prudent in invading people's privacy. *Reality check,* Jem told herself. Willy-nilly use of any of her abilities now would only prove General Cranky's point.

Thane was watching her, his expression neutral. Waiting to see what she'd do. He had changed because of her. For her, he had stretched his ethics into the gray zone. But he could only go so far. Any further, and it'd break him. *No, never*, she vowed. Cranky and the others didn't have to worry. This man was her control. He'd keep her off that slippery slope.

"Will you help or not?" Kaleb demanded after her silence had stretched past his patience.

"Yes, we will. However, your plan needs rethinking. You might be her son, but Aaron Leise is her legal guardian. We'd be kidnapping your mother."

Thane's subtle chin dip was agreement and thanks.

"You said your mother was the rightful habitat manager by contract and inheritance. Please explain. We need to understand the dynamics."

He took a swallow of beer.

"The Mandoria Management Corporation was founded by my great-great-grandfather. The Ellison Mining Company, which has exclusive mining rights for Mandoria, granted it a contract, in perpetuity, to maintain and oversee the habitat. When I left, they had five active mines on the surface."

"I don't think I've ever heard of a perpetuity contract," Thane said.

"I'm guessing there was something between my ancestor and Ellison's. Friendship, secrets, maybe blackmail. Doesn't matter. As long as the conditions of the contract are observed, it's binding."

"What are the conditions?" Jem asked.

"Maintain the habitat and all the required services in good condition, provide free accommodations for Ellison's employees, and…"

That was fairly standard to attract workers. Her room on Pappia, the Euphrates's mining moon, had been free, too, until she became an Independent.

"And..." Thane prompted after several heartbeats of silence.

"A direct descendant as manager."

It took a moment. "You are next in line to take over the Mandoria Habitat?" Jem said, startled. Why would anyone want to be in charge of that hell-hole? He must have read her expression.

"It didn't used to be that bad," he said, defensively. "A bit rough, yes. You can thank Aaron Leise for what it has turned into. I watched it sink: the fights, the knifings, the influx of questionable entertainments and services. Pretty much anything goes now as long as the habitat isn't endangered and he gets a percentage of their revenue."

"Challenge him," Thane said. "You're no longer a minor. Since your mother is unable to fulfill the contract's obligations, it should fall to you as next in line."

Kaleb's features turned stony. "I told him something similar the day I turned eighteen. He said that if I ever did, Mom would be having a fatal heart attack."

Jem sucked in a sharp breath. She might end up having to whisk the woman away after all. "Kaleb, how much risk will you face if you show up there?"

"I'm his backup for when Mom does die, so Aaron won't kill me. Won't risk me getting away again, either. Previously, his security kept me from leaving the habitat. I couldn't get off until Richardson came recruiting for Beckett. He signed me on after I told him I could fix just about anything mechanical. When two of Aaron's men tried to stop me from boarding his ship, Richardson burned them where they stood."

That Jem could believe. She'd seen the psychopath kill a man similarly on the *Hidden Trove*.

Giving a blasé shrug, Kaleb added, "Most likely, he'll have me kept from boarding a ship again. Although, he may find it simpler to just lock me up somewhere."

"That's not the worst risk," Thane cautioned. "Unless he's ready to retire, you'll need to be dead or similarly disabled for him to stay in charge."

"Did have a couple of near-accidents before I left," Kaleb drawled.

The guy definitely had to go. "What happens in the worst case: you and Mom both gone?" Jem asked.

"If gg's line dies out, the contract will move to the oldest in his brother's line. If and when that line dies out, the Ellison Company will auction off a new contract."

Jem and Thane traded glances.

"I'll talk with my granddad. He'll be able to advise what steps we can take. We'll get your mother back on her feet—if possible," Thane warned. "After so many years of drugging, there may be real brain damage now."

Kaleb's hand fisted on his knee. "I know. But she'll be free from him."

"At the moment, I'm kind of stuck here," Jem told him. "I'll need to talk to General Kowalski when he returns. In the meantime, we can work on plans for when I get unstuck. How are you for funds? Do you have any J-crystals left?"

***

It was late evening before they made their way back to the estate. They'd stopped to visit with Katrina and Shiloh for a bit, and then had a pleasant dinner at a small diner tucked away from reporters.

Yawning, Jem plopped down in front of the computer in Thane's old bedroom. Their bedroom. She hadn't had a chance yet to check her email. Not that she usually got a lot, aside from those frigging job offers, but she'd been gone for weeks and hadn't bothered to have any of it forwarded.

She scanned down the list, looking for anything that couldn't wait until tomorrow. Like, hopefully, a message from Boyd explaining why he'd left so suddenly. Not saying anything to Gordon and Gwen during his brief visit hadn't surprised her, but surely he wouldn't—*Yes!*

She clicked on the text message.

"Jem. Sorry to leave so abruptly, but I need to drift for a while. Nowhere in particular, just…contemplating the universe. You and Thane stay safe."

"Well, that tells me a whole lot of nothing," Jem said crossly.

"Tells what?" Thane said, padding out of the bathroom.

315

Momentarily distracted by his bare chest, Jem relayed Boyd's unhelpful message.

He shrugged. "It seems like we've lurched from one crisis to another for the last couple of years. We're looking forward to getting away from everything ourselves. Why shouldn't he?"

"Well, yes, but…for how long? He vacated his apartment, Thane."

He kissed the top of her head and simply said, "Jem."

She sighed. "I know. As long as it takes." But it felt…off.

About to close the screen, her gaze landed on the last item. The file was only a few hours old. Uh-oh. "I have a text message from Rolfe. It's marked urgent."

"Crap," he said, looking over her shoulder as she opened it. It was short and blunt.

"Contract offer increased. There are sniffers. Rolfe."

Jem gave a tired sigh. "Well, isn't that a fine way to end the day."

Thane reached around her and turned the computer off. "I got a better one."

Chapter 50

The *Wave Queen* sailed out of the Stohlass private marina and turned northward, Thane content at its helm. They had spent all of yesterday at GG's, relaxing and visiting with family. They'd talked with adults and played with babies—even Shiloh's triple toddler brothers. Now it was just him and Jem and wind and waves.

And sun, he added with a smile as Jem raised her face toward it, her hair fluttering in the same wind filling their sail. Her happy, relaxed expression stoked a deep warmth in his chest. It wasn't often there, not with the way their lives had been. Especially of late. They were looking forward to recuperating in the peace and quiet of their home. They didn't plan on leaving the fjord's security until the start of Founding Week festivities.

Too bad we can't take off and drift anonymously like Boyd for a month or two.

They were gliding past Sunshine Cove when movement caught Thane's eye. He couldn't make it out at first, but it quickly resolved itself into a drone coming in over the treetops.

"Damn reporters," he growled, alerting Jem.

Shading her eyes, she looked in the same direction. "I'm going to buy every damn paper in Azusa and then—"

"Something's wrong," Thane broke in. Too big for a video drone. And it wobbled, as if too heavy or the operator was inexperienced. It almost— *"Bail!"* he yelled instinctively when the drone made an unmistakable dive toward them.

Instead, Jem flung herself against him as he surged to his feet.

The boat exploded around and through their phased bodies. When the debris settled, they were standing deck-high off the water. He mouthed several of his strongest curses. Jem tugged on his arm and nodded toward the shoreline. *Thank Thor they hadn't been too far off the coast,* he thought as they started 'walking.' One part of him marveled at the feat, while the other nine-tenths continued to cuss out whoever had blown up Jem's boat.

They hadn't gone far when two watercraft came racing in their direction.

Thane tensed, then realized they were from Sunshine. They would have heard the explosion, come to investigate and help. He motioned for Jem to drop them into the water.

She did.

Thane rose to the surface, sputtering and coughing from the mouthful of water he'd swallowed. Jem treaded next to him. He started yelling, waving an arm at the boats floating next to the debris. One suddenly cut sharply in their direction.

***

They waved good-by to the Shore Patrol crew that had seen them safely to Spine Ridge Fjord. They closed and secured the solid door to their underground home.

Jem turned into him and buried her face in his shirt.

"We're home," he said soothingly and wrapped his arms around her. "We're safe and—" he broke off, realizing what his shirt's growing dampness meant. *She's crying.* His strong, resilient sig-ner was crying. The silence of her tears somehow made it worse. He curled her tighter against him and rested his chin on top of her head. There was nothing else he could do at the moment.

They had given their statements to Sunshine Cove's Enforcers. In response to the expected "who'd send an explosive-laden drone" question, they'd both shrugged. They both had enemies. The way the enforcers had eyed Jem, they suspected she'd been the primary target. They were undoubtedly right, and that was without knowing about the termination contract.

The enforcers had promised to canvas the area and citizens for clues. *"Sunshine is more village than town,"* one enforcer had told them proudly. *"It would be hard for a stranger to go unnoticed."*

They had thanked the locals gratefully, both those that had rescued them and the ones that had purchased dry clothing. When Stuart had called to say he would drive up to bring them back to GG's, Jem had declined.

I want to go home, she'd said.

Now, he stood with a wet shirt trying to comfort the woman he loved after some fucking, low-life, son-of-a-bitch bastard had tried to blow her up. The fact that he would have died too was beside the point. Eyes narrowed to slits over her head, his Tracker brain churned with plans.

Chapter 51

"Still no word on your attacker?" General Kowalski asked.

"No sir. A Sunshine Cove local did spot an unidentified male at about the right time. He was on one of the coastal pull-offs—no big deal attention-wise. No one saw him launch a drone. No one saw him leave." Jem shrugged. "Maybe it was him, maybe it wasn't."

They were on a video call, both of them relaxing at home. In Jem's case, her second home at GG's estate. They were staying there for the week's festivities. It'd taken Kowalski longer than he'd liked to make it back to Midgard. After the official visit to Commander Johnson's family—he'd been posthumously promoted to full Commander—he'd been drawn back to Earth for formal questioning by the Military Council. Several had wanted her to return likewise, but General Estrada had submitted the videos of her recorded testimony. All of them.

Jem had silently laughed at Kowalski's miffed tone when he complained about how they wouldn't take *his* recorded testimony and then sent him home by commercial liner.

He'd updated her on Admiral Gleason's improving condition and the Military Council's reshuffling as they filled the newly vacant positions. Lieutenant Corrigan had briefed him about the investigation of their boat attack. Not that it had gone very far. Suspects ranged from someone Consortium-based to any one of the crazed "too dangerous to live" crowd.

"The only clue—if you can call it that," Jem continued, "is that the woman who spotted him got the impression he was an off-worlder from his clothes.

Thane is running a number of checks on port records. He's even tapped Kenneth Brower to keep a street watch. Nothing unusual or hinky on either high or low end so far."

The general assured her his office was also keeping a close eye on port arrivals and the commandos had a go-bag ready at all times. Nicholas and Stuart were doing the same, minus the go-bag. Someone would have to be, well, a ghost to slip through all that.

"You're sure it wasn't a Palmyra mercenary?" Kowalski pressed.

"Yes, because Trystan Rolfe says the contract is still floating as unfulfilled. We asked."

"Uh-huh. You're sure *he's* not thinking about it?"

Jem gave that a few minutes of honest thought. "Pretty sure, otherwise I don't think he would have warned us. He offered me a job."

His lips pursed. "That's a disconcerting image. You...on his team."

Jem rolled her eyes. "Thanks. Anyway, here's something else you might find disconcerting." She told him about Kaleb's situation and that they intended to help him once that one-year clause was up. Only a couple of weeks now.

Kowalski sighed. "I was an idiot to even consider it, much less the original five years."

"No, sir," Jem said with a lopsided smile, "You were right about us needing time to stabilize after everything." The attacks on Thane's family. Her revelations. "I'll let you know before we go. Leave word in my postbox if something comes up. I'll keep check."

At his skeptical look, Jem held up her hand. "Promise." She also couldn't help noticing how tired he appeared. The man had a lot on his shoulders. "Anything else, sir?"

After a moment he said, "Commander Johnson had a daughter in Mars City. Lovely young girl. Her mother said that's why he took the aide position with Anton. So he could visit her on a semi-regular basis when they were at Military Command."

He stared off to the side for a moment.

"Technically, I'm still on leave. Lieutenant Corrigan was a bit dismayed when I told her I'd report in on Monday. Seems there's a big pile of reports waiting." His smile didn't reach his eyes. "Founding Week still has a few days left, so I'm going to spend them with Honey and the boys. Enjoy my family. What about you?"

"Ditto on family. We'll be attending Azusa's Founders Ball Saturday night."

"Then we'll pick the world up again on Monday. Have fun." he said.

Jem leaned back in her chair. A stream of memories flowed past her inner eye, the only place she'd see some of the faces now. A tiny bloom unfurled in her chest. Part sadness, part regret, part nostalgia.

After a moment, she wandered off in search of her own family.

Chapter 52

They stood beneath sparkling chandeliers, holding slim flutes of champagne and watching the ebb and flow of people. The Founders Ball was in full swing, the last of the official events. Azusa's Ball was being held this year in the newly finished Tri-Peaks Conservatory. Situated northwest of the city proper, it gave breathtaking views of city, ocean, and mountains.

Gwen and Gordon, as benefiting the patriarchs they were, circled slowly around the room, stopping here and there to speak with someone. Reyna and Lee were chatting in a small group next to the terrace doors. Erik and Lana, along with Susi, were in another group. Andi and Nicholas, Seth and Gina were doing the circulating thing. More of Thane's cousins were scattered throughout the room.

"I can't help but notice," Jem said, "that the family seems to be staying in pairs. Strength in numbers?" The better to corner their quarry?

"Probably," Thane said beside her. "Speaking of which…"

When Jem followed his gaze, she was wordless too. Katrina, on the arm of Kaleb. The Kid. Socializing? She'd bet his knife was hidden somewhere under that nice suit. Behind them came Shiloh, beaming at them from beside Major Markowitz.

"Kaleb," Thane said coolly when the two couples joined them.

"Thane," Kaleb returned just as coolly.

All three women rolled their eyes.

"Major, you look outstanding in your dress—" Jem sputtered to a stop." His medals and insignia stood out sharply on the crisp, black formal jacket.

Especially the shiny silver leaves that had replaced the gold ones on his lapels. "Congratulations, Lieutenant Colonel Markowitz," she said with a wide grin.

"When did this happen?" Thane asked, giving him a light shoulder thump.

"Last week." His grin dimmed a bit. "Admiral Gleason put in the recommendation before he left Anderson Station." A momentary pall wafted across their group, thoughts of the admiral and all that'd happened. Markowitz broke it with a chuckle. "General Kowalski tells me Admiral Gleason is trying the hospital's good will. They're about ready to catapult him out a window."

There were more chuckles.

"By the way, I spotted Miss Lexington arriving behind us," Katrina said. "Everybody grab a drink," she added, snagging two herself from a passing tray. Handing one to Kaleb, her tone anticipatory, she said, "The sparks are about to fly."

Markowitz gave Shiloh a puzzled look.

She patted his arm. "Sorry, Elijah, I forgot to tell you. You're standing on the front line."

"Oh? Major or minor skirmish?"

Shiloh grinned. "Very major, my Maj—Colonel."

Jem nearly choked on her drink at her first glimpse of Tia in the flesh. There was a lot of it.

Tia wore a cream-colored floor-length gown. The front was split down the middle to her waist, the two sides barely covering the nipple-half of each breast. As she walked, Jem could see the side was split up to her thigh. She turned to speak to someone, revealing the back was comprised of two strips, starting at each shoulder and crisscrossing down to her waist. *Probably all that was keeping it from falling off.* And she was draped in jewelry.

"Battle stations," Jem murmured.

Markowitz snorted. He paused a server long enough to take glasses off his tray. He angled Shiloh and himself on Jem's right side. Kaleb and Katrina took a similar position on Thane's left, forming a half-circle.

Jem took a sip. *Walk into my web.*

The waiting was over. They'd ignored the whispers and sideways glances. They'd emboldened Tia with their passiveness. The trap was set and Jem was looking forward to springing it.

"That's Dillon VanBuren she's holding onto," Shiloh said. "His father runs a major import/export business out of Odinheim."

"Hope he's smarter than he looks," Jem said.

"Nope," Katrina replied. "His sister is being groomed to take over the company. Since the top end's not working so well, his father might be trying to make use of the bottom end."

Markowitz choked on his champagne.

"I've been here a month," Kaleb said. "I've stopped being surprised at what the females in Thane's family say."

Markowitz cast a wary look at Shiloh.

Shiloh flapped her hand. "Just a cousin."

"Here she comes," Jem said softly. She'd been covertly watching Tia make her way across the room. Whenever she drew near one of the Stohlass family members, they'd turn their back on her or walk away. Did that sting, or did it embolden her? Either way, she was now deliberately aiming for their group.

"She must be wearing a whole jewelry store," Thane muttered.

Several necklaces wove around her neck and draped large settings on and between her breasts. Long earrings dangled to her shoulders and crusted combs sparkled in her hair. Rings covered her fingers and at least five bracelets clinked on each wrist. All were covered in rubies, diamonds, and emeralds.

Tia and her date stopped at the edge of their half-circle.

Shiloh looked her up and down. "Well, at least we know the rocks are real."

Jem managed to keep a straight face, despite hearing Markowitz's low-pitched "*uh-huh*."

Tia gave Shiloh a disdainful glance, eyed Thane for several baleful seconds, then switched it to Jem. "I'm surprised they let you attend. But then, you undoubtedly paid enough."

Jem gave her a puzzled look. "I'm sorry. It was free for us. Is that what it took for you to get through the door? A bracelet, maybe a ring?" First strike to her, from that tightening of Tia's jaw.

"Oh, no. No one stopped us from walking in," her black-haired rock said with a smile. "I'm—"

"No need," Tia interrupted, "I'm sure Miss Wilmont knows who we are."

Horror crossed his face. "J-Jem W-Wilmont? The thief and assassin everyone's talking about?"

The flash in Tia's eyes was satisfaction. *You poor slob.* She's using him as a springboard.

"Yes," she replied politely, "I'm Jem Wilmont. No to the rest of it."

There was a general 'drifting' of people toward their group. Miss Lexington was undoubtedly counting on it. *So am I.*

"If she was, Law Enforcers would have arrested her by now," Thane said coldly, using one of the responses designed to steer the conversation.

"Oh, she's no doubt bought her way out of numerous handcuffs," Tia said in a mocking tone.

Inattentive to the growing crowd, Miss Lexington missed the affront on several faces, including Enforcer Captain Kelding and FLEA Assistant Director Reis.

Her first mistake. Now, to push her into the next one.

"I assure you, Miss Lexington, I've never bought my way out of anything. I prefer to put my credits to use helping others instead of myself." Jem let her distaste at the garish display of jewelry show. "Nor do I feel the need to flaunt those credits."

Jem wore a simple, one-shouldered sheath dress that shimmered in shades of green that enhanced her bi-colored gaze. A single necklace of thick, interlocking silver links draped across her collar bone. A small cluster of diamonds and emeralds dangled below her earlobes, and the dark combs holding her hair back were unadorned. The visual difference between them was a galaxy apart.

"I sincerely doubt you do anything that doesn't benefit yourself somehow," Tia said coldly.

"Well, that's where you'd be wrong," Gwen said from the crowd's edge.

Tia's faint smile was a giveaway as she glanced sideways, then back.

Jem hid her smile. *Yes, you got your audience, but it's not going to go like you planned.*

"She's helped numerous people over the last few years, and I can give you a list, if you'd like," Reyna said from beside her mother. "In fact, Jem, those two sisters on Minos Four you protected from assault? Their parents have a free meal reserved at their restaurant for you the next time you're there."

Thane had collected a number of stories about a mysterious do-gooder, back when Kurzvall had deceived him into tracking her. He'd shared his Jem-file with the family as ammunition to combat the rumors. Reyna had even contacted a few of them to get their full stories. Jem had told the family that, barring the mostly classified stuff, they were free to tell others what they knew.

"If you need even more proof," Reyna continued, "Miss Wilmont is the founder of the Hands of Hope Foundation."

Tia's eyes narrowed as murmurs sped through the crowd. Jem waited quietly.

"So I've learned. Between your bank balance and the Foundation," Tia sneered, launching her next attack, "there is no way you gained all that money in just a few years. Not honestly."

"She's back to calling you a thief and assassin," Katrina said nonchalantly.

"Of course she is, and I have obtained proof of it." Tia said haughtily to several whispers in the crowd. "She destroyed a lab, killing its employees on Earth and killed a man on Pappia. It's all documented."

Oh, ho. Now they were getting to the nitty-gritty. Jem took a sip, as if thinking about it. Let the tension build for a few seconds.

"Yes, I worked at the Myerstone Lab, but I had already left it for other work when its power generator exploded. Investigated. Documented. As for Pappia, the man I killed there was about to kill Thane, who was injured. It's *documented* as justifiable self-defense. I am not an assassin and I have *never* killed for money or any other personal gain." The deaths on Tarragona were about survival.

"Do you have anything else to support your wild claims?" Jem asked dismissively, sensing a change in the murmurs at Tia's selective choice of facts. She saw several irritated expressions. Their plan was working.

"You said she was a killer," the black-headed simpleton at her side said. "That she kills to..." Even he recognized the venomous look Tia gave him and wisely took several steps away. Leaving her standing alone.

Exactly where Jem wanted her.

"You are most certainly a thief," Tia snapped, apparently sensing the shifting attitudes. "The amount of credits you acquired over the last several years is astronomical. How else do you explain all those credit spikes when, supposedly, you're working at menial jobs? Bartender. Waitress. Mucking out stalls? Really?"

Silence.

"How do you know her history of menial jobs?" Thane asked, his tone accusatory.

"How do you know her bank accounts' history?" Katrina asked, her tone icy.

Tia's expression blanked.

That's an oops. Franklin Lexington could have queried her account balance, pretending a pending financial action. That did not entitle him to the account's history. Much less her now-closed Earth account. Somebody at the banks had done a no-no.

Jem responded with a mischievous smile.

"First, I was traveling around the Republic, working and living sparingly on what I earned from those menial jobs. Since I wasn't spending it," she waved her glass, "the compounded interest from my parent's insurance, granny's estate, and investments pumped them up." She had to call those first two cash deposits something.

"That would build fast," someone in the back of the crowd called out.

"Second, I received a very large advance from Reginald Kurzvall, now of the Consortium, for recovering his ships from Beckett's pirates. That was further increased by a hefty penalty when he tried to renege on paying the rest of it."

Frustration flashed across Tia's face. *Anything else,* Jem thought smugly.

"You are a thief," she insisted vehemently. "You stole a backpack full of Jaguide crystals right out of their vault. You want proof? How about a copy of the Repository's Security Chief's report?"

Total silence. Even the servers were frozen along the back wall.

Shit, damn, crap. The one thing they hadn't planned for. Shocked, her back stiff, Jem's blood pounded from the weight of all the eyes on her. Tia's held triumph. Those messages she'd been getting. One of them. Did another contain the video of her teleporting?

"The military will be very interested in knowing how you acquired that *classified* information, Miss Lexington," Markowitz said in a hard, ominous voice.

Tia appeared surprised, then annoyed. "Why would the military care about or protect a thief? Did she offer to buy a new frigate or two? You're obviously on *good* terms with the family," she said in a snide tone.

Oh. My. God. The woman's arrogance knew no bounds. She was throwing everything away in the name of vengeance. This had to be handled.

"I was kidnapped and given a choice, Miss Lexington," Jem said in ice-coated tones.

"Really?" she scoffed.

"Steal Jaguide crystals for Beckett, or he would drop a Delgado on Azusa." There were sounds of gasps and more than a few curses.

Tia's cheeks flushed. "You expect us to believe that? How convenient and problematic to prove," she said derisively.

"I was there."

Jem's head whipped around. Kaleb was giving Tia his coldest stare. He'd also just outed himself to the authorities.

"I was on the *Hidden Trove*. Not only did she have to steal them, she had twenty-two hours to do it before Richardson signaled Beckett to launch the Delgado. The clock was down to eleven minutes when she returned with the crystals. Disheveled and exhausted. Richardson actually looked disappointed."

"Beckett orchestrated the Branson Hotel Fire, here on Midgard, and immolated millions on Magnus," Jem reminded the slack-jawed woman. "I didn't have any doubt that he would do as threatened."

"Are you saying you were one of Beckett's pirates?" Captain Kelding said, stepping forward.

Oh, crap. Kelding hated Beckett and his pirates with a passion.

"No. I was a mechanic. A skill Beckett needed."

Beckett's tendency to draft people with skills he needed, whether or not they were willing, had become well known. Kaleb's spin was a safe one—one part truth, one part a leading assumption. Kelding's pursed lips, however, said 'talking to you later.'

"As for it being classified, that was to protect both Jem and the Repository," Andi said. Standing next to Reyna, she practically skewered Tia with a disgusted stare. "It was to keep other criminals from forcing Jem into repeating it or hitting other high-level targets."

"By kidnapping a family member," Shiloh said coldly.

"And you just blew that, bitch," Katrina said pointedly.

"Your arrogance has put our entire family at risk," Gordon said, his voice vibrating with anger.

Tia's gaze darted across the crowd. The faces weren't friendly.

Instead of making me a pariah, you turned me into a hero.

Jem handed her glass to Thane and took two steps toward the aggravating woman and resisted, barely, the urge to punch her. "You have evidently gone to great effort and cost to dig into my life. Why? Because Thane refused to marry you? Or sell out Baron Financials to your father's predatory company?"

A fiftyish woman spoke up. "She said there were rumors that Thane's grandmother did the Living Inheritance because Miss Wilmont threatened her if she didn't. And that she also, um, ensured Katherine wouldn't inherit it."

Ugh. That would be giving Thane heartburn on several counts.

"No, I didn't threaten Helga Baron, and no, I didn't poison her niece. That is malicious gossip intended more to hurt Thane and his family than me. I am already…unpopular."

Guilt flashed across several of the closest faces.

"Miss Lexington also implied that the Stohlass family knew and profited from your—those activities," a bald-headed man said.

The woman beside him nodded vigorously. "She said that's why they and their company were doing so well."

"That's BS," said a loud male voice.

"Uncle Erik," Thane whispered, stepping up behind her as people searched out the speaker.

"As CEO of Stohlass Enterprises, I can categorically state that we have not received one credit from Miss Wilmont, stolen or otherwise. Our growth is due to a lot of hard work, sound investments, and fantastic management."

"Miss Lexington claimed she and her father were *working* to get Miss Wilmont brought to justice," said a woman Jem recognized as Gwen's long-time friend, Maria Jorgenson. "That we could count on *honest* services when L-RAM opened their offices here." She gave Tia a contemptuous look. "I laughed in your face and told you what I thought of *your* so-called honesty."

"It doesn't exist," a male voice called out.

The crowd scanned the crowd again, focusing on a trim, white-haired man. He pushed his way to the front.

"She wined and dined Sean Rheinhart, CEO of a private banking firm on Regus One and a man old enough to have known better. She talked up the benefits of being an L-RAM subsidiary. They got engaged. As soon as the corporate paperwork was completed…" he paused for a beat, "she broke the engagement and her father broke the company. It doesn't exist anymore. I should know," he said, anger finally breaking free. "I'm Carlos Rheinhart, Sean's uncle."

My, the galaxy is getting smaller. Jem's lips curled as the crowd's attention returned to Tia. The previous unfriendly looks were now downright hostile. "You are pathetic. Go home and don't come back."

"*Ever*," a voice sang out that she was sure belonged to Seth.

"Not yet," Markowitz said, stepping forward. He motioned to Reyna's husband. "Agent Twobears, I hate to ruin your evening, but I need to borrow your federal facilities."

Agent Garner stepped out of the crowd. "I'll accompany you." She took hold of the shocked woman's arm. "We wouldn't want any claims of impropriety."

"I'm a Rockefeller Lexington," Tia squealed. "You can't arrest me."

"I believe they are," Gordon said smugly.

***

They held hands in the near darkness of Gwen and Gordon's family room, a single lamp providing illumination. The Founders Ball had been a success, both in its original purpose and in the exposure of Tia Lexington's manipulations. Latecomers had been floored by the gleeful accounts of what they'd missed. She'd seen changes in the expressions of people as they looked at her, as they came up and spoke to her. So, yes, she could count tonight as a win for herself, too. By how much remained to be seen.

It was well after midnight now and everyone else had filtered off to their homes or beds. She and Thane would leave in the morning for their fjord home. She needed it. Needed *this*, the peaceful quiet, she admitted to herself, leaning her head against Thane's arm. She felt…drained. Lethargic. Decompression, Gordon had called it when she'd mentioned it. Said he occasionally experienced it after a long, hard trial. It was the brain saying "go away, don't bother me."

Thane gently tugged her upward. He turned the lamp off as they passed it on their way out.

Chapter 53

The next two weeks were bliss. She read. She slept. Jem soaked up sun during the day and made love with Thane at night. Thane had spent a fair amount of his time on vid-calls to Andi or the Bocharova Shipyard as they oversaw the work on his new ship. He'd jetted into Azusa this morning. He and Andi were taking a shuttle down for a final inspection and to bring it back.

Jem was eating lunch at the counter dividing her kitchen and living area when Freya announced a video call for her from General Kowalski. She sighed and switched to the chair at the counter's comm-niche and activated it.

"General, how are things going?" *Problem-free, yes?*

"Good, good," Kowalski said beaming. "Anton has returned to light duty and is reviewing aide applications. We should expect to see him sometime later this year."

"I'll look forward to it. Anything new about Tia Lexington?" She'd been transported to Earth for both military and civilian investigations. The Azusa news links were gleefully reporting her problems.

The general flashed a toothy smile. "That's my other news. We may have a name for your boat assailant. Things are getting lava-hot and she and her father are throwing each other in the pool. Miss Lexington has refused bail—says she's safer in jail."

"The assailant?" Jem said, focused on the more important statement.

"Gary Hagerty. According to Tia, he's her father's main troubleshooter. Combination of investigator, enforcer, and fix-it-any-way man. Says he paid her a visit about a week before the drone attack. He asked if removing you from the picture would make Thane more *amenable*. She told him to leave you alone but, if her father had authorized it as part of the *acquisition package*, she said Hagerty could have implemented it after it became obvious Thane wasn't cooperating. That in fact, also according to Tia, this wouldn't have been the first time such a tactic had been employed, either as retaliation or warning."

"Think she's telling the truth?"

"The interviewing enforcer believes it. Her report states that Tia hates her father and appears determined to take him down, regardless of the consequences to her. The latest wrinkle in this saga is her claim he's an unfit parent and has petitioned the court to have her younger brother, Asa Rockefeller Lexington, placed under the guardianship of his maternal great aunt."

"What about their mother? Is she deceased?" Jem asked, confused.

"No. Under the divorce section of their extensive prenup—it's eleven pages—she gave up all rights and custody of any children in return for a single, substantial sum…per child."

"That's disgusting. She went into that marriage exclusively for money. No way I'd let that woman get her hands on the boy." Maybe that also explained, somewhat, how Tia had turned out.

"That's also the general opinion of LE and the judge overseeing the case. Tia will probably get her wish, what with all that's being exposed about Franklin Lexington. Besides his dubious business philosophy, she maintains her father is behind the Repository theft report, even personally meeting with and paying a very large amount to the individual selling it. Interestingly enough, the file was logged into UPMS under a L-RAM Earth account with Gary Hagerty's ID at the same time we know he was here, whether plotting mayhem or not."

Someone had spoofed his ID and password, like she'd done with General Morelli.

"Hagerty has disappeared—probably switched to an established alias. An alert has gone out to all Republic FLEA and port offices. I've doubled that here as he may still be on Midgard. You and Thane watch your backs," he added in a concerned tone.

"We will, but he's more likely looking for safe harbor with things falling apart.”

“Maybe. Naturally, Franklin Lexington is disavowing any knowledge of Hagerty’s doings and is calling his daughter a liar, among other things, on all her accusations. Oh. He claims he had no idea his daughter was stirring up trouble. She was only supposed to be laying the groundwork here for a future Lex-Rock Asset Management office.”

Jem made a loud, unladylike sound.

“No one else is buying it either. The man kept too tight a rein. The Jaguide authorities have been notified of the breach in their security. They weren’t happy and promised to find the greedy bastard. Fortunately, the report the guy purloined was an earlier one: it had the what and who but not the how. We’re all guessing he didn’t know or wisely kept that to himself.”

“Or holding out for more money,” she muttered grumpily.

“The Lexington family is facing some serious charges and,” Kowalski chuckled, “if they’re very unlucky, hit with espionage charges by the Jaguide authorities. Needless to say, the L-RAM company is also taking a massive hit.” Promising to keep them abreast of news, he signed off.

Jem returned to her sandwich and thought over everything as she munched.

She’d have to ask Gwen about L-RAM. Thane’s grandmother was closely following the company’s status. As for Tia Lexington, Jem didn’t feel any sympathy for her. The woman’s hubris and self-entitlement had brought it on herself. And if she could take her even-worse father down, great. One less Kurzvall-type in the universe. She did, grudgingly, give the woman credit for looking out for her brother.

She was dozing in the terrace’s shade when Freya announced a video call from Thane. Jem hurried back to the comp. Thane’s smiling face blinked into view. “Everything went okay? It’s here?”

“Almost. We found one item that needed fixing. Mr. Bocharova promised to have it ready by tomorrow and that gave me an idea. Why don’t you sail in on the *Ghost Wind*? We’ll spend the night here at GG’s and head down after breakfast. I’ll make the final payment and we’ll bring the *Tracker* home together.”

Thane's grin stretched ear to ear and he was practically bouncing—she squinted at the screen. "You aren't bouncing, are you? We don't need another Andi in the family."

"I heard that," Andi said, somewhere off-screen.

Jem laughed and agreed to the plan. She signed off with a large smile of her own. It didn't take long to pack a bag and close down the house. Standing outside the front entrance, she gave Freya the Lock-and-Watch command. She listened as the door bolts snapped into place before heading down to the dock. Her new boat was slightly larger than her old one. It also had a military-style satellite communication panel, courtesy of General Kowalski. Alerts could be sent or received independently of normal phone traffic.

She called the Stohlass security office, leaving word with the young lady on duty that she was on her way. It was one of the safety features they'd recently implemented. There were several security protocols in place if she didn't arrive within the expected timeframe.

A short time later, she motored out of the fjord and cruised down the coastline toward Azusa. Unlike Thane and many other Midgarders, she rarely used sails if the engine worked.

***

Jem stood with Thane in the Globe's shadow as they waited for Andi to verify the med-room's panel had been fixed. "Shouldn't she be done by now?"

"Has been awhile," Thane acknowledged. "Knowing Andi, she's probably rechecking several things. I know she's still a bit concerned about how the interfacing between the Altus navigation module and Thor is working. Fortunately, we won't need it for the hop over to Azusa."

After installing and activating Thor, Andi had decided to replace the computer brain's thirty-year-old navigation module with the newer one. Thane hadn't elaborated on it, other than to say there had been "hiccups."

Jem tilted her head to one side. Then the other. "It looks…fatter? Maybe?"

Thane barked out a short laugh. "Fatter? Guess you could call it that. The main globe's diameter is about a half-meter wider. Not enough to change the transit time."

"So, what's its full name?" she asked. "*Lone Tracker Two*?" He'd been referring to it these past weeks simply as *Tracker*.

"*Tracker's Gem.*"

Jem spun around on her heel.

"*Tracker's G-E-M,*" Thane said, leaning down to kiss her. "The old name didn't fit anymore and, in truth, I had already planned on renaming it. Andi helped me with all the technical filings and it's now official. *Tracker's Gem*, Midgard registry by owners Thane Stohlass Baron and Jem Seaborne Wilmont. Surprise," he added gently.

Jem stared open-mouthed for a couple of seconds, then launched herself into his arms. She didn't have to say it, the "I love you" was in her hug.

Just as it was in the tender kiss on her head.

"Here they come." Thane nudged her head with his chin. "From the wide smiles on their faces, everything's ready. Let's finish this and go home."

Epilogue

Judge Brian McDonald congratulated the new couple and wished them well. His clerk would get their digital signatures in passing. Checking his schedule as the two men left, he found they were the last for today. Good. He normally enjoyed his turn in the Marriage Court, but today had not been a good one for him. He shifted in his chair; winced. No more trampolines, regardless of how much his grandkids wheedled.

He activated his intercom. "Janice, I'm going to leave a little bit early today."

"Sir, there is a walk-in couple waiting. I can have them schedule for another time."

He sighed. "No, send them in. Please have anyone else schedule."

His aches receded into the background when the man and woman walked in. *Well, well, well.* He didn't need the file being forwarded to his terminal to know who they were. He'd definitely have something to share with the wife tonight.

They stopped in front of him and waited expectantly.

Right. He flicked on the recorder and opened the file.

"You both attest to be Midgard citizens and of legal age," he said formally, scanning the first block. The woman had recently changed her citizenship. Not a problem, as Earth years were almost the same as theirs. Hmmm. *That's unexpected.*

"I see your prenup is on file, although I can't help but notice it's the standard court-issued one." And time-stamped about ten minutes ago. There were no conditions, no caveats, none of the fancy legalese he'd seen for its duration or in case of termination. Very unusual, as there were considerable resources on both sides. The survivor would inherit quite a chunk, minus whatever was committed in a will or other legality.

"Do either of you wish to reconsider your prenup?" he offered.

He received two "No, your Honor." He studied them for a moment longer. Very well.

"Thane Stohlass Baron. Are you obligated by prenup or marriage contract anywhere else, on or off Midgard?"

"No, your Honor."

"Do you enter into this contract and union of your own free will?"

"I do."

"Jem Seaborne Wilmont. Are you obligated by prenup or marriage contract anywhere else, on or off Midgard?"

"No, your Honor."

"Do you enter into this contract and union of your own free will?"

"I do."

"Do you have rings?" Excellent. Not everyone favored the old tradition. "Please place the rings on your partner's finger." Watching, he found it very telling that the two richest people on the planet had chosen simple silver bands. Probably titanium.

"You have both chosen to join together into a life partnership. A partnership that must be blended, balanced by the skills, needs, and dreams of each other for it to remain healthy and happy. Your rings are a symbol to the Universe of your commitment to each other," he finished, happy at being able to recite that last line

Folding his hands on his desktop, he said, "If you have a personal pledge, please face the other and recite it."

"You have my heart. You have my soul. I will cherish and be true to you until my last breath," Thane said with a soft smile.

"My heart is yours. My soul is yours. I will cherish and be true to you until my last breath," Jem said, gazing up at him.

Beautiful. "Congratulations. May you have many years together."

He added his digital signature to the file, closed it and sent it back to his clerk. Turned off the recorder. Giving into impulse, he quirked an eyebrow and said, "You do realize this is going to be a hot topic in about thirty minutes?" That was about the length of time it'd take for the nosy society reporter at Channel Two to see the updated public database.

They exchanged a look he'd have to describe as resigned amusement. Miss Wilmont gave him a wry smile.

"When aren't we?" she replied.

Very true. "I wish the best for you both in the future. Please stop at the clerk's desk."

McDonald watched them leave, still holding hands as they disappeared through the door. He hoped their future would go well. They deserved it.

The recent newscasts were now a lot more favorable toward Miss Wilmont after the revelations Miss Lexington had flung into the open. He, along with many of his fellow judges, had followed the reports out of Earth closely. Not only about L-RAM, either. From hints sprinkled here and there, he'd bet his next year's salary Jem Wilmont was somehow involved in the on-going military headlines.

He logged off his terminal. If he hurried, he could beat Channel Two in surprising his wife.

Author's Note

The Ash Ceremony is Midgard's primary funeral rite. Family and friends will gather and after the ashes have been scattered, with rivers and ocean the popular choices, someone will recite the *Liturgy*. Everyone joins in as a chorus on the last two lines.

The Liturgy of Passing

The time has come and you move on
To whatever waits for us beyond.
While in our midst you no longer stand,
We know you'll always be close at hand.
You'll dance with the rain and all its kin.
Your whispers will sail astride the wind.
We'll feel your caress in the warm summer light,
And know you stand watch thru darkest nights.
A part of you will live in us,
And continue on till all is dust.

Titles by R. D. Chapman

<u>Blurring Reality Series</u>
Shattered Reality
Blurring Reality
Tangled Reality
Reality Kicked

<u>D'Accio Investigations Series</u>
At Any Cost

About the Author

R. D. Chapman has been an avid reader all her life. A retired empty-nester living quietly in Nebraska with her husband, she draws on a lifetime of experience ranging from cook to software developer to craft characters and stories. She writes in a blend of SF&F, urban fantasy, and mystery with a smidgen of humor and romance. When not writing, she loves spending time with the three Rs: Reading, cRocheting, and Relaxing.

* * * * *

Thank you for reading *Reality Kicked*. If you have enjoyed this book, please consider leaving a review, as they are essential to expanding my sales and readership. Even a few simple lines will help. Thanks!

www.ingramcontent.com/pod-product-compliance
Lightning Source LLC
Chambersburg PA
CBHW022008310726
48972CB00006B/1571